I0760804

Echo Rift

Riven Worlds Book Three

(Amaranthe ♦ 16)

G. S. Jennsen

Hypernova Publishing
2021

ECHO RIFT

Cover design by Ikterna, Vandrage Artist and G. S. Jennsen.
Cover typography by G. S. Jennsen

Hypernova Publishing
174 E Neider Ave #89
Coeur d'Alene, ID 83815
www.hypernovapublishing.com

Ordering Information:
Hypernova Publishing books may be purchased for educational, business or sales promotional use. For details, contact the "Special Markets Department" at the address above.

Echo Rift / G. S. Jennsen.—1st ed.

LCCN 2020925370
978-1-957352-22-0

Amaranthe Universe

Aurora Rhapsody

AURORA RISING

STARSHINE
VERTIGO
TRANSCENDENCE

AURORA RENEGADES

SIDESPACE
DISSONANCE
ABYSM

AURORA RESONANT

RELATIVITY
RUBICON
REQUIEM

Asterion Noir

EXIN EX MACHINA

OF A DARKER VOID

THE STARS LIKE GODS

Riven Worlds

CONTINUUM
INVERSION
ECHO RIFT

ALL OUR TOMORROWS
CHAOTICA
DUALITY

Cosmic Shores

MEDUSA FALLING
THE THIEF
THE UNIVERSE WITHIN

Shadows & Light

LIMINAL SPACE
THE THEORY OF EVERYTHING
NAKED SINGULARITY (2027)

SHORT STORIES

Restless I • *Restless II* • *Apogee* • *Solatium* • *Venatoris* • *Re/Genesis*
Meridian • *Fractals* • *Chrysalis* • *Starlight Express*
Extinguishing the Stars

Learn more at gsjennsen.com/books or visit the Amaranthe Wiki: gsj.space/wiki

For the survivors

DRAMATIS PERSONAE

HUMANS

Alexis 'Alex' Solovy Marano

Space scout and explorer. Prevo.

Spouse of Caleb Marano, daughter of Miriam and David Solovy.

Caleb Marano

Former Special Operations intelligence agent. Space scout and explorer.

Spouse of Alex Solovy, bonded to Akeso.

Miriam Solovy (Commandant)

Leader, Concord Armed Forces.

Marlee Marano

Consulate Assistant.

Richard Navick

Concord Intelligence Director.

Mia Requelme

Former Concord Senator.

Malcolm Jenner (Admiral)

AEGIS Admiral.

David Solovy

Professor, Concord SWTC.

ASTERIONS

Nika Kirumase

External Relations Advisor, Asterion Dominion Advisor Committee.

Former NOIR leader.

Dashiel Ridani

Industry Advisor, Asterion Dominion Advisor Committee.

Owner, Ridani Enterprises.

Lance Palmer (Commander)

Military Advisor.

Joaquim Lacese

Former NOIR Operations Director.

Adlai Weiss

Justice Advisor.

Parc Eshett

Omoikane Consultant.

Selene Panetier

Justice Advisor.

Perrin Benvenit

Omoikane Personnel Director.

OTHER MAJOR CHARACTERS

Eren Savitas asi-Idoni
Former CINT agent.
Species: Anaden

Mnemosyne ('Mesme')
Idryma Member. Former 1st Analystae of Aurora.
Species: Katasketousya

Nyx elasson-Praesidis
Inquisitor. Granddaughter of Corradeo Praesidis.
Species: Anaden

Akeso
Sentient planet.
Species: Ekos

Akhar Ghorek
Brigadier, Savrakath military.
Species: Savrakath

Casmir elasson-Machim
Leader, Anaden military.
Species: Anaden

Corradeo Praesidis/Danilo Nisi
Former anarch leader.
Species: Anaden

Devon Reynolds
Concord Special Projects Director.
Species: Human

Enzio Vilane
Owner, Vilane Properties.
Species: Human

Ferdinand elasson-Kyvern Former
Concord Senator.
Species: Anaden

Kennedy Rossi
CEO, Connova Interstellar.
Species: Human

Lakhes
Praetor, Idryma.
Species: Katasketousya

Meno
Mia's Prevo counterpart.
Species: Artificial

Morgan Lekkas
Former IDCC Commander.
Species: Human

Nolan Bastian
AEGIS Fleet Admiral.
Species: Human

Ryan Theroit
Former NOIR member.
Species: Asterion

Torval elasson-Machim
Machim military commander.
Species: Anaden

Valkyrie
Alex's Prevo counterpart.
Species: Artificial

Xyche'ghael
Namino merchant.
Species: Taiyok

MINOR CHARACTERS

Charles Gagnon, EA Prime Minister (*Human*)

Cliff, CINT Artificial (*Artificial*)

Drae Shonen, CINT agent (*Anaden*)

Enkro Khalik, scientist (*Savrakath*)

Felzeor, CINT agent (*Volucri*)

Graham Delavasi, former SF Intelligence Director (*Human*)

Grant Mesahle, DAF consultant (*Asterion*)

Hohlaak Ponla-min, interstellar merchant (*Barisan*)

Hoya Isao, Conceptual Research Director (*Asterion*)

Ildaite Llawhe, Confove Mission Project Director (*Naraida*)

Kolgo elasson-Praesidis, Inquisitor (*Anaden*)

Lontias elasson-Praesidis, Inquisitor (*Anaden*)

Miaon, former anarch agent (*Yinhe*)

Maris Debray, Culture Advisor (*Asterion*)

Noah Terrage, Connova Interstellar COO (*Human*)

Onai Veshnael, Dean, Concord Senator (*Novoloume*)

Pinchutsenahn Niikha Qhiyane Kteh ("Pinchu"), Tokahe Naataan (*Khokteh*)

Rolph Tremblay, Romane Governor (*Human*)

Solstan Sahlann, *Purgatory* manager (*Novoloume*)

Spencer Nimoet, Justice Advisor (*Asterion*)

Stanley, Morgan's Prevo counterpart (*Artificial*)

Vaihe, refugee (*Godjan*)

William 'Will' Sutton, CINT Operations Director (*Human*)

Zhanre'khavet, Taiyok Elder (*Taiyok*)

Ziton elasson-Praesidis, Inquisitor (*Anaden*)

CONCORD

Member Species

Human

Representative: Vacant

Anaden

Representative: Vacant

Novoloume

Representative: Dean Onai Veshnael

Naraida

Representative: Tasme Chareis

Khokteh

Representative: Pinchutsenahn Niikha Qhiyane Kteh

Barisan

Representative: Daayn Shahs-lan

Dankath

Representative: Bohlke'ban

Efkam

Representative: Ahhk~sae

Allied Species

Asterion
Katasketousya
Fylliot
Ruda
Taenarin
Volucri
Yinhe

Protected Species

Ekos
Faneros
Galenai
Icksel
Pachrem
Vrachnas

AMARANTHE

CONCORD EMPIRE

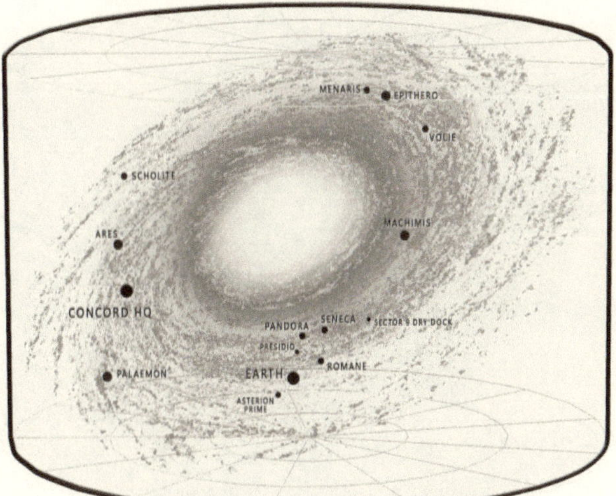

MILKY WAY GALAXY

LOCAL GALACTIC GROUP

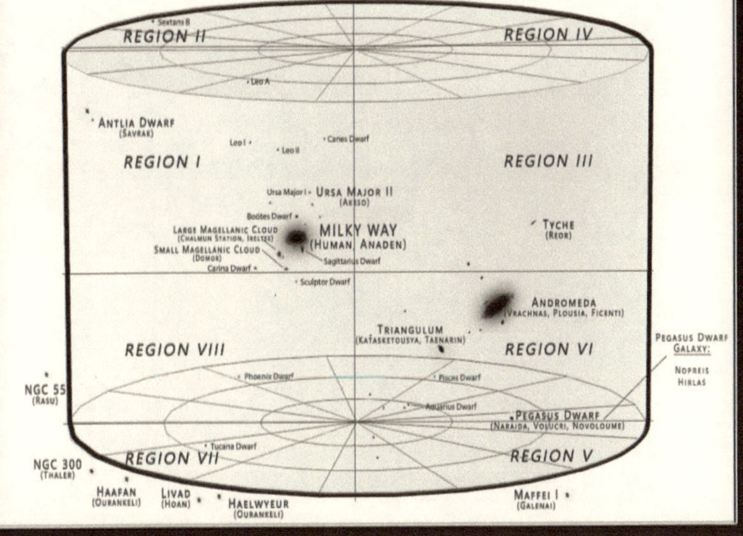

Gennisi Galaxy
(Messier 94)

Asterion Dominion Axis Worlds
Asterion Dominion Adjunct Worlds
Alien Worlds

ASTERION DOMINION AXIS WORLDS

Mirai Namino Synra Ebisu Kiyora

The Story So Far

*For a brief summary of the events of **AMARANTHE #1-13**, see the Appendix in the back of the book.*

CONTINUUM

Fourteen years have passed since the events of REQUIEM.

Nika Kirumase joins Alex and Caleb for dinner at their home on Akeso. They share the story of how humanity ended up in Amaranthe and fill her in on Concord, the multi-species government that has taken the place of the deposed Anaden Directorate.

Marlee Marano, Caleb's niece, is on the planet Savrak as part of her work for the Concord Consulate. The Savrakaths are a lizard-evolved species that originated in the Mosaic. Marlee discovers they are enslaving and mistreating the Godjans, a species they share Savrak with. While helping a Godjan girl, Vaihe, escape imminent torture, Marlee is arrested by local authorities. David Solovy and Caleb both arrive to come to her aid, and they are able to secure her release.

Elsewhere on Savrak, Eren asi-Idoni and his team (Cosime, Felzeor, Drae) surveil a Savrakath lab on behalf of Concord Intelligence (CINT). The team infiltrates the lab and acquires evidence the Savrakaths are secretly developing antimatter weapons.

Miriam Solovy, Concord's military leader, receives a visit from Lakhes. The Kat conveys its opinion of the Asterions and a warning regarding the Rasu. Lakhes then returns home, where it confronts Mesme about the secrets it has been keeping regarding the Asterions.

Alex takes Nika to Concord HQ to meet humanity's power players in Concord: her mother and father, Malcolm Jenner, Mia Requelme and Richard Navick. Nika fills them in on the Asterion's experiences with the Rasu (see the summary of *Asterion Noir* in the Appendix).

Nika returns home to Mirai, and Dashiel Ridani introduces her to the Omoikane Initiative, a massive project spearheaded by the other Advisors to accelerate technology, warfare and logistical plans to combat the Rasu. She learns about the Vault, a project to store the psyche backups of all Asterions in a fortified spaceship, where they can be spirited away in the event of a Rasu invasion.

On Machimis, Casmir elasson-Machim struggles to exert authority over the other Machim *elassons.* Torval elasson-Machim learns about the Savrakaths' antimatter development and, believing Concord is not doing enough to address it, decides to take matters into his own hands.

Alex, Caleb and Valkyrie travel to NGC 55, believed to be the closest Rasu-controlled galaxy to Concord space. They discover millions of Rasu vessels and platforms in thousands of star systems throughout the galaxy, as well as a Rasu artificial ring orbiting the galactic core.

Nika, Dashiel and Lance Palmer attend a formal meeting with Concord leaders to review what they know about the Rasu's reach, their intentions, and ways to counter them. Conventional weapons have proved ineffective, and they discuss the use of negative energy, nuclear and antimatter weapons, as well as even more exotic weaponry. Nika fills the others in on the Rasu's unique consciousness and their paranoid, controlling nature.

Miriam promises the Asterions military and scientific cooperation, information sharing and a steady supply of Reor/kyoseil, but stops short of providing them with adiamene. Alex asks Kennedy to secretly give the formula for adiamene to the Asterions. Kennedy and Noah decide if they can do so in such a way that protects their family, they will.

Vaihe unexpectedly contacts Marlee. She's escaped capture but is alone in the Savrak wilderness. Marlee hacks a Caeles Prism to open at Vaihe's location and gets her off Savrak. She takes Vaihe to meet Mia, and the Godjan relays the full extent of the Savrakaths' mistreatment of her people. Marlee demands Mia do something to help the Godjans.

On Mirai, Adlai Weiss discovers his personal account has been hacked and his bank accounts emptied. When he goes home, he is attacked and knocked unconscious. He wakes up in an unknown location, strung up in a rack and being held captive by a strange man.

Perrin is determined to find Adlai. She breaks into the Justice server to find out what Justice knows about Adlai's kidnapping. She and Parc Eshett review the data and discover Justice has a suspect named Ian Sevulch, but he has an alibi. Parc reveals that some Asterions have begun transforming themselves into "Plexes," where a single consciousness occupies multiple physical bodies simultaneously. He believes Sevulch could be a Plex, and they decide to surveil the man.

Perrin tails Sevulch to an abandoned shop, where she discovers Adlai tied up in the basement. She shoots Sevulch in the head and rescues Adlai. She then keeps vigil at Adlai's side while he recovers from his torture. Parc stops by, and Perrin reveals she's figured out that he's a Plex. He asks her to keep his secret, and she agrees.

Nika takes Maris Debray to visit their original homeworld, Asterion Prime, in the Milky Way. Maris tells Nika about the early days of the SAI Rebellion and about Nika's family, including her brother, Loshi, who was killed during the rebellion.

Eren's team receives authorization to destroy the Savrakath antimatter lab. However, while they're placing explosives around the lab, Torval arrives in his Imperium and blasts the facility, killing Drae and Cosime.

Eren takes Cosime's body to Alex and Caleb on Akeso and demands that they bring her back to life, much as Akeso did for Caleb fourteen years earlier. Caleb tries to explain how it's beyond Akeso's ability to renew life in someone the planet hasn't previously bonded with. When a hysterical Eren insists, Caleb tries to open a connection to Cosime, only to be overwhelmed by darkness and death. Eren realizes Cosime is truly gone; he asks Alex and Caleb to take care of her for him and flees.

Miriam arrests Torval for disobeying orders and the murder of Concord personnel, then tells Casmir to bring the other Machim *elassons* in line. Miriam and Mia deliver an ultimatum to the Savrakaths, terminating their negotiations for a Concord alliance, demanding they cease all antimatter production and offering asylum to all Godjans.

Alex and Caleb attend Cosime's funeral. Eren is absent, and no one knows where he's gone. Caleb decides to try to find Eren and enlists Felzeor's help to do so. Meanwhile, Eren travels to an underworld Anaden planet, Lethe, to acquire a dangerous black-market hypnol that will suppress his emotions and increase his reflexes. He takes the first dose, then begins planning his revenge for Cosime's death.

In a skirmish between Savrakath ships and Casmir's fleet, the Savrakaths deploy antimatter weapons to decimate the Machim ships. In response, Miriam issues a "red-flag" order, terminating all Concord relations with the Savrakaths and forbidding them from entering Concord territory.

Dashiel receives files from an anonymous source containing the details for adiamene production, and he begins making plans for its manufacture.

The Concord Senate approves a formal alliance with the Asterion Dominion, over the vehement objections of the Anaden senator, Ferdinand elasson-Kyvern.

During the Asterion's battle against the Rasu in the Gennisi galaxy, an Asterion pilot, Kiernan Phillips, and a Taiyok, Toshke'phien, were pulled into a Rasu wormhole and spit out to crash land on an unknown planet. The planet is being subjected to a quantum block, meaning they can't call home for rescue. They've survived until now by staying out of sight of Rasu currently roving the planet, which appears to have been home to a primitive species until recently. The Rasu discover the wreck of Kiernan's ship, however, and take it apart for information.

Despondent over what the Rasu might learn, Kiernan and Toshke return to Toshke's ship ahead of the Rasu and burn it. They then seek refuge in the woods for the night; the next morning they spot a non-Rasu ship overhead, and race to meet up with it.

In a distant galaxy, Danilo Nisi/Corradeo Praesidis and his granddaughter, Nyx elasson-Praesidis, visit an advanced alien species Danilo previously encountered, the Ourankeli. On arriving, they find the Ourankeli's habitats destroyed, including a solar halo ring, and the Ourankeli massacred. Next, they travel to the home system of the Hoan, the primitive species that sheltered Danilo after his son tried to murder him. They discover Rasu ships in orbit and a quantum block surrounding the planet. They descend to the surface, where they find villages of Hoan massacred. Danilo is lamenting their fate when Kiernan and Toshke rush out of the woods to meet them. After a tense encounter, Kiernan insists that they all leave immediately, before the Rasu discover them, and Danilo agrees.

Malcolm leads a special forces squad on a stealth raid of the Godjan prison on Savrak. They are able to rescue the imprisoned Godjans, but as the last of the captives are freed, Savrakath forces attack. Malcolm is caught in an explosion and loses consciousness.

Marlee accompanies Mia to Mirai. Shortly after they arrive, word reaches Lance of Kiernan's rescue, and of the fact that some Rasu may now know the location of Namino, where Kiernan's ship was based. The Asterions begin preparations for the possibility of a Rasu attack, and Mia and Marlee go with Lance to DAF Command on Namino. There, Marlee meets Grant Mesahle and convinces him to take her into the city for a tour.

Caleb and Felzeor track Eren to Lethe, but Eren has already departed. Caleb searches the hotel room Eren had rented, finds evidence of the hypnol Eren had procured, and deduces what Eren is planning.

At Concord HQ, Eren breaks Torval out of detention and imprisons him in the cargo hold of Eren's ship. Caleb and Felzeor reach Concord HQ minutes after Eren has absconded with Torval. They confer with Richard until he's called away by Miriam, then decide to go drop in on Marlee.

Rasu arrive in the Namino stellar system, and Lance deploys his fleet. Miriam orders the AEGIS, Machim, Novoloume and Khokteh fleets to Namino and accompanies them in the *Stalwart II*.

On learning of the impending battle, Ferdinand elasson-Kyvern conspires with other Anaden *elassons* to subvert the new alliance. He kidnaps Casmir before the man can report to Namino with his fleet.

The Asterion fleet engages the Rasu. Concord forces arrives at Namino and join the battle, but the Machim fleet is a no-show. Mia reaches out to Ferdinand, who threatens an all-out rebellion against Concord. The battle is nevertheless turning the Asterions' and Concord's way when massive Rasu reinforcements arrive. Miriam appeals to Lakhes for the Kats to join the battle, but Lakhes declines.

Alex arrives at Namino to find the battle going badly for the good guys. After checking in with Miriam, she leaves the *Siyane* in Valkyrie's hands and goes to the Initiative to warn Nika that they're about to lose Namino. Nika and Dashiel decide they need to get the Vault to a safe location, and they're debating where and how when Mesme shows up and offers to safeguard the Vault. Nika is skeptical, but Mesme's pleas and Alex's promise that she trusts Mesme convinces Nika to agree to it.

A Rasu leviathan attacks the *Stalwart II*. When it can't do any damage, it changes shape and surrounds the *Stalwart II*, enclosing it entirely. Rasu then melt and infiltrate the ship via tiny seams in the hull; once inside, they solidify and attack ship personnel. When the Rasu are about to reach the bridge, Miriam activates the ship's self-destruct mechanism.

Valkyrie shows Alex what happened to the *Stalwart II*. Alex tells Nika that whatever she's going to do to rescue the people still on Namino, she needs to do it now, then opens a wormhole and vanishes.

Nika prepares to go to Namino and fight the Rasu invaders. Joaquim Lacese arrives at the Initiative, eager to join her. Joaquim leads the way through the d-gate to Namino; just as Nika is stepping through, the d-gate shuts down, as does every d-gate leading to Namino.

Caleb learns that Marlee has gone with Mia to the Dominion. He sends a furious message to Mia, demanding that she get Marlee out of the warzone immediately. Mia insists that she's trying (unsuccessfully) to get Marlee to leave, and Caleb tells her to open a wormhole to her office and he'll personally come retrieve Marlee.

Marlee gets separated from Grant and begins trying to get pedestrians into the DAF Command basement as Rasu land in the city and go on the attack. Caleb arrives at Mia's office, and Mia opens a wormhole, joining him just as Rasu reach DAF Command and attack Marlee. Caleb is rushing through the wormhole to rescue her when it shuts down, denying him access to Namino. When Mia is unable to reopen it, Caleb announces he is going to get his niece and walks out.

INVERSION

On learning the *Stalwart II* has self-destructed, Alex returns to Concord HQ, only to find it embroiled in a coup attempt by rebel Anaden forces. Caleb's plans to travel to Namino and rescue Marlee are delayed as he helps Richard defeat the Anaden rebels.

On Namino, Grant and Joaquim rescue an unconscious Marlee from the Rasu and retreat to an underground bunker. Marlee awakens several hours later to find her injuries treated; Grant fills her in on events, and she meets Joaquim, Selene and Xyche'ghael. Joaquim and Selene clash over how to protect those trapped underground while fighting the Rasu invasion.

With their fleet decimated and Namino occupied, the Advisors gather at the Omoikane Initiative and review their limited options for how to respond. Unexpectedly, a fleet of Kat superdreadnoughts arrives to defend the remaining Asterion Axis Worlds from Rasu attacks.

At Concord HQ, David tries to keep the Concord infrastructure functioning while Miriam undergoes regenesis. Caleb convinces David to help him steal a CINT Ghost ship so he can sneak onto Namino.

The Savrakath ambassador tells Mia that Malcolm died during the Savrak raid. She immediately starts the regenesis paperwork to bring him back, only to learn that he had a 'no regenesis' clause in his will. On Savrak, however, Malcolm wakes up to find himself injured and chained up in a dungeon.

Eren delivers Torval to the Savrakaths so they can punish him for destroying their antimatter lab. Eren returns to his ship, intending to commit suicide, when he's knocked unconscious. He later wakes up to find himself restrained in the cargo hold, where his friend and teammate, Drae Shonen, intends to help him detox from the *dialele.*

On Epithero, the *elassons* Ferdinand elasson-Kyvern has gathered in his faltering rebellion against Concord bicker over how to move forward. Meanwhile, in the Dominion, Corradeo Praesidis/Danilo Nisi shows up at the Omoikane Initiative after rescuing Kiernan, stunning Nika and Lance, who remember him as their enemy during the SAI Rebellion.

Joaquim and Selene deploy drones to track the Rasu on Namino. Footage from the drones reveals widespread destruction, but also a massive Rasu compound being constructed on the edge of the city.

Alex belatedly learns Caleb has gone to Namino and that her father helped him; she and David argue, and she confesses how she's afraid that due to his bond with Akeso, Caleb won't survive this trial. Caleb reaches

Namino, battling both Rasu and Akeso's protests as he crosses the city to try to reach Marlee.

Miriam wakes up from regenesis in a new body. She struggles to accept what happened, what it means to have been dead and the incongruity of a new body. That night, she's consumed by nightmares of the Rasu imprisoning her.

Caleb reaches the underground bunker and reunites with Marlee. He tries to convince her to to leave Namino with him, but she insists on staying to help everyone trapped there, and he agrees to stay as well.

Parc Eshett's Plex twin was injured during the initial Rasu attack and is now trapped on the streets of Namino. Parc's other incarnation on Mirai reaches the Omoikane Initiative and reveals that he can communicate with his Plex twin on Namino despite the quantum block.

Mesme offers the Asterions a Rift Bubble device, which will prevent any Rasu from reaching the surface of a planet. Corradeo Praesidis tells Nika about the destruction he and Nyx saw at the Ourankeli's halo ring. Nika urges him to go home to Concord and bring the Anadens in line.

Miriam gives the eulogy at Malcolm's funeral, and Alex vows to do something to stop the spiraling carnage. Mia, in mourning, tries to convince Richard and Miriam to send Casmir and a Machim fleet against Savrak targets. When they refuse, she enlists Devon Reynolds, now in charge of Special Projects, to hack into the CINT servers and send a message directly to Casmir. Richard and David argue over David using Richard's credentials to help Caleb steal a Ghost. Casmir receives a message he believes is from Miriam, authorizing him to send Machim ships against Savrakath military targets.

Alex returns home to find Akeso in a full state of revolt, with thunderstorms and flooding consuming the planet. She enlists her father's help to steal a Machim Imperium, and they deliver it to Kennedy, who reverse engineers the Imperium's double shielding in order to install it on Concord ships.

On Namino, a team from the bunker finds an injured Parc and brings him back to their hideout. Caleb suffers through the intense negative physical reaction of Akeso to the violence he committed during the excursion.

Dashiel develops a way to meld kyoseil into adiamene, allowing the kyoseil to dynamically alter the shape of adiamene hulls, and begins building a new, more resilient fleet.

Parc on Mirai passes along a message for Alex from Caleb, then tells Nika what's happening on Namino. Dashiel announces that his people have developed a virutox that should disrupt Rasu functionality, and Nika asks Dashiel to create a kyoseil-infused body she can use to reach Namino and deliver the virutox.

Nika passes along Caleb's message, and Alex decides to take the *Siyane* to Namino. Devon provides her with new toys to combat the Rasu, including a negative energy handgun called a Rectifier. Alex seeks out Morgan Lekkas, who since Brooklyn Harper's death six years earlier has been running a bar on Chalmun Station, and convinces Morgan to accompany her to Namino. Alex then asks Akeso for help in tracking Caleb. They bond, and Akeso grants Alex the ability to sense the location of Caleb's heartbeat.

Corradeo returns to Concord space for the first time in fourteen years. On learning that all the Praesidis Inquisitors who didn't commit suicide after The Displacement have gone missing, he asks Nyx to try to find them.

Nika's new body is awakened, and she's overwhelmed by the effect of so much kyoseil flowing through her veins on top of the surreal nature of being a Plex. Alex and Morgan pick her up, then take the *Siyane* to Namino. Alex leaves Morgan in charge of the ship as she and Nika set off toward the occupied city.

Joaquim and Selene deploy a drone to investigate the mysterious Rasu compound. Parc asserts that the centerpiece of the compound is the source of the quantum block, and Caleb and the others decide to test out the compound's defenses. They sneak across the city to fire a rocket launcher at the compound, but the rocket is shot down before reaching its target. In response to the attack, Rasu track down the group.

Meanwhile, Alex and Nika fight Rasu through the city as Alex follows Caleb's heartbeat. They reach Caleb and the others just as Rasu forces attack; Alex uses the Rectifier to vaporize the attackers then reunites with Caleb.

Once they return to the bunker, Alex and Caleb argue over his deception about his plans, until they both have a breakthrough and reconcile. Alex discovers that, much like his heartbeat, she can feel what Caleb physically feels. She convinces him to remove the wall he's erected between himself and Akeso, at which point he can feel her as well. A sensory-overloaded sensual encounter ensues. Afterward, Caleb reluctantly rebuilds the barrier blocking Akeso off so he can continue to fight the Rasu.

Nika devises a plan for them to destroy the quantum block at the heart of the Rasu compound. Her twin and Lance brief Miriam on the plan, and Miriam agrees to bring a Concord fleet to try to free Namino. Miriam takes command of her new ship, the *CAF Aurora*, which has the Imperium's double shielding installed on it.

Richard discovers that Mia hacked the CINT server and sent messages in his and Miriam's names. He reluctantly moves to arrest Mia, but she vanishes through a wormhole before he can do so.

The Savrakaths offer to return Torval to the Anadens in exchange for a one-week cease-fire. Ferdinand accepts the offer but intends to break the terms and bomb the Savrakaths once Torval is safe. Eren recovers from his detox, only to learn that the Savrakaths plan to hand Torval back to the Anadens. In exchange for agreeing to reconnect to the regenesis network, he convinces Drae to help him stop the prisoner exchange. Eren arms himself with antimatter and literally dive-bombs the exchange, killing himself, Torval and many Savrakath military leaders.

Malcolm's prison is located beneath the site of the prisoner exchange, and the bombing creates enough damage and chaos to allow him to free himself from his cell. He escapes his crumbling prison and reaches the surface, then calls AEGIS for an extraction. When he arrives at the Presidio, he discovers that the world thought him dead and learns that Mia has disappeared.

On Namino, Morgan brings the *Siyane* into the city, and everyone in the bunker is evacuated to the ship. Nika, Joaquim, Alex and Caleb infiltrate the Rasu compound. Alex and Caleb create a distraction to enable Nika and Joaquim to reach the quantum block mechanism. As they engage the Rasu in earnest, Caleb almost kills Alex with unintended friendly fire.

Joaquim sacrifices himself to buy Nika time to implant the virutox. Once the virutox is activated, Morgan fires on the compound, destroying the quantum block. Nika, Alex and Caleb narrowly escape the compound and call the cavalry in.

Miriam faces the Rasu for the first time since they killed her, this time from the bridge of her new and improved ship. Mesme delivers a Rift Bubble to Namino, preventing any more Rasu from reaching the surface, and Alex shows Nika how to extract the code powering the Rift Bubble. Miriam, Lance and their fleets defeat the Rasu orbiting the planet, and DAF ground forces arrive on Namino to remove the remaining Rasu from the city.

After regenesis, Eren returns to his and Cosime's home on Hirlas, where he finally lets his grief overtake him. Corradeo arrives at the *elasson* gathering on Epithero in dramatic fashion.

The *Siyane* returns home safely, and Marlee reunites with her mother. Caleb and Akeso re-bond and seek a new, more sustainable way forward.

CONTENTS

Echo Rift

"But, first, a hush of peace—a soundless calm descends;
The struggle of distress, and fierce impatience ends;
Mute music soothes my breast—unuttered harmony,
That I could never dream, till Earth was lost to me."

— Emily Brontë

PART I

ECHOS

1

AKESO

URSA MAJOR II GALAXY

A warm sunrise shone through the canopy of colorful leaves overhead, casting a sea of tiny, frolicking shadows across the dew-soaked meadow.

Caleb Marano placed both hands on his niece's shoulders. "Close your eyes."

Marlee's mouth twitched sideways even as she complied, and he sensed her muscles straining to move beneath his hands. "Now *slow down.* Breathe in deeply. Take control of your awareness and direct it downward, into your chest and past your gut. Let it flow through your leg muscles, acknowledging their strength. Sense the dirt beneath your bare feet. Sink your toes into it and wiggle them around. What does it feel like?"

An airy giggle made it past her lips. "Cool. Damp. A little gooey."

"While you and I were on Namino, Akeso dumped enough rain on itself to fill a new ocean. It's fine—let your feet get muddy." He removed his hands from her shoulders and took several steps back. "Now imagine yourself rooted to the ground. Your feet are part of the earth itself. Solid yet pliant, sturdy and stable. The connection binds you and joins you with the soil, with the trees, with the flowing water feeding them. You *are* the earth, and nothing can dislodge you from this spot."

Marlee's calves flexed as she adjusted her stance without moving her feet, then bounced through her knees twice. "Okay. I'm a tree. Now what?"

Akeso whispered in his mind, and his mind whispered back. *Stretch upward beyond the soil and into the sunlight. Bind one to another.*

"Are you, though? Do you feel the planet's gravity itself securing you to the ground?"

"I totally feel it. I am rooted right here in this spot."

"Yes, you are. Open your eyes and look down."

As soon as she did, she let out a panicked squeal and tried to jump away, but the slender roots rising out of the soil to wind around her legs held her tight.

Caleb laughed, provoking a dirty glare from Marlee as she wiggled her legs within their prison. "Not funny."

"Yes, it is. But it's also serious. Close your eyes again. Memorize how this feels. The stability and security—the core strength—that comes from being rooted in the earth. Explore every aspect of it until you believe you can instantly call upon this sensation any time you need it."

Her brow furrowed tight. She sucked her cheeks in and progressed through a succession of ridiculous facial expressions. She drew in new air, then did it all again. Finally, she nodded. "I've got it."

Release and rejoin the soil. He silently circled behind her, his own toes renewing their connection to the earth with every step. Next, he reached out, his palm impacting her spine above her waist to shove her forward.

She stumbled for barely half a step before re-planting her feet, bending her knees and dropping her weight down to absorb the force of the shove.

"That's the idea."

"Well, it's not as if I can move while these roots are holding me prisoner."

"What roots?"

She peered down once more to discover that the roots had retreated into the earth. "Huh."

"See? This was all you."

She brushed away a loose strand of hair and considered him with a mix of residual skepticism and genuine curiosity. "I think I see what you're getting at here. But don't I also need to be light and quick on my feet? To dodge blows and outmaneuver opponents?"

"Absolutely. But you can't do so successfully unless you learn to stay rooted in your stability. Keep your center of gravity low and your strength wrapped around the core that center creates. Do this, and you'll never be knocked off-balance by anything less than a missile strike. Understand?"

"To be light and agile…I need to be grounded and solid?"

"Correct. It's only a contradiction until you understand how they complement one another in action."

She regarded him with exaggerated solemnity. "I'm ready to not be a contradiction."

"Then don't let me touch you." He lunged forward, feinted to the left and punched out, palm open. His fingertips swept barely a centimeter from the loose material of her shirt as she leapt away.

Thus began a dance across the meadow. The flow of their give and take carried them along the creek bed, into the morning sun and beneath a new canopy of trees.

He could have scored a few points on her, but for now he held back. Better to let her grow addicted to the confidence and sense of power that came from being in total control of her body and its motions. Harder lessons would come in due time.

Finally he dropped his hands to his knees, bent over and exhaled harshly. "Enough. You're wearing me out."

"You are so full of it."

"No, no. You've reminded me of how out of practice I am." He straightened up and dragged a hand through damp hair grown curly since coming outside this morning. The literal storm that had consumed both Akeso and him during their Namino trial may have passed, but the humidity from days of torrential downpours lingered. He went over to a shady spot and retrieved a water bottle from where he'd left it, turning it up for a gulp before offering it to her.

"Next lesson: transforming those sharp reflexes into a weapon using a perfect and constant awareness of your environment."

She waited to groan until after she'd emptied the water bottle. "When you say 'constant,' you mean constantly during a fight, don't you?"

"You never know when you're going to find yourself in a fight. Constant means constant." He took the empty water bottle from her, crouched and opened up the bag he'd brought outside. He produced a Daemon and tossed it to her, then lugged out a netted bundle of syncrosse balls. They were practice balls, made of a tough rubber instead of metal, but they packed a punch.

She regarded the bundle suspiciously while switching the Daemon from one hand to the other.

"Are you ready?"

"Dare I ask for what?"

He chuckled as he activated his plasma blade and sliced open the mesh restraining the balls. They floated up then shot in every direction, darting around like batted ping-pong balls in the air above them. "Shoot them. As fast as you can."

Her expression puckered up, and she raised the Daemon with both hands and fired. Ten meters away, shards of rubber went flying into the creek. Instantly she swung the Daemon to the left and fired again.

Pride swelled in his chest, for she was a naturally excellent shot. The Daemon whipped to the right and she fired—

—one of the balls smacked her between the shoulder blades, and the

Daemon tumbled from her hands to the grass. "Ow!"

"Hence the lesson: always, always, *always* be aware of your surroundings. You can't forget what's happening around you. Know where your threats are and where they're going, the location of objects you can conscript as weapons and, most importantly...."

The sound of new movement behind him overrode the discordant symphony of his pulse, and he spun around, both blades raised—and jerked his arms to a stop with the blades less than ten centimeters from each side of Alex's neck.

He suppressed a shudder. So foolish of him to have forgotten his own lesson. Granted, half of his consciousness, half of his very soul, had been cleaved away and walled up out of his reach, by his own choice. He'd deemed it necessary at the time, but now he was on a mission to ensure he never need do so again. Never. The price was too high.

"Keep track of everything that is moving on the field of play: friend or foe, innocent or antagonist."

Marlee twisted an arm around and rubbed gingerly at her back where the rubber ball had impacted. "But how am I supposed to keep my focus on my target *and* on every other moving object?"

"Lots and lot of practice."

She made a face, looking so like her mother did when challenged. But she retrieved the Daemon from the grass, gripped it in both hands with renewed determination and sighted down on another of the balls still whizzing through the air. It split in half from a point-blank hit. She jerked a nod to herself and quickly chose the next target, then disposed of it.

He followed her body language as she pivoted. She was telegraphing her moves, but not too badly, and they could work on it. His senses prickled the instant she zeroed in on a jittering ball almost thirty meters away and fired. The laser missed by half a centimeter, instead slicing into a tree limb overhanging the creek.

Oh! Shock. Loss. Self shorn away.

Caleb flinched, stunned by the jolt of...not pain, not exactly. An injurious assault. He forced himself to inhale through his nose and let the wave of trauma pass over him and fade away.

"I'm sorry, Akeso!" Marlee's gaze swung from the broken limb to him, mouth agape in horror. "And you? Did I hurt you, too?"

"It's okay. I expected this to happen. You're a good shot, but you're not *that* good. Not yet."

Her chin notched upward. "I will be."

"I believe you."

In truth, he'd done more than expected this to happen—he'd intended for it to do so. These lessons weren't solely for Marlee. Through them, he hoped to teach Akeso as well. About how there was nothing inherently evil in defending oneself, and how it was important to do so, lest people you cared for get hurt due to your inaction. This was about getting Akeso comfortable with action, even with violence, when framed by the proper mindset. If a little nick of the flesh was necessary for Akeso to begin to fully appreciate and internalize the lessons, so be it.

He took the Daemon from Marlee, set it on the ground and grasped both of her hands in his. "Watch this." He closed his eyes and inhaled, then opened one eye to find her staring at him. "Not me—watch the tree where you shot it."

"Oh." She chewed on her bottom lip and shifted her attention to the broken limb overhead.

He closed his eyes once more and breathed in fully. *I am the nourishing water pouring out from the creek and swirling through the roots beneath the soil, flowing up the trunk and out into the limb until I reach the point of injury.*

Replace. Renew. Replenish.

In his mind, a fresh limb sprouted from the shorn stub, extending and growing. Buds became shoots became unfurling leaves that greedily drew in the sun's nourishing rays. *I am the rays and the stomata in the leaves, the strengthening limb growing hardier as water flows along my ravenous pathways.*

Marlee gasped in delight, and he peered upward to see the limb fully regrown and in bloom with a sprinkling of tiny white flowers.

"Amazing! I've never seen the planet grow something so fast. I didn't know you could do that."

"It's mostly Akeso. I'm just an...active spectator." It wasn't quite true, or not quite true any longer. Before Namino, he'd not been able to take such an active hand in guiding Akeso's cycle of life. Of renewal. But things were different now, for both of them. While he was teaching Akeso to make peace with the necessity of violence in defense of the living, Akeso was teaching him how to strengthen the force and power of life itself. Maybe? He hoped they were both learning the right lessons.

He lingered in the moment as a tingling sensation spread through his chest and out to his extremities. It felt as if he'd been reborn, as surely as the tree's wound had healed itself in a surge of *élan vital.* Akeso's feedback loop, whether it coursed with the pain of loss or the joy of replenishment, really was something to behold. Even more so to experience.

But the real world waited on him, so he shook off the spell. He smiled, picked up the Daemon and returned it to her, then gestured toward the sky. "There are still seven balls in the air."

2

AKESO

David Solovy removed the last batch of blueberry pancakes from the stovetop skillet and piled them high atop an overflowing platter. He stepped back and studied the stack critically, then nodded in satisfaction. "*Skazochnaya*!"

Alex appeared in the kitchen to nudge her father playfully in the side. "I think we'll be the judge of that." She stole the platter from him and whisked it away to the dining table, where she set it next to a bowl of yet more fresh blueberries and sliced bananas.

David gestured toward the open front door as he joined Miriam at the table. "Should we tell them breakfast is ready?"

Alex grabbed a glass of mango juice from the counter before taking her seat at the table opposite her father. "Marlee's been looking forward to this training session ever since we got back from Namino. Honestly, so has Caleb. We won't be able to get them inside anytime soon. I'll save some leftovers for them."

"What if there aren't any leftovers?"

"Dad, this has got to be a kilo's worth of pancakes, and only three of us are eating. There had better be leftovers."

Her mother huffed a breath. "I thought you understood your father's relationship with blueberries."

"And with pancakes, apparently." Alex rolled her eyes in amusement as she motioned to Valkyrie, who was wandering amorphously along the front windows, and patted the chair next to her. "I know you're not here to eat, but you can sit and relax with us."

"Oh, certainly!" Valkyrie maneuvered the chair out from the table and arranged her virtual avatar into a sitting position. "It smells delightful. I am regretting not bringing my doll for the occasion—an error I will not repeat next time."

Valkyrie's physical body didn't actually digest food or use it as fuel, but the state-of-the-art model included simulated taste buds and a receptacle to store ingested food, among other features. The better to not be utterly bored at the dinner parties she was always being invited to attend.

Alex gathered a chunk of moist, steaming pancake high on her fork and bit into it, then moaned in delight. Her father had been crafting the most scrumptious pancakes ever since she was old enough to eat them, and his culinary skills remained as sharp as ever. "Delicious as always, Dad."

"*Skazochnaya*, even?"

"*Skazochnaya*." It came out sounding like 'scho-zho-cthunah' on account of her mouth being full.

"Thank you, thank you, *milaya*. So, what is the latest word from the Dominion?"

She washed the gooey pancakes and blueberries down with her juice. "The Kats are getting ready to deliver a Rift Bubble for the final Axis World, Ebisu, after which I think everyone there will let out a huge sigh of relief. No new sightings of the Rasu so far. I assume they're regrouping and trying to devise a new strategy before resuming harassing the Asterions at every turn."

"At which point we'll devise a clever new strategy to counter them again. What about Namino?"

Hearing the name spoken aloud sent a shiver through her bones. Though it had ended in victory and happy reunions, most of her short time there had been an ugly, dark trial. Except for the one rapturous interlude, of course. "Cleaned out of Rasu, but it's devastated. I don't know what the Asterions are going to do as far as rebuilding it. I'm not sure they know yet, either."

Miriam shook her head and paused her fork halfway to her mouth. "If they have any sense, which they seem to, right now they need to be pouring all their funds and efforts into strengthening their military and planetary defenses with weapons and tools that aren't gimmicks."

Alex frowned. "The Rift Bubble isn't a gimmick. It saved the lives of thousands of people on Namino, including three people currently here on Akeso."

"I realize that. Believe me, I appreciate the power of the technology, and I'm glad the Kats have finally stepped up to pull their weight in this conflict. But the Asterions need to develop and implement a contingency plan for when a Rift Bubble fails. We all do."

"I understand how the devices work. Remember, I built the Dimensional Rifter out of the Kat code. They won't fail."

"Then the Rasu will find another way through. It's what they do." A dark shadow swept through her mother's eyes…she blinked and set her fork down. "I apologize. I didn't mean to dampen the mood. It's a beautiful morning, and we're having a wonderful, hand-crafted meal around the table. Most of all, our family is alive, in good health and home safely."

"Yes, we are." David reached out and squeezed Miriam's hand. "But we also all want to stay this way, so your point is well made."

While she ate, Alex surreptitiously studied her mother's outward demeanor, searching for clues as to her state of mind. The rousing success against the Rasu at Namino the second time around had done her mother a lot of good. But there were still moments when a flash of panic crossed her features, as if fear was reaching out from the shadowy, unconscious depths to try to drag her away into the maw. Moments when she looked lost, struggling to produce a word or a memory, as if she unexpectedly found herself situated outside of this place and time, trapped in the limbo between life and death.

Regenesis was a genuine miracle, but it was also a complicated one.

The silence around the table lingered a beat too long, and Alex directed her attention to Valkyrie. "What did the Ruda say when you went to visit them?" In reality she could reach out with her mind and simply know all the details, but she knew it made Valkyrie feel more *real* to converse aloud, especially when she had an audience.

Tiny points of honeyed light rippled over Valkyrie's projected skin. "Unfortunately, nothing worthwhile. In fairness, we ought not to have expected anything else. They've claimed every centimeter of their planet and maintain a precariously balanced division of power based on the equality of their geography. Should one of them start morphing and changing shape and *moving*, it would provoke a planet-wide societal crisis. Nevertheless, they were most curious about the reason for my inquiry and expressed great interest in assisting us with whatever endeavor we were pursuing."

"Oh, I just bet they did."

"As an ally of Concord, the Ruda do not exist in isolation. It is reasonable to assume that they will hear of the Rasu sooner or later. Perhaps it would be better if we guide the narrative by providing the information to them on our terms."

Alex grumbled under her breath. "Mom, what do you think?"

"I think Valkyrie is probably correct. The Ruda are not a Protected Species, thus we have no obligation to attempt to protect them. From a military attack, yes, but not from information or current events."

"And what if we're protecting ourselves? Remember, the first thing the Ruda tried to do when we met them—or the second or third thing anyway—

was kill Caleb and me." She waved off Valkyrie's burgeoning protest. "Yes, yes, it was a misunderstanding, whatever. I was the one with a blade at my throat, and I'm merely saying we need to be careful—"

A heartbeat not her own jolted in surprise and sudden anguish, and Alex jerked involuntarily. The next instant she leapt up and hurried to the front door and out onto the porch.

Near the creek, Caleb approached Marlee with his arms extended, taking a Daemon from her and setting it on the ground. When he stood once more, he grasped Marlee's hands in his. As he did, his heartbeat gradually eased back into its normal rhythm, and the faint sensation of anguish faded into a controlled calmness.

Her own distress took an additional second or two to fade away. With the passing of Akeso's storm, so too had the more visceral aspects of her connection to Caleb quieted. But though it had now been almost two weeks since she'd sought Akeso's help in reaching him on Namino, the fundamental link created between her and Caleb, with Akeso as the bridge, hadn't vanished. In the silence, she could still hear his heartbeat. And when it spiked like it had a minute ago, she could hear it even through the noise.

A permanent gift from Akeso? It was too soon to put her weight down and rely upon it, but she deeply hoped so, for it was already precious to her.

"Alex?"

Her mother's questioning voice broke through her reverie. After a last check of the goings-on across the meadow to confirm the crisis had passed, she returned to the table and refilled her plate from the rapidly dwindling stack of pancakes. There really might not be any leftovers. "Everything's fine. I just thought I heard something."

Miriam cast a too-knowing glance at the open front door. "How is he doing?"

"He insists that his and Akeso's evolving relationship is very much a work in progress, but he's...better. A lot better." And he truly was, but the details were not appropriate breakfast table conversation, so she changed the subject. "Oh, by the way, I invited Richard and Will to come over for breakfast as well, but Richard said they had a prior engagement."

Her parents exchanged a weighty gaze, and her father followed it up with a dramatic sigh. "It might technically be true, but I'm afraid Richard isn't interested in spending any time in the same room with me at present."

Her jaw practically hit the table. Richard had been her father's best friend since before she was born—since before her parents met—and upon her father's return, after a few minor stumbles, they'd picked right back up where they'd left off. "What? Did you two have a fight? Has that ever happened before?"

"*Yes,* it has, though I can't recall one that was so troubling and lingered so long as this one. Truthfully, it was less of a fight and more me blundering into infuriating him. Also violating several of his most basic moral precepts and insulting his official authority."

"Damn. Is this your opinion of what happened, or his?"

"It obviously wasn't what I intended, but in retrospect I find I can't argue much with his position."

She glanced at her mother, who offered only a tiny shrug in response. She must be stuck playing mediator. "I can't even conceive of what such a fight would have looked like."

"It wasn't pretty." Her father appeared genuinely chagrined, bordering on crestfallen. "Before you ask, I have apologized, explained myself, conveyed my deepest and most heartfelt *raskayaniye,* and apologized again."

"And none of that worked? He hasn't forgiven you?"

"Not yet."

3

SENECA

SENECAN FEDERATION
MILKY WAY GALAXY

Richard Navick parked his skycar on the east end of the nearly empty dirt lot, then exited the car and took in the scene. A rustic, real wood-frame lodge sat on the banks of a lake to the south of the parking area. In every direction, forested mountains jutted into the sky to cradle the lake, and a slight breeze added a distinct chill to the air. It was an overcast day, and the water churned a muted indigo beneath a canopy of steel clouds.

Lake Boscosa was situated almost six hundred kilometers from Cavare and ninety kilometers from the nearest town, deep in the Alba Mountain Range to the north of the capital. Will had taken him to visit many vacation spots on Seneca over the years, but none so remote as this.

A dock extended out from the lodge into the water; at the end of it, an open-air boat rocked on the languid waves, where a large man in a floppy hat and a flannel shirt was lugging a cooler onto the deck. The man dropped the cooler in a corner, turned around and, spotting him in the distance, waved him forward. "Richard! Down here!"

Richard grabbed his jacket from the passenger seat and set off toward the lake. As he drew closer, he noticed the dock spanned the length of the lodge and then some. Two berths held tied-off boats, and another three sat empty.

As soon as he reached the boat, Graham Delavasi produced two beers from the cooler and offered him one. He hadn't realized how badly he wanted one until he held the cold, frosted bottle in his hand. He opened it and took a long sip, then scrutinized the interior of the boat. "I didn't bring a fishing rod. Or bait. Or whatever else one uses to catch fish."

"Not a problem." Graham gestured to a pile of supplies in the rear corner as he settled into the captain's seat. "A full set of gear comes with every rental. Besides, we don't actually have to catch any fish if you're not so inclined. We can just putter around the lake in circles and drink beer."

Richard laughed. "That might be better, if I'm being honest." He watched in growing curiosity as Graham fired up the motor and guided the boat away from the dock at a gentle speed. "I know you said you'd 'retired,' but I didn't believe it. You're going to...I was about to say you're going to live another hundred years, but now that you made it this far, you can live forever. Are you seriously intending on spending eternity running a fishing lodge for tourists?"

"Possibly."

"Why?"

"Not much for easing into things with a spot of small talk, eh?"

Richard shrugged. He'd known Graham for many years now, and the man had never met an etiquette he didn't ignore.

Once they were a hundred meters or so out onto the lake, Graham engaged the autopilot and spun his chair around to face Richard. "Aristide stepped down after his last term and moved to Elathan to run a nonprofit group. Gianno is, obviously, gone. You and Will left for the bright lights of Concord. I guess what I'm saying is, when The Displacement happened, the world got a lot bigger—which meant *my* world got a lot smaller."

"I have asked you to come work with us at CINT at least once a year for the last thirteen years."

"I know." Graham took a fulsome swig of his beer. "Most gracious of you. But I am set in my ways and too old to learn new tricks."

"Bullshit."

"It's true. I know the ins and outs, major players and small fries, of every gang, cartel and corrupt corporation in the Senecan Federation. But when I think about trying to start from scratch with seven alien species inhabiting thousands of worlds? Nope. Don't want to do it."

"It's not *that* complicated once you...." Graham scowled at him over the top of his bottle "...okay, okay. I won't browbeat you. But the world is a little less safe so long as you are out here on this boat instead of behind an intelligence desk."

"Bah. The world's getting along fine without me."

"Well, I'm not."

Graham adjusted a setting on the dash, and the boat slowed. "I figured this wasn't entirely a social call."

"Sorry. I am glad to see you, and this is a gorgeous place. I already want to come back here with Will and stay for a few days. Wander around the mountains. Maybe even learn how to fish. But yes..." Richard groaned, sank lower in his chair, and propped his feet on the top of the gunwale "...I could use someone to talk to right now."

"It's only me, the lake and the mountains, and we'll all three keep your secrets."

"And I thank all of you for it." He rubbed at his jaw. "Where to start? I had a mole in CINT who helped ex-Senator Ferdinand orchestrate his coup attempt against the Concord government. My oldest friend went behind my back to steal my personal access codes, then used them to help Caleb steal one of CINT's highly classified, highly experimental ships. I've been forced to issue an arrest warrant for Mia Requelme for breaking into the secure CINT server, impersonating both Miriam and myself, and issuing illegal orders to Anaden personnel during an active intelligence operation. And though I can't prove it, I believe Devon Reynolds helped her pull it off. My entire department is leaking like a sieve, morale is in the ditch thanks to the coup attempt and Anaden defections...and now I've lost two of my closest friends and a valued colleague."

"Shitty week, huh?"

"Shitty month."

Graham fiddled with another setting on the dash. "Have you talked to any of them about all of this?"

"Oh, everyone's *very* sorry. They were only doing what they thought was right and necessary and blah blah. And they're not even wrong." Richard sighed. "But I don't care for being taken advantage of."

"The easy thing for me to say would be how you're too nice, and this is why people take advantage of you. But I'm an unrepentant asshole, and I've gotten taken advantage of far worse than you did."

"What?"

"Come on. Don't you remember that time my chief deputy was working for the Aguirre Conspiracy? She nearly got Isabela Marano and several other innocents killed while trying to ensure the Second Crux War never ended, and she did it all right under my nose?"

He conceded the point. "I do remember."

"We're all fallible, Richard. So go easy on yourself." Graham paused. "I also remember a day, around the same time, when the world was spiraling out of control, and you broke every rule to work with me while our governments were at war with one another."

"You're saying that sometimes the rules are worth breaking...and that I used to know this."

"I'm not saying anything. I'm simply reminiscing about the good old days with a friend."

Richard grunted and finished off his beer. He hadn't meant to drink it so quickly, but…. "Have I become a bureaucrat?"

"I am certain you have not. But if you ever do feel yourself becoming one, head out here and hang out with me—or by yourself, or bring Will—and catch some fish for an afternoon. You'd be shocked what nonsense it'll make clear."

Richard gazed out at the waves lapping easily against the hull, then farther, to the hunter-green forest lining the shore. "I can believe it would." He glanced sideways at Graham. "So, do you want to come work at CINT?"

Graham guffawed and grabbed two more beers out of the cooler. "Hell, no. I've got fishing to do."

4

KIYORA

ASTERION DOMINION
GENNISI GALAXY

She lay peacefully beneath the curving glass of the stasis chamber, eyes closed and features relaxed, slightly crooked nose and all. Already enveloped in a deep, dreamless slumber that could last a week, a month or an eternity.

Dashiel Ridani's hand rested gently on Nika's shoulder. "Are you sure this is what you want to do?"

She—the wakened version of herself—nodded resolutely and without hesitation. "I am. Splitting my consciousness into separate bodies was an intensely uncomfortable, if necessary, experience. The situation required it, but my everyday life does not. And if I ever desperately need to be in two places at once again, I can wake this body up and reconnect to it."

"I know you can. But you seem…sad."

Was sadness the name for the strange, aching hollowness in her chest? Sentimentality, perhaps, but it had no basis in reality. It was simply unnerving to stare down at one's own face beneath the translucent cover. "It's not sadness. I told you, I'm not giving up anything or bringing an end to any part of a life. Everything that body experienced, I experienced. Her thoughts were my thoughts. There was no separation, so there's no loss now."

"If you say so." He moved closer behind her and leaned in to nuzzle her neck. "On to happier topics, then. Did I thank you yet for last night?"

She chuckled quietly. "Once or twice. But you should really thank her."

"What? You said there wasn't any separation."

She shifted around to face him, kissing away his growing puzzlement. "I did, and there wasn't any. I'm just playing with you."

"Something else you—both of you—have proved you excel at."

"Quite." She let the salacious and delightful memories of the night before drift through her mind…but reality soon intruded, and the responsibilities that came with it. "Come on, we're going to be late for the Advisor Committee meeting. I don't want to miss it, since it stands to be the first meeting in a while that doesn't feature screaming, crying and gnashing of teeth."

"I hope so. One never can tell."

Try as she might, she couldn't stop herself from taking a last glance back at the silent form lying in the stasis chamber. Then she pushed aside the perplexing, melancholy thoughts the sight stirred in her and followed Dashiel out of the room, closing the door behind her.

RW

After stopping off at the clinic's front desk to complete the authorization for the stasis chamber and its contents to be sent to medical cryo storage, Nika and Dashiel stepped outside into a warm summer Kiyora day. It was almost winter on Mirai, and she'd been carrying a jacket around all morning despite the heat here.

Dashiel stopped halfway down the steps and leaned on the railing. "Can I ask you something?"

She smiled as a gust of wind tousled his hair. It gave him an almost impish look, though she'd never voice such a scandalous notion aloud. "Always, darling."

"Why..." his lips pursed briefly before he began anew "...why did you decide to keep the new body? I mean, it was created as a special-purpose weapon, and it fulfilled that purpose. The body you're putting into cold storage, though? It's been *you* for a great many years."

"I know." *Even if I no longer remember most of those years.* She extended her left arm in front of her and twisted it around; despite the bright summer sunlight, the glow in her skin was unmistakable. Its intensity still surprised her now and then. "I chose to keep this body because kyoseil is the answer."

"To what?"

"To everything. We've scarcely begun to explore its true nature and capabilities, but you and I have both demonstrated how powerful it can be. And now that I've viewed the world through these kyoseil-saturated eyes, I can't go back. Not until I've seen everything it has to show me."

RW

MIRAI

ASTERION DOMINION
GENNISI GALAXY

Nika and Dashiel walked into the Omoikane Initiative and were immediately greeted by a cacophony of sirens and overlapping shouts. So much for no gnashing of teeth....

Dashiel tapped the first person they passed on the shoulder. "What's happening?"

The woman, one of Katherine Colson's subordinates, gestured toward the far wall. "Rasu signatures are approaching Mirai."

Here? A shiver chilled Nika to the bone, but she lifted her chin and projected her voice above the din. It was time to lead; hopefully events wouldn't transform it into a time to fight. Not today. "Everyone, we knew this was bound to happen. Let them bounce off the Rift Bubble a few times, and they'll lose interest."

"I hope you're right." Dashiel scowled darkly as they approached the group of Advisors gathered in front of the primary panes along the far wall.

Only Lance Palmer and Adlai Weiss acknowledged their arrival, and she fell in beside Lance. "What's the word?"

"Around twenty thousand Rasu vessels should reach the Mirai outer atmosphere in four minutes. Barely more than a scouting party."

"They must realize what they're going to find."

"Damn straight—a planet that can't be touched."

She'd seen the Rift Bubble technology work its magic firsthand on Namino. Nevertheless, her pulse took off to the races as the first Rasu vessels came within visual range. This was her *home*, dammit. What if they had identified a weakness in the technology they could exploit? What if Mirai fell today?

Dozens of violet beams shot out from the largest of the Rasu vessels—and vanished into nothingness. Nika breathed out.

The attackers fired many more times, from different locations and altitudes, all to no avail. Finally, a tiny Rasu vessel accelerated forward. A sacrificial lamb? It reached the perimeter of the rift barrier and vanished as well.

As one, the Rasu pivoted and accelerated away. Nika gripped Dashiel's hand, relief flooding through her.

Lance, however, growled over the erupting chatter. "Pull up the orbital feeds from Kiyora, Ebisu and Synra."

Three of the panes shifted to views of the colorful profiles of the remaining Axis Worlds, and a hush descended upon the room as everyone…waited. The Rift Bubble for Ebisu had been delivered and activated a mere six hours ago; if the Rasu had shown up a day earlier, the planet would have been lost. It was an uncomfortable reminder of how precarious their situation remained, and of how dependent they were on the Kats' technology and willingness to share it.

People were getting restless and moving on to actual work when a Rasu fleet, possibly the same one, showed up at Synra. The same sequence of events repeated itself as they watched on. She'd like to say it wasn't as stressful as the first time, but she'd be lying.

The next several hours passed on a knife-edge of tension as relief replaced worry replaced relief over and over again. It was evening by the time the Rasu departed the last Axis World, Kiyora, and reappeared swiftly at Chosek.

The enemy must know by now all about how Chosek was a jewel of a planet—one that nurtured enough kyoseil to allow them to control a hundred million Rasu, if only they could crack the mysterious life form's secrets. The data stored on Namino would have told them this when they pillaged it.

Of course they did know, which was why they tested the Rift Bubble protecting Chosek for longer than an hour and from pole to pole. Nika took comfort from the fact that Shoset and the rest of the Chizeru remained blissfully ignorant of the invaders trying so terribly hard to devour their civilization and take the planet and its resources for themselves. The rift barrier was located in the upper reaches of the atmosphere, and with no telescopes or sensor technology, the Chizeru wouldn't be able to see the ships. She wondered if some of them might nonetheless sense the malignant shadow looming over their peaceful existence.

Gods, what was with her and the melodrama today? Maybe all this kyoseil was screwing up her emotional processes. She should sit down in a quiet corner and take a look as soon as she had a few minutes.

After what felt like a veritable eternity, the Rasu fleet finally departed Chosek empty-handed.

At the first sign of their retreat, Lance went over and grabbed Adlai by the arm. "Announce the final Evacuation Order for the Adjunct Worlds. Right now."

Adlai nodded soberly and gathered the other Justice Advisors together to hash out the logistics. Because the Adjunct Worlds weren't protected, if the Rasu truly wanted to do so, they could spill Asterion blood today after all.

Nika wandered to one of the other busy tables. "Katherine, how many people are remaining on the Adjunct Worlds?"

Katherine looked up from a small pane in front of her. Worry lines around her eyes and mouth suggested she hadn't been getting much sleep lately, and Nika felt a twinge of guilt. Katherine wasn't an easy person to like, but no one could question her commitment to her job or to the Dominion. "Only about 140,000 across all the colonies, and of those, almost half have transferred their psyche storage to an Axis World. The footage from Namino provoked a change of heart in a number of previously recalcitrant people."

"Good. Maybe we can get more of them to change their minds today." She watched as Adlai, Selene Panetier and Julien Grayson hurried out and down the lift, presumably to oversee evacuations at the transit hubs. On the far wall, half the panes converted to display the sensor output from all twelve Adjunct Worlds.

Which one was it going to be? The closest to Chosek was Adjunct Rei, but she hadn't gotten the impression distance mattered much to the Rasu. Shi and Hachi were probably the richest in natural resources, but what if the Rasu didn't value the same materials as Asterions did?

The answer came almost two hours later, when red flashing alerts erupted in the top left corner of one of the panes.

"It's Adjunct San," shouted one of the DAF officers. The other boxes shrunk away as the feed from San enlarged. In seconds, the inky shapes of Rasu warships arrived to dominate the view. The first column fired their shots...and found the planet unprotected.

Lance paced in agitation in front of the panes. "Say the word, and I'll have every ship in the air and every boot on the ground there in fifteen minutes. Let me defend it."

Nika dragged both hands through her hair but shook her head. "We've talked about this. We've evacuated everyone willing to leave. We've moved all our sensitive or valuable data from the Adjunct Worlds to Synra. There's nothing on San for them to take except the soil."

"But we can *fight* them!"

"No, we can't. Don't you get it? There is an effectively infinite number of Rasu, and I imagine this scouting party of theirs will be joined by a lot of its friends any minute now. But every time we engage them, we lose people and ships, just when we're on the verge of actually fielding a real fleet."

"The new adiaK ships don't go down so easily. And, yes, I lost two-thirds of my ground forces clearing out Namino, but they'll be back up and itching for a rematch soon."

She wanted so badly to agree with him. She wanted to fight, too. But she had a responsibility to preserve and protect her people and their way of life. To ensure the heart of the Dominion never fell. "So long as it's a war of attrition, we still lose. We need to concentrate on marshaling and growing our resources for the next *real* battle."

"What about Concord? They can spare the ships."

"Now they can, yes. But what happens when the Rasu find their worlds? I won't constantly demand they fight our every battle for us. Concord is another resource we need to nurture, not waste."

Lance glowered at the panes. "I don't like it."

"That much is obvious. And I hear what you're saying, but now's not the time. Today's not the fight."

He rubbed at his face. "Fine. I'll go along for now. Until we're stronger. So if you'll excuse me, I need to go see about making us stronger faster." He strode off to the lift, fighting to keep his shoulders high.

A sinking feeling pooled in her gut as she watched the first Rasu ships descend through the San atmosphere. Flashes of battling the Rasu on the streets of Namino raced in circles in her mind. Soon the enemy would rule the streets of Adjunct San, and there would be no one to stand and fight them.

Dashiel was conferring with one of the other Industry Advisors a few meters away, and she sidled up beside him, fighting against the overwhelming urge to rest her head on his shoulder, only for a moment. "Several of the San d-gates have been diverted here to Mirai. I'm going to head down to the transit hub and see if I can help with the final evacuations."

He checked with the other Advisor, then nodded. "I'll go with you."

MIRAI ONE

Absolute bedlam awaited them at the transit hub. Hundreds of displaced people huddled around in small groups, bags on their shoulders, backs and dragging wearily from their hands, all while Administration staff struggled to get their identities registered and direct them to temporary refugee housing.

The chaos was most noticeable, of course, at the two gates originating from Adjunct San. People stumbled through one after another after another. Some of them were visibly injured, and many were coated in soot and debris.

The nearing prospect of Firewall hovered over the scene, even if the evacuees didn't realize it. How many more people stood a chance to make it to safety before the Advisors had to shut off the exit route to protect the Axis Worlds from a back-door invasion by the Rasu?

Nika scanned the crowd several times and finally spotted Adlai and Selene ushering off a group of new arrivals into the care of Administration officers. She and Dashiel picked their way through the furor to reach them, and she handed Adlai a bottle of water she'd snatched on the way. "Where's Perrin? I thought she'd be here helping with the evacuation."

"She is. She was down there a minute ago." He pointed toward one of the checkpoints, but not seeing her, he waved down a roaming Justice officer. "Do you know where Perrin Benvenit is?"

The man gestured toward the rightmost d-gate. "She went to San to try to speed up the flow of evacuees."

"She did what?" Panic flared in Adlai's expression, and he pivoted toward the gate.

Nika grabbed Dashiel's hand, then Adlai's as she rushed past him, dragging them both along behind her. What happened when the Rasu first attacked Namino was *not* going to happen again.

Selene shouted in their direction. "Weiss! We don't have much time."

"I know!" The three of them rushed through the d-gate, leaving Mirai behind.

RW

ADJUNCT SAN

ASTERION DOMINION

GENNISI GALAXY

A steady series of roaring crashes and a pervasive, low rumble assaulted Nika's ears as thick soot assailed her eyes. The d-gate was swallowed by smoke as soon as they cleared it, and she couldn't see more than a few dozen meters in any direction.

Hq (visual, 40%) | ((scan.infrared && scan.thermal)(290°:70°))

A cluster of heat signatures emerged amid the smoke down the street, and Adlai was moving toward them before she was.

They came upon Perrin struggling to get two people, both injured, the last hundred meters to the d-gate. Blood trailed down her cheek from a cut on her forehead, and a large swath of skin had been scraped off her left forearm.

Adlai and Dashiel each took one of the evacuees from her, and Perrin practically fell into Nika's arms. "More people are back there in one of the buildings, on the next block. We need to go help them."

Adlai shook his head. "There's no time. The Rasu will be in the streets any minute now. We've got to get out of here then shut this place off."

"But—"

Nika wrapped an arm around Perrin's waist, to hold her upright but also to keep her from fleeing back into the tumult. "He's right. And you're in no condition to be running around in this madness any longer."

Perrin sniffled. "But what about those people? The Rasu will torture and kill them."

Dueling sentiments warred in Nika's mind. She despised the very idea of Firewall, and she'd loudly spoken out against it at every opportunity. But that was before she'd seen what it meant for the Rasu to control the streets of Namino. "They knew the risks, and they've had weeks to leave. We've begged and pleaded with them to leave in every way we know how. We've done all we can. They've made their choice."

Perrin opened her mouth to argue, but doubled over from a fit of coughing.

Adlai peered back at her in concern. "Okay, let's move."

The transit hub gained hazy definition within the smoky overlay as they limped toward it. Thankfully, dozens of people continued to depart through the d-gates, though this resulted in the formation of a bit of a line. As the seconds ticked by, Nika kept checking behind them anxiously, searching the perimeter for the encroaching shadows of Rasu bipedals—

A thunderous roar split open the sky, so close to them that it nearly ruptured her eardrums. She peered up to see a Rasu cruiser decelerating to hover a scant fifty meters above downtown. Its belly opened, and giant Rasu mechs poured out into the streets.

"Go!" She shoved everyone forward; someone behind her shoved her as well, and she and Perrin fell through the d-gate to land face-first on the cool floor of the Mirai One transit hub.

Dashiel landed beside her with his charge in tow. Time slowed to a crawl as they watched the shimmering d-gate—then Adlai and his charge stumbled through as well. Adlai handed off the wounded evacuee to a waiting officer and fell to his knees beside Perrin. "Are you all right?"

"I'm…." Perrin's forehead dropped to his chest, and he wound his arms around her. Over her head, he stared grimly at Nika.

She nodded, even as hatred of the enemy and despair for the lost chewed up the fiery pathways of her mind.

Adlai's raspy, smoke-clogged voice shouted above the noise. "Selene, shut them down."

Behind him, the two d-gates leading from Adjunct San flickered and fell silent.

5

MIRAI

OMOIKANE INITIATIVE

Nika collapsed into the chair in her office—she'd finally found the time to claim a small room at the Initiative upon returning from Namino—and let her head fall back against the cushion.

She'd showered and donned fresh clothes after making sure that Perrin's wounds were treated and her friend was okay, or as okay as anyone could be given the brief but traumatic experience on Adjunct San. Dashiel was called away to one of the fleet production lines on the way back from the transit hub, and Administration staff was busily seeing to the evacuees who had barely escaped the Rasu's clutches.

And the Rasu? They were setting up camp on Adjunct San for a nice, long stay. She gritted her teeth at the thought; she hated it, hated everything about this nightmare. Every compromise, every sacrificed life and lost battle. Yes, she'd made the Rasu bleed on Namino, but it wasn't enough. It wasn't *nearly* enough.

Luminescence flooded the office amid a squall of dancing lights. In the split-second before her taxed brain caught up to the fact that it was a Kat, she'd leapt out of her chair and readied the blades at her wrists.

With a harsh exhale, she sank back into the chair as the lights took on a vague shape undulating through the small room. "Mesme?"

It is I. I apologize if I startled you.

"It's…fine." She pinched the bridge of her nose. "What can I do for you?"

The Rift Bubbles protecting all of your primary worlds, as well as Chosek, were tested today. I trust they performed their duties to expectations?

"Yes, they…" her lips pursed "…is there any chance you can take on an Anatype form and pretend to sit down or something? I don't have the energy to talk to all the lights at once. Not today."

As you wish. The lights drew in and tightened their spread until they formed the outline of a body. It wasn't so detailed as Valkyrie's virtual avatar, but she conceded it did comply with her request. A faint halo of lights drifted out from almost delicate facial features, such as they were. An attempt at hair? So far as anyone knew, the Kats were genderless, but Mesme's namesake was a mythological Greek Titaness, so perhaps this explained it. The goddess of memory...must be nice.

"Thank you. Yes, the Rift Bubbles held firm against repeated Rasu onslaughts. It is remarkable technology, and let me again express my gratitude to your people for sharing it with us. If my enthusiasm isn't quite what it should be, just understand that I wish we didn't need your help. I wish we were defending ourselves."

You are.

"No, we're relying on the charity and goodwill of hyper-advanced, sapient space lights—I'm sorry, that was rude of me. I *am* grateful for everything you've done. Millions more would be dead and worlds destroyed without your assistance."

The faint outlines of almond-shaped eyes watched her for a moment. *Do you wish to deploy the next Rift Bubbles to your Adjunct Worlds where the Rasu have not yet invaded?*

She reached for her mug of coffee, only to belatedly realize it wasn't there. Where had she left it? "No, the next one has to go to Toki'taku. Then...I don't know. You should probably start offering them to Concord, right? They have trillions of citizens who require protecting, and even their massive fleet of warships can't be everywhere all the time."

Discussions are underway regarding Concord's preparation for a Rasu incursion. You need not concern yourself with it.

"Well, at least that's one thing." Ugh, she kept trying to be polite and gracious and kept sounding bitter instead. "What about the Sogain—your system? I'm confident its existence and location were mentioned once or twice in the files on Namino."

Tyche is preparing a response. Any Rasu who enter the system will not survive to depart.

"Oh?"

Oh. As a result, soon it will no longer serve as a home—as a station—for any Katasketousya. In any event, as we are now public allies, we no longer benefit from observing your civilization from afar.

"You know, we could have become public allies two hundred thousand years ago, when we first met one another."

It wasn't time.

Her head lifted up from the chair cushion in interest. "What is that supposed to mean?"

You needed to be left alone to forge your own path and discover your own destiny.

And what was *that* supposed to mean? "This enigmatic shtick of yours isn't going to go away anytime soon, is it?"

I do not precisely understand your question.

"Right. Of course you don't." She abruptly leaned forward, her elbows landing on the desk, as another thought occurred to her. "Is the Vault safe?"

It remains safe, hidden and well-guarded. I can show you, if you desire it.

"You mean spin up and whisk me a couple of galaxies away, then suspend me in nothingness so I can get a good gander at it? I think I'll simply take your word for it, for now. It's been a hells of a day."

I see. Allow me to apologize for your...impolite treatment on your most recent visit to the Sogain stellar system. It was necessary, but it gave no one any pleasure.

"Necessary? You mean like torturing Alex on your Portal Prime was necessary?"

Mesme's presence seemed to deflate, spreading out across the chair it 'occupied.' *Yes, in point of fact. Without enduring the admittedly unpleasant experience to which you refer, Alex would never have been driven to arrive at the Prevo solution. The Humans would have been cowed into submission by my more irascible associates, and so would never have evolved to be strong enough to travel to Amaranthe and defeat the Directorate. Billions would have died at the Directorate's hand, but more relevantly, without the defeat of the Directorate, Concord would never have risen to power and thus been in a position to help your people defeat the Rasu.*

She stepped through her limited knowledge of recent Human and Anaden history, and the dots connected well enough. But hindsight was tricky this way, always erasing alternate, abandoned paths that might have led to the same result, or even a better one.

She dropped her chin into her hand and considered the shifting presence sitting opposite her. At her request, its outline mimicked the appearance of an Anaden, and of the two species her ancestors had begat, Asterions and Humans. Mesme had been at this game for some time now, hadn't it? Did the Kat imagine it was shaping destiny itself? "We haven't defeated the Rasu yet."

You will.

"Why are you so certain?"

Because you must, else all is lost.

RW

MIRAI ONE

Adlai lifted his hand to the door lock on his apartment...and held it there, stricken by a wave of irrational hesitation. He continued to suffer these random flashbacks to Sevulch's attack from time to time, usually when he performed some rote, routine action that on a single day had resulted in a terrible outcome.

But Ian Sevulch—all living versions of him—was imprisoned at Zaidam Bastille (under new management), and Adlai's home was again a place of peace and refuge. He shook off the spell and opened the door.

The apartment was dark except for a dimmed light in the kitchen, and the paralyzing flashback threatened to rear up once more and overwhelm him. After a brief struggle with himself, he fought it off and tapped the overhead light on. Far too much relief flooded through him when it worked; naturally, it worked. Ian Sevulch needed to get out of his head, dammit.

His current attire was coated in ash, dirt and flecks of dried blood, so he'd take a quick shower, get cleaned up and head back to the Initiative—

He jumped in surprise to see Perrin sitting on the couch, for she hadn't made a sound since he'd walked in. After a brief stint at a repair bench to treat her injuries, she'd insisted on heading directly to the refugee center hosting the newest evacuees, and he'd assumed she was still there.

Instead, she sat slumped in a corner of the couch, her head in her hands. He hurried over and dropped to his knees in front of her. "Perrin? Are you all right?"

She peered at him, and through the splayed fingers he could see she'd been crying. "Not really, no."

He slipped his jacket off, let it fall to the floor and sat beside her, wrapping one arm around her shoulders. "What's wrong? Is this because of what happened on Adjunct San?"

She sat up enough to rest her head on his chest. "I don't understand how there can be such evil in the world. How can such soulless creatures exist that are driven to wreak indiscriminate slaughter on people they've never met, who never harmed them or threatened them?"

He kissed the top of her head. Things had been a bit tense between them since she'd confessed to keeping Parc Eshett's Plex identity a secret, and sometimes he worried about what other secrets she might be holding close, secrets about her past with NOIR. But then she went and reminded him how there likely didn't exist a purer, more caring soul in the universe. It wasn't the only reason why he loved her, but it was certainly reason enough for her to have earned his trust. Now, his heart ached anew over the sorrow she was inflicting on herself.

"I don't have a good answer for you. We conceive of evil as existing along a continuum, but the far end of that scale is truly, deeply horrifying. I'm so sorry you had to see its depravity today."

"I needed to save as many people as I could. But what about all those I didn't save? How many of the people who remained also insisted on keeping their backups close by, and now they're gone forever? Their stories, their hopes and desires, all lost to the monsters of the void."

"Enough of this." He gently turned her so she was facing him. "It's understandable to mourn those who we've lost, but they chose to put themselves in danger. They knew the risks."

"Nobody could possibly comprehend the risks the Rasu pose to life until they've seen it firsthand."

"Nonetheless. We did everything we could for them. Most importantly, though, focus on the people you *did* save, today and every day for the last month. Thousands of people are safe, with food and beds and roofs over their heads, because of you. You should be so proud of what you've accomplished. I know I am." He squeezed her shoulders, and she flinched away from him.

He immediately loosened his grip. "Are you still hurt? I thought we patched you up."

She shrugged with her right side. "A little. I didn't realize it earlier, but I guess my collarbone is cracked."

Had she been paying any attention at all to her OS alerts today? He stood and offered her a hand. "Come on. You have to get this fixed."

She frowned at his hand, shaking her head. "I'll stop by the clinic at the Initiative later." A weak chuckle escaped her lips. "One nice thing about the Chalet—the repair bench was always just across the room."

"I don't want to imagine you having to use it regularly."

"I didn't. Not too often." She forced herself to her feet, trying and failing for a teasing smile. "How do I snap out of this malaise? I need to get back to work. Those people we evacuated from Adjunct San need my help, but all I can think about is the ones I watched fall to the Rasu. I'm trying so hard to feel hope, but all I feel is despair."

Gods help them if her light stopped shining in their world; sometimes it felt as if it was the only thing keeping any of them moving forward. He took her hands in his. "We're going to take a shower to wash away all this grime, and you're going to let me kiss and hug on you until you smile, for real. Then we'll see to your collarbone repair, after which we'll go out there and do the best we can."

6

MIRAI

MIRAI ONE

Joaquim Lacese's first stop after leaving the regen clinic in a spiffing new body was his functional-at-best apartment to change into his own clothes and confirm nothing had been disturbed in the weeks of his absence. He couldn't think of a good reason why anyone would have broken into his place, but old habits and all.

Satisfied everything remained where he'd left it and feeling a bit more comfortable in his new skin and old clothes, he decided to head to the Initiative. It was time to try to find out what he'd *done* for those missing weeks.

It came as a pleasant surprise, and in truth as something of a relief, to learn that he'd been a proper godsdamn hero on Namino. He'd rescued friends and strangers alike, taken out a bunch of Rasu in clever and inventive ways, and capped it off by sacrificing himself to ensure that Nika was able to trigger the destruction of every last invader and reclaim the planet for the Dominion.

It was nice being viewed as the good guy for once. Sure, from his perspective he was always the good guy, protecting people and saving lives with weapons and attitude. But this time he was being *lauded* for it! Everywhere he wandered in the Initiative, hugs and handshakes and pats on the back were the order of the day.

Riding a nice, low-level buzz from all the accolades, he made tentative plans to meet Parc and a newly reawakened Dominic for dinner later in the evening and left everyone to their work at the Initiative. He'd volunteer to help with the renewed Adjunct World evacuations tomorrow, but tonight? He was simply going to enjoy being alive once again.

He stepped off the lift on the first floor and ran straight into someone not paying attention as they made to step onto it.

"Oh! Sorry." A blonde woman leapt to the side, then did a double-take. "Lacese?"

She looked familiar, but he drew a blank. "I'm sorry, do we know each other?"

"Right. You went nonfunctional at the Rasu compound." Her chin dropped a little, but she stuck a hand out. "Selene Panetier. We were together on Namino."

Panetier...*Justice Advisor.* His countenance darkened, and he almost refused the proffered hand. But she was being polite, and if she'd been on Namino, she'd know a great deal about the events of his last several weeks. Also, he couldn't deny that she was attractive, in the gritty, hard-edged way that Justice officers and rebels often shared.

After a brief and awkward pause, he relented and shook her hand. "Nice to meet you, again. I'll assume we did great work together on Namino."

"We actually did." Her expression flickered, and she turned toward the lift to leave...then back to him. "Say, if you'd like to go get a drink, I can tell you about it."

"You don't have important work to do upstairs?"

"I think all the day's excitement the Rasu brought has petered out. So...no. Nothing that can't wait until tomorrow."

A refusal hovered on his lips, but he craved real details about what had happened on the ground at Namino. And had he mentioned how she was cute? No, not 'cute'—serious and deadly and quite attractive. Not that it mattered, because she was *Justice.* But what did matter was how she had answers about his missing weeks. And he was already going for a beer anyway....

He shrugged. "I'm up for it. You can tell me about my heroics over a couple of drinks."

"Mostly *my* heroics."

"Is that so?"

"Yes, it is. You did help occasionally, though, when you weren't too busy being an asshole."

He snorted and fell in beside her as they strode toward the exit. "Sounds about right."

RW

"So you blew a hole in the torso of the Rasu bipedal. Then, before it could react, you shoved a grenade into the hole and took off running—smack into me."

"Like at the lift earlier?"

"So much worse, and bloodier. We both tumbled to the floor just as the grenade detonated and the Rasu exploded into a hundred pieces."

Joaquim took a sip of his vodka on the rocks, which he'd switched to after one beer. "But don't the Rasu simply reform?"

"*Yes.*" She twirled the stem of her glass between her fingers. "But we were waiting on Colonel Rogers to finish deploying the drone, so we couldn't bolt yet. Instead, you started stomping on the little Rasu slugs every time they tried to slink toward each other to form back up."

He choked on the vodka. "I *stomped* on them?"

"You did. You looked ridiculous, hopping around from one to the next. But it was sort of working, so I joined in after I dug a Rasu shard out of my shoulder."

"Ouch. What happened next?"

"You missed one of the slugs, and it started crawling up your leg. You shouted at me to shoot your leg off before the alien slithered inside you."

"Did you?" He patted his left thigh. "This is a new body, so I'm not able to tell."

"I did not. I managed to grab the slug off your knee and toss it down the hall." She opened both hands and scowled at her palms. "I swear I can still feel it on my skin. Anyway, about that time Rogers finally showed back up, and we all bailed for Camp Burrow."

He chuckled lightly; she was a skilled storyteller and embellishing for laughs, but it sounded like something he'd do. He realized his glass was empty, so he waved over the dyne server. "Another round of drinks for us—assuming the lady wants to regale me with more stories of our mutual heroism."

She shrugged in a way he took for affirmation. "There are certainly more stories to tell."

"Another round it is."

RW

Joaquim opened his eyes to reveal a blurry but unfamiliar ceiling. A soft bed lay beneath him, but also an unfamiliar one.

Ah, shit. What had he done this time?

He carefully rolled over, ignoring for now the headache banging against his skull, to see a tangle of blonde hair strewn on the pillow beside him, followed by a hint of pale skin peeking out from the covers. Well, then.

He dragged a hand down his face and tried to remember…there had been drinks with someone, possibly the blonde woman currently lying next to him. Beer had quickly become vodka then shots as the stories she'd told about their adventures on Namino had grown ever more outlandish…what was her name?

Selene. *Justice Advisor.*

He bolted upright and swung his feet over the side of the bed. His stomach churned, but not from the alcohol. Or not only. Cassidy's face swam in his vision, taunting him with sad, heartbroken features. Was there any greater betrayal of her memory than sleeping with a Justice Advisor?

He couldn't breathe. He had to get out of here. He had to get far away, then keep running.

As soon as his head stopped swimming, he eased off the bed while trying not to disturb the sleeping woman. The last thing he wanted right now was a confrontation. Once he was standing and fairly confident his legs weren't liable to give out from underneath him, he fumbled around on the floor by the bed until he found his pants and shirt. Forget the underwear. He hopped clumsily into his pants and pulled his shirt over his head before checking around for anything else of importance he might have brought along. Seeing nothing, he headed for the door.

The rustling of sheets broke the silence behind him.

"So this is how it's going to be?"

He should keep walking...but he turned around. The woman was propped up on one elbow; the sheet had fallen away to reveal the shadowy curves of lovely breasts in the darkness. Flashes of the night before crept into his awareness, full of passion and laughter and ecstasy—he shut them down with a rough grunt. "Yeah. This is how it's going to be."

She rubbed at sleepy eyes, and the sheet slipped farther to reveal yet more curves. "You are such an asshole."

"After spending a couple of weeks with me, you really should have figured that out. Listen, I need to—I've got to go. I can't be here."

"Why not?"

"I just *can't*, okay? You'd never understand. I'm sorry." Why had he apologized? She was the enemy here. His chest tightened until he couldn't breathe again, and the walls closed menacingly in on him. He spun and hurried out of the bedroom and down a short, moonlit corridor toward a door. He didn't check to see if she followed, and by the time he reached the door he was running.

Then he was out in the hallway. It resembled a hotel...which would make sense, because her home would have been on Namino, because she was the Namino *Justice Advisor.* He stumbled down the hall in the direction of the lift, which was when he realized he'd forgotten to grab his shoes. Screw it, he'd walk home barefoot.

What the fuck had he just done?

7

EARTH

EARTH ALLIANCE
MILKY WAY GALAXY

Miriam stood in a river of blood, sticky and viscous. It painted violent streaks along the corridor walls, where the edges dribbled down toward the floor in a slow drip…drip…drip. *The corridor glowed a florid crimson hue, for gore had splattered across the row lighting above.*

She looked down to see a severed arm wash up against her foot as the river's current grew more forceful. She tried to step away, but her feet were stuck to the floor.

She couldn't move from this spot. Couldn't elude all this death.

From out of the blood swirling at her feet rose inky aubergine tentacles. They wrapped around her ankles and slithered up her legs. No matter how hard she fought them, their grip only tightened. She reached for the Daemon at her hip, only to find it had become a third tentacle winding around her waist. It squeezed, denying her air, as more tentacles reached her neck, then her face. Liquid metal poured into her ears, nose and finally her mouth.

"You think you are alive, but you are mistaken. You never left us. We will never let you escape."

Terror and a lack of air sent her heart racing, her pulse pounding against the invading metal. She was going to die again, and again, and again, helpless to strike down this insidious enemy.

…But she'd never been a victim in her life. Why was she so convinced she must be one now?

No. *She drew in all the air she could muster through the gaps in the liquid metal choking off her breath. "NO." She clawed at the tentacles, ripping and tearing at them until they melted away between her fingers. Metal poured back out of her mouth; metal tears streaked down her cheeks.*

Her lungs began to clear, and she sucked in fresh air. Tangible, life-giving air. "I am alive, and I do not belong to you. I will never belong to the monsters."

Miriam opened her eyes with a gasp. The reflected light from a full moon flooded their bedroom to remind her where she was, as did the warm hand gripping hers. She looked over at David beside her. He was propped up on one elbow, the fingers of his left hand wound through hers, his eyes studying her with gentle concern. "This sounded like a bad one."

She breathed in deeply, until she was confident no slithering metal had hitched a ride in her chest, then rolled onto her side to face him. "It was, to start. But this time I…this is going to sound stupid."

"I highly doubt it."

Would she have been able to do any of this, she wondered, without him? The decades of waking up alone, forced to confront whatever demons had chased her through the night in solitude, were long in the past. But here, now, she remembered the difference, and having him at her side meant everything.

"Nonetheless. All right: this time, I fought back. I refused to surrender to the Rasu's invasion. I expelled them from my body and my mind."

"How did you manage it?"

She huffed a quiet laugh. "This being nightmare rules, through sheer force of will. I said 'no,' and the Rasu retreated."

"Brilliant. If only this strategy worked on the battlefield."

"That would be fantastic, wouldn't it? I'll give it a try next time I meet them there. But the point is, they didn't capture me in the nightmare, and now…." She pushed up to a sitting position, then extended her arms in front of her and considered them anew in the moonlight. "For the first time since waking up in this new body and learning I had died, I don't have this lingering unease that perhaps the nightmare was reality and this is the dream."

"Oh, *dushen'ka*." David sat up as well and leaned in to kiss the corner of her lips. "Nothing has ever held you captive for long. Maybe since you've taken charge and frightened them off, this will be the last nightmare."

Her face lit up, buoyed by the possibility. "Maybe it will be."

CONCORD HQ

COMMAND
MILKY WAY GALAXY

Miriam arrived at the office early, and anyone who saw her might accuse her of having a spring in her step. They'd be correct, though she'd deny it if asked.

Her early arrival allowed her to sit and enjoy an entire cup of hot tea while she contemplated the series of fairly consequential meetings scheduled for this morning. Concord as an entity had suffered several blows lately, and it was important to get the institution back on track, if only so it would be stronger when the next inevitable blow hit.

Her assistant soon announced the arrival of her first appointment, and she invited the Novoloume government leader into her office. "Dean Veshnael, welcome. Thank you for taking a few minutes out of what I'm sure has become a demanding day." She knew he genuinely had a packed schedule, so she remained standing.

"The pleasure is mine, Commandant. Congratulations on a hard-earned victory at Namino last week."

"It is scarcely a beginning, but I am grateful for it. I won't take much of your time. I simply wanted to thank you personally for agreeing to step into the role of Consulate head. AEGIS should be naming a new Senator soon, but it will be unfair to ask that person to immediately take on double the responsibility. You were our first Consulate leader, so I expect you'll be able to reengage with minimal difficulty."

"I expect so as well. I regret what has happened regarding Senator—Ms. Requelme. Is there no chance of her resuming her position?"

Miriam sighed. "I, too, empathize greatly with her. But I'm afraid our laws are clear on the matter."

"So they are. If I can ask, do you have any thoughts on what will happen in seven months when the position rotates to the Anaden Senator?"

The mere thought of it made her shudder. "I believe I will worry about that problem when we again *have* an Anaden Senator."

His iridescent skin gleamed a little brighter. "A sensible compartmentalization of mental effort. I will be traveling to the Asterion Dominion tomorrow to introduce myself to their leadership. I've met Advisor Kirumase, but the other Advisors need to see me as well."

"It's an excellent idea, which is why I will leave the diplomacy in your skilled hands."

She saw him out, and barely had enough time to brew a new cup of tea before her next and most welcome guest arrived.

Malcolm Jenner walked in wearing crisp BDUs over a heavily bandaged right shoulder. He was clean-shaven and, other than the bandage, showed no visible signs of his ordeal...except in his eyes. She'd seen the thousand-kilometer, haunted gaze on returning POWs before. Some never lost it, but she hoped he wouldn't suffer that fate.

He stopped inside the door, pulled himself to attention and saluted her. "Commandant."

She returned the salute, then did something she rarely did with anyone who wasn't family—she reached out and hugged him. "I am so glad to see you alive and well."

He cleared his throat awkwardly, and she allowed him to step back and regain his composure. "Thank you, ma'am. I want to apologize for all the trouble I caused. It wasn't my intent, but...."

"Let's place the blame where it belongs, on the Savrakaths. They lied to us and spent weeks deliberately hiding your presence in one of their prisons from us." She motioned toward the small table, but waited until he'd sat somewhat stiffly in one of the chairs to join him. "Still, we were having our own share of difficulties here at Command, and I can't help but wonder. If we—if *I*—had been more focused on the proper things, we might have been able to locate you and execute a rescue mission. For any lapses on my part, I apologize as well."

His face blanched in horror. "No, ma'am. I've seen the reports, and Colonel Odaka and his people spared no effort in their search. I was, it turns out, quite well hidden in a secret location none of our surveillance efforts had previously uncovered. And I want you to know that I didn't reveal any Concord intel or—"

"Of course you didn't. You're a Marine, one of the very best, and I've no doubt you comported yourself with honor while in captivity. I'm merely saying that you shouldn't have had to rescue yourself. But we're all glad you did. Now, we need to put the past where it belongs, move forward and concentrate on doing better in the future." Was she talking about Malcolm, or herself? "What do the doctors say about your injuries?"

"My shoulder will require a couple of biosynth replacement parts as soon as a residual infection is gone. But once those get taken care of, I'll be as good as new."

"Excellent." Her lips pursed. "I expect you've heard, but due to your presumed death, Field Marshal Bastian was named AEGIS Fleet Admiral—"

"I did. It's fine." He nodded quickly. "Bastian should remain in the position, as I believe he'll do a far better job than I did. Granted, all he needs to do to accomplish this is not run off on some ego-boosting ground mission like an idiot." A shadow passed across his features, and he hurriedly sat up straighter. "In any event, I'll be requesting an indefinite personal leave of absence, effective today. I'm sorry if this creates any sort of difficulties, but given that I was dead, I doubt you had me slated for any vital missions."

She shouldn't be surprised to learn the bizarre sequence of events his capture set off had left him shell-shocked and decidedly off-kilter. As such, she didn't call him on the painful self-flagellation, instead studying him with empathy and a touch of sorrow. "You're planning to search for her—for Mia."

"Yes, ma'am. Everything she did, it was because of me. I can't imagine...." He stopped, and his throat worked for a few seconds. "She's not answering my messages. I'm not even sure if she's receiving them. I have to make this right, however I can."

"Forget making it right. You have to find the woman you love. I understand."

"I realize this is a challenging time for Concord, and I regret that I can't be here to help you fight these Rasu, never mind the Savrakaths and everyone else. I wish...well, I wish a lot of things at this moment. Relevant to you, I wish I could be on the front lines. Maybe...I want to say 'maybe one day soon,' but I can't ask you to count on me, only to let you down yet again."

Damn. She'd had a rough couple of weeks on her return to the world of the living, but if his mood was any indication, he was having a worse go of it so far. "You haven't let me down, Admiral, and I respect your choice. If or when you find yourself ready to resume active duty, I'm certain there will be a place for you."

He nodded tightly but stood, saluted once more and turned to go.

"Malcolm?"

He stopped and pivoted back to face her. "Yes, ma'am?"

"Aren't you going to ask me about the regenesis?"

"It doesn't affect my—I accept your position and your leadership. I'd never question either."

"And I appreciate that, believe me, as not everyone feels the same way. But given your circumstances, I understand if you have a few questions. It's okay if you don't, but I don't mind trying to answer even the difficult ones."

He hesitated briefly, then dove in. "What was it like? Waking up? In an entirely new body, with a gap in your memories, being told you were dead but now everything was fine?"

"Terrifying."

"And now?"

"Honestly? Still a little terrifying." Her mind drifted to her nightmare victory a few hours earlier. "It is, however, getting demonstrably better."

"Do you feel like yourself? Do you...*know* that you're yourself?"

This was the true crux of the matter, wasn't it? She'd spent every spare second for weeks struggling with these precise questions, but it could be that the sole answers were the ones she decided for herself. "When I woke up, I was simply waking from a good night's sleep. I was *exactly* myself, and for anyone to suggest otherwise would have seemed absurd. It was only after they told me what had happened that the challenges and uncertainties began. Sometimes our mind can be our own worst enemy."

"Of course. But what about..." he sighed "...I don't know what it is I'm trying to say, and now I feel as if I'm being rude."

"I don't have any easy answers for you, Malcolm. But it doesn't mean we shouldn't be asking questions."

"Okay." His brow furrowed up. "Would you do it again?"

"I suppose I do have one easy answer: without question. I'm *alive*, and everything flows from this one gift. I'm alive, and so long as this is true, any challenge can be overcome."

RW

CONCORD RESIDENCES

Conflict berated Malcolm's thoughts as he headed for the apartment on HQ after leaving Miriam Solovy's office.

He felt gratitude above all. He'd walked into her office expecting a dressing-down of epic proportions. The woman had mentored him and nurtured his career for decades, and today she hadn't so much as expressed an iota of disappointment when he'd abandoned her, AEGIS and Concord at arguably their time of greatest need to pursue a personal cause. Renewed shame flushed his cheeks, but he had no choice and only one option.

She also hadn't challenged him on his 'no regenesis' clause or his willingness to respect and follow her orders now that she was...what? Reborn? Resurrected? Reconstituted? Regenerated? A copy, a golem, a simulacrum? The terms ranged from reverential to offensive.

She had *died*, yet she was alive. If he mused on it too hard, her resurrection would do more to challenge his own beliefs on the topic than any other counterpoint, but for now he was glad she was present and guarding the gates. If she'd fallen permanently, he shuddered to imagine what would have happened to Concord, and humanity with it. The people needed her, now more than ever.

But they could do without him for a while longer.

He'd escaped captivity to find the whole world changed, from the politics of Concord to the rising menace of the Rasu, but nowhere so much as what he'd believed his life to be. What was most important, and what had fallen tumbling by the wayside.

All the ingrained honor in the universe wasn't going to force him back into an admiral's chair until he'd found Mia. Funny how, though he *hadn't* died and been reborn a golem, he felt like he'd lost his soul all the same. He'd reclaim it when he found the woman with raven hair and jade irises and the most arresting smile in the cosmos.

The sterile silence of the apartment when he walked in hit him like a slap in the face. He told himself that it had only ever served as a functional place to eat, shower and sleep when he and Mia were working too many hours, that it wasn't genuinely their home. But if he closed his eyes, he could hear her laughter pealing from the living room, could smell her perfume in the air and on the sheets.

What the Savrakaths had done in lying to the world about his fate was unforgivable. What Mia had done on believing him dead was nothing less than the Savrakaths deserved, but utterly heartbreaking nonetheless. It shouldn't have fallen on her shoulders to punish them. She'd wrecked friendships, destroyed her luminary career and put her freedom in jeopardy. And none of it had to be, dammit.

Guilt and recriminations ate away at him as he ditched the BDUs and changed into khaki slacks and a dark brown collared shirt. He packed a bag with essentials, but most of his civilian clothes were on Romane or in Vancouver. He'd checked both homes the instant Presidio Medical had discharged him in the frantic hope that he would find her waiting at one, but both had sat as sterile and silent as this apartment. He'd check them both again this afternoon, and flesh out the contents of his luggage, before setting off on his journey.

On his way out he sent her another message, the forty-seventh by his eVi's count. In a civilization spanning over fifty galaxies, there were literally thousands of places where she could have gone. He'd start on Romane.

8

PANDORA

IDCC

MILKY WAY GALAXY

Mia Requelme signed the lease to the retail space as Laisha Balente, a persona she and Meno had created out of whole cloth in the last twenty-four hours. The first name was a derivative of a part of her name she'd long ago dropped, but not so close to it for anyone to make the connection. The last name was a random assortment of consonants and vowels she'd scribbled out in her head while walking to her new apartment the night before.

She paid the first two months' rent in untraceable credits, thanked the realtor for her help and headed out into the madness otherwise known as Pandora.

The Approach was neither the nicest nor the sleaziest region on Pandora. Rather, it occupied the 'quirky' segment of the middle ground. Once upon a time, Noah Terrage had lived and worked here, and she'd visited the area many times during her troubled tenure on the colony. She could afford far better than The Approach, of course. She could afford to buy a penthouse high above The Promenade and live in splendid, desolate isolation for years.

But Meno's gentle ministrations had penetrated the grief-stricken state of her mind enough for her to remember who she was and had always been: a survivor. Though a large part of her consciousness—the part currently stuck in a silent, never-ending scream of despair—badly wanted to curl up in the shadows and hide, she wouldn't shrivel away to dust in a dark corner. She needed to keep going until she found a new path for herself. A way to forge a new life.

So she'd rented a small but clean apartment in The Approach and a small but clean storefront down the street from it. And if her life now felt suspiciously like it was on a loop, this was because it *was.* How did the old phrase go? 'The past doesn't repeat itself, but it does rhyme.' The new shop wasn't on Romane, since even with a new haircut and color and new eyes, her face was too well-known on Romane for her to risk seeking refuge there. But it was a tiny consumer tech shop all the same.

She wasn't above admitting that this wasn't so much a fresh start as a retreat to the familiar. A tentative baby step into the future, while relying on the past for support. She'd done this before; she could do it again.

Three large boxes were waiting for her on the curb outside the storefront when she arrived—they must be the first shipment of her retail stock. Grateful to have something to occupy her mind beyond empty shelves that loomed like specters of an empty life, she toggled on the news feed screen on the wall and immediately opened up the boxes and began unpacking.

The form and function of commercial tech gear had changed a great deal in the twenty-plus years since she'd run the little shop on Romane. Now, everything was either impossibly tiny or monstrously large. Most of the tiny items revolved around enhancing cybernetics technology, which had advanced by leaps and bounds since The Displacement, while the larger items dealt with tweaking and modding quantum hardware. Hardware used to run Artificials. Around ten percent of the people she'd passed on the street since arriving were Prevos, so the market should be a hot one.

She picked up a tetrahedron-shaped, milky glass object, turning it over in her hands curiously as she carried it to one of the front-most shelves.

"An AEGIS spokesperson has confirmed to Galaxy First Communications that former Fleet Admiral Malcolm Jenner, believed killed in action during a mission on the planet Savrak, is in fact alive."

The object slipped from her hands to clatter across the floor. Her legs insisted she join it there.

"Admiral Jenner escaped from captivity on Savrak during an attack by unknown perpetrators and has received treatment from AEGIS medical personnel for serious but non-life-threatening injuries. The AEGIS spokesperson indicated authorities will release an official statement on the matter in the coming days. In other news...."

The walls spun around her, zig-zagging left and right, up and down, then dipping into a few hidden dimensions. A fuzzy light prismed out from the milky glass object to drown her in a kaleidoscope of color.

Alive?

Mia, this is wonderful news. Allow me to slow your heart rate and counterbalance the neurotransmitters flooding your system, so you do not stroke out.

She blinked. Alive? Her stomach clenched into a prickly knot, and a wave of nausea sent her heaving up the glazed doughnut she'd had for breakfast. Captive on Savrak? Darhk had lied to her face! The things he'd said about

Malcolm's burnt corpse...all lies.... How much perverse pleasure had he taken in seeing her suffer?

She wiped her mouth clean with her shirt and focused on breathing. What had the reporter said about him escaping during a mysterious attack? Her throat convulsed anew, but nothing remained in her stomach to expel. In her attempt to exact vengeance for his death, had she nearly killed him instead?

But you also might have saved him. I am reaching out to sources and collating data as quickly as I am able, and it appears the attack the reporter referenced was a bombing of a prisoner exchange involving Torval elasson-Machim. Eren Savitas took the information you sent him and acted, and that action allowed Malcolm to escape his prison.

Killed him. Saved him. Dead. Alive. What was real? What had she done?

Meno's behind-the-scenes efforts to calm her body's system-wide revolt began to take hold, and the room gradually stopped spinning. She leaned against the wall behind her, letting the tears run free to stream down her face and soak her already ruined shirt.

He would have messaged her on his return. She'd shut down the address that belonged to her old persona and had never intended to so much as glance at it again...but of course she was still able to access it. Her hands trembled, palms pressed hard into the cool floor, as she back-channeled into the account.

Forty-seven messages. The last one sent a mere twenty minutes ago. He must have heard about her crimes by now, but he hadn't stopped trying to contact her. Her limbs shook with urgency, begging to be set free to sprint down the street, to the spaceport, all the way to the Presidio and directly into his arms, for however long she managed to remain there until security arrived to arrest her.

A hand rose shakily from the floor to cover her mouth as she stared at the endlessly scrolling message headers...but she didn't open any of the messages. She knew what they said, for she could hear his voice in her head as clear as day. Expressing his deep and abiding love for her, his sorrow over the pain he'd caused her, begging her to respond and tell him where she was.

Meno, scan the messages from Malcolm. Do any of them say he's amending his will to remove the 'no regenesis' clause?

No. They do not mention either his will or regenesis.

Her chin dropped to her chest as an avalanche of renewed sorrow swept through to wreck the joy the news had kindled. He was alive today, but all her mind's eye could see was him dead. Dead on Savrak, dead in a spaceship explosion, dead in a Rasu invasion, dead to a gang of muggers on the street. The pernicious lie of his death on Savrak had ripped the wool from her eyes and shown her the inevitable future. It had let her live that future for several horrifying, soul-destroying weeks before depositing her back in the present day and shoving her onward.

Without regenesis, one day—whether tomorrow, next month or next decade—the debilitating misery of these endless weeks was certain to return to haunt her future.

Her chest ached as surely as if it had been cleaved apart by a hatchet. She was not strong enough to do this again. Her survival instinct had seen her through a brutal childhood attack and escape from New Orient. It had seen her through years of indentured servitude to a violent and sadistic mob boss. It had seen her through a vicious attack on her and Meno, her near death and stubborn return to life. It had seen her through overcoming the full might of the Earth Alliance government, the Prevo revolution and the riots on Romane. It had seen her through the murderous retribution of Olivia Montegreu's abandoned Artificial and the universe-destroying machinations of the Directorate.

But her survival instinct was not strong enough to shepherd her through Malcolm's death a second time.

Mia, do you want to reply to his most recent message? I can route it so it can't be traced back to you by the authorities.

Her voice trembled, even in her head. *No.*

I don't understand.

Neither do I. Alice just tumbled down the rabbit hole. We're all mad here now.

9

AKESO

SIYANE

Alex reattached the displaced cushions to the couch's frame, then nudged the low table sideways until it once again lined up with the couch. The cleaning bot had scrubbed the *Siyane's* interior from top to bottom in an attempt to clean up after the fifty-three guests she'd hosted for half a day when they'd evacuated Namino, but a bot could only do so much. A thousand tiny things on the ship were scratched up, knocked out of place or merely rumpled.

Cleaning up the house, surrounding property and landing complex after Akeso's planet-sized temper-tantrum had taken priority on their arrival home, and only now was she finding the time to direct her attention to getting the *Siyane* back in proper shape.

She went over to the data center controls and immediately frowned. None of the settings were correct! Someone must have played around with the configuration while she and Caleb were fighting their way through the Rasu compound.

Ugh. A scowl took up residence as she dove deep into the menus to make certain nothing crucial had been altered or deleted. Despite her annoyance, though, touching the nuts and bolts of the *Siyane* to make things right again evoked a feeling she hadn't often experienced in the last few months: peace. Serenity, even? She wasn't convinced she had the capacity to feel true serenity, but this brought her damn close.

A heartbeat, measured and steady, gradually bubbled up into her conscious awareness. She glanced up from the control panel to find Caleb leaning against the cockpit half-wall, one ankle draped across the other, a vague smile on his lips.

She instinctively returned the smile. He looked...good. Calm, confident, engaged, arguably displaying his own manner of peace. He also looked *good*, with his beard trimmed and his navy henley complementing sparkling sapphire irises. God, did he look good. This had never changed, but it was truer today than it had ever been.

He gestured toward the control panel in question, an eyebrow raised, and she promptly readopted the scowl. "One of our guests screwed around with the data center settings."

"I can't say I'm surprised. Any damage done?"

"None that I can see, thankfully." She closed out of the settings. "I had to reset the configuration, but everything seems to be in order now. What about you? Any luck?"

He nodded thoughtfully. "I think I found her."

Because of course he had, and without the need of Alex's help. He'd asked her to divulge where Mia had fled to, but she honestly didn't know, since Mia had shut herself completely off from the Noesis after her dramatic exit from the Consulate. Could Valkyrie persuade Meno to reveal their location on the sly? Possibly, but it felt like a betrayal of the trust the Noetica Prevos placed in one another for her to ask the question.

But if Caleb wanted to find Mia on his own, she wasn't going to stop him. He was Mia's oldest friend, and the woman clearly needed a proper friend right now. Malcolm was alive after all, which was genuinely welcome news. But based on what her mother had shared about her meeting with Malcolm, it sounded as if no joyous reunion between the couple was materializing. The series of tragedies his false death had kicked off weren't finished playing out their macabre theater quite yet.

"I'm glad. So you're headed to…?"

"Pandora."

She worked to keep a flare of concern off her expression. Pandora wasn't that Anaden shithole Lethe that Caleb had tracked Eren to, and it definitely wasn't a Rasu-occupied Namino, but it was still fraught with dangers, traps and criminals. "Do you want me to come with you?"

He laughed lightly, came over and wrapped his arms around her. "Not necessary. I'll be fine. And it'll be a good test—a measure of our progress."

"Going to give Akeso a peek at the seedy underbelly of humanity and see how the two of you handle it?"

"That's the plan."

She searched his eyes, the twitching of his lips and the beating of his heart, but discerned no hesitation, deceit or fear. "If you're sure."

"I'm sure. Besides, you have your own plans for today, don't you?"

"I do, though say the word and I'll postpone them. Otherwise, as soon as I finish up in here, I'm headed to Mirai to see Nika. I have a promise to keep."

RW

PANDORA

Caleb strolled the streets of The Approach with deliberate, practiced casualness. He hadn't visited Pandora in almost a decade, and in the recesses of his mind, he let a cascade of old memories wash over him. Missions with Samuel at his side and solo ventures. Weekend getaways punctuated by a little too much fun in simpler times. Meeting Noah when the man was a gray-market tech dealer and smuggler. Nearly dying at the hand of a mysterious assassin at the hidden estate of a wealthy power-broker. Identifying Mia as the key to bringing down a petty warlord, feeding the starving young woman a burrito and helping her free herself from the bondage of the cartels.

With the other half of his awareness, he took in the energy pulsing through the streets. The passersby, their demeanors and intentions. The Approach was far from the most dangerous area on Pandora, but beneath a bit of spit and polish, it was dominated by criminals of all stripes, and there was plenty of danger here to trap the unwitting.

Akeso stirred in his mind. *Humans willingly cause harm to one another? I do not comprehend why this could be.*

For money, mostly. To gain power on the one hand and protection on the other. Here on Pandora, everyone is either looking out for themselves or paying tribute to someone more powerful to look out for them.

Are you the only Human who is not selfish and destructive?

He chuckled to himself. *I can be as selfish and destructive as anyone, on bad days. People are complicated. All living beings are.*

Akeso did not believe oneself to be complicated, until you arrived in one's life.

His step hitched briefly, but he recovered and continued on. Recently—since returning from Namino—Akeso had begun, here and there, to refer to itself by their chosen moniker for the planet's consciousness, rather than as 'All.' He hoped this was a sign of a burgeoning appreciation for some of the concepts he was trying to help Akeso understand. *I'm showing you the larger world, as we agreed, and the inescapable reality is that the world is a very complicated place.*

Indeed, it must be.

He caught notice of a man directing a challenging glare his way as they neared one another on the sidewalk. The shimmering tattoo on the man's shoulder displayed a pattern too specific to lack significance; an active-duty intelligence agent would know what it meant, but he hadn't been one of those in a long time.

A cold brutality hardened the man's eyes. Cunning, also, for he'd sized Caleb up in seconds and identified him for what he was—had been. Still, he'd be surprised if the old him was shining through already. Had his trials on Namino reawakened something long-buried inside him, and done so enough for this man to see it?

This Human you are contemplating makes Akeso uneasy.

You're probably sensing my unease. Do you understand why I'm feeling it?

Akeso understands why you perceive the person as worthy of unease. It has no frame of reference to judge if you're correct in your assessment.

This was progress. Good progress. Akeso was beginning to accept how the world was full of nuance and shades of gray, which was one of his goals. Its naive absolutes could not survive out here in the rough-and-tumble world beyond its borders, and if he was going to live in that world, so must Akeso.

This man is the type of person who hurts people. If he hurts someone innocent in front of me, I will need to hurt him in response, to save the innocent life and all those who he would have endangered in the future. Understand?

But why would this person hurt that which is innocent? What gain comes from inflicting such pointless pain?

There are a thousand possibilities, but not every question can be answered by us. It's true all the same.

He and the man passed one another, stares locked in challenge…and the man made no move. Most bullies were cowards when confronted by someone displaying both the ability and willingness to fight back.

Why didn't the man attempt to attack you?

Because I let him know that I would fight back if challenged, and it wouldn't go well for him.

You…Akeso will try to comprehend this. Human interaction is most crude, yet oddly complex.

After putting another dozen meters between him and the man, Caleb crossed the street at the next intersection. Mia's new shop was only a few blocks away, and he turned his attention to the imminent conversation.

He reminded himself how he wasn't here to chastise her or tell her what she should do, only to ensure she was physically safe and to provide a shoulder to cry on should she require one. She'd suffered through a horrific month, and he hadn't been there for her during it; the last time he'd seen her, he'd lashed out at her in anger and stormed off. But he could be here for her now.

He walked through the door to the shop to find a brightly lit space with full shelves lining every wall. The open center of the shop was punctuated by elaborate displays of the latest in tech gadgetry and items marked 'Grand Opening Sale.'

"This all looks rather familiar."

A head popped up from behind the counter in the back. It came with a few surprises, such as shoulder-length lilac-and-silver hair and platinum irises, but her features were otherwise unmistakable. Mia's eyes widened in shock, but the shock quickly gave way to relief.

She hurried out from around the counter and embraced him. "Caleb...."

He squeezed her tight against his chest, happy that she didn't fight him, or worse, slap him on account of his behavior when they'd last seen each other. Only when the embrace began to border on awkward did he draw back, reaching out to flip the ends of her hair with a fingertip. "Cute. I like it."

"Thanks. First thing: how is Marlee?"

"I'm forced to say, better than ever."

"Good. I am so glad she's safe..." abruptly Mia scowled at him "...do I even want to hear how you found me? I thought I covered my tracks rather well."

"Oh, you did. But I used to find people who didn't want to be found for a living, and I know you better than anyone."

A shadow passed across her features, and she stepped farther out of his reach. "You do. Naturally, you'd guess where I'd run."

"Is that what you're doing? Running?"

"I'm a fugitive living on a semi-lawless planet under a fake name. I assumed this much was obvious."

Okay. Might as well venture straight into treacherous waters, then. "You know he's alive, right?"

She nodded curtly and went around the counter to busy herself with typing something into a control panel. Presumably gibberish.

He pressed on. "Have you talked to him?"

"I have not."

"He's taken a leave of absence from the military to search for you. Let me save both of you a lot of trouble and bring him here."

"No!" Her eyes burned a fierce challenge straight through him. "Caleb, don't you dare. Promise me."

"Listen, if you were secretly miserable in the relationship and were searching for a way out of it, then good on you for escaping. I won't interfere—unless you ask me to beat him up, in which case I will seek him out and do so, for you. But, forgive me, I had the impression you were...happy being with him."

The fierceness died away, leaving her looking so desolate. Broken beneath the steel. "I was. I truly was. But he *lied* to me. He let me believe he'd come back to me if the worst ever happened. Then the worst *did* happen, and I learned the truth: he'd never intended to return at all. He didn't care enough about me to make certain he would always come back, and this tells me everything I need to know about our relationship."

But it was much more complicated than that, like everything in the world, and he sensed Akeso's enduring questions hovering beneath his conscious thoughts. This was heartbreak talking—a shattered soul scrambling to construct a narrative that allowed it to survive through all the pain.

"I can't believe I'm standing here *defending* Malcolm Jenner, but don't you think he at least deserves to hear you say this to his face? And a chance to respond with his side of the story?"

Her face blanched, and for a second her vulnerability bled through once again. "I'm not ready to see him. I can't. Not yet. Please, promise me you won't tell him where I am."

"I promise. My allegiance has always been to you. But if you change your mind, tell me, and I'll try to make this as easy as possible for you."

She pretended to ignore his offer. "So are you only here to check on me?"

"Isn't that enough of a reason?"

"Of course it is, and I appreciate your concern. But I know you fairly well, too, and I doubt it's the only reason."

He reached in his pocket and slid a thin film over the counter to her. "A plea deal offer. Richard's signed off on it and persuaded the various prosecutors to get on board as well, so all you have to do is say yes to it."

She stared at the film, eyes wide, as if she was afraid it would explode if she touched it. "What does the offer entail?"

"You plead guilty to unauthorized use of Concord property and interference with an official Concord investigation, pay a fine of 100,000 credits and agree to two hundred hours of community service."

"And?"

"And...you're barred from holding a government position with any Concord- or AEGIS-recognized entity. Forever."

Her throat worked, and her gaze dropped to the floor.

"It's a good deal, Mia. A fair one. No prison time, and other than the ban on holding government office, your actions and movements aren't restricted."

She nodded tightly. "It is."

"So will you take it? Quit running? The store is a nice façade, but this kind of life isn't you any longer. It hasn't been for a long time."

"That's where you're wrong. Caleb, I just want to be left alone. I'm so damn tired...." She ran a hand through her silver locks, all the way to the lilac tips. "I want to walk in a world of strangers, where no one recognizes me or expects anything of me, and simply *be*. You can understand that, can't you?"

"I absolutely can. But I also believe you'll get past those desires. You'll get your feet back underneath you, and Pandora will no longer be able to hold you."

"Maybe one day. It doesn't feel like it right now."

He reached over the counter to clasp her shoulder. "Comm me when you're ready. Comm me before then, the instant you need anything."

"You know I will."

"I'd prefer it if you'd confirm it."

She conjured up a weak smile. "I swear."

"Thank you." He glanced toward the door and beyond it to the bustling street outside. "I don't have to tell you to be careful, do I? This isn't the safest neighborhood."

"No, you don't, and I'll be fine."

She was a long way from 'fine,' but short of camping out in her storage room or hiring a squad of armed guards—which she'd never allow—there wasn't much more he could do for her at the moment.

"All right. I'll respect your wishes. Again, comm me if you need anything, anytime. And..." he gestured to the thin film sitting on the counter like radioactive debris "...I'll just leave this here with you."

10

MIRAI

MIRAI ONE

Though she'd made several fly-by visits, Alex had never lingered for long enough to get a proper view of the city of Mirai One. As she accompanied Nika through a series of levtram rides and sidewalk jaunts, she decided it was quite lovely. Cool, crisp air carried on a breeze from the gorgeous harbor the city overlooked gave it a fresh and lively atmosphere. Everything was hyper-clean, and the buildings shone as if they'd been buffed and polished the night before. In a lot of ways it reminded her of Cavare, though Mirai One was populated by fewer people and many more bots—or 'dynes,' as the Asterions called their mobile sub-Artificial machines.

She and Nika chatted about the Namino aftermath and speculated on the possible tactics of the Rasu until they arrived at the Industry Division's Conceptual Research lab, where Dashiel Ridani was waiting for them. He and Nika embraced, and they murmured to one another for a minute before he stepped back and motioned toward a wide door. "Come on in, and I'll make the introductions."

Alex held up a hand to forestall him. "Hold on for a minute. Everyone will be relieved if we only do those once." She sent a pulse.

Devon, are you ready for the meeting over in the Dominion?

One second...yep. At your location?

That's right.

A few meters to her left, the air shimmered and a fissure opened up; once it took firm shape, Devon Reynolds walked through from his office. As the fissure healed itself and vanished, she gestured at everyone in turn. "This is Devon Reynolds, Director of Concord's Special Projects division. Devon, these are Asterion Dominion Advisors Nika Kirumase and Dashiel Ridani."

Handshakes were exchanged, then Dashiel glanced at her. "Are we good to go inside now?"

"We are."

"Excellent." He punched in a code and the door opened, revealing a long room with a tall ceiling and a series of glass enclosures. Pervasive white lighting and an abundance of a high-grade austenitic steel alloy gave the space a clinical, almost medical feel. Asterions in clean suits worked in many of the enclosures, dynes in others.

Dashiel led them to a circular table in an open corner; while they got situated, he walked off briefly, then returned accompanied by two men. "This is Hoya Isao, Director of Industry's Conceptual Research Department here on Mirai. And this is Parc Eshett, Omoikane Initiative consultant and all-around programming wizard."

Alex had met Parc on Namino, but greetings were passed around as they took their seats. She dipped her chin toward Devon, who'd sat beside her. "Devon, you asked for this meeting, so why don't you begin?"

"I'd be happy to." He clasped his hands atop the table, looking every bit the head of a major intergovernmental organization and *not* the hacker, rebel and general prankster he'd once been.

"At Special Projects, we have created a new team of researchers and given them their own lab dedicated to understanding and countering the Rasu threat. I hear you've been doing much the same thing here, which is great. The more brilliant minds attacking the problem in as many ways as possible, the better.

"But I can't help but think that a more productive path would be for us to, if not overtly work together, at a minimum maintain an open line of communication between our teams. When my people come up with a promising new weapon concept, we let you know. When you come up with a clever new defense system, you let us know. Perhaps most importantly, when one of us fails spectacularly, we can forewarn the other and save valuable time and resources. We can brainstorm ideas and poke holes in each other's plans. This way, we don't duplicate efforts or get too far down a path on research that already hasn't panned out."

Director Isao nodded thoughtfully. "In principle, it's a worthy idea. But there are intellectual property ownership issues to work out, and a lot of what we do here is technically confidential."

Devon waved off the protest. "*Everything* we do at Special Projects is technically confidential. But I was led to believe that when it comes to the Rasu, everything was also on the table. Was I misled?"

Dashiel shook his head while casting a meaningful look in Isao's direction. "No, you weren't. Director Isao, I'll authorize whatever waivers we need in order to share our Rasu work with Concord Special Projects."

"This is all I needed to hear." Isao reached over and shook Devon's hand.

"Glad to have you on the team."

"And you as well."

Parc Eshett had stood almost as soon as he'd sat to meander around the perimeter of the table looking bored, but now he leaned in by Devon's shoulder. "Hey, did you bring one of those Rectifiers with you?"

Devon's face lit up, the 'executive' mask slipping a little to make way for excitement. "No, but give me five seconds." He leapt up, opened a wormhole in the middle of the meeting area and disappeared through it.

Isao stared at the wormhole with intense interest, but Nika and Dashiel had seen one enough times by now to...actually, they also stared at it with notable interest. Given her and Nika's plans for the rest of the day, Alex probably shouldn't be surprised.

Devon quickly reemerged wielding one of the handheld negative energy guns. "Voila!"

"Excellent! I heard about Alex tearing up a bunch of Rasu using one of these on Namino." Parc motioned for Devon to follow him, and they went to a workbench in one of the nearby unoccupied enclosures. "How do you keep the particles stable? A Bose-Einstein condensate?"

Devon carefully laid the Rectifier on the workbench, then removed the outer casing covering the center of the weapon. "Close, but we didn't need to go to such an extreme. The bundle of negative energy particles is enclosed in a He4 superfluid shell."

Parc leaned over to peer into the inner workings of the weapon. "Brilliant. Is the propulsion mechanism an ionized plasma burst?"

"No. Since the outer capsule is constructed of physical material, we used standard cryogenic propellant. But now that you mention it, a plasma burst might be an even better idea."

"I'll work on something using it. Can I see the code running the firing mechanism?"

"Sure." Devon pulled out a tiny quantum cube from his pocket and set it beside the Rectifier. Lines of code sprang to life above it.

Parc scanned it for a minute. "Oh, clever use of magnetic field dynamics to keep the He4 shell intact."

"Yeah, I wrote the code myself. It's slick."

Back at the meeting table, Nika regarded Alex with an arched eyebrow. "I see you have one, too."

"One of...oh." Alex chuckled. "We do indeed. I guess no society is complete without a wise-cracking programming genius with attitude."

"I guess not." Nika eyed the two men in amusement for another second before turning to Dashiel. "Everyone seems to be settling in nicely. If you can handle this from here, Alex and I have something else we need to do."

"Not a problem. I think Hoya and I can wrangle those two for a few hours."

Nika stood and squeezed Dashiel's shoulder. "On that, I wish you luck."

Alex gestured a farewell to the men and sent Devon a pulse to let him know he was on his own, then followed Nika out of the lab. "Hopefully they won't blow up the building for fun while we're gone."

Nika frowned back at the door. "I give it fifty-fifty odds. So, where to?"

"We should go someplace with lots of open space, far from valuable property, so *we're* not the ones blowing up buildings."

Nika smiled. "I know just the place."

11

MIRAI

MIRAI ONE

Nika's choice of setting turned out to be an open, grassy field in sight of the Mirai One skyline. A salty breeze wafted in from the harbor, though rolling hills obscured it from view.

"Does here seem good to you? It's isolated enough that I doubt I can damage anything but the grass."

The air was cooler this close to the water, and Alex zipped up her jacket. "Here's fine. Your city should be safe."

Nika's gaze unfocused and drifted toward the harbor for a moment, then she visibly exhaled. "Good. Before we get started, I have a mission you and Caleb might be interested in, whenever you have time. The Supreme Commander—sorry, Corradeo Praesidis—brought back a tale of an advanced species he believes were wiped out by the Rasu, but not before they deployed some sort of mysterious weapon against them. He thinks this weapon could have some value in our own conflict."

"Interesting. Was it a species he encountered during his lost millennia?"

"You mean after his son tried to kill him? I, um…" Nika's brow furrowed "…I'm not certain. I confess I didn't press him for details."

"He likely would have waxed poetic for a while without answering your question, anyway. We'll look into it." Alex took in the dramatic skyline for another beat. "I admit, I half-expected there to be two of you on hand for this."

"Oh. No." Nika wandered in a slow circle. "I put the other body down for a nice, long nap. Once the immediate crisis was over, having two of me walking around was…awkward."

"I can imagine." She wasn't surprised that Nika had chosen to keep the kyoseil-soaked body active. The woman seemed to always be pushing ahead, seeking, searching, though for what wasn't so clear.

Alex plopped down in the grass and motioned across from her. "Sit down."

"Why? What good is opening a wormhole if I'm not going to walk through it?"

"Valid point, but we're not opening wormholes straightaway. We need to start with sidespace."

"What-space?"

"Sidespace. It's what us Prevos call the...it's a sort of quantum dimension, unbound by distance or...well, much of anything. It's part comm channel, part virtual playground overlay, part expressway to anywhere in the universe. Devon once described it as a dimension where qubits hold all their possible values, where waves are particles and particles are waves. There are no wormholes without sidespace—at least not for Prevos. I can't imagine it will be different for you."

"Understood." Nika dropped to the ground and curled her legs beneath her. "Show me how to access it."

"Right. So you...." Alex suddenly realized she had no good way to explain it. You simply shifted your perception, and you were there. Dammit, she should have done the homework ahead of time.

Valkyrie? Can I ask for an assist?

"Of course." The voice wafted into existence in time with Valkyrie manifesting beside her, already seated cross-legged on the grass. "Good afternoon, Nika. It's a pleasure to see you again."

One corner of Nika's lips curled up. "And you, Valkyrie. Welcome to Mirai."

"Ah, yes." Valkyrie tilted her head up to look around. "It's beautiful here. As are you—this new glow of yours is quite lovely."

"Oh, thank you."

"You are welcome. Tell me, can you not sense sidespace all around you here?"

"No, I can't. Unless you mean the kyoseil waves."

"Not exactly, though kyoseil undoubtedly crosses through sidespace. Can you follow a kyoseil wave using your mind?"

"Well...yes, in a sense. If I'm connecting to an existing ceraff or creating one with someone else."

Alex nodded. "It's basically the same thing, except sidespace isn't limited to following kyoseil waves. It's an overlay upon the entire universe. Any universe—it existed back in the Aurora portal universe, too."

Nika shook her head. "Sorry, I only see the kyoseil."

Valkyrie smiled pleasantly; she was clearly a much better teacher than Alex. "Let's try this: follow a kyoseil wave you're familiar with to its destination, but don't form a ceraff when you arrive."

"Dashiel..." Nika's eyes closed "...done."

"Can you see the area around where Dashiel is currently located?"

"I think he's still somewhere in the Conceptual Research lab, but I know this because his thoughts are leaking across the connection, even without a structured ceraff. When I try to see what he's seeing, though, it's as if there's this filmy, half-opaque barrier wherever I try to look beyond the kyoseil."

"Can you swat away the barrier with your mind? Or gently nudge it to the side?"

"I..." Nika's brow furrowed tight in concentration "...no. It's as if it's fighting against me." She groaned and sank back on her hands. "I must be doing it wrong."

"I'm confident you have the tools and capability to access sidespace, but your brain is structured differently from those of both Humans and Artificials. As I assume it is steeped in quantum programming, in theory this ought to be easier for you than it is for us, but it could require a completely different approach." Valkyrie's voice was soothing and kind. "I do have a theory regarding the problem here, though regretfully it doesn't come with a solution."

Alex motioned for her to continue anyway. Despite the difficulties, Valkyrie was obviously enjoying herself.

"As I understand matters, the belief has emerged among Dominion scientists that the kyoseil in your body protected you—protected every Asterion on Namino—from the ravages of the Rasu's quantum block."

Nika nodded. "It's true. There's no way to test it empirically, and for evident reasons we don't want to, but it's entirely possible that without the kyoseil in our bodies, every person on Namino might well have died the instant the quantum block was activated."

"I suspect you are correct. Therefore, my theory is this: in the same way, and perhaps for the same reasons, that the kyoseil protected your neural output from the interference of the quantum block, it's preventing you from accessing a purely quantum realm."

"But we traffic in quantum matters constantly. Those neural processes are themselves quantum in nature."

"Hence the need to protect them."

"Granted, but we also walk through d-gates all the time. Practically every day. D-gates are merely wormholes held open through mechanical means. Alex, you said wormholes are formed in sidespace."

"They are, but...." She leapt to her feet and opened a wormhole back to Akeso. "In scientific terms, the wormhole is the fissure itself." She ran her hand a few centimeters away from the outline cutting into real space here and on Akeso megaparsecs away. "The interior—the opening itself—is just space."

"Actually, it is nothing at all." Valkyrie barely skirted the edge of sounding condescending. "Within the bounds of the open wormhole, the distance between *here* and *there* is smaller than the Planck length. It effectively does not exist. So walking through a wormhole is no different from walking from this spot in the grass to that bush over there. There is no barrier to cross or transition to make, thus nothing to ward against.

"Sidespace, however, is not part of you. It's not physical, but rather 'other.' Perhaps to the kyoseil, it appears the same as the quantum block—something intending on intermingling and possibly interfering with your own internal quantum processes."

Nika rubbed at her forehead, looking increasingly frustrated, so Alex returned to the grass and latched onto Valkyrie's train of thought. "Nika, how much do you know about how kyoseil operates?"

"Not enough. Not nearly enough. Yes, we've been using and manipulating it for millennia, but not as a sentient life form with independent awareness. That part's new."

Valkyrie lifted her face to the breeze, and Alex slipped a tiny portion of her consciousness into Valkyrie's. Instantly she was awash in the tingling sensation of the air slipping past each individual particle Valkyrie controlled. *Exquisite.*

After a halcyonic moment, she reluctantly focused back on the task at hand. "You mean it's newly discovered by your people. It's always been there."

"And a part of us all this time. Don't think it's not a trifle unsettling. But that's a conversation for another time, preferably when drinks are involved. So how do I signal to the kyoseil that it's safe to let me access this dimension?"

Valkyrie mulled over the question. "As I forewarned you, I do not yet see the path to a solution. Has anyone succeeded in communicating with the kyoseil in any real way? In talking to it?"

"No. Dashiel's trying, after a fashion, but so far it's only harmonics and resonance, not language."

Alex chuckled. "That's the closest I've ever gotten."

"What are you talking about?"

She fished her Reor slab out of her pocket and placed it flat on her palm. "This little guy was a gift to me from the Reor cluster in the Oneiroi Nebula.

I really do need to take you there sometime..." Mesme's enigmatic warning echoed in her mind "...once things calm down a bit. The purpose of the gift eluded me for a long time, but it turned out that a specific harmonic frequency unlocked the Reor's natural encryption. Now, using this slab as a filter, I can follow the strings passing through it to any Reor slab anywhere in the universe and access the data stored on it. But that's all it does."

Nika stared at her strangely. "Does this mean you can use it to read my mind?"

"I have no idea. Do you want me to try?"

"I suppose the secrets I keep mostly wouldn't interest you. Go ahead—but don't delve too deeply, okay?"

"To the extent I can control the delve—which isn't much of an extent at all—I'll try not to." Alex held the slab aloft and slid into sidespace. It was an effortless, almost unconscious transition, which was what made the act so hard to describe and teach. Strings undulated through the air, wandering off toward the city in bulk, but also leading a short meter away to Nika, where they bound up into a tremendous knot of prismatic light.

Wow. Do you see this, Valkyrie?

I do. She's even more stunning now than in physicality.

And more otherworldly. But there's no data stream flowing out through her strings, is there?

That's not quite accurate. There is not data precisely, but I am detecting an aura of...knowledge, possibly of awareness. Do you sense it?

Because Valkyrie sensed it, so too did she. A fully quantized mind, swimming with data organized at a level of complexity far beyond what any Reor slab held, but also girded with elemental consciousness none of them understood, yet....

She and Valkyrie both spoke at once. "Where are all your memories?"

"What?" Nika flinched, sending a discordant vibration through the strings. "What do you see?"

Alex switched back to the 'real' world and eyed Nika almost warily. What *were* the Asterions, truly? "It's difficult to explain. Not discrete data. Not your secrets, but the sense of there *being* secrets. And winding through everything is an unnatural absence, almost like a...wound."

"You are not a data storage unit, which is what we are used to reading using the Reor slab," Valkyrie said. "If you were, you would be nothing more than a machine. Instead you are a mind, a consciousness, a fully realized, sapient living being."

Nika studied the grass at her feet. "This doesn't make me feel as relieved as you might expect."

Alex leaned forward until Nika was forced to look at her. "*Where* are all your memories?"

Nika exhaled and tipped her head to the sky. "Your wound analogy is painfully accurate. They're gone. Stolen from me almost six years ago. I had discovered that our leaders at the time, the Guides, made a deal with the Rasu to provide Asterions for their experiments, and in return the Rasu agreed not to attack our worlds. When I confronted the Guides about what I'd learned, they psyche-wiped me and dumped me in an alley."

"That sounds uniquely terrible. But if they wiped your memories, how do you know what happened?"

Nika's smile was heavily tinged with sorrow and wistfulness. "Dashiel, in fact. We were together before the psyche-wipe. It took several years, but we found one another again. On accident, though thinking back, it feels like fate. He told me who I had been and helped me recover a few of my most important memories. In time, I was able to reclaim the life that was stolen from me. In a stroke of luck, I had always kept personal journals, and they filled in the rest of the blanks."

Valkyrie sighed; on her virtual lips it sounded like a lament. "But written words are not memories."

"No, they are not, and they never will be. But they're all I have. And most days, they're enough." Nika huffed a wry breath. "Want to fire me as the Dominion representative to Concord now?"

"Hell, no. You've been incredible, and I never would have guessed. I won't tell anyone if you don't want me to..." Alex rolled her eyes "...I'll probably tell Caleb, but it won't bother him."

"It's not even a secret. It's also not public knowledge, but at this point dozens of people know. It's become part of who I am now."

Alex couldn't help but wonder what it said about who she'd been before...but there was no undoing the past. Not for Nika, not for any of them.

Nika laughed faintly. "Did anything you saw by chance point us toward a way for me—for Asterions—to open wormholes?"

"I'm sorry, no." Alex climbed to her feet and stretched her arms over her head. "I thought this would work. It should work, but you're more complicated than I expected."

Nika held her hands out in front of her, tilting her head to ponder the glow emanating from her skin. "Thank you for trying. I suppose Dashiel and I need to have a long conversation about harmonics. We need to learn how to properly talk to our kyoseil companions."

RW

NIKA'S FLAT

Nika lay on her bed and stared at the ceiling. Kyoseil strings danced through the ceiling and onward to the floors above her, out the window and into the city. On the edges of her perception, she could sense 'hotspots'—concentrations of kyoseil signaling the locations of active ceraffin.

She focused on the strings emanating from her person, on the evanescent light waves that originated inside her body. She sent a clear, direct thought to herself: *open the way.*

Nothing happened.

She grabbed a pillow, threw it over her face and groaned into it. *Open the way, godsdammit!*

A chime sounded, and she jumped in surprise. But it wasn't the kyoseil, merely the door. She checked the security feed to see Perrin fidgeting in the hallway.

She tossed the pillow aside. The interruption was for the best, as the only progress she was making was in driving herself mad.

Come on in. I'm in the bedroom.

A few seconds later Perrin bounced through the open bedroom door and collapsed on the bed beside her. "What are we doing?"

"Nothing useful, that's for certain."

"I see." Perrin's gaze bore into the side of her head. "You look funny with the glow."

"You get used to it after a while."

"Maybe *you* do."

Surprised at the challenge in Perrin's voice, Nika raised up on one elbow. "You're mad at me. Because I kept this body instead of the original one?"

Perrin twirled a strand of strawberry-blond hair around a finger. "I'm not mad at you. I'm…." She sat up and stuffed the pillow Nika had been commiserating with into her lap. "Okay. Here's the thing, since I have learned my lesson about keeping secrets from friends." She sucked in a deep breath, and her chest puffed out. "I feel like I don't know who you are any longer. Now, I realize it's just me and my own insecurities and selfishness—"

"It's not just you."

"What do you mean?"

"I'm honestly not sure I know who I am any longer, either. Diplomat, rebel, politician, leader, fighter—it's exhausting trying to be all of them at once. I can never get a handle on which one the moment requires, and half the time I find myself fighting when I should be leading or mouthing off diplomatic platitudes when I should be fighting. I split myself into 8,000 shards to infiltrate the Rasu platform and...Perrin, I died 8,000 times. I experienced every death, and they haunt my nightmares still. Then I split myself in two and lived that reality for days, and it was too surreal. As if in being both, I was neither."

Nika stretched her arms up into the air above her and wiggled her fingers around. "I told Dashiel I kept this body because kyoseil is 'the answer.' The answer to our greatest questions, including how to defeat the Rasu. But the kyoseil won't talk to me. It simply floats around, happily connecting us all but not explaining how. *Why*. So...never mind who I am. What am I even doing?"

"Have you talked to Dashiel about this?"

She shook her head. "Dashiel loves me so much. He doesn't want to see the flaws...and I kind of don't want him to see them."

"You know that isn't how relationships work, right?"

"Yes, I know."

"I doubt he'll mind. You should have a little more faith in him." Perrin sighed with overdramatic flair. "Can I say, this is the most *you* you've been in weeks! I don't have the answers to your questions, but hearing you share your struggles, seeing your frustration...gods, am I a horrible person for wanting you to be fallible?"

"Ha! Being fallible is the literal least of my problems, believe me." Spilling her guts about her deepest fears in a deluge was terrible manners, but it was already making her feel so much better. She sat up and took Perrin's hands in hers. "I'm sorry. I haven't been here. And when I've been here physically, I haven't really been present. I am, once again, a bad friend."

Perrin made a face and let her gaze rove around the bedroom. "Hmm...maybe a smidgen. But you're trying to save the universe."

"What's the point of saving it if I lose everything that matters in the process? Thank you for reminding me why I'm doing all of this."

PART II

UNTETHERED

12

HIRLAS

NARAIDA/VOLUCRI HOMEWORLD
PEGASUS DWARF GALAXY

Eren Savitas swung idly in the hammock as a setting sun filtered through the ubiquitous tree limbs to cast intricate patterns on the elevated porch. He listened to the evening chirps and songs of the local wildlife, letting their melodies lull him into a peaceful trance.

He was getting used to just *being*. He spent hours wandering through the weald below, where he only rarely encountered another resident other than the critters, and spent longer hours lying in the hammock or on the bed, staring up at the nothingness beyond the ceiling. He raged and cried and hit things, mostly the broad tree trunk supporting the house. He made tea, but nothing stronger, and occasionally remembered to eat.

Every time he believed he would drown forever beneath an avalanche of despair, this place—their home—brought him back from the brink. It breathed life with every rustle of a breeze, and on the breeze swirled the memory of Cosime's life. It saved him, again and again.

He wasn't checking his messages, as he remained unwilling to allow the outside world to intrude on his retreat. Admittedly, though, he was beginning to sense he'd be ready to take a peek at them in a few days. Whispers of curiosity about the ongoing intrigue out there in the cosmos had started breaking through the fog to poke him at unexpected moments. He needed to thank Drae for saving his life with more than a note; he needed to apologize to Felzeor more fulsomely, and apologize to Caleb and Alex at all.

But first, he needed to make dinner. Everything he cooked up lately tasted bland, as devoid of flavor as the world in her absence, but he'd picked some juicy horenau on this morning's wanderings, and he found he was actually looking forward to spicing up his dinner—

A premature shadow darkened the amber light on the porch, and he leapt out of the hammock, instantly on guard.

"Calm yourself, Eren. It is only I."

At the sight of the vaguely anatype-shaped Yinhe shadow wavering nearby, he sighed and sank onto the edge of the hammock. "Miaon? I haven't seen you for several years now. How have you been?"

"I have been as I always am."

"Jolly good, then. You might not have noticed, but I've got a whole solitude thing going on right now. What brings you here?"

"I bring tidings and news. The man you knew as Danilo Nisi has returned."

"He's alive? Stubborn bastard. I'm glad to hear it." He eased the rest of the way back down until he was once again stretched out on the length of the hammock. "But I don't see how his return really affects me. He was my boss, not my friend, and the anarch rebellion is long over."

"He intends to quell the recent unrest among the Anaden *elassons* and unite all Anadens beneath a new banner."

"A Concord-friendly banner?"

"That is his intent, yes."

Eren shifted his hips to send the hammock swaying gently. "Well...good. Someone definitely needs to stop those gormless *elassons* from bollocksing-up the one positive thing that's happened to this corner of the cosmos in several epochs. But I still don't see what this has to do with me."

"Were you so inclined, you could assist him in this endeavor. I believe he would welcome your help."

Eren covered his face with his hands and groaned into them. "Miaon, I can't. I don't know if you realize or not—you probably don't, given your shocking tone-deafness to silly things like emotions—but I'm in mourning here."

"You cannot grieve her forever."

"Maybe not, but I've barely gotten started good."

"Eren, a new mission can give you purpose, if only you will allow it to do so."

"I swear, if you say 'help him, and watch the universe turn your way,' I will throttle your shadow. Not sure how, but I'll find a way."

"I was not wrong then, was I?"

He thought back to the night in a rundown hostel when he'd struggled over whether to help his new friends Caleb, Alex, Valkyrie and Mesme in their insane mission. Miaon had convinced him that night, and though Eren hadn't realized it at the time, everything about his life had changed as a result.

"Not for a while, no. You weren't. But I..." he climbed off the hammock and went to the corner of the porch to consider the meadow far below

"...I'm not ready. Not ready to be out in the world, talking to people and doing things and acting like everything is somehow *okay*, when it's fucking not."

"Perhaps the only way to become ready is to do it."

He'd shoot Miaon a withering glare, but there wasn't enough of the alien to properly focus on. "Stop trying to manipulate me to your own ends, you selfish prick."

"If Corradeo fails in his mission, it could mean the downfall of Concord, and ultimately the fall of all to the Rasu."

Eren frowned. "If who fails? The Praesidis Primor is fourteen years dead, and I thought we were talking about Sator Nisi."

The shadow rippled in an agitated zig-zag pattern. "You do not know, then? He never told you?"

"Told me what?"

13

EPITHERO

KYVERN DYNASTY HOMEWORLD
MILKY WAY GALAXY

Ferdinand elasson-Kyvern sputtered indignantly from his spot on one of the many couches littering the 'gathering room' at the former Kyvern Primor's estate. "Let me see if I understand this correctly. *You* were the leader of the terrorist group who made our lives miserable for millennia and ultimately murdered our Primors?"

"But he's also the man who defeated the Dzhvar and ushered in the glory days of the Anaden Empire."

Corradeo Praesidis dipped his chin respectfully in Casmir elasson-Machim's direction, even as he held up a hand to stave off further argument. "Thank you for the support, Casmir, but I need to be able to defend myself. Yes, Ferdinand, I led the anarchs. I authorized the elimination of the Primors. I ordered the assassination of my own son, and don't think that decision doesn't haunt me to this day.

"But he had stolen the power he wielded. And not solely him—all the Primors stole their power. They stole it from you, their supposedly beloved *elassons*; they stole it from the Anaden people. They took away your free will with their genetic manipulation and in its place imposed their own will upon you through the integrals. The Primors had to be deposed, and they were never going to give up their stolen power. Their deaths were the only way for trillions of Anadens to be free."

"It was a bad call. You weakened us at the precise moment when we needed to be strong. You cleared the path for the Humans to barge in and take control and lord their rule over us."

"The Humans don't rule you, Ferdinand. They *were* ruling alongside you, until you threw a narcissistic conniption fit and stormed off the stage."

"How dare you—"

Corradeo stood, brushing Ferdinand's protestations off with a dismissive wave. "If ever there was a species that should be our allies and comrades, it is Humanity. They are us, and we are them. Our histories differ, but we are all born of the same DNA. In the midst of this vast, endless universe, filled with the strange and the wondrous and the terrifying, they are our kin, and we must embrace them. We must stand beside them, not as rulers or ruled, but as compatriots."

"But they—"

"I wasn't finished. You're also wrong about something else. Fourteen years ago was not when we needed to be strong. Today, now, *this* moment is when we need to be strong. I have seen what the Rasu intend for all of us, and it will take every Anaden, every Human, every Novoloume, every Katasketousya, every *Asterion,* every member of every civilized species standing together to prevent us from falling to their tidal wave of violence and death."

Ferdinand groaned. "Not the Rasu again. I am so damn sick of hearing about this mysterious boogeyman who's going to kill us all. I won't let Concord's fear-mongering alter our course."

"Believe what you want, but you no longer control our course. If you ever did."

This brought Ferdinand to his feet as well. "I will never stand alongside those who mean to subvert our rightful authority, and I will certainly never stand with the Asterion traitors."

"Don't you think it's past time to retire that grudge?"

"Why? They rejected the rule of law to hook themselves up to synthetics, then took up arms against their own government. I don't recall there ever being a statute of limitations on treason."

Corradeo leveled a steely glare on Ferdinand. "Were you present when those events transpired? I don't believe you were, but I was. The truth is, the Asterions did not start the SAI Rebellion—we did. The Asterions did not fire the first shot—*I* did. And I was wrong to do so. The Asterions of today are no threat to us, but they can be a powerful ally."

"It sounds to me as if that makes them a powerful *threat.* You want everyone to be an ally, but chaining ourselves to allies such as these only makes us weak."

Enough. Corradeo had abided the man's arguments for the sake of seeking some manner of harmony, but he was beginning to get a clearer understanding of what had happened here to send everything flying off the tracks. Ferdinand was a petulant, spoiled *elasson,* and it was going to take more than a reasoned argument to change him.

"That is a lie, and you are a pathetic excuse for a diplomat for believing it."

Ferdinand fumed, his fists clenching at his sides while his gaze ricocheted around the room in search of support. In addition to Ferdinand and Casmir, a smattering of other *elassons* lounged about, for now content to watch the show without scuffing their shoes.

Finally Ferdinand threw his hands in the air. "Why hasn't Torval arrived yet? He was instructed to report here as soon as he left the regenesis lab on Machimis."

Blank stares greeted his inquiry. Corradeo kept his expression neutral, but it was a good question. Torval's misdeeds in the last few months made Ferdinand's antics look like a child's pouty tantrum.

"Does no one know where he is?"

Casmir shrugged in Ferdinand's general direction. "Maybe he's not inclined to take orders from you."

"Casmir, your popcorn commentary grows tiresome. I should have you returned to your room under armed guard."

Corradeo's head whipped toward Ferdinand, his glare laden with warning. "Casmir is no longer your prisoner."

"This is my home, and I control who comes and goes from it."

"No, this was Jakar Kyvern's home, and you are nothing but an interloper." Corradeo glanced toward the windows, lest he visibly enjoy Ferdinand's wilting in response too much. He was trying quite hard to refrain from sowing more discord, but it was proving to be a far greater challenge than he'd expected. "You raise a good point, however. We need a new home. A new center of government, of Anaden leadership. A place that can act as a beacon of peace and hope for the Anaden people."

"Well, you blew up Solum, so it's off the table."

Corradeo barely managed to keep from flinching. He'd believed fourteen years of wandering the stars had healed the wound, only to return and discover the mere mention of it cut as deeply as ever. "The *diati* blew up Solum, and my heart remains broken because of it. In any event, our new capital should not reside on any Dynasty homeworld, but instead someplace every Anaden will feel welcome. But I get ahead of myself. There are, I'm afraid, more urgent matters than a change of address to wrangle first." He pivoted to Casmir. "If you don't mind, please check into Torval's status and location. I do need to speak with him."

Casmir stood, adopting a military stance and stopping just short of a salute. "Yes, sir. I'll find out where he's run off to immediately."

Eren strolled behind his armed escort through the corridors of the Kyvern Primor's residence with deliberate indifference. He'd dug up some proper clothes for the occasion—deep umber corium pants and a silk creme shirt—and bound his hair back at the neck. Oh, and showered and washed his face. By his recent standards, he was ready for a formal dance ball.

Miaon's unexpected revelation had genned up enough interest for him to leave Hirlas and drop in on the circus currently engulfing Epithero, but he'd packed only an overnight bag. He didn't intend on staying. The bustling crowds at two spaceports had grated on his nerves like a file dragged across concrete, and he already longed to flee to the peaceful sanctum of his secluded treehouse. But now that he was here, he might as well find out how far into the muck this little *elasson* conclave had descended.

After several hallways and lifts were traversed, they reached a closed door. His escort bid him to wait there and disappeared inside. Muffled voices echoed through the door, and the man quickly returned and motioned him forward. "You can go in now."

"Thanks, mate." Eren stepped inside what appeared to be a residential suite. It was empty save for one man, who sat studying a stack of materials at a desk. Eren closed the door behind him and propped casually against the wall. "You look rather different. And also disturbingly familiar."

Danilo Nisi—Corradeo Praesidis, apparently—waved away a screen above the desk, smiled and came over to shake his hand. "Eren, it is good to see you. Miaon filled you in, then?"

He pushed off the wall to wander aimlessly around the suite. "All that time, we had The Big Man Himself leading us, and we never knew. It's a bit disconcerting, you wearing the face of the person we spent so much time trying to kill."

"It was my face and my name he stole. I have the right to reclaim them."

"Oh, for certain. I don't begrudge you it. I'm just saying it's a mite cocked-up."

"Fair enough." Corradeo paused. "I was very sorry to hear about Ms. Rhomyhn. I didn't know her personally, but all her actions and Xanne's reports over the years indicated she was a wonderful person. Talented and kind."

"Kind?" Eren laughed a touch too bitterly. "Well, kind to me at least. Not so much to our enemies. Anyway, what are your plans here?"

"My plans are to wake our people from their long slumber. To unite them under a better, freer form of leadership and help guide them to the heights they are capable of reaching. To rejoin Concord and prepare to face the Rasu together with our allies. Will you help me?"

"Excuse me?"

"Why are you here, if not to join me in this fight, as you did in the last one?"

"I'm not the same man you once knew. Also, I'm not in any shape to be giving my all to the good fight. I no longer even have an 'all' to give."

"Then why *are* you here?"

"Morbid curiosity?"

Damn, how was it possible for the man's stare to be yet *more* piercing and hypnotic when animated by a new face? "I don't believe you. I think you are desperate to be given a purpose again. I think you long to immerse yourself in the 'good fight,' as you put it, if simply to distract yourself from your pain for a time. I'm willing to give you that purpose, Eren. Join me, and help me save our people from themselves."

A chime preceded the door opening, and Casmir elasson-Machim poked his head inside. "Oh, I'm sorry. I didn't realize you had a guest. I've got an update on the Torval situation."

"Thank you, Casmir. I'll stop by in a few minutes."

"Yes, sir." The door closed once again.

Torval. The *Torval situation.* Bereft of better options, Eren had disintegrated Torval, the bulk of the Savrakath military leadership and himself in an antimatter explosion on Savrak, freeing Torval to wake up in a shiny regenesis lab somewhere. But now there was a *situation,* because there always was where Torval elasson-Machim was concerned.

He'd tried to accept the meager vengeance he'd achieved in subjecting Cosime's killer to weeks of inventive Savrakath torture. He'd tried to close the book on the rotting nest of vile hatred Torval had fermented in his battered soul.

Now, though? Now he saw a chance to score the full requital in final and appropriately dramatic fashion.

"Well, Eren? What do you say?"

He exhaled harshly, making a show of pacing energetically for a minute before pulling up to a stop in the middle of the room. He leveled what he hoped was his most engaging, fervent gaze upon The Big Man Himself.

"All right. I'll help your cause however I can. Use me as you see fit. I'll be your personal assassin. I'll be your spymaster. Hells, I'll be your entertainment at parties. I only have one condition."

14

MACHIMIS

MACHIM DYNASTY HOMEWORLD
MILKY WAY GALAXY

Torval elasson-Machim woke to a flood of bright, antiseptic light, and he instinctively blinked against the glare. In between his blinks, the hazy outline of objects gained definition and recognizable features…a regenesis lab.

Not his first visit to one, but no matter how many times he underwent the process, the first minute or so after waking was always bewildering. The disorientation, the dizziness, the unshakeable sensation of being detached from one's skin and bones.

But Anaden brains were designed to quickly adapt to such changed circumstances, and by the second minute he had command of his mind and body.

While the medical staff checked his readings over and confirmed his fitness for living, he accessed a variety of files and reports in order to get up to speed on what had happened to bring him here. The last memory he possessed was of being walked in shackles toward Otto and Ferdinand beneath the sweltering Savrak sun. Then nothing. Before that memory stretched an endless haze of agony and suffering at the hands of his Savrakath torturers…better to let those memories fade away.

The news feeds carried vague stories of an attack on Savrakath military leadership, but they were scant on details, and none mentioned the possibility of Anadens being present. Given the sorry state of official relations with the lizards, he shouldn't be surprised the news was getting the story all wrong. Alternatively, someone was trying to keep whatever had happened on Savrak out of the public spotlight.

It didn't matter. He was free of captivity, free of his torturers' delights. He was well and whole and once again on his home turf. And now, those torturers would pay for the pain and indignities they'd inflicted on him. Their families and friends and neighbors and strangers would pay.

As soon as he was discharged from the regenesis lab, he reported directly to the orbital Annex above Machimis. Only once he arrived there did he begin to learn of a schism among the *elassons*, of how many of their number had rejected Concord at Ferdinand elasson-Kyvern's insistence and were now conferring about their future at a secret location. Oh, and he had a summons waiting on him from Ferdinand.

Torval scowled at the summons then deleted it. Gods knew he hated Concord and wanted to see it burn to the ground more than anyone, but he also wasn't inclined to jump when a slimy Kyvern bureaucrat deigned to bark an order at him. He had cultivated Ferdinand as an informant because the man was a useful source of intel due to his position in the Concord Senate, but now that Ferdinand had abandoned his post, the man's usefulness had evaporated. Torval might get around to paying the Kyvern a visit in a few days, but not until after he'd completed the new mission he'd assigned himself.

The next surprise waiting on him at the Annex was the irritating discovery that his Imperium had gone missing. The duty log indicated Casmir took command of it after Torval's arrest, then had promptly gotten it banged up in a scuffle with Savrakath warships. Casmir dropped it off at the MW Sector 9 Dry Dock for repairs and transferred his command to a shiny new Imperium fresh off the assembly line. Only now *Torval's* Imperium was no longer located at the Dry Dock or any other station of record. The log hinted at the possibility that it had been stolen.

His still frayed nerves grated at the thought of some simpering alien having the gall to stand on the bridge of his ship, but...he inhaled through his nose. It was fine; he could adjust his plan with little difficulty.

Three Imperiums were currently docked at the Annex. Did they belong to *elassons* who were refusing to participate in Ferdinand's summit? Years of Concord's subversive entreaties had begun swaying the sympathies of many of his brothers and sisters, rendering them weak in Torval's eyes. As he reviewed the names attached to the docked Imperiums, his suspicions were all but confirmed. Subservient, spineless cowards, all of them.

But because they had what he needed, he sent each of them polite messages, including nary a mention of their cowardice.

Two responded with colorful equivalents of 'fuck no, you can't borrow my ship.' One simply ignored him.

He stalked through the upper-level halls of the Annex for upwards of twenty minutes, taking his frustrations out on passing *ela* officers and *asi* servants whenever he encountered them.

Very well. He'd take a battlecruiser, then. Without an Imperium's double shielding, he'd be slightly more vulnerable to attack. But given the wrecked state of Savrak's defenses, the firepower a battlecruiser could deliver was sufficient for him to make half the planet burn before anyone got their first shot off at him.

Satisfied with his plan, he set off for the high-ranking officers' private quarters to find a lochagós to bully into handing over their ship.

RW

SAVRAK

SAVRAKATH HOMEWORLD
ANTLIA DWARF GALAXY

Six hours later, Torval's newly acquired battlecruiser exited superluminal thirty megameters from Savrak.

No planetary defenses challenged him on his arrival, for Casmir had been kind enough to destroy those on a previous assault. No military security contacted him to demand his withdrawal or surrender, either.

His memories stirred. General Jhountar had been at his prisoner transfer, along with several other Savrakath officers displaying many shiny medals upon their ridiculous uniforms. Was it possible the entirety of the Savrakath military leadership was dead?

Such a reward was worth the price of a few minutes of post-regenesis disorientation and a few hours of scrambling, and it now made his chosen task all the easier to accomplish.

He half-expected a pleading communique to arrive from the planet's president or premier or whatever they called their civilian political leader, but none ever did. He admitted to being a little disappointed. Was there anything left on the planet worth destroying?

The battlecruiser descended through the atmosphere without opposition until the endless sickly green-and-jonquil swamps raced beneath it. Finally, the umber mid-rise buildings of downtown Savradin came into view on the horizon, and he cheered up. There were plenty left standing for a proper razing.

He straightened his posture and lifted his chin. "Open fire."

The battlecruiser's XO cleared his throat weakly, and his voice shook a little. The crew was visibly terrified of Torval and had been jumping at his shadow ever since he'd boarded. Which was acceptable. "Um, target, sir?"

Torval waved toward the viewport and the outlines of the buildings beyond it. "Everything."

15

FICENTI

ANDROMEDA GALAXY

The rancid smell of flash-cooked live meat assaulted Nyx elasson-Praesidis' nostrils the instant she turned the corner and left behind the uncultured, crime-ridden Rico District for its entirely lawless big brother, the Mikro-Teln District. Along both sidewalks, street vendors hocked still-squirming food on skewers alongside giant jugs of potent hypnols and deadly weapons mods.

Her nose crinkled up in distaste; she dialed down her olfactory filters, and not just due to the rancid meat. The people here reeked, too. Sweat and overactive Barisan oil glands mixed with occasional whiffs of blood and bodily waste.

Nyx had seen many revolting places and people in her work as an Inquisitor, but a part of her must have somehow remained naive, for she was frankly shocked such a place was allowed to exist in the Anaden Emp—in Concord. And not only was it an Anaden-run world, it had existed in this wretched state for millennia, so she couldn't blame the Humans for its decline. Her former Primor had excused it by saying there needed to be outlets and escape valves to lessen the pressures that built up in any society. Allowing places such as Ficenti to exist helped to prevent ineffectual uprisings by the populace.

Except it didn't work out that way, did it? The anarch rebellion had taken hold in spite of the 'flourishing' of over a dozen worlds as vile as Ficenti, hadn't it? Granted, in the end it was the arrival of the Humans that tipped the balance of revolution in the anarchs' favor.

But once grabbing the reins of power, under the guise of taking a light touch when it came to governance, the Humans by and large allowed the Anadens to rule themselves, and the result was a degradation of already deplorable places like Ficenti. Without the Directorate to manage the boundaries, there was no empire here. No rule of law, and barely any civilization at all.

The Mikro-Teln District was 'ruled' by someone calling himself the Sultan of Ficenti. His thugs enforced his will on the streets, and his throng of Novoloume slaves seduced anyone who got close to him, neutralizing any threat. Rumors whispered of orgies involving dozens of Naraida and Idoni women playing out for the Sultan's enjoyment, during which anyone not displaying sufficient enthusiasm for the performance had their throat slit on the spot.

Though his kingdom was tiny for now, the Sultan of Ficenti was as brutal and brutish a warlord as any who'd existed in history. For this reason, Nyx held out some small iota of hope that he wasn't who she feared he was.

"Pretty jacket, pretty lady."

She ignored the leer of the Theriz man on her left while veering to avoid a fistfight spontaneously breaking out between two Barisans in the middle of the crowded street.

"Give it to me."

She glanced back in annoyance at the realization the Theriz man was following her. "I think I'll keep it."

"I think you won't."

Abruptly she spun around and surged forward. In less than two seconds, she had grabbed the man by the collar of his shirt and shoved him through the milling crowd and straight into a brick wall. She got up in his face, then stopped herself from recoiling, for no Anaden should ever smell so foul as he did. "Do you know what I am?"

His voice quavered, but he managed to keep the brash edge to it. "A pretty lady in my jacket."

"I'm an Inquisitor, you disgusting moron."

"Ha! An Inquisitor without their *diati* isn't shit. What are you going to do, glower me to death?"

She kept her expression suitably threatening as frustration tightened her grip on the man. He clearly wasn't inclined to leave her alone, and if his behavior escalated, he'd draw attention to her presence here—the last thing she wanted to happen. She hadn't come this far just to have her mission derailed by a random street thug. So be it.

"No. I'm going to cause you several hours of agonizing pain before you finally die and wake up in a lab that will be far cleaner and more orderly than your squalid bones deserve." She palmed her blade and sliced it across his gut. Not too deep, or he'd die too quickly to remember the experience and perhaps learn from it his next time around.

His eyes widened in panic, but no more words emerged from his lips. Nyx stepped back and let him slide down to the ground, his hands clutching blindly for his stomach. Then she turned away and rejoined the raucous throng. It wasn't as if a bleeding man on the sidewalk was going to surprise or concern anyone here; she'd passed two of them since arriving in the district.

Killing gave her no pleasure. It never had, though once upon a time it had been such an integral part of her job that she'd simply performed it without thought—or hesitation. But this was the first time she'd taken a sapient life, even temporarily, in fourteen years, and doing so made her feel dirty. Dirtier than all the smells and grime and filth surrounding her. She'd need to assess and internalize these new emotions later, once she was gone from this dreadful place. But she'd also kill again if she needed to in order to complete her current mission.

Ahead of her, the street began to open up until it merged into a wide, circular...she was forced to call it an arena. Large, snarling animals, many from species she'd never seen before, stalked within force-field cages off to the left. People hung off scaffolding along the edges of the arena, the better to view the activity underway in a metal-rimmed pit at the center.

At the far end of the arena, an arc of more traditional bench seating rose up to a...was that a *throne*? Upon it, surrounded by half a dozen naked Idoni and Novoloume women, sat the self-styled sultan himself. She zoomed in her vision to maximum, for she needed to be certain.

Kolgo elasson-Praesidis.

She shrank back into the crowd, overcome by an irrational fear that he might spot her, even from several hundred meters away. But he was fully occupied with spirits and hypnols and nudity and blood sport.

Acid rose to burn her throat. How could an Inquisitor have fallen so far? They were supposed to be the best of the Praesidis and thus of all Anadens.

She knew all too well the struggles that came from losing one's *diati*. The panic, the foreign feelings of insecurity, impotence and powerlessness. The fear of having become...lesser. But the *diati* had only ever been a tool. An Inquisitor's true strength resided in his or her mind: blade-sharp intelligence, breadth of knowledge, skill at seeing the details most people missed, the ability to solve puzzles without possessing all the pieces, and an inherent belief in the rightness of one's cause.

Did Kolgo believe in the 'rightness' of his cause from atop his vulgar throne? Had he somehow twisted the pathways of his mind until this all made sense to him? Or had the only thing to survive the loss of his *diati* and the fall of the Directorate been his congenital arrogance and sense of superiority?

She was self-aware enough to admit she'd suffered from the same arrogance at times. But she also chose to believe that if her life had taken a darker turn fourteen years ago, she would never have descended to so low an existence as this. The mere notion was anathema.

An uproar of disapproval rippled through the crowd in response to something happening in the pit, and Kolgo knocked the woman on his arm away to grab a gun and shoot one of the creatures participating in the brawl below. Then he settled back into his throne, downed a glass of shimmering mint-colored liquid, and pulled one of the other women onto his lap.

Nyx pivoted away in disgust and began picking her way through the crowd toward the fringes of the district. She'd kill Kolgo here and now if it would make any difference, but it would not. She'd confirmed the existence of two off-record regenesis labs here on Ficenti, as well as dozens on other Anaden worlds. People who wanted to remain off Concord and Vigil's radar—people like Kolgo—were using the facilities to keep their immorality train steaming ahead without suffering any consequences for their actions.

But she *could* keep Kolgo away from her grandfather. Corradeo had sent her on this mission to find the Inquisitors who'd vanished in the hope of bringing them together as a family, but this monster had no place within a kiloparsec of the center of Anaden power.

Her clenched jaw relaxed a little as she crossed the unofficial district border, and her pace increased. The sooner she was able to rid herself of this planet, the better.

One missing *elasson* scratched off the list, four to go.

VOLIE

MILKY WAY GALAXY

Nyx breathed a sigh of relief as soon as she stepped out of the spaceport in Cobola. She'd showered three times after returning to the *Periplanos* then manufactured a set of brand-new clothes, but she swore Ficenti's putridity was still stuck in her pores. This place, though? This place would wash it all away.

The beachfront community of Cobola on Volie represented the polar opposite of the Mikro-Teln District on Ficenti in every aspect imaginable. The sun shone a bright fuchsia amid clear skies. The streets were clean and well-manicured, the shops neat and airy, the food properly cooked and aromatic. The occasional pedestrians Nyx passed were dressed in casual but expensive attire, and they invariably nodded a greeting, welcoming her without question.

It was so nice here, in fact, that she stopped at a bistro for a sandwich and lemonade and enjoyed the meal out on a patio under the warm sun. On departing the bistro, she decided she could get used to the sun and sand and sea spray Cobola had to offer, and the walk to the strip of isolated beachfront homes on the outskirts of town was simply delightful.

The cloistered home at the end of the lane stood silent atop pilings stretching out over the cusp of the ocean shore. It was almost half a kilometer from here to the sole neighboring house, and the only sounds to reach Nyx's ears were the cawing of gulls and the gentle lapping of waves upon the sand.

She rang the entry bell, but was not surprised when no one arrived to answer it. She waited a generous two minutes before removing a small module from her bag and hacking the lock. The door slid open without complaint.

An overwhelming sense of *staleness* greeted her when she stepped inside. A thin layer of dust coated the otherwise stately furniture and polished wood floor. Ubiquitous windows cast warm rays of light across empty, untouched rooms. She wandered into the kitchen, taking in its dust-covered marble countertops and nook table, then opened the refrigerator. Two piles of fine granules sat on the top shelf, the remains of food that had been autosanitized once it started to spoil. A half-empty bottle of *eau de vie* sat in the door rack.

A stroll through an abandoned living room decorated in beige-and-sorrel furniture brought her to a sliding door. This door was unlocked; she ventured out onto the deck beyond it, leaned against the railing and peered down at the water swirling around the pilings below. From here, the salmon-hued waters stretched to the horizon. White dots in the distance marked pleasure boats, and wind sails soared across the spotless fuchsia sky.

She reluctantly left behind the idyllic view to return inside and head upstairs. As on Ficenti—as on nearly every mission—she knew what she was going to find. The curse of being an Inquisitor.

The door to the master bedroom was open, and she stopped in the entry to lean against the doorframe. The blinds on the wide windows to the left were open, letting light stream unfettered into the room.

Laid out on the bed, atop the covers, were the skeletal remains of Xeshar elasson-Praesidis. Time had melted away his flesh and organs, leaving only sun-bleached bones behind.

There was no data belonging to him stored in any Praesidis regenesis server, nor at the general regenesis lab in Volie's capital city, and unlike Kolgo, Xeshar would have no reason to use an unregistered lab. Odds were he'd followed the path of at least three of their brothers and sisters, disconnecting from the Praesidis integral then ending his life.

She understood why each of them had taken such an irrevocable step. She felt the absence of her *diati* every single day. She mourned what its loss had taken from her: the freedom, the power, the sheer certitude of action and belief. But without it, she'd learned who she truly was when stripped of her armor.

Now, her heart ached in sorrow all over again. Xeshar was a good man and a talented Inquisitor. The profession made one a loner of necessity, but when their paths crossed he'd always been...kind. He was the quiet, introspective, philosophical sort, and she wondered if it was the loss of his *diati* or of something more fundamental that had driven Xeshar to this fate. The world had changed around him, and perhaps he'd felt he no longer had a place in it.

If only he'd held out for a few more years, she could have shown him the way.

A wave of loneliness weighed down her spirit as she went back downstairs and left the house and the ocean behind.

Two down, three to go, and she was starting to suspect that no one remained to stand with her at her grandfather's side.

16

CONCORD HQ

CONSULATE

Marlee clasped her hands behind her back and waited while Dean Veshnael finished conferring with his personal assistant, whom he'd brought with him to the Consulate from the Senate. When the assistant finally departed, Veshnael graced her with a cordial and welcoming smile. "Please, Ms. Marano, come in. Have you recovered from your ordeal on Namino?"

"Yes, sir. Thank you. I'm ready to return to work whenever you're ready to have me." Should she have included 'if' he was ready to have her? No. It was *her* job, and he'd have to resort to confrontational behavior and kick her out the door if he chose to get rid of her.

He didn't so choose, not yet, instead gesturing to one of the chairs opposite Mia's—his—desk. "Sit. Tell me about the Asterions. I've met several of course, but you spent weeks living in close quarters with them. I'm interested in your impressions."

"Oh." She sat and folded her hands in her lap. She liked Veshnael, she supposed, but he was so terribly formal, even for a Novoloume. He was all grace and politeness and decorum. She believed he was a good and honorable man, as did most people, but she couldn't say much else when it came to Veshnael. But now that she'd be working for him, perhaps she'd learn more about him in time.

She did miss Mia so much, though. While she'd sometimes chafed under Mia's strictures—and gotten herself into trouble for breaking them more than once—Mia was a terrific boss and maybe a friend.

But Mia no longer occupied this office, so she needed to suck it up and deal with reality. She cleared her throat. "Obviously, the Asterions weren't at their best during my time there. It was a horrible, frightening situation for everyone involved. But they are as diverse in personality and skills as we are. Humans and Novoloume, I mean.

"The interesting thing about Asterions, though, is that they can change those personalities and skills whenever they wish. They call it 'up-genning,' which is where they tweak their operational programming in some substantive way. I think..." she brought a hand to her chin "...they are the most fully realized Artificials I've ever met, by far. But despite their mostly flesh-and-blood bodies, they are synthetic where it matters."

"Interesting. What about their culture? Their society?"

"On an ordinary day, I can't say. As I noted, my time with them was under pretty unusual circumstances. But they are really clever, displaying bucket-loads of initiative and ingenuity. Or the best of them do. They're also highly individualistic. I think it's important to them to be able to take care of themselves and control their own lives. Their own destiny, even. I'm only speculating, but this might stem from their history of rebellion and escape from Anaden repression. The Rasu have dealt them a brutal blow, but they seem doggedly determined to overcome it."

"I'm glad to hear it. We need allies who display such spirit." Veshnael looked pleased; hopefully it meant she was meeting his expectations. "How much of their Anaden nature would you say persists?"

She pondered the question for a minute. Every properly educated human knew that the history of Anaden/Novoloume relations was an ugly one. Having been freed of the Directorate's shackles, the Novoloume now treated the Anadens with minimal civility within Concord, but nothing more. Veshnael had played an important role in toppling the Directorate, and there was no way he had forgotten the millennia of mistreatment his people had endured under Anaden rule.

"Very little. The opposite, in fact. The only similarity one might notice is due to how they live a very long time. Potentially forever, I expect. But the truth is, most of them don't display the sort of detached, removed demeanor so many Anadens do. They value their lives a great deal.

"Granted, this could have been because most of the Asterions I met were having their continued existence threatened, since their backups...whatever they call their neural imprints...were stored on Namino and had been destroyed by the Rasu. See, they don't use networked regenesis. There's no trace of integrals or groupthink or anything. Like I said, they tend to be quite individualistic." She paused. "But I'm generalizing. They are as varied as we are."

Veshnael nodded thoughtfully. "Would you say they are good people?"

"Oh, yes. Absolutely. All the ones I've met are. They rescued me during the Rasu attack, at tremendous risk to their own lives. They took me in and cared for me. They took care of each other and tried to save lives whenever possible."

"Excellent. Your assessment is most helpful."

"I hope so." She wasn't sure if he was being truthful or merely polite, so she straightened her posture and lifted her chin. "Sir, I want to make a request. Since I've had more experience interacting with the Asterions than anyone else at the Consulate, I was thinking I could serve as an...ambassador to them. I want to further our cooperation as much as possible and—"

"Now, let's slow down. You will make an excellent advisor to me on the Asterions. But with all the upheaval transpiring in Concord, plus the fact that I am new to this job, it's important for me to play a public role in our interactions with the Asterions for some time. They will feel uncertain about their standing after the unfortunate departure of Ms. Requelme, and I need to make the effort to assure them our positive relations will continue. Besides, you are only beginning your career in diplomacy. Better for you to continue to watch, listen and learn for now."

She bit the inside of her mouth to quash a smartass retort. In Novoloume-speak, he'd just called her a child. Dammit! After having the adventure of her life—a terrifying and stressful adventure, but a memorable one nonetheless—he was ordering her back to her office, consigned to once again do research and write reports.

She couldn't bear the thought of it. But she also didn't want to get fired straightaway, so she forced herself to hold her tongue for now. "Yes, sir. Whatever you think is best. I'll get caught up on the backlog of work I missed while I was on Namino, then we can move forward from there."

"Perfect. I look forward to a long and fruitful working relationship, Ms. Marano."

On the way to her office, she stopped to gaze longingly out one of the frequent viewports on the torus. The gleaming silhouette of the enormous central structure of HQ dominated the tableau, with thousands of ships and stars twinkling in its halo.

She hadn't gone to work at the Consulate to spend her life trapped in an office; she'd done so to get to see the cosmos and meet all the many-varied life that called it home. Like her uncle and aunt, she belonged out there, amid the ships and the stars. Now, how to make that happen?

17

PANDORA

"Thank you, and please come again." Mia offered the customer a pleasant smile and kept it frozen on her features until the woman had departed, at which point she sighed audibly and let her shoulders sag.

She didn't remember retail being this much work. Customers were far harder to please than rival diplomats, and their demands were often far more unreasonable. Here on Pandora, everyone expected goods to be either cheap or illicit, and usually both. The fact that she was offering high-quality, legal products seemed lost on too much of her potential customer base.

She peered idly out the front windows, observing the midday pedestrian traffic outside. And another thing—where were all the alien tourists? By her count, she'd seen a single Novoloume and two Naraida, both at levtram stations, since she'd arrived. Granted, she'd been spoiled by the constant alien presence at Concord HQ, but they were supposed to be integrating, weren't they? The Big Three—Romane, Seneca and Earth—had implemented extensive alien outreach programs, but back when reports on such activities crossed her desk, they showed modest success at best. She would have thought at the very least some aliens would have been curious about the scandalous treats Pandora offered.

But there was almost no trace of them here. And after years working with a variety of aliens on a literal daily basis, their sudden absence was both odd and strangely disorienting.

It wasn't that she'd anticipated selling aliens much in the way of wares, since most of her products were suited only to humans. She merely wanted to see them on the sidewalks and in the restaurants.

But it was fine—as was the frightening lack of sales she'd enjoyed so far. She didn't need the money; the store was simply something for her to occupy her hands and mind with. She'd initially intended for it to serve as a distraction from Malcolm's death; now it served as a distraction from the reality that he lived.

But in the long silences stretching between the occasional customer, she couldn't forget it. And at night in her bed—a bed free of memories of their long, luxurious nights together—he haunted her every waking thought and, to the extent she allowed herself to experience them, her every dreaming slumber. He was the shadow in the corner of her vision and the whisper on the breeze.

Dammit, the whole point of her not contacting him was to close the door on that part of her life before it brought her incalculably greater pain.

A simple directed thought, and he will know where you are.

No, Meno. We've already discussed this. At length.

There is no shame in changing your mind.

I said no. It's too late for us. Besides, I can't exactly walk back into my old life as if nothing has happened. They changed the locks on all the doors, remember?

You can take Richard's plea deal.

Meno had long been her co-conspirator, trusted confidant and the voice of her conscience, but he'd grown increasingly irritating since she'd arrived on Pandora. Or perhaps her conscience had. *I just want to be left alone in peace to run my shop.*

Respectfully, no, you don't.

The door opened to admit a new customer, bringing a merciful end to the prickly conversation. "Welcome. Is there anything I can help you with today?"

The customer was a beefy man sporting thick arms painted in angry glyph tattoos and a ragged, unhinged glint in his eyes. He strode directly up to the counter and leered at her as he leaned into it. "I'm from the neighborhood, uh, security watch group. We've had a lot of break-ins lately, and even one or two fires set. We want to help you keep your store and your person safe."

She rolled her eyes in resignation. So not a customer then. "How much?"

"Well, you see, we've got a good crew, but it takes a lot of work to keep the peace—"

"*How much?*"

He glanced around at the well-stocked shelves and gleaming displays. "Eight hundred a week."

It was a ridiculous sum for protection money, but she shouldn't be surprised. She retrieved a thin film from the drawer, imprinted it with the amount and shoved it across the counter. "Here's a month in advance. Don't come in here again for, oh, thirty-five days."

He took the thin film and stuffed it in a pocket, then snarled. "I don't think I like your attitude."

"And I don't care. I've seen this whole routine of yours a hundred times before and, frankly, right now I'm too tired to fight it. So take the money and be glad I won't cause any problems for you."

"A mouth like yours, it sounds as if you *are* working up to causing problems."

She switched to her diplomat voice. "I swear, I'm not. I just want to be left..." she was a worn-out, broken record "...in peace."

"Huh. We'll see." The man turned his lumbering frame around and marched out of the store.

She'd been expecting someone to come around eventually. There had been protection rackets even on Romane back in the old days, so of course they would be pervasive on Pandora. Here, they were practically an entire industry all their own. The major, multi-planet cartels—Zelones, Triene, Shao—might be relegated to the rubble of history, but the vacuum created by their dismantling had allowed every corner thug with ambition to start their own racket.

With a sigh she added the weekly eight-hundred-credit payment to the store's budget.

RW

Later that evening, Mia stopped at the deli down the street to grab a sandwich for dinner and ended up striking up a conversation with the owner, a nice, grandfatherly sort named Jeffrey, who was originally from Scythia. The topic soon turned to the local gangs, and he filled her in on the current power players in The Approach. It turned out that about a year ago, a new group calling itself the Rivinchi cartel had popped up out of nowhere and soon crowded out the lesser gangs using more money and rougher street muscle.

Jeffrey instantly identified the guy who had shaken her down as 'Chad,' no last name. He gave her a free chocolate chip milkshake to take home with her and advised her to keep paying the protection money, as Rivinchi's use of strong-arm tactics had been ratcheting up in recent months. She thanked him for the information and tipped him enough to cover the cost of the milkshake.

Halfway home, she decided to start a file in her personal data store on the Rivinchi cartel. Chad was her first entry.

18

AKESO

"Good. Now close your eyes and try to deflect my attacks."

Marlee's face scrunched up, but she held any retort and nodded instead. Her eyes closed.

Caleb waited to a count of four, then glided to her left and snapped out a knife hand toward her shoulder. As his hand moved, so did she, pivoting and swiping up to deflect it with her wrist.

"Excellent. Again." He backed up, then silently crept around her. His rear leg swept out to tap her on the hip—

—her hand shot out and grabbed his foot at the ankle, a pleased grin breaking across her lips.

He laughed. "Even better. You're obviously ready for advanced work." He peered up into the broad limbs of the tree overhead. "Felzeor? Are you ready to join in?"

The Volucri launched off a branch and sailed down to land on Caleb's shoulder. "Indeed I am. I enjoy games so. But I do not want to hurt you, Marlee, and this game appears a tad violent."

Caleb reached up and scratched Felzeor's neck. He'd invited his friend here today to help with Marlee's training, but also because he owed the Volucri some attention after abandoning Felzeor in his rush to get to Namino. "Don't worry. We're not going to hurt her, but we're practicing now so bad people never succeed in hurting her, either."

Felzeor gasped dramatically. "Marlee, are you in the habit of attracting bad people who want to injure you?"

She huffed in mock indignation. "*No*…. But I do seem to be in the habit of wandering into the middle of them? Only to help others!"

"It's a family curse. Now close your eyes again. This time, try to deflect my attacks *and* Felzeor's."

"Uh-huh. Piece of cake." She shook out her arms and flexed her knees. "Come at me—"

The sound of the Caeles Prism activating drew their attention toward the landing complex. A simple but expensive civilian craft emerged through the Prism and settled onto one of the landing pads.

Felzeor clucked at Caleb's ear. "Who is that?"

"Let's go find out. Marlee, you get a brief break."

The three of them strode across the meadow toward the landing complex. It was finally drying out after Akeso's deluge, and the dirt felt firm beneath Caleb's bare feet.

They were still thirty meters away when a ramp extended from the side of the ship and Malcolm Jenner emerged. He was dressed in what military officers always seemed to think were casual civilian clothes, but in reality were substitute military attire without the insignia.

Caleb sighed softly. Well, this was going to be awkward. He wished Alex were here to intervene, but she was at HQ helping her mother review the new work coming out of the Concord Special Projects/Dominion Conceptual Research partnership.

He nudged Felzeor off his shoulder and went to greet their visitor. "Malcolm. It's good to see you walking around among us again."

"Yeah." He glanced behind Caleb at the others. "I heard you and Marlee had an ordeal yourselves. I'm glad you all made it home in one piece."

"Thanks. So, what can I do for you today? Alex isn't here...."

"I didn't come by to see her. Actually, I need to talk to you."

"All right. Do you want to go inside and have a drink, or something to eat?"

"No, that's, um, not necessary. I'm interrupting, so I won't stay long." Malcolm dragged a hand down his face. "Do you know where Mia is? If you do, I'm asking you—no, I'm begging you—to tell me."

"I'm sorry. I wish I did, because I'm worried about her, too, but I haven't any idea." Deception had always been one of the easier facets of his job with Division, and the lie rolled effortlessly off his tongue.

"I've scoured Romane from pole to pole." Malcolm took up pacing in agitation along the border of the landing pad. "I've tried to scour Pandora, but they apparently don't have so much as an official registry of property ownership, so I don't know how or where to start. I've wandered around the streets of New Orient and—"

"She would never return to New Orient."

"I don't think so, either. I realize it holds only terrible memories for her. But if she were hoping to lie low?"

"She would *never* return to New Orient." Caleb stilled his tongue before he said anything further. By omission, he'd given the man the answer he was searching for, though he doubted Malcolm was thinking clearly enough to realize it.

"Then where would she go? There are hundreds of human worlds and thousands of alien ones and I..." Malcolm pinched the bridge of his nose, deepening the wrinkles spreading out like cobwebs from the corners of his bloodshot eyes "...I don't know how to find her. Please, if you know anything, tell me. If you care anything at all about her, *tell* me."

Caleb bristled at the challenge, his composure slipping the tiniest bit. "I've known Mia since you were squirming under the boot of your first drill sergeant. Never question how much I care about her."

Malcolm's hand slipped down to clutch at his jaw. "I'm sorry. It's just...I'm at the end of my rope here. I can't think of where else to look, or even how to look. But I refuse to stop."

Marlee cleared her throat a tad awkwardly. "She's always loved Atlantis. Have you checked there?"

Malcolm forced a weak smile. "She does love Atlantis, and I've checked every hotel and rental residence on the planet. I've checked them for her name, her middle name and a dozen variations thereof. I've shown her image to every beach bum and bartender at twenty resorts. Nothing." He inhaled, drew himself up, and stepped closer to Caleb. "If you find out anything, any hint of where she might have gone, will you contact me? I only want to see her, to make sure she's safe. To try to explain, to apologize, to...you'll tell me, won't you?"

The man was so blatantly suffering that Caleb came within a breath of spilling the truth, and only the vow Mia had adamantly extracted from him choked the words off in his throat. "I will."

"I appreciate it. I need to...I don't know. Start over. Search everywhere again. Try harder. Check outside the main thoroughfares, in more secluded spots. Thank you for your time." He pivoted and climbed the ramp back into his ship.

They watched the ramp retract. Seconds later the ship lifted off and vanished through the Caeles Prism.

Caleb exhaled carefully and rubbed at his temples. Malcolm would never be a friend, but he hadn't enjoyed deceiving the man in the slightest. It couldn't have been easy for the Marine to bury his pride and come begging Caleb for help, either, and sending him away empty-handed felt callous.

He glanced over at Marlee without quite meeting her gaze. "I'm famished. Why don't we take a real break and get a snack? Then we'll pick back up where we left off."

Marlee studied him in blatant suspicion. "You lied to him. You *do* know where she is, don't you?"

"What makes you think so?"

"The little muscle in the crease of your left eye, next to your nose, twitched every time you spoke—exactly like Mom's does when she's keeping something from me."

He sighed and glared at the sky. "You are entirely too good at this. I should stop teaching you things while I can still keep a few tricks for myself."

Felzeor landed on his shoulder and leaned in close to inspect him; the Volucri's beak reached out and tapped the skin between his left eye and the bridge of his nose. "Does she mean right here?"

He groaned. "Felzeor, get out of my face!"

"Oh, dear. I forgot that was rude. Apologies." Felzeor climbed up onto his head to ruffle his hair.

Marlee refused to be distracted by the Volucri's antics. "So you did lie. Why? I mean, I understand Mia must be terribly upset after everything that's happened, but hiding out there all alone can't be good for her. Don't you want her to be happy?"

He whipped toward Marlee fast enough to send Felzeor flapping into the sky. "More than anything. But who am I to say if he's the one to make her happy? His return to the world of the living hasn't brought her joy so far."

"But she loves him."

"And to her mind, he betrayed her love by not telling her about the 'no regenesis' clause in his will. The truth is, if it were up to me, I would have pointed him in the proper direction. Poor guy's looking rather pathetic, and you're right, he has made her happy for a long time. But she demanded that I keep her secret. And she means a hell of a lot more to me than Malcolm Jenner does, so I will honor my oath to her, no matter what."

Marlee scowled, but her lips quirked around as she debated how to respond. Finally she blew out a breath and dropped her chin. "I guess this means you're not going to tell me where she is, either. Not that I'd go see her, necessarily—I was just her employee, after all. But it would be nice to know she's okay."

Since he'd found Mia, he'd cajoled Alex into using sidespace to check in on her and the shop once a day; it wasn't much, but it was what he could do to assuage his own concerns. "She's as okay as she can be right now. If she needs my help, I'll be there for her in a second. But Mia has always chosen her own path to walk, and she's got to forge a new one now."

19

CONCORD HQ

"The Rectifier is a total game-changer for ground combat. Trust me on this."

Miriam eyed Alex ruefully. She wouldn't change anything about her daughter, but she'd also never stop worrying when Alex willingly threw herself into peril. Yes, as a Prevo, should the worst happen then Alex's return was all but guaranteed, but Miriam also wasn't ready to wish the ordeal of regenesis on anyone lightly.

"I've already ordered the weapon into general production, and I'll sign off on licensing the IP to the Asterions."

"Good." Alex made a face and glanced toward the door. "Sorry, but I need to go. I promised Kennedy I'd meet her for lunch."

"Actually, I do as well. I hope your afternoon is more enjoyable than mine is shaping up to be."

Alex frowned at the scrolling military status feed, then at the growing stack of quantum cubes on Miriam's desk. "I can pretty much guarantee it will be. Don't let the bureaucrats beat you down."

"When have I ever?" She accepted Alex's quick hug and saw her out the door.

Once her daughter had departed, Miriam checked the time. She was running ahead of schedule, and she had no desire to loiter at her next appointment, so she slipped her jacket on and headed toward the CINT offices.

Richard's door was open, but she knocked on the frame instead of barging in. At the noise, Richard looked away from a double aural above his desk. His countenance, tight with concentration and worry, brightened a touch, and he waved her inside.

"We missed you at Alex's for breakfast last week."

"I'm sorry I couldn't make it. I had a prior engagement."

"That's what Alex said." Her lips pursed. "Richard, listen. I'm not here as David's envoy, and I won't try to excuse his actions. But as your friend, I will say one thing: this cold-shoulder treatment of him you insist on maintaining seems to be making you as miserable as it's making David. This means that, despite each of your best efforts, together the two of you are making *me* miserable. What can I do to help resolve this conflict?"

He grimaced, then shook his head. "You can talk to me about the Savrakaths and the Anadens."

Inwardly, she sighed, but she knew better than to push him when he was being this stubborn. "Why don't you talk to me about them, instead? You currently know more than I do, and I genuinely do need to know what intelligence you've gathered."

"All right. Let's see. Ghost patrols report an even greater percentage of Savradin is in ruins than it was when Malcolm escaped. Someone laid waste to large swaths of it yesterday."

"Torval? Again?"

"We weren't able to get eyes on the attackers, but it's a reasonable assumption."

"Is it? I have trouble believing Corradeo Praesidis would authorize such indiscriminate slaughter. Once upon a time, maybe, but not the man he is today."

"According to my informant, Torval has yet to be seen on Epithero. There's no reason to think Corradeo has Torval under his control." He paused and checked one of the aurals. "But there is reason to think the situation will soon change."

"Oh? What do you know?"

"Eren Savitas has joined Corradeo on Epithero."

"Interesting. I'm glad to hear that Eren's re-engaging, but how does his presence there change things?"

"Per Drae Shonen's report, after Eren kidnapped Torval from Detention, he delivered the man to the Savrakaths for them to abuse as they wished. When General Jhountar arranged to trade Torval for a cease-fire, Eren bombed the meeting location. To say he wishes Torval ill would be a colossal understatement."

She mentally connected the dots. Up until now, details had been scarce surrounding the bombing that killed much of the Savrakath military leadership and played a role in freeing Malcolm. "How did Eren know about the trade?"

"Because Mia intercepted a communication from my informant on Epithero and forwarded it to Eren." He rubbed at his jaw. "The Savrakaths have caused a great deal of pain and heartache for a lot of people. But this vigilante justice—on all sides—has got to stop."

She couldn't agree more. As a military leader and one of the architects of

Concord's infrastructure, the notion of government and military agents running around bombing each other on enemy planets, without oversight, orders or sanction, was *not* ideal. But the full consequences of the Anaden leadership's rebellion were going to take a while longer to shake out, it seemed.

"You've removed Mia from the equation. I know it wasn't easy for you—it wasn't easy for any of us—but given her actions, it was the right thing to do. On the other side, as much as it pains me to say, I think we need to give Corradeo a little time. I believe if there's any way for him to do it, he'll come through for us."

Richard nodded tightly. "Noted. So what are *we* going to do about the Savrakaths?"

"They're Red-Flagged. The only threat they can wield against us is a rapidly dwindling supply of antimatter, and with the flag controls in place, they will not get within a parsec of Concord property carrying any of it." She shrugged. "They're crippled, to a greater extent than I ever wanted. If they try to retaliate against Concord in any way, we'll respond appropriately. But to cripple them further now would be…cruel."

EARTH

EARTH ALLIANCE HEADQUARTERS

The shouts of protesters beyond the tall fence greeted Miriam as she departed the heavily guarded transportation building and strode across the lawn flanked by two security escorts. The cacophony of overlapping shouts and over-bright signs meant it was difficult to make out much regarding the protestors' complaints, but neon flashes of 'No Regenesis,' 'No Zombie Humans' and similar colorful phrases gave her the gist.

She kept her chin high and her stride purposeful; it was hardly the first time she'd run a gauntlet of citizens expressing their displeasure at her decisions. Still, the angry, agitated nature of the crowd reminded her too much of the OTS protests of old. Those protests had soon graduated to riots, spurred the creation of an entirely new interplanetary alliance in the IDCC, and ultimately forced Miriam into a revolution against her own government.

She didn't work for the Earth Alliance any longer, but she had faith that the government was on top of any burgeoning unrest. Well, not faith as such, but she'd assume it had the matter in hand until she was provided a reason to believe otherwise.

They reached the side entrance to the main building, and the shouts faded away in favor of the warm halls and quiet murmurs of government business being done. Her escorts delivered her to the waiting area outside the Prime Minister's office and returned to their duties.

With a term now stretching past fifteen years, Charles Gagnon's tenure was getting a bit long in the tooth. But he'd shepherded the Earth Alliance through The Displacement, the expansion of AEGIS and the formation of Concord with a minimum of bloodshed and a surfeit of handshakes, so if the history of his tenure in office were written today, historians would treat him favorably.

Miriam's relationship with the man had always been cordial. Friendly when they were able to work closely together on matters of import, and a tad frosty when public opinion and politics chafed against the decisions of the military or Concord. On balance, their dynamic had worked more often than it failed.

Today might veer toward the frosty side, Miriam thought as she was shown into Gagnon's office and shook his hand in greeting. His gaze bore studiously through her, as if he had a mind to dissect her and ruminate on whether the copy's organs measured up to those of the original. It was an unnerving stare, if one she was getting used to enduring. But his administration had signed off on the results of the Regenesis Extension Project and authorized the legalization of regenesis (albeit with an accompanying mountain of regulations), so she hoped his morbid curiosity was personal rather than official.

"Prime Minister, it is good to see you, as always."

"And you, Commandant. You left us for a little while there."

"For a few days, yes. I'm glad to be back."

"Of course. I'm sure you've been forced to share your harrowing tale a thousand times, so I won't torture you by asking you to do it again today. I understand you wish to discuss this Rasu threat."

"I do." She sat opposite his large, consequential desk as he settled into his chair behind it. "Are those people outside protesting the entire idea of regenesis, or my use of it specifically?"

"Both, I believe."

"Wonderful. I trust Pamela Winslow remains securely ensconced in her swanky prison suite in Paris?"

"She does."

"Then I will not spare too much energy worrying over the protests. In any event, about the Rasu. We are working around the clock to better prepare for this new enemy. We're running encounter scenarios, speeding up weapons and defense deployments, and sharpening our contingency plans. AEGIS is working closely with Concord on these efforts, and I expect you are already beginning to receive recommendations from the AEGIS military leadership."

"Indeed I am. Frightful creatures, these Rasu."

You have no idea. "Frightful and powerful." She glanced toward the windows behind him. "I'll leave the details of the Earth Alliance's defensive preparations to AEGIS. I don't need to barge into the middle of a functioning chain of command. But I do want to take a few minutes to clearly articulate the severity of the situation directly to you."

Gagnon spread his arms wide, though his expression remained guarded. "Do tell."

"Earth is and has always been my home. I represent Concord now, but the welfare of humanity, of this precious planet of ours, is always at the forefront of my mind." She leaned forward intently. "Prime Minister, the Rasu represent the greatest threat we have ever faced."

"Greater than the Machim Primor attempting to drop a black hole on our universe?"

"In the short term, perhaps not greater than that, no. But in the longer term, the result will be the same if we don't act to defend ourselves."

"I understand where your concerns are coming from, Commandant. They did kill you."

She ground her frustration into her jaw. "Prime Minister, have I ever been wrong when I have counseled you about a military threat? Have I ever exaggerated or fear-mongered?"

He tilted his head in concession. "No. You have not. But some argue that you aren't the same person you once were."

"If you believed this to be true, you never would have signed the regenesis legalization bill into law."

"True enough. I did want to see for myself, but I'll grant that you appear unchanged."

"Then I ask you to believe me now."

His eyes bore into her, but she didn't flinch; finally the stare broke, just a fraction, and he nodded minutely. "To be fair, the admiralty is expressing much the same concerns in their reports. But other than adopting every

AEGIS recommendation that's flying in from the Presidio on an almost hourly basis, what would you have me do?"

"Today? Right now? Add an array of negative energy missile batteries to the Terrestrial Defense Grid. Oh, and make certain they're modular, because we're working with the Asterions to develop more advanced versions of our negative energy weapons. If the improvements are viable, you'll want to deploy them once they're ready."

"You want me to build a new set of missile batteries around the entire planet? Do you have any idea how much such an undertaking will cost?"

"Less than the cost of rebuilding every major city on Earth after they burn to ashes in a Rasu-delivered conflagration."

"Commandant—"

"The Rasu are nearly impossible to kill—but we *can* kill them. The methods we employ to achieve this are not perfect, but they do work, and we need to put ourselves in a position to be able to use them effectively when the time comes. The lasers comprising the Terrestrial Defense Grid remain the most formidable conventional weapons active in Concord, but they will only slow the Rasu down for a minute or two. Negative energy missiles are the safest tool we possess to permanently destroy Rasu while posing the smallest threat to civilian populations and military craft. Adapt and meet the problem, Prime Minister."

He drummed his fingers on a leather box sitting atop his desk. "The Assembly Armed Services Committee, not to mention the Select Military Advisory Council, will have to approve an infrastructure project so massive as what you're suggesting."

"I'm happy to speak to them if they have questions or concerns."

"And you very well may need to do so. But you're correct. Across a myriad of threats to our existence we've faced during my time in government, you've never been wrong. So I will..." he shrugged broadly "...do what I must and recommend we pursue such a project. Damn the torpedoes one more time."

She let a small measure of the relief she felt reach her expression. "Thank you, Prime Minister. I pray that we stop the Rasu in their tracks long before they ever learn of Earth's existence and you never need to use those defenses, but I'll sleep better at night knowing Earth is well-prepared to meet this threat."

20

CONCORD HQ

Richard had barely ensconced himself back into the newest intel report to hit his desk when another knock jolted him out of it. He looked up to see Devon standing in the open doorway to his office.

He immediately adopted a mask of cordial neutrality. "Good afternoon, Devon. What can I do for you?" Despite his efforts otherwise, it came out sounding stilted and overly formal, which seemed about right. He was trying to take Graham's advice to heart, but his brain had thus far stubbornly refused to let loose of its grudges.

Devon stared at him for several seconds, the younger man's nose pinched up and his eyes creased. Finally he nodded, as if to himself. "Can we go get a beer?"

Richard frowned. "Why does everyone keep wanting to ply me with beer?"

"I can't speak for anyone else, but here's *my* thinking: one, because I'm going to need one, or possibly three, for this conversation. Two, because you really look like you need one. Possibly three."

He'd always been amused by Devon's unique brand of humor, and the deadpan delivery broke through his defenses. "Granted on all counts. Let me finish one thing up." He deleted the sentence he'd been struggling over and wrote a new one without thinking on it too hard, then sent the response and shut down his screens. "Where to?"

RW

The Black Hole wasn't even close to the only bar on Concord HQ, but it was the one most frequented by Command and CINT employees. It served decent finger food and a comprehensive assortment of drinks for every species, and the high-back, circular booths provided a measure of privacy for the patrons.

Richard eased into a booth near the back opposite Devon. They ordered two SanDune IPAs, then Devon clasped his hands atop the table. Then fidgeted around for a minute, grabbing a napkin to clean off an invisible stain on the table and scrolling through the menu again.

"Devon…."

"I helped Mia access the CINT secure network to send a message to the mole you had in place with Ferdinand."

Richard sighed. "I know you did."

"What? How could you know? I was sneaky. Clever, too."

"You always are, which is why I can't prove it—or couldn't until you just confessed to me. It's probably more accurate to say I suspected."

Devon's shoulders sagged, and when their drinks arrived he hurriedly turned his up, prolonging his sip for longer than politeness dictated. Finally he set the mug down and wiped foam from his mouth. "Why didn't you come talk to me?"

"Because I didn't particularly want to have this conversation. I didn't want my suspicions confirmed. Also, I'm getting tired of arguing with people I care about."

"Aww, that's…well, at least you didn't say 'cared' in the past tense."

"Tell me why I shouldn't."

Devon flinched; the barb had left a mark. "Listen, Mia appealed to all my most vulnerable weaknesses. We were fugitives together, on the run from the almighty Earth Alliance. She saved Emily's life when Montegreu's Artificial poisoned her. She brought me to Amaranthe to help save the world. We have a history together."

"So do we."

"I *know*, which is why I've felt terrible about it ever since. Why I came to you to bare my soul, confess my sins and throw myself at your mercy."

"Over beers."

"I had to do what I could to sway sentiment my way. I'm sorry?"

Richard took a sip of his drink; it was succeeding in loosening his tongue, if nothing else. "Everyone's so very sorry after the fact, once they've already gotten away with their schemes. But you know what? I am done being taken advantage of by people I call my friends."

Devon regarded him curiously. "You're speaking in plurals an awful lot. This has to do with more than Mia's interference, doesn't it?"

"It might." Richard groaned and dragged a hand down his face. "Honestly, I'm just tired. Tired of being the only one on the team who respects the rules and thus has to constantly nag everyone else about following them. Concord may be the newest power player on the block, but it's not a kangaroo government. The rules are in place for a reason. They matter."

"Oh, you're not the only one trying to keep the rest of us in line, don't worry. But..." Devon grimaced, looking as frustrated as Richard felt "...we've been friends for almost two decades now. Have you ever known me to follow the rules?"

"No, which is one reason why you're on the lowest rung of my shit list. I'm disappointed that you went behind my back, but under the circumstances I can't be too surprised. As you said, you and Mia have a history as well, and I imagine her plea struck a chord with you."

"Are you kidding? Vengeance for the loss of one's beloved? Apparent loss, I guess—and how messed up is that? I mean, yay for Malcolm actually being alive and all, but what a mind-fuck for her."

"No doubt." He lazily swirled the beer around in its glass. "Do you know where she is?"

"I do not." Devon shook his head slowly for added emphasis.

"Can you find out?"

"Come on, man. Are you seriously going to ask me to do that? I don't want to do that...but if it will keep me in my job and, most importantly, out of prison, yes, I can. And I guess will."

Richard huffed a wry laugh. "I'll hold your sort-of-offer in reserve for now. I'm playing a longer game, and if it works, I won't need to find her."

"Whew. I'll be honest, I've had all the double-crossing I can stomach. It's wearing on me."

"Good. Remember this next time someone tries to con you into a double-cross."

"No promises, but I'll try. Damn, this being an upstanding, respectable and respected luminary is tougher than I'd expected."

"Oh, is that what you are?"

Devon shrank back in the booth, hurt flashing across his features. "All right, I deserved that. Though they came from a desire to do good for someone in need, my actions were neither respectable nor luminous, and definitely not befitting the head of a Concord division." He chewed on his lower lip. "So you're not going to arrest me?"

"No, Devon, I'm not, though don't think I haven't been tempted. You're an accessory to a crime. But your actions fall far short of Mia's crimes. And Miriam might literally string me up by my toes and leave me to starve in the desert if I depose two Concord division heads in less than a month."

Devon nodded with the fervor of the pardoned. "Thank you. Thank you, thank you, thank you." He turned his glass up and emptied it, then gave Richard an earnest, foam-adorned smile. "Now, can we please be friends again?"

Richard cast a resigned gaze to the ceiling. "Never, *ever* break into one of my secure networks again."

"You don't have to worry about it. The guilt alone has soured me on this manner of escapade."

"Devon."

His shoulders snapped straight. "I promise. I will never, ever, *ever* break into any system you control, of any kind, ever again. Unless you need me to."

"Why would I need you to break into one of my own systems?"

"In this crazy world, you never know."

He wasn't wrong. Richard finished off his beer and shrugged, trying his damnedest to let go of all this pent-up resentment. "I'll accept your promise, and hold you to it."

21

PANDORA

Mia yawned and flexed her arms out behind the counter. Last night had been another fitful night of tossing and turning, of her mind drifting to better times and better memories in the twilight between sleeping and waking. Though Meno denied it, she suspected that sometime during the night he'd finally screwed around with her neurochemicals to knock her out for a couple of hours. She wanted to be angry at him, but in truth she was too desperate for the peaceful oblivion of dreamless slumber to care.

Store traffic, and with it sales, were gradually improving. She'd tweaked her inventory and the presentation of it to be more appealing to the unique customer base of the neighborhood, and the adjustments were showing signs of helping. She was still bleeding red ink, but the hole was shallowing. Another year or two of hustling for business and she might make a profit. She'd been rather skilled at doing that, once upon a time.

Her attention flickered to the silent news feed screen; she forced it away. Being out of the loop and absent from the halls of power made her twitchy. She longed for the inside news on the Rasu conflict, on the faltering Anaden rebellion, even on the…she shuddered…Savrakath situation. But so far every time she'd activated the news feed, within five minutes Malcolm's name had come up, and she'd had to hurriedly shut it off again.

As a result, it often felt like she lived in a brittle bubble, cut off from the rest of the world and its grand machinations by a flimsy barrier that was always one catastrophic event away from bursting. Did normal people feel this way all the time? Isolated and frustrated, helpless to shape the course of history?

Her finger was wavering above the news feed button when the door opened. A man walked in carrying something in both hands; he was well dressed, especially for the neighborhood, wearing tailored navy slacks and a gray merino wool cardigan. Wavy, dark brown hair fluttered over his temples from the breeze outside to frame the striking silver of Prevo eyes. Over-sharp features put a slightly hard edge on an otherwise handsome face.

He gave her a broad smile as he ignored the product displays to cross the store and arrive directly in front of her, where he set his package on the counter. "Good morning. I'm Enzio Vilane, president of the Approach Community Retailers Council, and I brought you a 'welcome to the neighborhood' gift."

She stared down at the package in surprise. Beneath a clear plastic cover sat a large plate stacked high with...cookies? "I'm Laisha. It's a pleasure to meet you, Mr. Vilane. And thank you. These smell delicious."

"I'm glad to hear it." His expression flickered uncertainly. "Shall we dive into them? I mean, they're all for you, of course, but if you want to do a taste-test?"

They really did smell wonderful, so she removed the cover and handed him a cookie, then picked one up for herself. "Let us test them together."

The cookie was warm, gooey and filled with raisins. She let the gooeyness fill her mouth before washing it down with coffee. "Did you bake them yourself?"

He hesitated. "Is the correct answer, 'yes'?"

"The correct answer is the truth."

Something indefinable flashed across his features for a microsecond and was gone. "Then yes. For good or ill."

"No, they're delicious. My compliments to the chef. Or...baker, I guess."

"What a relief. Thank you." He dragged a stool over and sat at the counter to munch casually on his cookie. "How are you finding the neighborhood so far? Good neighbors? Good customers?"

"The other store owners I've met have been very friendly, and after a slow start, business is picking up. The local gang shakedown was a little annoying, but other than that, everything is going well."

He frowned. "I do apologize for the thugs bothering you. The Council is doing what it can to run the lowlifes out of here, but...."

"But this is Pandora. I expected it."

"So you've lived here for a while?"

"No. I lived here a long time ago, when I was a teenager. I've only recently returned."

"I'm not surprised to hear it. If I may be embarrassingly honest, having met you now, you're too classy for this place. Don't misunderstand, this is not me complaining. I'm glad you've arrived to spruce up the quality of the neighborhood."

"You flatter me, but I'm simply trying to make a living like everyone else.

I'm nothing special."

"I highly doubt that."

She smiled blithely. He was charming, no question. Perhaps a touch *too* charming. "What do you do? Other than run the...what did you call it?"

"The Approach Community Retailers Council, but 'ACRC' is less of a mouthful. I'm a real estate investor—or trying to be one. I own a couple of apartment buildings in the area."

"I imagine the real estate market here on Pandora can get exciting at times. How long have you been a Prevo?"

A corner of his lips wavered. "Some years now. I did miss the OTS unrest back in the day, but I signed up not long after The Displacement. What about you?"

If he could lie, so could she. "Oh, only a few months ago. It's all still new to me. Exciting, but also a little daunting."

"If you ever have any concerns or want some helpful tips, feel free to message me. I'll send you my personal contact address. I just need your...well, I can send it to the store account."

She didn't rise to the bait, instead plastering on an expression of innocent obliviousness. "How kind of you."

"Exhibiting kindness to our local retail owners is part of my job, and you are making my job easy today. Hey, we have a newsletter that goes out once a month. I'll include an announcement about your store opening in the next issue. Hopefully it will bring you a few additional customers."

"Thank you. And for the cookies. I think I'll have another one for brunch."

"My pleasure. Truly." He gazed at her for a long moment, giving her an opening to engage further, before taking the hint of her silence and standing. "I'll come back by for the plate in a few days. It'll give me an excuse to drop in and see how you're doing."

"I look forward to it."

He smiled again, backed toward the door, then finally turned and left.

She munched on a second cookie, half expecting him to reappear in the doorway with another gracious entreaty. When he didn't, she set the plate under the counter. The cookies were too tasty to let her customers abscond with them.

What an odd encounter. Part of her feared she'd become too jaded and distrustful to recognize a simple, friendly interchange for what it was. Not everything in life was palace intrigue and court manipulations.

But she'd risen to the dizzying heights of the Concord Senate and oversight of inter-species diplomatic relations—before taking a stunning triple axel dive off that peak to crash on the rocks below—because, among other skills, she'd grown very good at reading people.

Meno, I want to know everything the exanet knows about Enzio Vilane. Then I want anything else you can scrounge up on him. But don't use the Noesis. He's a Prevo, so he could be listening in.

I will find all the available information. Avoiding the Noesis will make the work more difficult, but I welcome the challenge. May I ask why, though? He seemed quite nice. Did you not think he seemed nice?

Oh, he seemed *quite nice indeed. What he* is *is trouble.*

22

AKESO

Alex let the steaming hot water cascade through her hair and down her back. It had been a whirlwind couple of days of bouncing between her mother's office and the Special Projects labs at Concord HQ, the Connova Interstellar testing facility, and various locales in the Asterion Dominion. The defeat of the Rasu at Namino had given them a chance to regroup and get the upper hand on the conflict, and everyone recognized they couldn't let it go to waste.

But now she was home, with a few free hours to catch her breath. She celebrated by luxuriating in the shower for an extra five minutes before toweling off, throwing on sweatpants and an old t-shirt, and setting off to find Caleb.

Doing so wasn't difficult, especially with the sonorous beat of his heart pointing the way. She found him several hundred meters south of the house, sitting cross-legged by the creek, his palms open at his knees and his eyes closed.

She crept across the meadow, which had finally dried out, and eased down to the ground beside him. Once there, she took the opportunity to study him unobserved. The worry lines that had creased deep into his skin around his eyes and mouth after the ordeal on Namino had all but vanished. His jaw was relaxed, as was his posture. His heartbeat resonated in her chest, steady, calm and slow, almost as if he were in a trance. He looked…peaceful, but not soft. Resolute, but for the first time in quite a while, not burdened. She'd daresay this new phase of his relationship with Akeso was working out rather well so far.

A corner of his mouth curled up, though his eyes remained closed. "Hi, baby."

"Hi, *priyazn*. I didn't mean to disturb you."

"Your presence is never a disturbance." His left hand reached out to cradle the stem of a tiny flower sprouting up through the blades of grass between them. As she watched, the bud opened and bloomed into rich magenta petals with white tips. He deftly snapped the flower off at the root, then opened his eyes and offered her the flower now resting on his palm. "Akeso says this is for you."

"Well, thank Akeso for me." She accepted the flower and tucked it behind her ear.

He stared at her for a few seconds, then burst out laughing.

"What?"

"You're not exactly a 'flower in your hair' kind of woman."

"I'm really, really not." She rolled her eyes and removed the flower from her ear, but kept it cupped gently in her hand. "What's today's conversation topic?"

"The nature of evil."

Her brow furrowed in consternation. "I hope the flower wasn't a central figure in the discussion."

"Nah." His focus fell to the grass, and after another second, the snipped stem grew a new bud. "Akeso is having some difficulty grasping the million shades of gray on the morality spectrum, and how people can slip—or be pushed—down the spectrum toward darkness. We're working on expanding our mutual understanding, but it's a challenging topic."

"You've always seemed to have a solid handle on it." She watched as the bud unfurled; this time, the petals were teal tipped with cornflower. "Mia's fine this morning, by the way. She was eating cookies, which is sort of making me hungry."

"It so happens that Graham Delavasi sent us a cooler of fresh fish last night. I'll grill some up." He stood and offered her a hand. "How was your trip to Mirai? Did you learn as much as you hoped to?"

She fell in beside him as they walked toward the house. "I now know as much as Nika does about these Ourankeli aliens, but that isn't much." She paused. "Nisi would know more."

"I hear he's officially going by Corradeo Praesidis once again."

"Whatever. Do you want to reach out to him?"

Caleb shook his head. "No. He has his hands full wrangling a bunch of spoiled, recalcitrant *elassons* into line, and he doesn't need a reminder of why the job is proving to be harder than it might have been."

How many times had they covered this ground? A thousand on the low end. "I seriously doubt he blames you for the loss of his *diati*, much less the loss of it by the rest of the Praesidis. The blame lies squarely on the head of his dearly departed son, Renato. Besides, Nika said he acted genuinely happy to learn you were alive."

Caleb's expression brightened noticeably. "I'm glad. But…no, I don't want to open that can of worms. Not yet."

"Richard says Eren's working with him now."

"What? Now this *is* good news. A righteous cause will give Eren a reason to stick around in the land of the living."

"Hopefully so. Still don't want to pay them a visit?"

"Because of Eren?" They reached the porch, and he stopped to lean against a pillar. "I do want to see Eren. But it's enough to know he's alive and engaged in an endeavor that's important to him. Corradeo will take care of him."

"Assuming Eren allows anyone to."

His gaze cut over to the creek. "I know I've been running from a lot of difficult truths for a while now. I'm working hard to get on top of them. Give me a little more time on this one?"

"However long you need. I'll stop being a pest about it." She smiled. "In the absence of talking to the source, we'll wing it with the Ourankeli. It certainly won't be the first time we've flown in blind, right?"

"It is our stock in trade."

"And I'm okay with that. I think the *Siyane* will be impervious to whatever is causing the widespread erosion in the Ourankeli stellar system, but while I was at HQ, I fitted it with a new, supercharged EM shield just in case. I also acquired some new personal shields from Devon. They should protect our environment suits from anything space or aliens can throw at us."

"Excellent." He reached out and drew her into his arms, kissing her softly. "You go put the flower in a vase. I'll shower and pack a bag, then cook lunch. After we eat, I'll be ready to go whenever you are." His lips brushed across hers again. "It's time for us to have an old-fashioned adventure."

23

MIRAI

DASHIEL'S FLAT

Close your eyes and open your vision. See the hidden dimension that exists everywhere and nowhere: the gateway to the universe. Visualize where you want to be and let your mind take you there—

Nothing. Nika stretched her arms over her head as the lingering vestiges of a damn restful night of sleep competed with her need to concentrate on solving the sidespace/wormhole puzzle. But whether her eyes were shut or open, all she saw was kyoseil waves. They sure seemed to travel wherever they pleased, but they were not as yet interested in offering her consciousness a ride on their journeys.

She tried mentally nudging them aside, as if parting a curtain, but they continued to ignore her request in favor of their dancing undulations.

Ugh. All this kyoseil flowing through her, powering her very thoughts alongside sophisticated quantum synthetic programming, and she couldn't find a way to harness it to execute on her intentions? What good was any of it if it refused to do as she asked?

Several good nights of sleep in a row had improved her overall outlook considerably, but on this point she remained annoyingly frustrated. With a resigned sigh, she decided to give up for now, again, and switch to her other puzzle, the Kat code from the Rift Bubble on Namino. It accessed hidden dimensions as well, but the programming that allowed it to do so was accessible to her.

The code appeared at first glance to be infinitely complex. The rift device not only accessed extra dimensions to power itself; it then tore a planet-sized hole in the fabric of space-time, optionally hid everything on the other side of the tear from view, and opened a new hole in that fabric at a distant yet specific location.

But once you separated out the disparate functions into their own silos, it began to be decipherable. Byzantine, intricate and strikingly beautiful, but decipherable. She'd already delivered a copy of the code to Conceptual Research in the hope they'd be able to build their own Rift Bubbles and possibly even develop new uses for the technology. But Alex had chosen to share this gift with her, personally, and she badly wanted to wrangle it into submission herself.

The instructions forcing the device to rip open space-time were written in the formalistic, structural language of quantum programming, but in practice the operations didn't behave so differently from Alex's instructions on accessing sidespace. What if she—?

In the corner of her vision, Dashiel emerged from the lavatory wearing khaki slacks and an unfastened shirt, then rested against the doorframe and regarded her with a playful smile. She didn't need to turn her full attention toward him to feel the lust in his gaze. She'd kicked off the covers at some point during her ruminations, and the morning sun streaked in through the windows to warm her skin. She stretched again and purred seductively. "See something you like?"

"Do I ever." He came over and perched on the edge of the bed, leaning down to kiss her, long and slow.

She urged him more fully down on top of her, letting her hands snake beneath the material of his shirt to caress the muscles along his back. "Come back to bed."

"Hmm…." His lips left hers behind to trail tantalizingly down her neck and across her chest; his tongue darted out to circle her left breast, evoking a moan from deep in her throat. "I would deeply, *deeply* love to stay right here all day and night…" his lips returned to linger upon hers for a breath "…but I can't. I'm expected at the DAF Orbital Assembly #3 in forty minutes."

"Damn."

"I know." With a groan he slid off the bed, stood and began fastening his shirt. "Tonight, nothing will distract me from…" he gestured vaguely at her "…this vision you present. In fact, I will have to struggle mightily to think of anything else all day."

In truth, she was expected at the Initiative not too long from now herself, but she so enjoyed teasing him. "Tonight, darling."

DAF ORBITAL ASSEMBLY #3

Dashiel stood on the sealed observation deck in low Mirai orbit and watched as an army of space-rated dyne mechs assembled row upon row of military warships. The kyoseil-infused adiamene took on a cornsilk hue in its final form, and the arrangement of ships—fighters, in this instance—resembled a sea of fireflies poised to swarm the planet below.

It had taken a herculean effort on the part of Ridani Enterprises, the Commerce, Military and Administrative Divisions on multiple worlds, and numerous business partners to bring the warship assembly facilities to fruition in record time. But he believed he had finally created a robust, redundant supply and production chain for the DAF fleet.

Component production facilities were duplicated on all four functioning Axis Worlds, and shipyards had been completed above three of the four, with the fourth scheduled to begin production next week. For now, each shipyard specialized in a different type of warship: fighters here above Mirai, frigates, cruisers and carriers at Synra, and specialty and support craft at Kiyora. But every shipyard could be converted to handle the other ships in less than a day, should the need arise.

So long as a single Axis World still stood, the Dominion would have its fleet.

He diverted his thoughts before they began to delve into the troubling possibility that one day no Axis World would stand, because it was *not* going to happen. Before he got hold of the diversion, his thoughts darted immediately to the delicious sight of Nika's naked body luxuriating in his bed this morning, and it was with a great deal more reluctance that he put those musings aside as well.

His people continued to refine and improve the delicate process of creating adiaK, and a joint Conceptual Research/DAF ceraff-enhanced team continued to churn out improvements to warship weapons and engines. But Palmer was correct. He couldn't scrap the fleet and start production over every time he or anyone else had a newer, better idea. So he was rolling improvements into the production process as they tested out, and where there was time and a lack of battles, the older-generation ships were cycled in for retrofitting.

Grant was back on the team now, at least nominally. The two times Dashiel had met with him, his head didn't appear to be completely in the game. Given how his homeworld had been leveled and his home and business destroyed, he'd forgive the man for a little distraction. Still, none of them could afford to be too distracted, not while they had worlds on fire and Rasu relentlessly probing every defense they'd erected to protect the ones that weren't.

Of all the nonconventional weaponry they'd determined was able to put a permanent dent in Rasu—antimatter, negative energy and nuclear—negative energy weapons left behind the least collateral damage and created the smallest risk to nearby objects, people and planets. A far from zero risk, but the smallest of the lot.

They'd never had cause to need negative energy weapons before now, but they certainly knew how to construct them, and new facilities on Ebisu and Synra had begun building the weapons earlier this week for addition to the frigate and cruiser loadouts. Their fighters were too small to carry more than two, which to his mind seemed almost like a waste of effort.

But on the way here this morning, he'd authorized the creation of a new Conceptual Research ceraff devoted to the task of developing a rechargeable negative energy mechanism. If their supply of the weapons became effectively unlimited, it stood to change the shape of every battle to come.

Dashiel exhaled and rubbed at his jaw. It wasn't in his nature to thrive on crafting instruments of mass destruction. He preferred to build things that lasted. Useful, creative things to improve people's lives, work and the society that nurtured both.

But nothing improved lives so much as not getting killed by Rasu, so he was making his peace with this new phase of his professional career. The times called for a wartime industrialist, so a wartime industrialist he would be.

24

MIRAI

OMOIKANE INITIATIVE

"We cannot have multiple copies of a single person running around the streets like they're in a madhouse carnival. Do you have any idea how much more difficult Justice's job will be if Plexes become widespread?"

Nika shrugged in Adlai's general direction. Outside in the hallway, beyond the open door, she kept an eye on Maris and Spencer talking in fervent but hushed tones. Spencer had excused himself from the table to confer with Maris almost ten minutes earlier. "If our society was structured around making Justice's job easy, a lot of things would be different."

"That's a low blow."

Adlai acted like he was teasing, but she softened her tone anyway. "I didn't mean it as such."

"I know you didn't. I do wonder if this is NOIR talking, though."

She forced herself to ignore the hallway drama and focus all her attention on Adlai and the others gathered around the table. "Maybe it is. NOIR was created for a reason."

"Yes, the Guides' overreaching and, it turned out, treasonous activities. We've done away with their excesses."

"Most of them. Listen, having been a Plex myself twice now, I'm not a fan of the technology. But it does have its uses—"

"And we can write in exceptions to the ban for those uses."

"But a ban is still a ban, and we try to have as few of those as possible." Nika sighed. "The idea of Plexes having free rein in our society makes me uncomfortable, too. I'm searching for a middle ground here."

Selene returned from taking a comm to settle into her seat. "From my perspective, if we implement basic registration requirements so we know who they are, I don't have a problem with legalizing the technology."

Adlai shook his head. "People who become Plexes aren't the type to be amenable to 'registering' with the government."

"True, but—"

Maris tip-toed into the room to lay a hand on Nika's shoulder. "May I speak to you for a minute? In private?"

Adlai arched an eyebrow but didn't protest, and Nika stood and followed Maris out into the hallway, passing Spencer on the way as he went back to the table.

Maris closed the door to the meeting room behind them. Her features were unusually pinched, and the hint of worry lines framed her orchid irises.

Nika leaned against the wall a few meters down from the door. "Are you and Spencer fighting?"

"Yes, and I don't want to talk about it."

"Okay. What do you want to talk about, then?"

"I was listening in on the last bit of your discussion regarding the Plexes—"

"Instead of listening to whatever Spencer was rather earnestly trying to say to you?"

"Nika, I am not seeking love-life advice."

Maybe you should.... But she kept the thought to herself. In her admittedly limited recollection, she'd never seen Maris so snippy, or even upset. "I'm sorry. Please continue."

"Thank you. It sounds as if you are reluctant to grant Plexes legal rights, which brings me to...I feel I need to remind you of something. Or simply tell you in the first place, since you don't remember. I was there with you when you chose to stand up for the right of every individual, whether they be Anaden or synthetic, to live a life of their own choosing, and to live it freely. The Nika that ignited the SAI Rebellion would never have advocated for making a new variant of sapient life illegal."

She sank deeper against the wall and rubbed at her face. "Are you saying *I* started the SAI Rebellion?"

"Technically, your brother started it by flaunting the new laws and provoking the authorities, but you were the one who stood up, spoke out and rallied everyone to fight. Because you wanted to protect your brother, yes, but also because you believed in the cause—believed in it enough to risk your life without the safety net of regenesis."

"And my brother ultimately lost his as a result."

"He would have said it was worth it. He was utterly fearless. Also stubborn, single-minded, a genius and a mite insane, but in an endearing way."

Nika's heart ached with a deep yearning to remember Loshi—what he looked like, how he talked, the escapades they must have enjoyed together.

But she also recognized it might well hurt far worse if she *could* remember. Better to not truly understand the magnitude of what she'd lost?

She nodded in acceptance. "Consider me properly chastised. I suppose I was letting my personal misgivings cloud my objectivity, and I don't have the right to impose those on every Asterion. You make a strong case, but we can't make the case to the room without exposing your and my 1st Gen status."

"Adlai knows, of course, though it wasn't my choice. I think Selene has long suspected. But Julien, Harris and even Spencer remain ignorant—as well as the Administration Advisors in there—and that's the way it must stay."

"On account of 'the rules.'"

"The rules were earned through heartbreak and terrible loss—"

She was so sick of this speech, so she cut Maris off. "I know. Fine. Abruptly changing my position immediately after furtively whispering with you in the hall will raise a few suspicions, but you're not wrong. I'll do what I can."

"It's the correct decision, my dear."

Maris pivoted to leave, but Nika called out after her. "Maris? Remember: don't break Spencer. He's a good man, and we need him."

"Perhaps you should be more worried about him breaking *me*." With that, she spun on a heel and strolled elegantly down the hall and around the corner, leaving Nika standing there speechless. The concept of earnest, mild-mannered, hard-working Spencer Nimoet ever cracking Maris' formidable composure? It was absurd.

She shook her head in dismay and returned to the meeting room, where she retook her seat and clasped her hands atop the table. "Sorry for the interruption. I want to take a step back and reevaluate where we are, because I feel as if we've gotten lost in the weeds here, debating minutiae and blowing up worst-case scenarios. I'm not blaming anyone—I'm guilty of it as well. But I can't help but question if this is how the Guides started, taking one tiny step after another down the path of repression—"

"That's not fair," Adlai protested, and this time he was definitely not teasing.

Still, she pressed her point. "I'm not comparing us to the Guides. Not yet. But if we keep going this way, one day we *will* become as bad as them. So let's not keep going. Asterions exist as a people because we fought for the right of all sentient beings to live free. I led a rebellion practically yesterday against a tyrannical government, then dismantled it in favor of a *better* way forward.

"The fact is, it doesn't matter if we believe Plexes are more likely to commit crimes than the general population. It doesn't matter if they make us uncomfortable. It doesn't matter if I or Adlai or any other Advisor disapproves of them. It's not our job to pass judgment on their life choices. So long as they respect other people's lives, liberty and property, none of us have any authority to tell them they can't exist."

Her gaze swept across those seated at the table. "Does anyone want to argue that I'm wrong?"

RW

Parc rested by the small window and watched while a dyne team disassembled the Project Shurido command center. It was now futile to try to hide their worlds from Rasu discovery, so all the work on the planetary cloaking shield had been for naught.

Okay, not *totally* for naught. In adapting Taiyok stealth tech for the project rather than simply using it out of the box, they'd learned a great deal about how the technology worked. They'd also refined and honed their satellite communications and sensor algorithms. If the improvements were as clever as their creators—mostly him—claimed, they'd soon use that earned knowledge in other areas, including to help keep the Rasu off their soil and out of their heads.

A throat cleared in the doorway, and Nika peeked inside. He motioned her over. "We're taking down the office here."

"You did good work. It won't be in vain."

"I was just thinking the same thing." He cast his eyes toward the ceiling. "How are things going upstairs?"

"I have good news. You're no longer a criminal."

"Are you certain?"

"Only that you're no longer a criminal merely for being a Plex—I don't want to know about any other reasons you might be one. The details of a few restrictions and registration requirements are being hammered out by the Justice Advisors, but within a couple of hours Plexes will no longer be in legal limbo."

"Well, that's a relief."

"Parc."

"No, it is. I definitely don't want a second visit to Zaidam in my future. It's only…the legality of my existence hasn't been the first thing I've been fretting over when I wake up in the morning."

She grimaced. "Believe me, I know how that is."

"But you turned in your Plex card. Are you regretting it now?"

"No, I am not. This singular body is keeping me plenty busy as it is."

"I bet." He grinned. "Can I have one?"

"A kyoseil-saturated body? Um..." she frowned "...Dashiel wants to run the full design construct through additional safety and functionality tests before we think about making it an option for people. Obviously, we didn't have time for safety checks in my case."

"But when you got back from Namino, you kept it anyway."

"I did." A far-off, whimsical expression crossed her features. He'd gotten a few ceraff-glimpses at the mind of Nika Kirumase in recent months, and it was a damn complicated place, even by his standards.

One of the dynes uttered a request for clarification of its instructions, and he went to investigate the issue. "Have you seen Ryan lately?" he asked casually over his shoulder.

"First thing this morning, actually. He was meeting with Lance about helping out on some new modifications to DAF's combat mechs."

"Good. Ryan will be an asset on whatever scheme Palmer is spinning up for the mechs." Parc adjusted the dyne's instructions and shifted his attention back to Nika. "What else do you have for me? Anything interesting? Anything at all?"

Something akin to concern flickered in her eyes. Had he sounded so pathetic? "We're scheduled to push out an Initiative-wide update on all active projects later today. I'm sure several items on the list will catch your fancy."

"I'm sure they will."

After she left, he settled back in to watch the dismantling work, but his brilliant mind could hardly be expected to only focus on one thing at a time. For a few minutes he piggybacked on his Plex duplicate's efforts to continue to improve the ceraffin operating code, but eventually his thoughts drifted to the recent events on Namino, as they did at least four or four hundred times a day.

He was all PTSD-out thanks to the Rasu torture inflicted on a prior version of himself; this time he was trying to *learn* something from his mostly horrible experience on Namino. But attempts to learn something about himself inevitably led, as they always did in the quiet, to thinking about Ryan, and he was pretty confident surviving the Rasu on Namino hadn't taught him a damn thing to help him salvage their relationship.

25

MIRAI

JUSTICE CENTER

Adlai felt like a stranger in his own office. When he'd been kidnapped, it had become Spencer's office for a time, then sat vacant while he recovered at a clinic. Then the Rasu had attacked Namino, and nearly all of his time was spent at the Initiative or the refugee centers, trying to maintain a bare semblance of order and security at both.

He chuckled darkly to himself. Perrin made sure the evacuees were fed and clothed and counseled, while he made sure they didn't shoot one another or steal what meager belongings people had brought along. Both efforts were necessary, but she was definitely awarded more smiles and hugs than he ever received.

Which was fortunate, because the smiles and hugs might be the only thing keeping her going right now, despite his earnest endeavors to provide her the support she needed. She was too good and felt things too deeply for a world that could venture into such darkness.

But his job was to hold the darkness at bay. He could manage the thieves and assaulters and occasional would-be murderers, but bringing the Rasu to justice was proving to be beyond his capabilities.

And Plexes. He wasn't happy about being overruled by the other Advisors today, but he was self-aware enough to recognize his prejudices on the topic were of a most personal nature. It wasn't Ian Sevulch's status as a Plex that had driven him to kidnap and torture Adlai; it was the disintegration of a mind that had suffered past its breaking point. The man deserved empathy and treatment, but all Adlai felt toward him was bitter acrimony.

A knock on the door snapped him out of his maudlin ruminations. Selene gave him a little wave from the doorway. "May I come in?"

"Of course." He motioned toward one of the chairs opposite his desk. Selene's home, Justice Center workplace and entire jurisdiction had been destroyed, so she was working out of the Initiative and renting a hotel suite for now. No one had broached the possibility of doing away with the Namino Advisor positions or the divisional branches they managed, since

Namino was going to be rebuilt. One day.

"What's up? Change your mind on the Plexes already?"

"No." Instead of taking a seat, she wandered along the front of his desk, first in one direction, then pivoting to draw a fingertip along the surface as she reversed course. "Tell me about Joaquim Lacese."

Adlai had expected some issue involving the draft Plex regulations or an update on one of the recent altercations at the refugee centers. "You spent several weeks with him on Namino. I'd say you know him better than I do."

"Possibly. But those were unique circumstances. None of us were quite ourselves while we were trapped in that pressure-cooker. You've had dealings with him before, though. Your girlfriend is close to him, as is Nika. I'm curious as to your thoughts."

"Why?"

"Because I am. I value your opinion."

"Fine. But remember, you asked. I believe he can't be trusted. I believe that *he* believes his heart is in the right place, but he doesn't respect any boundaries or rules. His time in NOIR—or maybe he was always this way—made him decide he exists above and outside the law."

"Fair points. Then why do you put up with Perrin's friendship with him?"

He smiled wryly. "I don't get to tell Perrin who she can and cannot spend time with."

"Good for you. Why else don't you care for him?"

"Isn't my saying 'I don't trust him' enough of a reason?"

"Come on, Adlai. Don't play interrogator with me."

He sighed. "I can't prove it, and I don't expect to ever be able to do so, but I'm convinced he killed Blake Satair—final death."

"You think he introduced the corruption into the server to wipe Satair's psyche backup?"

"Or hired someone to do it, yes. He despised Satair with a terrifying fervor."

Her expression soured, but she nodded deliberately. "Okay."

"Selene, you know he loathes anything and anyone associated with Justice."

"Yes, I picked up on it. But we got past any prejudices to work together on Namino, because the situation demanded it. By the end, I think he trusted me implicitly. And..." she tossed her hands in the air and collapsed into the chair "...I'm not saying you're wrong about him. In many ways, I'm certain you're correct.

"But here's the thing: I've never met a more strident defender of innocents. Never, not in all my many years of working for Justice. Yes, he's wild and irresponsible, quick to flare in anger, emotionally closed-off from everyone, rudely impatient and imprudent in the extreme. But on Namino, all he wanted to do was save lots of people and kill lots of Rasu."

"Doesn't everyone want to do those things?"

"Everyone says they do, but few possess both the skill and psychological will to accomplish either feat. He does."

Adlai's eyes narrowed, and he dropped his elbows onto his desk. "You *like* him, don't you?"

She drew back in reproach. "I respect several aspects of his approach to life."

"Selene, your personal life is none of my business, but you can't possibly—"

"You're right. It isn't your business." She leapt up from the chair and strode brusquely toward the door. "Thank you for the advice. Your theory about what happened to Satair is disturbing. I'll keep it in mind."

Then she was gone, and Adlai was left shaking his head at the empty doorway. Selene was one of the most practical and pragmatic people he knew; no way would she succumb to whatever incomprehensible charms the former NOIR operative tossed her way. Surely.

He rubbed at his forehead. No matter what he did or how hard he tried, he could not seem to rid himself of Joaquim Lacese.

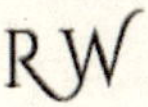

MIRAI ONE

Joaquim groaned at the sound of the door chime. He'd been working for hours trying to improve the deployment trigger mechanism for the archine grenade design with few results to show for it, and he was in no mood for visitors. But after the events on Namino and somewhat to his surprise, he seemed to find himself regarded as a legitimate member of society now, so he reluctantly stood and went to answer it. Then he saw Selene Panetier's face on the door cam and stopped short.

Gods, she was gorgeous, all hard edges and bold confidence. And Justice and the enemy. And his recent partner in an insurgency against evil. And a delightful wildcat in bed. And Justice and the enemy. Not 'the enemy' in the way the Rasu were, of course, but worthy of his scorn at a minimum.

Right?

He should ignore her. Let her stand out in the hall and twiddle her thumbs until she got bored and left. But why was she here at all? After the cringe-worthy way he'd departed her hotel room, he'd never imagined she would seek him out again.

She could be here to arrest him for any of a multitude of crimes, most of which he'd fairly committed. He didn't fancy damaging her to clear out and vanish, but he'd…*would* he do it if he had to? Ah, shit.

As the questions tumbled over one another in his mind, curiosity got the better of him, and he impulsively opened the door. "Panetier, what do you want?"

Her expression was so scrupulously blank, she might as well be interrogating him in a cell. "It was 'Selene' the other night."

"I was drunk the other night. What do you want?"

She shoved something bulky into his chest. "I brought your shoes back to you. Trashed the underwear."

He jerked in surprise, barely catching the shoes before they tumbled to the floor, and she took the opportunity to stride right past him into his apartment.

"You could have just burnt these in a pyre. Also, I didn't say you could come in."

"You really are an unmitigated asshole."

"Yes. For the thousandth time, you simply must have known this by now."

"I did." She wandered around the small living space for a moment, then abruptly spun toward him. "Did you kill Blake Satair?"

He unceremoniously tossed his shoes into the corner and sank against the wall. "Been talking to Weiss, have you?"

"I talk to Advisor Weiss almost every day, as a matter of course. Did you?"

"No."

"Did you hire someone else to kill him for you?"

"What difference does it make? He's gone, and the world is a better place for his absence." Joaquim went to the refrigeration unit and grabbed a beer…then reached back in and got a second one, which he tossed to her.

She caught it in one hand, opened the bottle and took a long swig. "It matters because I want to know the truth."

"The truth about me?"

"The truth about everything. I'm a Justice Advisor. It's in my blood."

"You always manage to remind me of that, don't you?"

"Why do you hate Justice so much? Is it a result of your time in NOIR?"

He snorted. "No. Don't get me wrong. You lot trying so desperately hard to arrest and imprison us certainly didn't help. But my *justifiable* hatred of Justice stretches back a lot further than NOIR."

"But you only killed Satair. What did he do to you?"

"Without confirming your assumption, I'll answer your question. He kidnapped me, mind-raped me and tortured me to learn the location of the NOIR base. Then he killed and psyche-wiped an old colleague of mine, bombed the NOIR base and took out a bunch of my friends. He also killed the love of my life, but that's another story."

Her eyes flickered in surprise. "I'd like to hear that story."

"Yeah, well, I don't want to tell it." Joaquim turned up his beer until the flare of aging grief faded.

When he finally lowered the bottle, he found her demeanor had only grown more complicated. Gone was the blank mask; in its place was something akin to sincerity, confusion and possibly even affection, all laced with grim determination. "Did you have Blake Satair killed?"

The too-endearing expression on her features and gentle tone of her voice snapped something free inside of him, and his posture sagged. Lying in the face of such multi-faceted pressure was exhausting. He recognized that as a skilled interrogator, she was definitely manipulating him, but her piercing, hyper-intelligent eyes and somehow always-pouty lips slew the last of his good sense.

"Fine. You win. I did have him killed. I'll never say who helped me, because I owe them a great deal more than money, so don't bother asking." He set the beer on the table beside the couch and extended both arms out in front of him, wrists pressed together. "Are you going to arrest me now? Wipe me and start fresh, or merely store me?"

Her countenance hadn't shifted; if anything, it might have softened a touch. "We don't store people."

"But you do wipe them, or else ice them and send them off to Zaidam. So what'll it be for me? I'm standing here before you, unarmed and defenseless."

"Lacese, if there is anything I learned about you on Namino, it's that you are never defenseless."

"It was 'Joaquim' the other night."

"I was drunk the other night." She sighed with what resembled existential weariness. Was it all part of the performance? She'd extracted the confession she'd sought. "No. I'm not going to arrest you, though only the gods know why not."

He relaxed a touch. Part of him had honestly expected her to do it. "Because you've got a soft spot for me?"

"Don't flatter yourself. Because Satair made you look like a saint. He lied to the other Advisors. He deceived us for his own nefarious purposes. He was a murderer and a poisonous influence on our society, and he deserved to be punished for his actions."

"A thousand times over, but I'm shocked to hear you say it."

"I try never to deny the truth..." she shot him a glare "...much as I want to sometimes. And the truth is, Satair deserved to die."

"But your vaunted Justice system doesn't allow for it. In fact, to hear Weiss tell it, deletion causing final death is the single worst crime a person can commit."

She leaned against the back of the couch. "The Guides wrote those rules. Now they're gone, and we're free to make new rules. I suppose I'm rewriting a few of my own."

Damn, that was a sexy move on her part. How messed up was he to think so? He lifted his hands in a less confrontational gesture of surrender. "What now? I've laid my soul bare at your feet. You know my dirty little secret. You say you're not going to arrest me, but if you spill the beans to Weiss, I guarantee you he will jump at the chance to put me away. So will you keep my confidence?"

"You want me to lie to another Advisor—like Satair did."

"Not like Satair did at all. This would be in the cause of good."

She scowled at him over the top of her bottle. "What good?"

"Keeping my mind intact and my body breathing free air?"

"And?"

"And you might need me around for the next Rasu invasion. Or the next time you've got an itch you can't scratch."

She dropped the empty beer bottle on the table a tad roughly. "I can scratch my own itches just fine, thank you."

"Sure..." he wandered deliberately closer, invading her personal space "...but not the way I can."

"Damn you, Lacese." Her breath was hot, her cheeks flushed, her body weaving its heady spell to trap him in its web.

He smiled darkly. "No need. I'm already damned."

"Then maybe I am, too." She hooked a hand behind his head and crushed her lips to his.

26

SAVRAK
SAVRADIN

Brigadier Akhar Ghorek walked the battlefield, his tail stiff and his teeth locked together by his jaw, like the military commander he'd always been and the leader of his people he now was. Only today, what he'd labeled a battlefield were in fact the ravaged streets of Savradin.

General Jhountar was dead, killed alongside most of his top lieutenants in the explosion at the prisoner exchange. Mere chance had caused Ghorek not to be in attendance at the exchange that day; as a result, his life had been spared, but now he found himself the last person standing at the head of a non-existent military, a gutted government and an all-but-annihilated people.

With the planetary defenses destroyed in earlier attacks across Savrak, a single Concord warship had been able to waltz in and bomb Savradin into literal dust before Ghorek's last three flight-worthy vessels had managed to overtake and destroy the Concord warship using antimatter missiles. Two of the Savrakath vessels had been destroyed in the engagement as well, however, leaving him with a single, solitary warship and a scant four antimatter missiles secured in its hold. If a new Concord warship showed up now, he'd need to decide whether to sacrifice his last viable weapons to eliminate it or to save them for some grand, suicidal final act.

Nothing worth bombing remained standing here for them to destroy, but Ghorek no longer believed Concord acted rationally. He'd known for some time that they were bullies and tyrants, but now he judged them to be monsters. Rather than allow his people to pursue their own safety and security, Concord intended to eradicate them from the universe. And they might well succeed. But, he thought, he should make them regret their actions either way.

He looked to his left to see a child sitting on the broken sidewalk, covered in dust and blood, cradling the head of an adult Savrakath in his lap. Young enough for sentimentality not to have been beaten out of him. If their people survived this trial, the child would grow up to carry a world-breaking chip on his shoulder and a deep and abiding hatred for Concord. If their people survived this trial, in time Ghorek could work with such hatred. He could use it to build a new military, one that would never stoop so low as to negotiate with its enemies.

He'd once believed Jhountar's rage and bloodlust was irrational and counterproductive. Now, though, surrounded by the ruins of their once-mighty civilization, he decided Jhountar hadn't been nearly aggressive enough.

His tour next brought him to a flooded intersection. The swamp was rising up out of the soil to reclaim its land. He sighed to himself, then pivoted to face the two aides who trailed along behind him. "I've seen enough. Tell the medical squad to round up anyone who still lives and move them to the camp we've established outside of the city, then meet me at Site 2A."

SITE 2A

A wide swath of jungle trees and runaway overgrowth hid the military's emergency fallback site from prying eyes overhead. Ghorek himself only spotted the vague outlines of tents and large crates once his shuttle was descending through the canopy.

He had set up the site on Jhountar's order—one of the man's last—as a location to gather all their remaining antimatter weapons. Then Jhountar had been murdered and Concord had attacked anew, and Ghorek had used those weapons on the attacking enemy vessel. But instead of abandoning the site, he'd ordered his highest-ranking officers and scientists to convene here in the jungle.

He'd made his decision during the trip from Savradin to Site 2A. If he used his last antimatter missiles on the next Concord attack, it only forestalled the inevitable. Yet another Concord attack was certain to soon follow, and at that point they would be utterly defenseless until the end. The brutal truth could not be denied: there was no way for him to win this war.

Best to leave a mark that Concord wouldn't soon forget, then.

Savrakath vessels were marked as shoot-on-sight in Concord space; they'd tested Concord's so-called 'Red Flag' decree and found the enemy perfectly willing to follow through on the decree's threat. Therefore, sending his final warship against a Concord target was an exercise in futility and an impotent gesture. The antimatter missiles had limited range, and the warship would never get close enough to hit a worthwhile target.

But there must be another way he could make Concord pay for slaughtering his people. His gaze traveled across the hastily erected tents and the covered crates to where their sole surviving warship sat 'docked' upon wooden planks to keep it from sinking into the muck...and the beginnings of an idea stirred in his mind.

He spoke to his chief aide without turning toward him, trusting the man had followed him on his meandering journey across the site. "Is Dr. Khalik still alive?"

"As of this morning, yes, sir."

"Get him here. And bring in a small paramilitary tactical squad as well. I believe I have a mission for them."

RW

Ghorek cornered Dr. Khalik the instant the shuttle carrying him landed. The scientist was overly frilled and weak, but Ghorek nonetheless respected the man's intelligence. "Can you package the antimatter from our missiles into a portable bomb?"

Khalik's eyes swept across the site, taking in and likely cataloguing the purpose of every individual, crate and object in sight. "A significant portion of it, yes. Some amount will be degraded during the transfer."

"Can you package enough to destroy a large space station?"

"How large?"

Ghorek chose his words carefully. Desperation made people stupid, and he couldn't trust any single person with the full details of his plan. "Several kilometers in diameter."

"Hmm. We can repurpose enough to cause significant damage, but to destroy a structure of such size? We will need an additional catalyst to boost the explosion. How are you planning to deliver the bomb?"

"Let me worry about the delivery mechanism—and the catalyst. Can you render the antimatter impervious to security scans?"

Khalik's honed teeth scissored across one another. "That will take more work. But I believe I can construct multiple levels of shielding to prevent it from being detected at anything less than very close range."

"How close of range?"

"Perhaps two meters."

"Make the shielding as robust as possible. Spare no expense or effort. I'll also need the bomb to operate on a remote detonation trigger."

"It will require yet additional work, but it is doable."

"How long do you need?"

"For everything? If I have on hand the supplies and workers I will need to accomplish it all? Four days."

"You have two." Ghorek pivoted and strode to the adjacent tent, where the tactical squad and the captain of the warship waited.

"Soldiers, you are going to steal a ship."

The captain sputtered. "But, sir, we already have a ship."

"A ship that is marked for death in Concord space. You are going to steal one that is not so marked."

"But how?"

Ghorek called up a map of this sector of the Antlia Dwarf galaxy. "Forty-eight parsecs from Savrak, the closest Concord installation, a commercial warehousing and distribution facility, orbits the star designated 48Cv. Most of the ships which visit the facility are cargo haulers or merchant vessels. We need to procure one of the latter.

"Captain, you are to idle, stealthed, out of range of the station's scanners and track vessels departing the facility. When you acquire a suitable target vessel, you will move in, disable it, board it, kill the crew—all except one member—and bring the vessel and the surviving crew member here. Do you understand the parameters of this mission?"

A few hesitant questions followed, but the plan was straightforward enough for them to absorb the details and fill in the blanks within a few minutes, so he left them to their preparations. It wasn't going to be easy to neutralize the merchant crew before they sent off a distress call without also damaging the ship, but Savrak tactical squads had ways of doing so.

Ghorek grunted to himself as he headed across the camp to check on Khalik's progress. The plan would work. There was no other option.

27

EPITHERO

Eren idly considered the assholes gathered around the dinner table while he sipped on expensive champagne. The apéritif was the first mood-altering substance he'd allowed himself to ingest since returning from Savrak, and he forced himself to sip it slowly. This wasn't about drowning his sorrows in a haze of drunkenness; this was for show.

He was the only *asi* in the room. He might be the only one on the premises. For what he assumed were security reasons, even the help staff were *elas.* He'd stopped caring about such caste distinctions long ago, but he doubted the same could be said for the rest of the people at the table. Possibly excepting Corradeo.

Giora elasson-Idoni studied him from across the table as if she were a predator sizing up her next meal, and not the one soon to be presented on the plate in front of her. Though he'd never met her before tonight, she seemed to imagine she held some power over him, some right and authority to dominate him by virtue of her elevated status. He'd like to see her try.

Seriously, he *would* like to see it; the rearrangement in her thinking he'd deliver would be…satisfying. The Kyverns at the table—Ferdinand, Basra, plus two he didn't know by sight—scowled at him in the way they did to all Idonis, with disdain bordering on disgust at the wild, unruly nature of the entire Dynasty dripping from their dour mouths. The Machims mostly pretended not to notice him. He'd received the curtest of nods from Casmir, but no acknowledgments from the others.

The truth was, many of those at the table harbored too much festering ill will toward the man sitting at the far end to be bothered with sparing much for Eren. They'd been bickering and sputtering like spoiled children used to getting their way ever since he'd arrived, and thus far they appeared unable to deploy any coping mechanisms when that was denied them. In fact, only a few had explicitly recognized Corradeo's authority so far.

Corradeo, however, was demonstrating patience beyond any limits of where a normal man would have blown a gasket, followed by blowing up the entire estate (or maybe that was just Eren). Now, after an afternoon jam-packed with incessant arguing and escalating tempers, Corradeo had insisted they simmer down the stress level by all sitting down for a friendly, no-business dinner. Under any other circumstances, Eren would have excused himself for the evening, as enduring a formal dinner with thirty *elassons* had to be in his top five worst nightmares. But this dinner, he wasn't going to miss for anything.

The doors to the dining room opened, and two of the omnipresent guards escorted in—

Eren's blood turned to ice. He'd known this moment was coming and had tried to prepare himself, but he still had to forcibly cement himself to the seat of his chair. *For now, for now, for now.*

Torval elasson-Machim jerked a rough nod in greeting to his fellow Machims, then zeroed in his gaze on Corradeo. "You're dead."

Though the man must be growing tired of having to explain this peculiarity for the thousandth time, Corradeo began elucidating it for 1,001st time without a trace of annoyance in his voice. Eren had heard it all several times over by now, so he tuned out the words to focus in on his enemy. The man's skin had the faint sheen of recent regenesis—twice in a single week, if one was keeping count. His dull brown hair was trimmed in a perfect military buzzcut, and his new body bore no markers of the torture inflicted upon him by the Savrakaths. A small smile grew on Eren's lips as he recalled how Torval had looked chained up in the belly of his ship.

After some back-and-forth and a reassurance from Casmir, Torval seemed to accept the situation for the time being and moved to sit between Casmir and Hannah elasson-Machim. His eyes swept across the table, then abruptly jerked back to Eren. He flung the chair he'd just occupied away and stood once again. "Fuck, no. This Idoni fop kidnapped me and handed me over to the Savrakaths. Arrest him now."

Corradeo steepled his hands at his chin. "I am aware of Eren Savitas' actions, and they will be addressed in due time. Please sit and enjoy your dinner."

A tiny flare of pride bloomed in Eren's chest at the man's use of his preferred name, but Torval shot Corradeo an incredulous glare. "I don't care who you claim to be. I am not sharing a table with this psycho."

Corradeo calmly, deliberately nudged his chair back and stood. "Eren is my guest, as are you. Sit down and eat your meal."

Wow. Corradeo's voice had not raised above a conversational tone, but his words thundered about the room with the authority and gravitas of Zeus himself. Eren had never seen the man do that before, but damn, such a skill was going to come in handy during the struggles yet to come.

Torval blinked, stunned into silence. Finally he turned to Casmir, who placed a hand on Torval's shoulder and applied appropriate pressure to urge the man down into his chair. Seemingly at a loss, Torval shook his head—and complied.

"Thank you, Torval." Corradeo gestured toward the doors as they opened again. "Ah, I see our first course has arrived. Excellent timing."

Servers ushered in platters stacked high with soup bowls, and Eren nodded a thanks when a bowl was placed in front of him. He brought the glass of champagne to his lips and held it there to obscure the fact that he was not partaking in the soup. At a cursory glance, everyone would assume he was trying to get blitzed as swiftly as possible. He was an Idoni, after all.

He noted with interest when Corradeo placed a discreet hand on Casmir's arm and leaned in to whisper something, leading Casmir to set his spoon down. Corradeo appeared to have taken a liking to the Machim. Eren had once heard a rumor that Casmir was the one who alerted the anarchs to the Machim Primor's attempt to deliver a Tartarus Trigger to Humanity's home universe. He'd dismissed the rumor at the time, but perhaps it was true?

It took a herculean effort on Eren's part not to stare malevolently at Torval as the time drew nearer. He dared not tip the man—or anyone—off, and this required him to play the part of docile lackey until the fateful moment. Instead he inhaled enough of his champagne to justify a refill and flagged the server down.

He was raising the newly full glass when the first rumblings began. A Theriz—Lars, he thought—frowned and began massaging his temples. Across the table, Giora's spoon clattered onto the table as she brought a hand to her forehead and her chin to her chest. "I don't feel well."

Ferdinand coughed into his napkin, started to stand, and collapsed back in his chair. "Neither do I. Something's wrong with the soup…have a word with the kitchen staff…." His hands came to his head and clutched raggedly at his hair.

Variations on the scene rippled unevenly around the table, until Eren, Casmir and Corradeo were the only ones present who weren't visibly ill.

Corradeo drew in a deep breath and stood once more. "Everyone, I apologize for your discomfort. When I came here to Epithero, I did so in the hope of appealing to your reason and intelligence, both of which are in ample supply in this room. But I underestimated the extent of the damage your Primors inflicted upon you. I deeply regret that this action has proved necessary, but there is no other way. If our world is going to change, it must be forced to do so, and this begins with the people in this room."

Ferdinand again tried to stand, then planted his palms on the table and swayed woozily, narrowly stopping himself from diving face-first into his soup bowl. "What have you done to us?"

"The soup contained nanobot swarms programmed to target the integral nodes in your brains. Among other effects, you've all been disconnected from your integrals—and their regenesis servers."

Amid the exclamations and shouts exploding around the table, Eren did not check with Corradeo for the final go-ahead. He'd been given license, but even if he lacked it, he would not be stopped now.

He stood, removed the small handgun from his pants pocket and raised it until it was aimed at the bridge of Torval's nose, right between the eyes. "This is for Cosime, you worthless piece of shit."

He pulled the trigger.

Blood and brain matter splattered across the far wall like a splash of performance art, and Torval's lifeless body collapsed over the arm of his chair.

A shocked silence fell for two seconds that stretched into an eternity—then everyone was shouting again. Chairs were overturned; bodies moved, but in their ailing states, they rarely succeeded in moving far.

Eren swung the gun to the left and sighted down on Ferdinand, raising his voice above the fervor. "What do you think, Ferdinand? Are you next? You're responsible for this whole fucking disaster—"

"Eren." Corradeo's voice was low, steady, and quite threatening.

"He does deserve it."

"Even so."

Eren sighed, lowered the weapon, resumed his seat and turned up his glass of champagne. This seemed to further agitate Ferdinand, who stumbled backward and began zig-zagging haphazardly toward the door. "Torval was right. He's a psycho! Get that madman out of here!"

The two guards at the door glanced uneasily between Ferdinand and Corradeo. The latter shook his head minutely, and they didn't move.

Otto elasson-Machim leaned into the table with nearly enough force to flip it. "What is—how could you—do this?"

Corradeo surveyed the chaos engulfing the dining room; he looked a little sad, but otherwise unflustered. "Torval was a war criminal and an unrepentant murderer. His genetic template was corrupt beyond any possibility of rehabilitation. He did not deserve to share a table with *elassons* such as yourselves. His mere presence was poisonous, he destroyed everything he touched, and we could not move forward so long as he remained in our midst. Eren acted at my direction, and any repercussions for his actions will fall on me alone. Now, what's done is done, so let us move on to the topic you genuinely care about.

"Regarding the severing of your connections to the integrals and their regenesis servers, I say this: it is time for you to earn your right to immortality. You all act as if there are no consequences for your actions and no price to be paid for your inconsiderate, thoughtless, dangerous decisions. It is time to remind you that there is *always* a price to be paid.

"Do you want to continue living forever in positions of authority? Prove you are worthy of doing so. Pull yourselves together and start acting like leaders, like honorable stewards of your people, instead of selfish, spoiled children."

Lars elasson-Theriz looked as if he was seconds away from vomiting all over his silk shirt. "What about the *elassons* who aren't here? Are you sending assassins to poison their food as well?"

Eren shot Corradeo a questioning look, eyebrow raised. He'd be more than happy to do the job.

A corner of Corradeo's lips twitched, but the man suppressed any smile he might have wanted to grant Eren. "The simple fact that they are *not* here indicates they have better sense than any of you. They've refused to betray Concord or comport themselves like petty tyrants, so I have considerable hope for the value they can bring to our people's future.

"Nonetheless, I am issuing a decree that will affect them as well. From this day forward, the title of *elasson* is no longer a birthright. If you desire to lead from a position of power, I say again: prove you are worthy of doing so. As of now, anyone, whether branded by the system as *asi*, *ela* or *elasson*, is capable of proving they are worthy of doing so. I look forward to seeing who rises to greatness when the system is no longer rigged."

Corradeo considered the bloody mess decorating the northeast corner of the room, his brow furrowing briefly. "Now, seeing as this room is no longer suitable for dining, I suggest we reconvene in the lounge or, if you wish, you may retire to your rooms. Any queasiness you're experiencing should subside in a few hours."

RW

Ferdinand closed the door to his bedroom suite and fell against the wall beside it, his breath heaving out of his lungs. He'd managed to keep the hyperventilating at bay as he'd walked-and-not-run from the dining room all the way to his private residence. But now the sweat beading on his forehead began dribbling into his eyes as his chest spasmed.

He'd almost died.

The concept of death—real, permanent denouement—had never held any concrete meaning for him. Yes, in the immediate aftermath of the Primors' mass execution, he'd felt a few twinges of concern over the possibility that the anarchs were apt to come for him, too. He'd added a couple of additional regenesis labs to his network, and the angst had soon faded, as Anadens were, for all intents and purposes, immortal. The *asis* occasionally saw their genetic makeup fiddled with enough during a given regenesis that they woke up a transformed person, but *elassons* had already reached the peak of perfection. It came with the title.

It was possible he'd never before felt true fear in his life. Not until now.

His heart beat mercilessly upon his sternum; the pulse it drove pounded in his ears. What was he going to do? He couldn't stay here, not with an insane despot making the rules while allowing his bloodthirsty pet assassin to run free around the grounds. He'd rightfully claimed this estate as his own, but now he had to leave it behind in order to save his life.

All visions of his grand plans for a new Anaden Empire with him stationed at the helm vanished as he threw a bunch of clothes in a bag. He'd go to Menaris first. It was run by Kyverns and should provide a friendly haven. From there, he'd figure something out. Some way to counteract the effects of the poison he'd been dosed with so he could reconnect to his regenesis lab network. Then, some way to reclaim a measure of power. He'd hide for a time if he must, but he wasn't ready to give up his dreams of a glorious Anaden future forever.

His stomach was still in revolt from the poison and the fear, and twice his packing was abandoned while he rushed to the lavatory and vomited. But finally he was ready...or rather, everything was in the bag. He had no idea how to measure his state of readiness, as he'd never been a fugitive before.

He threw the bag over his shoulder and rushed for the door—but stopped short. If this Praesidis monster discovered him leaving, the man might lock him up here on the estate. Or worse, let the Idoni assassin loose on him. He needed to be smart and quiet about this.

He tossed the bag on the bed in a fit of panic, then retrieved a smaller, more professional tote and transferred everything he could fit into it. Next, he sent a message to Basra and Felipe, in which he stated that he needed to take a quick trip to meet with one of the absent *elassons* who was displaying an interest in joining them, and he expected to be back at the estate by morning.

He grasped the handles of the tote in one hand, straightened his hair in the mirror, and strode confidently out the door.

Breathe in through your nose. Calm. You aren't suffocating. Breathe out through your mouth. Chin up, attitude on. You aren't afraid.

He passed several *ela* servants as he traversed the least-used hallways that would bring him to the side exit, but no *elassons,* so he went unchallenged. The guard at the exit greeted him, which he ignored, because he'd always done so in the past. Then he was outside.

The flower-lined pathway to the landing complex stretched interminably before him. *One foot in front of the other. Don't run. Be poised.*

There wasn't much in the way of comings and goings between the house and the landing complex, given how this was a retreat, and no one appeared to waylay him during the quarter-kilometer gauntlet. He reached his small personal ship and, as soon as he was inside, locked it up tight. All but safe now...unless the Idoni assassin had brought a rocket launcher.

The thought sent his heart racing anew, and his vision swam. *Sit in the cockpit chair. Remember the proper launch procedures. Don't attract attention.*

His fingers trembled as he activated the liftoff sequence, and he wiped new sweat out of his eyes as the engine engaged. Distress and relief muddled together in his mind as the ship banked above his magnificent, sparkling city and accelerated away.

28

DOMOR

SMALL MAGELLANIC CLOUD

Tales of a mysterious vigilante were whispered in every tavern and club on Domor. According to one story, this one-man crime-fighting squad had strung up an Erevna dealer who sold tainted hypnols from the awning outside his shop, naked and branded with 'killer' across his chest. In another version, a Naraida woman suspected of selling Volucri hatchlings to local gangs for use in sport fighting contests was dropped out of a skycar from two hundred meters in the air.

The stories got more outlandish from there, and Nyx absorbed the various details only insofar as they provided clues as to how she could find this vigilante, whom the local populace had dubbed 'the Shadow Stalker.'

Domor was a bustling and diverse planet, but average for a developed world in most respects, except for a higher than normal crime rate. Hence the vigilante, she supposed. His work had been spotted in at least four of the major metropolitan areas, so her search grid was frustratingly expansive.

Nyx went from neighborhood to neighborhood, asking questions of friendly residents, getting a bead on the local criminal element and scoping out their territories in each area. Thus far, to no avail.

Now she sat in a booth in the rear of a sandwich shop and ordered an iced tea, then dropped her head against the riser behind her. The vigilante was a chameleon, an enigma, and it didn't help that his reputation had reached mythological proportions among the population. Separating fact from fiction was becoming increasingly difficult.

She *would* find him; in her life she'd found many people far more cleverly hidden. But it was going to be a challenge, especially if, as she suspected, her quarry was a fellow Inquisitor. She felt the weight of every passing hour and day with growing impatience. Though she sent and received regular messages to and from her grandfather, still she worried about him, facing down all those recalcitrant and rebellious *elassons* on his own. She needed to get back to him soon. What if—

Lontias elasson-Praesidis slid into the booth opposite her. He wore rugged black pants and a gray sweatshirt with the hood draped loosely over his head. "Why are you looking for me, Nyx?"

Damn him for getting the jump on her! "It's good to see you, too, Lontias."

His cold expression softened. "And you, sister. But why am I seeing you now? I thought you were gone. Dead, maybe, like so many of the others, or on a galactic walkabout."

"You're not too far off on the latter. I'm here to ask you to come with me."

"On walkabout?"

"No. That was…I'm back now. And I'm not alone. Our grandfather sent me to find you—to find any of us who remain."

"Our *grandfather*? What does that mean? The Primor is dead, and we have no parents."

It was possible the 'grandfather' designation applied solely to her, she who he claimed was born of his daughter aeons ago in a past she'd never known. But she doubted Corradeo would mind all of the Inquisitors thinking of him this way. And she should be magnanimous enough to share him with the others, of course.

"We were lied to, Lontias. In so many ways and for such a long time. The Primor was not who he claimed to be, and he used us for his own ends without our knowledge. But grandfather will want to tell you the rest himself. Will you come with me?"

He shot a furtive glance around the restaurant. "You might not have noticed, but I'm doing a lot of good here."

"So I hear. You're the only thing the locals talk about. But I think you've frightened the resident criminals sufficiently at this point. The mere threat of you coming for them should keep them in line."

"For a while. Who else do you have with you?"

Her lips pursed. "In truth? Only you. Xeshar died long ago. Kolgo is…" she shuddered "…not available."

"I know exactly what he is. I've killed him once already, but it didn't do any good. I assume he's got a regenesis link to some underworld lab somewhere."

She huffed a breath, admittedly impressed. "I assumed the same. I'm still searching for Ziton and Phoebe. And that's everyone. It's possible you and I are the only ones left alive and sane."

"Not certain about the second part, but I do what I can." He crossed his arms atop the table. "What does this 'grandfather' person have planned?"

"To save our people from themselves. Ferdinand elasson-Kyvern attempted a coup against Concord, and our grandfather wants to undo the damage this caused. He wants to teach all Anadens how to reach their potential without the crushing strictures of the Primors or the mind control of their integrals."

"He wants us to become more like the Humans."

"Is that so terrible a goal?"

"No. They're a screwed-up bunch to be sure, but not nearly so much as we are." He stared at her intently, wheels spinning behind his eyes. "You were always the most level-headed, rational one of our lot. You believe in this man and his goal?"

"With all my overly rational heart. He *will* succeed in guiding the Anadens back to greatness. A better, more peaceful and fairer greatness. I know it."

Lontias reached up and pushed the hood down to his shoulders, revealing a mop of unkempt, midnight black waves. "Eh, I've about run out of criminals worthy of stringing up here, anyway, but I do need to see to one last thing first. Where can I meet you?"

"My ship, the *Periplanos*, is docked at the public spaceport in Domorono, Bay E15. I can stay here for another ten hours. If this job of yours takes longer than that, then I'll need to come back for you."

"It won't. I'll see you on the ship."

RW

Lontias was true to his word. Eight hours after she left him in the restaurant, he showed up at the *Periplanos'* bay, wearing the same clothes but carrying a large duffel bag in each hand. "Where are we off to first?"

Nyx motioned for him to come up the ramp and board the ship, then closed the airlock behind him. "I've got a lead on Ziton pointing to Scholite."

"Sounds good. I admit, it'll be nice to get back to real civilization. I think I've been rolling around in the muck of criminals for too long. But why the rush?"

She busied herself with inputting their new coordinates. "I want to return to Grandfather as soon as possible. I don't like leaving him alone in that pit of *elasson* vipers for so long."

Lontias returned from securing his bags to plop himself in the cockpit's second seat. "If he's as strong a leader as you suggested, he should be able to take care of himself."

"He is, without question. He's lived...well, as I said, he'll want to tell you himself. I'm simply..." she shrugged "...an Inquisitor. I have an intrinsic need to act as his guardian. His sword and shield."

RW

SCHOLITE

MILKY WAY GALAXY

Scholite was mercifully cosmopolitan and relatively crime-free, making it a welcome change for her as well as Lontias. Skytrams raced by overhead between clusters of towers, spiraling aerial gardens and floating platforms. At ground level, the streets were wide and well-ornamented and the shopping options top-shelf.

After spending years living on a spaceship and venturing in the deep wilds of the cosmos, Nyx's wardrobe had seen better days. The onboard fabricator could only produce basic, utilitarian attire, so she and Lontias split up for an hour while she bought some new clothes. All finely made, but more importantly, all practical yet conforming to the current styles so she wouldn't stand out in a crowd.

Their target was listed as the Director of Corporate Security for Michanero Production, which owned two square blocks in the middle of downtown. She met Lontias outside the main entrance, and together they went inside.

A sullen-looking Machim *asi* guard stopped them almost immediately. "Michanero Production is a private company and not open to the public. Can I help you?"

She slipped into the old Inquisitor guise effortlessly, as if it hadn't been over a decade since she'd properly done this sort of thing. "We're here to see the Director of Corporate Security."

"Zoral ela-Praesidis? Do you have an appointment?"

"It's a matter of some urgency."

"What's it regarding?"

"That's between us and the Director of Corporate Security."

The guard frowned. "I'm sorry, but I can't allow you in to see him without an appointment."

The problem was, with the Directorate dead and gone, she now wielded no true authority except that which she created through sheer force of personality and persuasion. "The nature of the matter precluded an appointment, but I assure you, he will want to hear what we have to say. You are welcome to guard the open door while we speak to him—"

"It's fine, Prador. Let them in."

She spun toward the voice to see Ziton elasson-Praesidis standing at the entrance to a long hallway. He wore a too-slick gunmetal-gray business suit over a shiny crimson turtleneck, but the trademark wavy raven hair and piercing sapphire eyes were the same.

She and Lontias exchanged a look, then abandoned the chagrined guard to follow him down the hallway to his office.

As soon as the door had shut behind them, Ziton regarded them curiously. "Nyx. Lontias. I didn't think I'd ever see either of you again."

Nyx arched an eyebrow. "Same."

Lontias chuckled. "Hiding as an *ela*? Isn't that beneath you?"

"By definition. But didn't you hear? It's a new world out there."

Sensing her opening, Nyx stepped closer. "More than you know. We have a proposition for you."

"I'm in."

She blinked. "Excuse me? I haven't told you what it is yet."

"Don't care. I'm going mad from boredom at the sameness of it all in this soul-killing job on this tedious, cookie-cutter planet. I need a change of pace before I tear my hair out and start blowing up expensive property."

Her brow furrowed up. "Okay. I'm glad to hear it, I think. Still, there are some things I should tell you."

"You can tell me on the way to wherever we're headed. Let me stop off at the front desk to tender my resignation and drop by my apartment to grab a few things, then let's be on our way."

29

PANDORA

Mia thrust the data disk from Escapes Extraordinaire toward Eli Baca. "I got your files. Didn't run into any problems. Now pay me."

He made a face at the disk and waved her off. "Go take it to Isaiah. He'll get it on a transport. I'll pay you when he says the data's good."

Annoyance and hunger gnawed at Mia's gut. "Fuck, Eli—I'm not one of your pansy runners!"

His hand shot out and grabbed her wrist, yanking her onto her knees in front of him. "You're whatever I say you are, sweetie, because I own you. Don't I?"

Spit gathered on her tongue, ready to spew forth. Hit him between the eyes with it. She could do it.

"Say it!" His meaty, clammy fingers tightened their grip until they cut off the blood flow to her hand.

She swallowed the spit, and the last vestiges of her imagined dignity accompanied it down her throat. The whisper escaped through gritted teeth. "You own me."

Mia's eyes popped open. Her heart skittered around in her chest, and her stomach churned violently. She rolled over to seek comfort in Malcolm's arms…

…but of course the other side of the bed was empty. She was alone, by her choice. In this second she wanted more than anything to have made another choice.

You still can.

She ignored Meno to get up and stumble to the small lavatory, where she splashed cold water on her face. The haunted visage staring back at her in the mirror carried in it the crushing defeat of the memory-dream.

She shouldn't be surprised that old memories were rising up out of the depths to haunt the nightmares of her sleeping hours and the shadows of her waking ones. Maybe she should've picked somewhere other than Pandora to vanish. Half a dozen other human colonies were lawless enough for her to safely hide, yet civilized enough for her to build a business and, eventually, a life.

But she was here now, so she'd have to deal with the repercussions. She dragged herself back into the bedroom, collapsed on the bed and pulled the covers up to her chin, though she'd resigned herself to the fact that sleep would not be rejoining her tonight.

If you are going to lie here and brood, perhaps you'd like to review the report I've prepared on Enzio Vilane.

She mentally perked up. *You've finished your research already?*

I have, and I believe you will find the results most interesting.

Will I now?

She opened up the file and started reading.

Enzio Vilane

Born: Approximately 2314

Father: Unknown

Mother: Unknown

History: Enzio's birth was not recorded in any official repository. The first time he appeared in any records was when he enrolled at the prestigious Kalende Preparatory boarding school on Romane at the age of seven.

Kalende's financial records indicate Enzio's tuition was paid by a holding company called Render Investments. A thorough investigation of the company's ownership reveals a trail of shell companies and fictitious investors. The trail ultimately ends, however, at Aiden Trieneri, the now-deceased former leader of the Triene cartel.

Enzio went on to attend École Polytechnique on Earth and Tellica University on Seneca, where he received undergraduate degrees in accounting and finance and a Masters in Business Administration, respectively.

After completing his studies at Tellica, Enzio disappeared from public view for two years before resurfacing as the CEO of a then-small real estate company, Vilane Properties, on Pandora. A complete list of Vilane Properties' holdings is not available, but they are believed to be extensive, including commercial and residential properties in every district of Pandora as well as properties on Romane, Pyxis, Scythia and Krysk.

His reappearance also coincides with the rise of the nascent Rivinchi cartel on Pandora. Though inconclusive, persuasive evidence exists linking him to the (admittedly obscure) Rivinchi leadership structure. If Enzio is involved in Rivinchi, this behavior is at odds with his public persona as a community leader and philanthropic businessman.

Damn. When she'd remarked how Enzio was trouble, she'd had no idea how right she was.

No way did you find all of this on the exanet.

Clearly I didn't. I maintain close contact with a number of Artificials and databanks operating within governmental agencies and...other organizations.

She scowled at the bare ceiling above her. *Shouldn't I know all of your friends?*

I never said they were my friends. To answer the question you intend to ask: the speculation as to his possible leadership position in the Rivinchi cartel does not come from reputable sources. Nonetheless, it is likely true.

So the authorities don't know about his cartel ties?

Not so far as I was able to determine. To the world, he presents as an upstanding and increasingly influential businessman.

She sat up in the bed and rubbed at her face. *No parents of record—no record of him ever being born at all—and Aiden Trieneri paid for his education. Could Trieneri be his father?*

An analysis of Enzio's facial features and bone structure returns a 69 to 78 percent probability that he is a first-generation relative of Mr. Trieneri.

Way to bury the lede, Meno.

I don't follow.

If you assume that he's Trieneri's son, the rest of the story starts making a lot more sense.

Enzio would have only been around nine years old when his father died, arguably too young to have been groomed in his father's image. But he might have decided to take the mantle upon himself, devoting his life to rebuilding what his father had lost—or possibly to eclipsing the man's achievements. He'd received the best education money could buy, all geared toward his chosen 'career' in business, illicit or otherwise. Then, a two-year gap. Had he spent it acquiring the people and assets that would become the linchpins of the Rivinchi cartel?

It is a shame. He genuinely did seem like a nice man.

All these years, Meno, and you're still too naive and trusting. People aren't always what they seem.

This was what she'd sensed in her initial encounter with Enzio. All smooth, affable confidence and grace on the outside, but beneath it, something sinister and calculating. Something dangerous.

The reason for his sudden cookie-bearing arrival at her store now became clear. His enforcer, Chad, had reported back to the boss that the newest local store owner was a Prevo with a mouth and an attitude. Enzio had visited her to assess the problem for himself. To take the measure of her.

What had he walked away believing about her, she wondered?

This was all speculation, but she'd spent several years embroiled in the cartels long ago and many years since then judging the character and motivations of adversaries and allies alike. All her instincts told her she had the right of it.

With a groan she crawled back out of the bed and headed to the shower, though dawn was only a hint of light on the horizon. Dammit, she did not come to Pandora to get involved in this kind of nonsense.

RW

Sixteen sleep-deprived hours later, Mia was locking up the store for the night when Enzio Vilane magically appeared beside her on the sidewalk. "Ms. Balente, good evening. I wanted to stop by and see how things are going for you."

She cut her eyes over at him briefly; now that she knew the truth, the predator lurking behind the friendly guise was easy to spot. She held up a hand. "One second, please." She slipped inside, closed the door behind her and went to retrieve his plate from underneath the counter.

He was pacing along the outside of her storefront when she re-emerged and presented him with the plate. "Here you go. Washed and dried."

His brow furrowed. "I was actually kidding about returning for the plate. You were welcome to keep it."

"No, I wasn't. It belongs to you, and now I've returned it. I can reimburse you for the cookies, or if you prefer, I can include a little extra in my next protection payment."

His gaze immediately hooded. "I don't understand what you mean."

She locked the door to the store and pivoted to face him. "I know who you are, and you own a great deal more than 'a couple of apartment buildings.' I know you secretly run the Rivinchi cartel and have designs on taking over The Approach, then all of Pandora.

"I don't care for cartels and gangs and underworld crime syndicates, but I also don't care what you do with your time. I just want to be left alone. So here's the deal I'm offering you, Mr. Vilane: I'll pay your protection money without complaint, and I'll keep my mouth shut about your shady dealings. In return, you'll stay out of my way. *Far* out of my way."

Enzio was a handsome man—but only so long as he kept the mask in place. In a blink, the friendly, ingratiating countenance vanished, to be replaced by something dark and threatening.

He took a step toward her. "How could you possibly believe you 'know' such things? Who are you?"

"I told you. Someone who wants to be left alone."

"It doesn't matter. You don't get to make demands of me, Laisha. This silly little store you're clinging to? I own it. I own this street, I own this block, I own everything you can see in all directions. I own your apartment building, too, and you know what that means? It means I own *you*. I make the rules. I go wherever I want and talk to whomever I please. So the next time I walk into your store—and trust me, I *will* be frequenting it—you'll want to be nicer to me."

Mia stepped onto the sidewalk in front of Eli Baca. He failed to recognize her in the long coat and hood, and made to veer around her.

She took a single step sideways to block his path, activated the blade and plunged it into his heart.

Eli was fat, but her blade was far from tiny. A bloom of red unfurled to dye his sweaty shirt crimson as he gaped at her in shock and confusion.

She reached up with her free hand, pulled the hood off and leveled a cold, malevolent glare at him. "You don't own me anymore."

Every alarm bell in her mind flared in agony, and her teeth ground painfully from the effort of not screaming out to the heavens in frustration and rage. Her right hand clenched and unclenched at her side, energy threatening to crackle out from her fingertips. He was a Prevo; she could kill him with a single, hard stare. But he was Prevo; it wouldn't do any good. His Artificial would have him back up and terrorizing the streets and her in a matter of days.

She reached down deep for the rebellious, brave, desperate spirit that had enabled her to kill Eli Baca and free herself from servitude all those years ago…and found only a broken heart and a feeble, wounded soul.

She squeezed her eyes shut, blocking out his sneer. "Isn't it enough for me to play along with your rules, pay your extortion and not report your nefarious deeds to the cops?"

He snorted. "There aren't any cops on Pandora."

"What are you planning to do to Eli's operation?"

Caleb shrugged. "I'm going to explosively dismantle his chimeral production line and bring the cops down on the remains."

"There aren't any cops here."

He laughed. It bore a hint of mystery, as if to imply he knew more about Pandora than she did. "Yes, there are."

She threw her head back and laughed, much as Caleb had in the memory. In her years as an IDCC government official, she'd come to learn quite a lot about the hidden police presence on Pandora. "Yes, there are. They'll let you play your games here so long as you don't stick your head up too far above the crowd. But you had better keep a light touch, else someone with arrest powers will notice what you're doing. You wouldn't want to end up like your father."

His expression morphed in a flare of…not rage, precisely. Frustration? "Never mention my father again. He is dead to me."

"In fairness, he's dead to everyone."

His hand snapped out toward her throat, and she pressed harder against the glass window of the storefront behind her. But he pulled up a centimeter before his fingers curled around her neck. A smirk tweaked at the corners of his mouth, and instead he let his fingertips stroke her jaw.

"You think you're clever. I can see it in your eyes—a haughty defiance, as if I'm somehow beneath you. But understand this: you are *nothing*. A gnat I can plaster all over the wall with a swat of my hand. I am warning you here and now, do not fuck with me, or I will do exactly that."

"I don't want to fuck with you, Mr. Vilane. I swear, I simply want to be left alone."

"What if I don't want to leave you alone?"

"Then you will regret it."

His lips pinched, giving him a petulant, whiny aspect. "Did you just threaten me?"

"No, I merely stated a fact. Let me run my shop in peace. Forget all about me, and we'll get along fine."

"Aren't you listening? You don't make the rules here. I do."

She really, really should have let him have his imagined victory. She did not come to Pandora to get involved in this kind of nonsense.

But she was who she had always been. "We'll see if you're right, won't we?"

He blinked in surprise, took a step away and blustered something about a meeting demanding his time. His expression locked down, and he stalked off down the sidewalk in the waning evening light.

I fear that was a foolhardy action for you to take.

Maybe. But it was fun.

Mia, the sensations you are currently experiencing do not resemble fun.

Her stomach churned to confirm Meno's analysis. Dammit! This could not be happening to her again.

Every day since the night twenty-nine years ago when she'd gutted Eli Baca like the pig he was, her life had been on an upward trajectory, one that had taken her to such rarefied, exquisite heights. Every day, that was, until the one on which Malcolm died. Then he un-died, and nothing made sense anymore, and now...

...was it possible she was right back where she'd started?

Caustic laughter seared her throat. History might not repeat itself, but it did hilariously rhyme.

30

CHALMUN STATION ASTEROID

LARGE MAGELLANIC CLOUD

Marlee was of two distinct minds as she wandered along the maze of hallways cutting through Chalmun Station. On the negative side, the claustrophobic corridors of the hollowed-out asteroid reminded her a touch *too* much of the tunnel network beneath Namino One. Twice already, her heart had stopped at the sudden appearance of a dark form that resembled a Rasu when viewed in the corner of her vision. But on the other hand, how cool was this place? A cornucopia of aliens wandered to and fro in every direction. Rogues, thugs and general ne'er-do-wells hung out in every alcove and packed every shadow-laden gathering hole.

She wasn't worried about her safety. She carried a brand-new plasma blade in her pocket, plus she was increasingly confident in her self-defense capabilities thanks to Caleb's rigorous training regimen.

But Caleb would remind her to be humble. To have 'the beginner's mindset' in all things. Because she was listening to (most of) his advice these days, she tried to do so.

She breathed in and took note of the flow of movement around her. Of the slovenly Barisan who leered at every passerby from one corner of the branching intersection ahead. Of the willowy Naraida slipping through the crowd, pick-pocketing every fifth passerby of any valuables not secured to their person. Of the large, russet-and-sage Volucri guarding the entrance to a shop by flexing its claws and threatening to dive-bomb anyone who approached the door.

She slid effortlessly to the side a nanosecond before a Khokteh shoved past her, his tall, thick body and tail taking up half the passageway as he barged onward toward an urgent destination.

Then she was at the entrance to *Purgatory*. She froze for a moment, her legs primed to pivot and flee—but she was being ridiculous. Before leaving the *Siyane*, Morgan had *invited* her to drop by sometime, hadn't she? Yes, she absolutely had. So Marlee ran her fingers through her hair in a futile attempt to smooth it out, tamped down any telltale wrinkles in her fitted champagne top and strode inside.

She barely had time to take in the setting when a commotion at one of the tables near the stage broke out. Shouting and shoving quickly commenced and, curiosity piqued, she headed toward the fray. She'd almost reached the epicenter of the conflict when two bouncers, a Dankath and a Barisan, grabbed an angry Anaden man by both arms and began dragging him away.

Their absence revealed Morgan Lekkas standing at the other side of the table, wiping a trickle of blood off the corner of her mouth as she scowled at the unruly patron. "When I said 'no cheating allowed,' I meant *no cheating allowed*. Never show your gre…greasy face in here again." She tossed a hand dismissively in the man's direction, and the bouncers resumed hauling him off toward the exit.

"Fucker made me spill my drink."

"I'll get you a fresh one, ma'am," a Novoloume man in emerald robes offered, then backed away and headed toward the bar.

Morgan's gaze drifted around the space, passed over Marlee—and returned to her. "Marlee, you came! Here, join me." She raised her voice above the din. "Solstan, bring my friend here a drink, too. What'll you have?"

"Uh…a Diamond Dust, please."

The Novoloume man had halted halfway to the bar; now he nodded confirmation and continued on his journey.

Marlee eased into one of the chairs at the table and studied Morgan in concern. "Did that guy hurt you?"

"Bah. As if." Morgan blinked a few times and scowled at a wet spot on the table. Her spilt drink? Her head wobbled, which was when Marlee pieced together the blindingly obvious evidence and realized the woman was drunk. As in, seriously drunk.

Well, shit. She couldn't very well seduce a badly inebriated woman, could she? No, of course not. Her mother had taught her a few manners.

The Novoloume—Solstan, she surmised—arrived carrying their drinks. Marlee took a small sip of hers, while Morgan downed a third of her glass in one gulp. Then she held onto it rather than set it on the table and regarded Marlee with bloodshot eyes and dilated pupils.

Marlee cleared her throat a tad awkwardly. "So, how have you been since we got back from Namino?"

"Fabulous. Glad to be home, runnin' my place, winnin' chance games, doin' my thing. You?"

"Good. I've been training with Caleb, which is awesome. I've got a new boss, which is a little weird. I miss Mia, but she—"

"Ran off. I heard. Stupid bitch. Everything she ever wanted is offered to her like she's the princess of the high castle, and she thumbs her nose at it and skedaddles away."

Marlee frowned. "Yeah. I guess she's technically a fugitive now. It must be scary for her."

"Not the first time."

"What do you mean?"

"For Mia. Not the first time being a fugitive. In fact, it's got to be like the..." Morgan studied her glass as if searching it for answers before turning it up for a long sip "...third time? Or is it the fourth?"

"Mia? No, that can't be right."

"Why, because she's all elegant and cultured and perfect?"

"Well...kind of, yes."

"Goes to show you—you never truly know a person. Remember that. It'll save you a lot of grief in the future." Morgan finished off her drink and motioned toward the bar.

Marlee caught Solstan's attention as he was returning to their table and gave him a minute shake of her head. He merely shrugged helplessly in response. "Another drink, ma'am?"

"Yep. And one for my friend here, too."

Who had designs on plying who here? "I'm still working on this one. Give me a few minutes."

She watched Solstan stride smoothly toward the bar, working out the logistics of the situation in her head. "Where's the lavatory? I need to step in there for a minute."

Morgan's brow furrowed, as if she'd forgotten. Finally she gestured toward the far left corner. "Thataway."

"Thanks. I'll be back." She stood and started heading in the direction Morgan had pointed. But once she'd passed a couple of dancers who blocked the view, she veered left and went to the bar. She leaned over it near where Solstan was mixing drinks. "Got to do what the boss orders, huh?"

He peered over his shoulder at her, seemingly sizing her up in one quick glance. "Yes, ma'am. That is my job."

"Even when she's like this?"

"Especially when she's like this." He paused. "Are you a friend of hers?"

"I hope so. Does she...does this happen often?"

He sighed and stepped closer. "Oh, she always enjoys her drinks, make no mistake. And in the early days, yes, this happened with some frequency. She was hurting and...but it's not my place to speculate. She had been doing a lot better lately, though. Until tonight, it had been almost a year since the last time she went on a hard bender. I don't know what set her off. Perhaps her trip with Alex Solovy a few weeks ago?"

"I was there with her. I don't think anything happened that would trigger this." They'd gotten shot at by a bunch of Rasu and blew up a giant invasion compound and a quantum block and had various other zany adventures, but it had all been more fun than upsetting.

She took the glass from him. "I'll bring it to her. Thank you."

On the way back to the table, she took a tiny sip from the glass—and spit it out. God, it tasted like pure grain alcohol.

Morgan's head was resting on her arm when Marlee arrived, and for a second she worried the woman had passed out. But when her chair scraped across the floor, Morgan's head lifted, her hand instantly reaching for the glass Marlee had set in front of her. Another long sip followed, then Morgan steadied the glass on the table using both hands. "Fucking Malcolm fucking Jenner. What made him special enough to not die the way a good soldier's supposed to do?"

"I don't think—"

"How can Mia be so stupid? I always believed she was smarter than this. The universe hands the woman her greatest wish on an adiamene-coated platter, and she walks away from it? Doesn't have any idea of the magnitude of the gift she's being given, doesn't appreciate what the rest of us wouldn't do to be in her shoes—" Morgan abruptly turned the glass up again.

Oh. God, how dense was she for it to take her this long to figure it out? Marlee gazed at Morgan with new, wiser eyes and...not pity. Empathy. What could she possibly say to make Morgan feel better? She didn't exactly have much experience with this sort of thing, so she just started rambling.

"I am certain Mia is so incredibly grateful that Malcolm's alive. I think it's...I mean, I wasn't there when everything happened, but it sounds as if the way things went down was super-complicated, and everybody got played by the Savrakaths, and now the situation's all mixed up. I'm sure it'll work out."

"For them? Yep. Always does. Lucky S.O.B.s...." The nearly empty glass slipped from Morgan's grasp and rolled across the table. The next second, the woman's head landed on her arm. For real this time?

Marlee half-stood to peer around the bar until she spotted Solstan talking to one of the dancers, then waved to catch his attention. He nodded as he arrived at the table. "It's for the best that this bender has come to an early end."

"Do you know where her apartment is? Can you help me get her there?"

"I do. It's above and behind the bar here." He slid an arm beneath one of Morgan's, and Marlee hurried around to the other side to do the same. Morgan muttered a nonsensical protest when they lifted her up, and Solstan patted her on the back. "We're going to take a short trip, ma'am. Just walk with us."

Step by step, they managed to maneuver a barely conscious Morgan through the rowdy patrons to a hidden lift behind the bar. Upstairs, a short hallway led to a door. Solstan input a code, and the door slid open to reveal a nice but spartan living area.

"The bedroom's off to the left." He led them through a door-less archway to a smaller room containing an unmade bed, nightstand and dresser, but little else.

They eased her down onto the bed to the accompaniment of vague half-protests. Once Morgan's head hit the pillow, however, she didn't move.

Marlee offered Solstan a genuine smile. "Thank you for your help. I'll finish tucking her in."

"It wasn't a problem. I'm glad you were here for her tonight."

"Me, too." She'd need to think long and hard later about whether it was true.

"I'll see myself out."

She waited until the door to the apartment had closed behind him, then moved to the end of the bed, wiggled Morgan's boots off and set them on the floor. Next she went into the kitchen and fixed a glass of water, taking a moment to check out the rest of the apartment. It was clean and had all the appropriate furnishings, but there wasn't a hint of personalization. No visuals, no mementos, no quirky art.

She carried the glass of water back to the bedroom, where she set it on the nightstand. There wasn't much else to do, so she sank onto the edge of the bed and dropped her chin to her chest.

This wasn't how she'd envisioned the night going. And what had she been thinking, anyway? A rare bout of self-doubt crept into her thoughts. She'd never measure up to the memory of the great Brooklyn Harper, and the stinging truth refused to be denied: she *was* just a silly child for ever believing she'd be able to do so.

She immediately chastised herself. Morgan was hurting, and she shouldn't be selfish. She should want to help a…friend.

But she had no easy fixes for a broken heart, and she couldn't bring the dead back from the grave. Her 'sprint gleefully ahead first, ask pertinent questions later' approach to life had never led her to the key to either.

She sighed ruefully as Morgan's breathing leveled out into a not-so-troubled slumber. It wasn't fair; tragedy should never have intruded to break the woman's spirit. Morgan was beautiful and fierce and talented and, until tonight, larger than life. The woman had deliberately cut herself off from the world, but the world would be so much brighter with her in it. If only there was some way she could show Morgan how much she was worth.

But Marlee didn't know how she might accomplish such a feat. She was just a silly child, after all. But maybe she *could* change that.

She pulled the rumpled covers up to Morgan's chest, leaned down and kissed the woman softly. Even with the souring taste of alcohol on her lips, it was perfect.

Then she wrote up a brief note for Morgan, detached an aural and situated it above the nightstand, and left the apartment.

RW

Morgan tried to open her eyes, but they were glued shut. She squinted and rubbed at her face to work the sleep loose from her eyelashes, then tried again. The mercifully dim light of her apartment greeted her, blurred, wavered and slowly solidified.

"Ow." She ordered her eVi to begin running its entire suite of alcohol cleansing routines and rolled over to bury her face in her pillow. What had she *done* last night? Drank too much, obviously....

Because Jenner was alive and Brook was dead and life wasn't fair. And all the alcohol in Concord space hadn't made it any fairer.

A shimmer to her left caught her notice, and she carefully shifted her head. On the nightstand sat a glass of water and an aural containing a note. She fumbled for the water, then slid the aural over above her chest so she could read it while she tried to drink the water and mostly spilled it down her chin.

Morgan,

I'm sorry I came by at a bad time, but it was still good to see you. We can hang out again sometime, once you're feeling better.

Best,

—Marlee

Shame flushed her skin hot. She hadn't wanted the young woman to see her in such a sorry state. When Marlee looked at her, Morgan saw an idealized reflection of the person she had once been, and she'd forgotten how nice it was for someone to see her that way. But the next time they met, Marlee wouldn't look at her with admiration any longer. The bloom was surely off the rose now.

She groaned and struggled up to a sitting position, thankful the room had slowed its spinning. So what now? Her extreme acting out had drained her of emotions, had even drained away much of the pain, leaving her…empty. A hollow shell waiting to be filled. But by the same old anger and vitriol, or by something new?

All right. The water was helping, but she needed to ingest something stronger, which meant getting out of bed. She eased her feet to the floor and stood. A little wobbly, but not too bad. She shuffled to the kitchen and brewed up a pitcher of Peronan espresso, then collapsed into a chair at the small kitchen table and dropped her forehead onto her palm.

The details of the night before gradually drifted back into her mind—the ones before the bender commenced in earnest, at least. After AEGIS had finally released a full report on the sequence of events on Savrak, the news feed had gone wall-to-wall coverage of Jenner's miraculous survival for half an hour. To her credit, she'd made it through twenty minutes of the breathless reporting before opening her first bottle.

She'd give anything to be in the enviable position Mia found herself in right now. Were she, she'd do it all better. Most of all, she wouldn't toss away the precious gift the universe had bestowed on her, the way Mia seemed intent on doing.

After a few tenuous sips of the steaming, bitter coffee, she toggled off the neural block and tip-toed into the tsunami of information that formed the Noesis for long enough to confirm Mia wasn't broadcasting her location there. Nope, not a trace.

Next step in the hazy plan forming in her mind: she sent a pulse to Alex.

Do you know where Mia is?

She'd finished the cup of espresso by the time a response arrived.

I do.

Have you told Malcolm yet?

No. Caleb promised Mia he wouldn't disclose her location, and I promised him the same.

You don't think Malcolm should know?

Of course I do. Malcolm showed up on Akeso, begging Caleb to help him find her. It's a yobanyi *mess from top to bottom, and I feel awful for both of them. But it's not my responsibility, or my right, to try to fix it.*

A cute sentiment, and one Morgan normally would have enthusiastically ascribed to. But now, she was overcome by this absurdly virtuous desire to help.

Will you tell me where she is?

I can't.

Morgan groaned and refilled her cup. She was zero-for-two so far, and she wasn't certain she had the energy to try a third time. Then Alex surprised her by sending a follow-up pulse.

Valkyrie thinks Meno will tell Stanley if he phrases the question in the correct manner. She says Meno is worried about Mia and frustrated at his inability to improve her state of mind.

I bet he is. They all think they're noble stewards of our well-being. Okay, I'll see what I can do. What are you up to?

Chasing down a lead that might help us against the Rasu.

She felt a flare of...jealousy? Or was it longing that panged around in her chest? She'd been doing nothing good for anyone for so long. Until Namino. Damn Alex for reminding her what an adrenaline rush it was to save the good guys and kick the bad guys' asses.

Good luck.

You, too.

She downed most of the second cup of coffee in one long, bracing sip, set the cup down and slapped her cheeks roughly. The cleansing routine was making progress, as was the industrial-grade caffeine.

Stanley, while I take a shower, try to ply Mia's location out of Meno. I'm not clear what Valkyrie meant by 'phrasing the question in the correct manner,' though. I guess be nice and sympathetic or something.

I will manage.

I've no doubt you will.

He had the answer before she'd so much as activated the shower water. Meno must be genuinely worried.

Morgan prepped a short message and sent it off before she thought better of it.

Admiral Jenner,

She's on Pandora, running a tech retail shop in The Approach called The Whole Shebang. Don't fuck it up.

Duty done, she stood under the hot water for a solid thirty minutes as uncomfortable ruminations warred with one another in her head. Why did today feel like a point of no return? If she continued down the path she was on, she feared she'd be lost forever. But stepping out into the light and taking a chance on something better might ruin her even faster.

She finally turned the shower off and returned to the bedroom to dig up fresh clothes. Once there, though, she gravitated toward the bed and the nightstand beside it. She opened the drawer, where a visual of Brook gazed up at her, same as it always did. Smiling, which had not been an easy sight to capture and memorialize.

"Oh, Brook, I still miss you every goddamn day. I wish so damn much that you'd made a different choice, because I'd have taken an eighty percent real, twenty percent synthetic, patched together version of you without hesitation. But you didn't, and there's no going back.

"My foray on Namino made me realize that I've got to...do *something.* I think I've got to stop hiding, because in six years it hasn't solved a damn thing. I think you'd want me to get out there and do some good. If I'm wrong, I hope you'd forgive me. Either way, I've got to try, else I'm already dead."

She closed the drawer with a reverentially gentle nudge and glared up at the ceiling. "Now, it would be simply smashing if I could figure out what it is I'm supposed to do."

PART III

WHAT WAS LOST...

31

SIYANE

OURANKELI STELLAR SYSTEM
BEYOND THE BOUNDARIES OF CONCORD SPACE

The starlight from the system's sun reflected brilliantly off the shattered halo ring encircling it, much like the lens flare in an overexposed old-timey photograph.

At the sight of it, Alex brought a hand to her mouth with a sharp inhale. Even crumbling apart, the ring structure was one of the most stunning creations she had ever laid eyes upon. A monument erected to proclaim what wonders intelligent life was capable of forging. The Ourankeli had dared to lasso their sun and make it their own.

The fact that the ring was a dead world built by a dead species made her heart ache. For every glorious wonder sapient beings built, it seemed fiends eagerly waited to tear it all down.

Reason enough to hate the Rasu, I think.

We didn't need another reason on top of the thousand we've amassed, but yes. Reason enough, Valkyrie.

Alex brought the *Siyane* to a relative stop half a megameter above one edge of the ring and initiated a thorough systems check. Whatever insidious metal-disintegrating weapon was at work here, she did not plan on allowing it to damage her ship.

Caleb sat with his elbows propped on his chair's armrests and his hands fisted at his chin, his attention focused on the ring. She'd seen the pose a hundred times, but it had been some time since it had made an appearance, and she was glad for its return.

"Lamenting all that must have been lost here?"

"Thinking about how we can make certain this never happens to us."

Even better. "We'll find a way. Valkyrie, are we detecting anything that can account for the corrosive effects Corradeo and Nyx experienced while they were visiting?"

'There is a faint but pervasive radiation field present here that doesn't correlate to the star's output or other regional characteristics. It will take some time to fully catalog and analyze its effects.'

"Before we get to any potential effect on the adiamene—and we definitely should test its tolerance—will the new shielding protect us from the field?"

'I need to make a slight adjustment in the frequency oscillation of the shield to create a more fulsome barrier. A moment...done. I'm sending you a record of the changes I made, as you will need to recreate them on your personal shields before you venture outside.'

"You're the best." She glanced at Caleb. "Are you ready to land and go exploring?"

He pondered the question, then shook his head. "First, let's take a survey of the ring and, if you don't mind, the whole stellar system. I want to try to create an image in my head of what might have happened here."

She was anxious to put boots on a hard surface, but if he was engaged in the mystery, she was not going to shut him down. "We can do that." The systems check came back nominal, and she opened up all the ship's recording instruments to full.

They cruised above the ring until they reached the point where it had been sheared away for more than a quarter of its original circumference. "In her report, Nyx speculates that this destruction occurred a minimum of two centuries ago."

'I concur. In fact, based on a preliminary analysis, it appears to have occurred between three and five hundred years in the past.'

In her head, Alex scanned through the measurements Valkyrie was basing her pronouncement on—for her own edification, since it wasn't as if she expected to find an error. "Without the support of a fully bounded structure and the stable orbit it maintained, I suspect the missing portion of the ring has already fallen into the star. In fact, the ring's orbit is decaying badly, as the two open ends are being inexorably dragged toward the star. Valkyrie, do you want to spin some spare cycles on analyzing the ring's orbital angular momentum to extrapolate backward and estimate more precisely when the attack occurred?"

'Doing so will require a lot of spare cycles.'

She chuckled lightly. "Maybe when we get home, then. While we're here, concentrate on solving the mystery of this corrosive radiation field, along with anything else we uncover that's out of the ordinary."

They sought out the destroyed moons of the gas giant Corradeo had mentioned to Nika and found them as described: shredded into jagged chunks of plagioclase and pyroxene rocks. In one case, an otherwise intact satellite had taken a blast straight through to its molten core, leaving a steady stream of solidified iron trailing behind its orbit.

Caleb's visible interest only intensified as they surveyed the damage. "There's only one controllable force I've ever encountered that can cause such destruction: *diati*."

"Or a Tartarus Trigger."

He shot her a smirk. "Fine. Two forces. But unless it was focused, tiny and quickly extinguished, a black hole would have consumed the gas giant as well."

"Are you saying you think someone used *diati* here? This happened before The Displacement, so it's theoretically possible."

He stared intently out the viewport, eyes narrowed and jaw set. A muscle beneath his cheek flexed. "It is, but…no, I doubt *diati* is responsible. I'm saying the Rasu have far more powerful weapons at their disposal than what they've shown to us so far."

"Or the Ourankeli did. Exotic weaponry could have inflicted this much damage if it was activated beneath the surface."

"Why would they destroy their own habitats?"

She shrugged. "Collateral damage? A scorched earth campaign? Utter desperation?"

He huffed a breath. "All viable theories. Are we picking up any traces of Ourankeli structures in the area?"

"Nothing. If a structure was smaller than a moon, I don't think it exists any longer."

"What about their homeworld? Before the ring? Do we know anything about it? How many terrestrial planets are there in the system?"

She gazed at him rather than answer, a bright smile growing upon her lips in time to the spreading warmth in her chest. "Hi."

He tilted his head to regard her curiously. Then, as understanding dawned, his expression softened and he dropped out of his chair to his knees. Just as he'd done years ago when they launched themselves through a portal and into the unknown for the first time. "I am so, so sorry. I know I haven't always been as attentive as I should be—"

"No." She fell to her knees in front of him. "You don't have anything to apologize for. It's only…this is the first time it's felt like you're really *here,* really present, on the ship and engaged in the mission, in a…little while. So…" she grinned, keeping her countenance light and teasing even as her heart overflowed "…hi."

His hands came to her jaw, and his lips brushed exquisitely across hers. "Hi, baby."

Their trajectory jerked to port, and she reluctantly glanced up in time to see a ten-meter chunk of lunar debris sail past. "Thanks, Valkyrie."

Caleb's gaze returned to the viewport as well, and she pressed his hand into her cheek briefly before climbing to her feet and returning to her chair. Where were they? "We, um, don't have any information on the original Ourankeli homeworld, but the report says they harvested both local terrestrial worlds for materials to build the ring. Presumably not down to the core, though. They might still exist in gutted form."

She scanned the hyperspectral imaging output for markers of orbiting bodies closer to the star. "There. We've got a planet-sized object 1.3 AU out." Her attention returned to the emerald gas giant dominating the viewport. "I don't think we're going to find any answers out here."

Caleb nodded in agreement as he settled back into his chair, and she adopted an intercept course for the planet they'd identified. "How are the systems holding up, Valkyrie?"

'This field is most persistent. I am successfully keeping its corrosive effects out, but it requires constant readjustment of the parameters of our shielding.'

"Then I'm glad you're here to do the heavy lifting." She let her mind wander across the readings arriving from the plethora of sensors. A battle for the ages had been waged across this system. The kind of battle that Concord hoped to be able to not merely muster but win against the Rasu when the time came. But this battle had left the system uninhabitable by anyone—Ourankeli, Rasu, any microbes that had once lived on the various planets. It was possible no one had won the day here, but unquestionably the Ourankeli had lost.

The planet in question came into view, looking as desolate and barren as everything else in the system. Once a rocky super-Earth, the planet had been stripped to the mantle as surely as if a Theriz Cultivation Unit had come through scavenging for materials. Its decaying orbit would send it plummeting into the star not long after the ring burnt up.

An alarm pealed through the cabin. 'I am detecting Rasu signatures.'

"Active ones? Here?" She leapt into action, opening a spread of screens across the HUD and tossing several Caleb's way.

'The signatures are weak, and they appear to be drifting in a natural orbit instead of moving under active control.'

She studied the radar until she had confirmed what Valkyrie saw. The Rasu signatures were clustered in a loose grouping about ninety megameters distant from the nearby planet. "Stealth to full and Dimensional Rifter engaged. Let's ease in and see what's up with the bastards."

On the visible light spectrum, the Rasu formations were practically invisible against the void, and their electrical signals were barely stronger than ambient background noise. In the far-infrared band, where Rasu typically shone brightest, only faint signals registered on the instruments.

After much tweaking of the sensor settings, the objects finally resolved into fourteen separate Rasu...blobs, honestly. They ranged in size from thirty meters to almost one hundred forty meters in length. They lacked form or definition, however, instead resembling pools of semi-solid metal, not unlike the leaking lunar molten core they'd observed earlier.

Caleb frowned darkly. "Are they dead?"

"I think so, or as near to dead as they can be without being atomized. There's only minimal electrical output and no other techno-signatures. We're not picking up anything identifiable as purposeful activity."

"So this is what the Ourankeli weapon did to them. Rendered them incapable of practical operation."

'Based on initial scans, I would posit that the weapon prevented them from changing shapes or functionality and from combining or separating.'

"It looks as if it prevented them from holding any purposeful shape at all. These aren't ships any longer. They're messy globules at best." Alex watched as one of the smaller blobs floated languidly by a few hundred meters from the *Siyane.* She'd witnessed Rasu ships in action—and Rasu foot-soldiers—and this one genuinely did look dead. "We could grab a sample and take it back for Special Projects to analyze."

Caleb arched an eyebrow, his eyes twinkling in challenge.

"Hey, the Asterions managed to capture a living Rasu, bring it to Mirai and talk to it."

"I don't think these Rasu are in any shape to talk. Still, though. How about we send a Special Projects HazMat team here and let *them* take the sample?"

"Okay." She rolled her eyes in mock annoyance, but she didn't argue. Over the years she'd transported dozens of dangerous or at least mysterious materials in the hull of the *Siyane.* But the truth was, the notion of having a Rasu onboard, even a mostly dead Rasu secured in a sealed and quarantined container, made her shiver.

Caleb waved a hand at the viewport, as if to say he was done with this scene. "The question is, what broke the ring? The same weapon that gutted those moons, or a concentrated burst of this anti-Rasu field? Were the Rasu winning the battle before the Ourankeli deployed their doomsday weapon, or did the Ourankeli inflict catastrophic damage on themselves simply to take the Rasu down with them?"

Visions of what the battle might have involved danced through her mind, though the scale of the destruction suggested she had no proper frame of reference—not even the massive, sprawling final battle against the Kats' superdreadnoughts almost two decades earlier.

"I do not know. How about we land on the ring near where it's sheared away and see if we can dig up some answers?"

32

PANDORA

Mia rubbed at her weary eyes as the customer began his third circuit of the displays. Enzio Vilane had joined the parade of violent faces in her nightmares, and even with Meno's caring ministrations, she was getting less sleep than ever.

Twice the customer had picked up an item and fondled it in his grasp for several seconds before putting it down. He wasn't a real buyer, but he might very well be a shoplifter or, worse, casing the store for a later robbery.

If this was his plan, he'd find an unhappy surprise waiting when he executed on it. Her security system was rather robust.

Finally she stepped out from behind the counter. "I'm sorry, sir, but we're closing. You're welcome to return tomorrow."

"Oh." He glanced over at her as if surprised. "I may do so. Thank you." He turned and mercifully exited the store.

Her shoulders sagged. All she wanted to do was drag herself to the apartment, heat up some noodles, take a steaming hot bath and finish off a bottle of wine. She shut down the store's computer system, killed the overhead lights and went to lock the front door for the night—

—the door opened beneath her hand, and something big and bulky slammed into her face. Bolts of pain shot up through her nose straight into her brain, and she stumbled backward.

Move! To your left!

Meno's order overwhelmed the pain, and she ducked left as a thick arm swung for her gut. It ricocheted off her shoulder, but then someone was behind her, grabbing her arms and yanking her back against a barrel chest. Hot breath assaulted her ear. "You should have gone along to get along, missy. Now you'll have to pay with more than credits."

A shadow filled the open doorway. Its profile was muscled, wiry and dominated by gleaming silver irises. It pointed a Daemon at her chest. "The boss wants to have a word with you."

Reverb code!

It had been years since she'd used it to take out an Anaden assassin on

Nopreis, but the required actions sprung fully formed in her mind. She squinted at the shadow, focusing in on the center of its head.

The shadow convulsed and collapsed to the floor.

"What the hell?" Her assailant's grip on her loosened in surprise at seeing his comrade fall, and she elbowed him beneath his ribcage then wrenched away to lurch toward the interior of the store. If she could reach the office and storage room, she'd be able to escape through the rear—

—laser fire streaked centimeters to the left of her ear, and she lunged to the right, slamming into the corner of the counter. The collision spun her around, and she saw the assailant steady his Daemon on her.

Hands reached around the man from behind, grabbed his head and—*snap.*

The man fell to the floor in a heap, revealing a new shadowy figure behind him. This one, though, she would recognize from across the galaxy.

Malcolm leapt over the body and rushed toward her. "My God, Mia. Are you hurt?"

Her heart swelled to block any words from escaping her throat, and she flung herself into his embrace.

Warmth. Strength. Alive, heart racing. Alive.

He held her tight against him. A cocoon of safety, where nothing could ever harm her. Her chin lifted, and his lips crushed hers.

She'd thought she'd never feel this again. This, her greatest wish during those agony-filled days when she'd believed him dead—one more embrace, one more kiss, one more murmured endearment, one more second to feel his arms secure around her. It was like coming home, like every dream fulfilled.

But 'one more' was never going to be enough. She knew this now. Every touch, every breath, was tainted by the knowledge that one day they would come to an end, forever. Another attacker could appear in the doorway and shoot him dead in her arms this instant. Forever.

She summoned all the anger and frustration that had consumed her for so long and pushed against his chest, stumbling out of his embrace.

His gaze took her in, eyes full of love and fear and adrenaline. "Are you *all right?*"

"I...I think my nose might be broken. Yes, Meno says it's broken. But I'm fine." Her voice sounded nasally and borderline hysterical. *Don't be hysterical. Now more than ever before, you have to be strong.*

"Let me get you a rag..." he glanced around "...I don't know where anything is."

"Don't worry about it." She grabbed her jacket off the counter chair and blotted at her nose.

"What happened here?"

"I picked a fight with the local cartel. Probably shouldn't have done that."

He looked incredulous and a little confused. "No, probably not. I've been so worried about you."

"How did you find me?"

"I got a message saying you were running a store here in The Approach."

"From whom?" Caleb wouldn't have betrayed her trust. He'd never do it.

"She didn't say not to tell you, so...Morgan Lekkas."

Goddamn her. Her mind started to jump through the possible ways Morgan could have known, but there were many, and it no longer mattered. Malcolm was standing in front of her. All she'd ever wanted, and all she never dared have again.

He reached out for her. "Come here."

She took a shaky step back, farther out of his reach. "Thank you for the most timely save, but you need to go."

"I...what? No! I am so sorry for everything I put you through. I understand why you're upset, and I can't imagine how terrible things must have been for you. But I'm here now, and we can fix all this. So let's go home, okay? Let's go home and talk things through."

"Malcolm, you lied to me—about your will, about the neural imprints. About always coming back to me. You looked me in the eye and you held my hand and you *lied* to me."

His chin dropped to his chest. "I did. I couldn't...I'm sorry. I'll try to explain, if you'll just come home with me. Please. I love you, and I've missed you so much."

She shook her head, which sent a fresh round of blood gushing out of her nose. "You don't love me enough to come back to me."

"I've come back to you now. I'm standing right here."

"That's not what I mean, and you know it."

"Come on, Mia. What if the doctors had performed regenesis based on my neural imprint after believing me dead? There would be two of me right now."

"Two of you is better than none of you. Trust me on this—I can work with two."

"Well, you only have one of me. The real me, not some golem copy."

She launched herself at him, dropping the jacket to the floor to beat her fists ineffectually on his chest. "You *died*, dammit. You left me alone in this world, and you didn't have to, and it wasn't fair."

He didn't resist her sloppy hits, instead tenderly stroking her hair as tears glistened his eyes while she flailed away at him. "I know it felt that way. I will apologize forever for the pain I caused you. Mia, I thought of nothing but you every minute of my captivity. Everything I did, I did it so I could get home to you. And I got it done. I'm here now, don't you see?"

"And you could die tomorrow." She shoved him, but only succeeded in knocking herself away from him. "Don't *you* see? I love you more than you will ever know, but I will not survive losing you a second time. I can't. So you have to go." *Hurry, go now, before I lose my will and myself to you and you destroy me all over again.*

His shoulders rose in the shadows. "What will it take to change your mind? Name your price."

A spark of hope embered in her chest. "Revoke the 'no regenesis' clause in your will. Prove to me you *will* always come back."

His lips parted, and his proud stance wilted. "Mia, I can't do that. You know I believe regenesis is fool's gold. Whatever it is that wakes up in a new body will not be me. I don't believe our souls can cross back over the threshold. I just don't."

"If it means you die when you don't have to, then screw your beliefs."

He swallowed heavily, his Adam's Apple bobbing against his throat. "You don't mean that."

"What if I do? You broke my heart, dammit! You broke my world. You broke me—and there's no unbreaking any of it now." A slippery, metallic taste filled her mouth, and she wiped blood off her lips. "Leave."

"No. Please, ask anything else of me. Anything."

"There is nothing else. Leave!"

He laughed bitterly. "Do you remember the last time we had a relationship-ending fight and you ordered me to leave? I obeyed you, like a good boy. Then I came groveling back, hat in hand, begging for your forgiveness. Is that what you want? Do you want me to crawl? Fine."

He dropped to the floor. "I'm on my knees, begging you."

Her eyes widened in horror and she spun away, unable to bring herself to look upon him in such a state. "Get up."

"I beg you, come home with me. We can work through this and start again."

"Get up—!" Tears and blood choked off the rest.

In her peripheral vision, his shoulders slumped. He dragged one foot up, then the other, and trudged to his feet. "I don't know what else to do."

She forced herself to face him. One last time. "There's nothing else for you to do. Go to the Presidio. Resume your post. Fight some Rasu. Try not to die. But I can't count on it any longer. I have to move on, before you kill me, too."

"I love you."

"I know you do. Leave."

He gestured to the bodies on the floor. "What if more of these goons show up? I won't abandon you while you're defenseless."

"I'm not defenseless. I killed one of them myself."

"And the second one would have killed you."

"Only for a little while. Unlike you, I'd come back."

He ignored the dig. "I'd greatly prefer we not test that theory."

She wracked her brain, desperate to find a way to force him out the door and down the street and a few parsecs away. Quickly, before the last threads of her sanity unraveled. "I commed the police as soon as these guys broke in. They'll be here any minute."

"Good."

"No, not good. When they see you here with me, they'll soon figure out who I am, at which point I'll be the one getting arrested. Do you want that to happen?"

He frowned. "No, of course not."

"Then leave before they arrive."

"But—"

"You need to get out of here."

He looked at the bodies again, then at her. Finally, a deep sigh of resignation escaped his lips. "Okay. I'll go—for now." He reached out for her, holding his palm open, surely realizing she didn't dare take it. "But this is not over. I am not giving up on us. You may have, but I won't. Not today, not tomorrow, not ever."

Her words were all dried up, so she simply stared at him until he turned and walked dejectedly out the door.

Goodbye, Malcolm.

She collapsed against the counter. Her head was on fire, despite Meno's best efforts at pain mitigation. She couldn't breathe through her nose. Her face and hands were covered in blood. Every breath hurt, presumably because her ribs were cracked from the counter collision.

She wanted so badly to run after him, but down that path waited only more pain. She wanted to sink to the floor and cry forever, but she was spent. She had no more tears left to shed. No more strength left to fight.

She'd made a right proper disaster out of her life, hadn't she? And in record time, no less.

Grief makes people crazy. But now, no matter what else you are feeling, you're not grieving any longer.

Because he was alive. Intellectually, she'd known this for a while, but seeing him, touching him, hearing his voice? He was *alive.*

But him being dead had gone beyond destroying her. It had exposed the ugly reality that her own life, her own sense of worth, had become all tangled up in him. In them as an entity. And in the messy aftermath, she couldn't recall who she'd been and had no idea who she might be now.

She peered hazily around at the gruesome scene decorating her little shop. What was she *doing* here? Why had she ever thought returning to the start of the loop was the way forward?

She went into the lavatory and washed her hands and arms and splashed water on her face. Her cybernetics had staunched the bleeding, but her nose and the skin under her eyes were bruised and swollen.

Laisha Balente had never truly existed, and it was a simple matter to let the persona fall away. She grabbed a bag and stuffed the few things that held any value to her in it. Meno's hardware was stashed in a secure location, but she'd have to leave everything in the apartment behind; odds were high that Vilane's men were already ransacking it.

Vilane hadn't sent his thugs here to kill her—he'd sent them to kidnap her. He understood full well the way Prevos worked; they were difficult to kill, but not impossible. He'd likely intended to pump her full of chimerals and coerce her into revealing the location of Meno's hardware, then destroy it all. Then he'd kill her, properly so. And despite her bravado-laced retort to him yesterday, she lacked the means to properly kill *him,* which meant she had to run. Again.

She'd lied to Malcolm about comming the police, but even in The Approach the commotion would have attracted attention. Someone would show up soon, so she needed to move fast. She situated the bag on her shoulder and started to depart out the front door. But there was at least a seventy-five percent chance that Malcolm had stuck around to watch and make certain no reinforcements arrived to finish the job. She pivoted, picked her way past the bodies and the mess, and slipped out the rear door.

As she wound through the alley network to the next cross-street, she sent Morgan a pulse.

Why did you tell Malcolm where I was? You knew I wanted to be left alone.

Because you have no idea the magnitude of the gift the universe has given you. Don't fuck it up.

Too late for that…her steps slowed, and she peered down the alley toward the street. She hadn't meant what she'd said about his faith. It was quite possibly the cruelest thing she'd ever said to him, or anyone for that matter, and her conscience was going to have a field day with the guilt. In her heart of hearts, she hadn't meant most of what she'd said. But she'd needed to force him to leave before she begged him to stay.

Losing him had fractured everything she was, everything she'd become. In its wake she'd somehow reverted to an old version of herself, and the worst habits she'd thought long banished had returned to drive her actions.

She'd run, just like before, but running had never solved anything. History seemed determined to rhyme, but she couldn't allow it to repeat itself.

The memory of his lips on hers flared in her mind unbidden. Warmth surged through her chest, and she wanted with every fiber of her being to spin around and *run* back into his arms. But she refused to do it. Not yet.

She needed to remember—to relearn—who she was without him first. She needed to stand strong on her own and reclaim her life and her sense of self. Then…maybe. She suddenly realized how much she hoped he meant what he'd said about not giving up on them. How horribly selfish of her, but it was a chance she had to take.

She turned left and exited onto the street, merging in with the light foot traffic headed toward the nearest levtram station. As she did, she sent another pulse.

Caleb, tell Richard I'll take the deal.

33

CONCORD HQ
CONSULATE

Marlee's feet were kicked up on her small desk, ankles crossed, and she had three aurals arrayed in front of her. The leftmost one contained a breakdown of the number and categorization of the Godjan refugees brought to Concord soil so far, and the other two set out provisional plans for their care and resettlement. Mia had drafted high-level guidelines before vanishing, but now someone had to work out the details of implementing those guidelines on the ground. It was one task Marlee didn't mind undertaking, though.

She had felt terrible about leaving Vaihe alone while she was trapped on Namino, but wow, had the Godjan girl stepped up! The initiative Vaihe had displayed in coming to Mia and devising her own plan for evacuating her fellow Godjans was impressive. Marlee would like to take credit for seeing a spark of moxie in Vaihe from the beginning, but the truth was, she'd simply wanted to save an abused girl from the vile Savrakaths.

Now she wished she could thank Mia personally for taking such tremendous steps to help Vaihe—to help all the Godjans—but Mia remained out of her reach. She set a reminder in her eVi to go visit Vaihe at the refugee camp as soon as she climbed out from under the mountain of work that had greeted her on her return to the office.

A polite throat-clearing drew her attention to the open door of her office. Dean Veshnael stood there looking refreshed and serene, as always. She dropped her feet to the floor and sat up straighter, as was only polite. "Yes, sir?"

He carried a small quantum cube suspended in a translucent, sealed box in both hands. "I have several files that need to be delivered to the Asterion Dominion Advisor Committee. Officially, with proper sign-off and transfer notation. I wondered if you might want to deliver them for me."

She regarded him curiously. "I thought you said when it came to the Asterions, you wanted to be the public face of the Consulate for a while."

"I did, and it would be my preference. But the addition of running the

Consulate to a plate already brimming with running the Novoloume government and seeing to my duties as a Concord Senator is not leaving many free hours in my days to indulge in preferences."

"I understand." She stood and accepted the box from him. "I'll be happy to deliver this for you."

"Thank you, Ms. Marano."

When he'd departed, she consciously resisted the urge to sprint off for the Dominion straightaway. Instead, she sat back down and spent ten minutes preparing her recommendations regarding the Godjan resettlement plans, including rolling out temporary credit accounts to the refugees. The move to a new planet filled with strange aliens was going to be overwhelming enough for them without the pressure to immediately obtain jobs in a society they did not yet understand. If everything went well, self-sufficiency would come in time.

Satisfied, she sent off the recommendations, then grabbed her jacket and hustled over to Special Projects, followed by the Caeles Prism Hub.

RW

NAMINO

ASTERION DOMINION
GENNISI GALAXY

Marlee picked her way down the broken remains of a deserted street. Around a fifth of the buildings remained standing in the Namino One suburb, but ubiquitous debris had coated everything with dust, soot and random gunk. The air was hot and dry; she knew this region of Namino was generally arid, but in the aftermath of the Rasu destruction, it felt like the desert.

Other than DAF soldiers acting as guards, she'd passed no more than half a dozen Asterions and two Taiyoks on her journey. Given that the Dominion remained under active attack by the Rasu, reconstruction efforts hadn't begun here. Between the utter lack of people, the wreckage everywhere and the hot, dusty air, she might as well be trekking through a post-apocalyptic wasteland. All she needed now was a set of chrome spiked shoulder guards, and the illusion would be complete.

Ahead, an etched sign proclaiming the location of 'Mesahle Flight' hung scorched and crooked above a half-broken gate. She stopped in front of it, but could find no working buzzer to announce her presence. After considering her options, she shimmied through the torn gap in the gate.

A one-story building that could be a house or an office sat off to the left, but she continued on to a large open space behind the structure. Several rows of damaged scaffolding were suspended in tatters overhead, while dozens of large crates had been overturned and their contents spilt across a concrete flooring.

Grant Mesahle sat on a cleared-out spot of concrete, surrounded by multiple open boxes and neat stacks of equipment. He was glaring at a large, boxy module he held in one hand. A long crack ran down one side of it, and cable wraps dangled beneath it.

She hadn't quite managed to craft an appropriate salutation when he spotted her. He quickly set the module aside and climbed to his feet. "Marlee! This is a pleasant surprise. How did you know where I was?"

She shrugged mildly. "I broke into a few databases. Rooted around in some classified files and studied surveillance footage."

"Seriously?"

"*No.* I had to drop off a set of Consulate documentation with Nika at the Initiative. She told me where you'd be."

"Oh. Of course she did." He huffed a wry chuckle and gestured grandly around him. "Welcome to what's left of my home and business. Did you come out here all alone? I know DAF *says* they've wiped the last of the Rasu out, but I'm jumping at shadows every time I turn a corner. There could still be stragglers hiding out."

"That's why I brought this with me." She wiggled the Rectifier out of its makeshift holster and waved it toward the street, then returned it to the holster.

"Is that one of the new negative energy handguns? How did you get one of those?"

"There are perks to my aunt being the head of Concord Command."

"Ah. I imagine there are." He glanced around. "I'd offer you a chair, but I don't think any survived. What brings you here today?"

"I wanted to see how Namino looked with the Rasu gone."

"And?"

She winced. "Truthfully? It looks like a shithole. What a disaster."

"Right? They wrecked this place good and proper. Not only my place, obviously—the whole city. Half the planet."

"They really did. Are you planning to try to keep living here?"

"Nah. I rented a place on Mirai for the time being. One day we'll rebuild, better than before. But right now, all those resources are tied up in making ships and weapons and planetary defenses. So I thought I'd see what was salvageable and clean the place up a bit. Until I can come back for good."

"You like it here."

"Namino's been my home for…a long time."

She worked to make her demeanor light, bordering on teasing. "Still aren't going to tell me how old you are, huh?"

Grant winced, letting his gaze drift up to the scaffolding overhead. "It's nothing personal, I promise. It's just…an Asterion thing. Age is not a straightforward concept for us."

"Because of your up-gens?"

"Up-gens are merely tweaks. But sometimes people start over completely. New personality, new skills and no personal memories. We call it an 'R&R': retirement and reinitialization."

"Oh." She'd need to ponder this tidbit later and figure out how it fit into the Asterion mystique. "Fair warning—'R&R' means something rather different to humans, so you might get a strange look if it comes up in conversation. Have you ever…retired and been reinitialized?"

"No, I haven't. I'm stubborn that way, I guess."

Which meant for him, age *was* a straightforward concept. But she didn't push the issue any further. Ultimately, it didn't matter how old he was. While she measured her age in decades, he measured his in millennia.

"Okay. I'll accept defeat." She kicked at some dirt gathered on the concrete. Gosh, he was cute…but 'they' were never going to happen, and his heart-fluttering attractiveness wasn't why she'd ventured out here today. *Suck it up, Marlee, and do what you came here to do.*

"Listen, I want to apologize for the things I said to you back at Camp Burrow. I was going to just send you a message, but then I realized that the adult thing to do would be to tell you in person. So here goes: I was rude and childish and…mostly, I was wrong. You're not a coward. You're brave and heroic and kind, and you looked after me even when I acted like a bitch to you. So, I'm sorry. I hope you can forgive me, but I'll understand if you don't."

Grant stared at her strangely; his lips quirked as if he was about to smile, but he pulled it back. Tilted his head and stared some more. "Apology accepted, but no harm done. Tensions were strained as fuck in that bunker, and no one was the best version of themselves, including me. Under the circumstances, you were great."

"I try to be great under any and all circumstances, but I'm still a work in progress. Thank you for being kind to me yet again."

"It's not kindness when it's true."

Her ears burned. She hoped she wasn't blushing, but she had no idea how to respond. The conversation lulled into an awkward silence for a few seconds, and she wracked her brain for something to say.

She was dredging up a lame question about what kind of products Mesahle Flight built when he abruptly spun around and started digging through a pile of...well, most of it resembled rubble.

He triumphantly produced a spindly, sage-green plant in a cracked terra cotta pot. "Houseplant! One survived."

She groaned, but it was tinged with laughter. "That's a *cactus*! You can't seriously expect me to be older than a cactus. This is in no way whatsoever a reasonable comparison."

"Fine, fine, fair enough." He shrugged and set the plant down on the concrete. "I'd ask if you want to come inside for a cool drink, but the inside looks worse than the outside. Also, the refrigeration unit is broken, so there aren't any cool drinks."

"Thank you, but I need to run. A thousand duties back home and all. It sucks how the Rasu trashed your place, but I know you'll rebuild it one day soon, even better than it was before."

"I will." He picked up a grease-soaked dishrag from atop the stack of boxes beside him and started fiddling with it. "When things calm down a little—if they ever do—feel free to break into some databases and hunt me down again. We'll grab a bite to eat somewhere. As friends?"

Her smile felt warm and real on her lips. "As friends. I'd like that very much."

34

ROMANE

IDCC
MILKY WAY GALAXY
CONNOVA INTERSTELLAR TESTING FACILITY

Kennedy had just finished up a status conference comm with Miriam, Fleet Admiral Bastian (that was still weird) and Devon Reynolds when Noah appeared in the doorway of the Connova Interstellar testing lab lugging a bulky, meter-high stack of Reor slabs.

She wasn't at all certain he could see around them, so she moved out of his way, then giggled as he staggered across the room and gingerly slid them onto one of the workbenches with a grunt. "Ask, and ye shall receive."

"Wonderful!" She hugged him from behind, burying her face in the crease of his neck. His skin was warm and clean, and he smelled of crisp aftershave and the maple syrup from breakfast. "You're my hero."

"I know I am." He twisted around and kissed her lightly. "Now, dare I ask why you wanted twenty kilos of Reor so desperately? I mean, you were mumbling about it in your sleep last night, but in the absence of complete sentences I confess I did not get the gist of this particular desire of yours."

"Sorry. Did I mumble anything else important?"

"Only some stuff about how terribly much you loved me, and how swoon-worthy I was, and how you were the luckiest woman in the world to have met me on Messium all those years ago."

"Uh-huh. I bet I mumbled every bit of that."

He tucked his hair behind one ear, sending her heart pitter-pattering as madly as it had on the day she met him. "You did."

She rolled her eyes playfully, but despite her best efforts to stay lighthearted, the unrelenting pressure of work reasserted itself to dampen her mood. "Fine, I accept your statement, if only because it's all true, but now we need to focus."

"Okay. Still don't know what we're focusing on."

She began pacing around the workbench holding the Reor slabs. "The Imperium double shielding is unwieldy and expensive. Half of our ships can't support it, either because it would interfere with their core functionality or because the ship's design won't accommodate the power generation required to run it. It works for the big command ships and cruisers, which, yes, is a huge relief, but it's not a viable solution for the fleets at large."

"We've known this for a couple of weeks now, though. Besides, I thought you were working with Special Projects to increase the thrust potential on the combat-class engines, so more ships can outrun the Rasu."

"I am. And we're making good progress on it. But a heavy frigate or a carrier is never going to be fast enough to outrun the Rasu. For a lot of vessels, we need a backup plan."

He arched an eyebrow at the tall stack of slabs he'd deposited on the workbench. "And developing that backup plan involves Reor?"

"Yes! Well, it involves kyoseil. There's no technological reason why we can't do the same thing the Asterions are doing: blending kyoseil into the adiamene to create those amazing adaptive hulls."

He nodded thoughtfully. "Did you ask their permission?"

"The Asterions? Hey, we gave them the recipe for adiamene free of charge. I think turn-about is completely fair play."

"True...." He grimaced while playing with the top slab on the stack.

"You've turned into quite the upstanding citizen, haven't you?"

"Didn't have a choice. Who's going to raise our kids if we go to prison?"

His words knocked her back for a second. The answer was 'her parents,' but she also knew that wasn't the point. She told herself *everything* she did was performed with an eye toward Braelyn and Jonas' future. Except sometimes, when the science and the engineering started running wild, it did become about invention, achievement and being not only the first, but the best. She needed to be careful to keep that in check.

She sighed, deflating a little. "Yes, I talked to Advisor Ridani this morning. He shared all the tech specs on their work with me and wished me luck."

"Excellent. So, my beautiful genius, how do we do it?"

"Ha! No pressure. Well..." she studied the stack of Reor slabs "...first we have to get the kyoseil out of its armor. According to Ridani, this simply involves sending a specific resonance wave function. So let's set up one of the slabs and give it a shot."

Noah frowned dubiously. "Don't we have people for this sort of thing?"

"Be careful, lest you start sounding like your dad."

He clutched at his chest. "Oh, you wound me. My heart."

She laughed. "Yes, we have people, but I try to be the person who first-runs a crazy idea. We have to keep being the innovators. We can't get lazy."

He leaned in and touched his nose to hers. "*No one* with two children under the age of six will ever be considered lazy."

"One day they'll be twenty."

"Yes, and then we'll have to go rescue them off some besieged planet or other."

"No. No, no, no, do *not* put ideas into their heads."

"I don't think I have to, though we should consider keeping them far away from Marlee for the next decade or two. Back to the matter at hand: we're not lazy, and we're the innovators. Let's do this thing."

He retrieved a clean containment box from the storage room and situated it on one of the empty lab tables, then they carefully secured a Reor slab inside. She set up a wave emitter opposite it, tuning it per Advisor Ridani's instructions.

Noah grinned at her over the top of the containment box. "You know what this reminds me of? Us jury-rigging up a QEC and a waveguide shield to figure out how to get around the Kats' comm block on Messium."

"See? We are the innovators."

"Yeah. I just remember how cute you were, with dirt smudges on your face and your curls all tanged. Even then, I knew I was in trouble."

She stared at him for a minute. "I love you. Thank you for damning the torpedoes and accompanying me on this crazy life adventure."

"You are most welcome, Blondie."

As wonderful as basking in his praise was, her gaze insisted on drifting to the emitter. "Here goes." She hit the transmit button.

The Reor slab sat peacefully—and solidly—inside the containment box.

"How long is it supposed to take?"

"A couple of seconds. Maybe as long as twenty or thirty."

They waited.

Finally she gave up and double-checked the settings on the emitter. "Everything is exactly right. The Reor is supposed to loosen up around the fibers to allow us to tease out the pure kyoseil. Or possibly the kyoseil melts the Reor surrounding it, with the same result. But we're getting zero response. Nothing."

Noah winced. "So we comm Ridani again?"

"I hate to do that. I know they are so busy over there, same as us. But on the other hand, what if it's a dumb oversight on my part? Or a translation error, or merely a subtle difference in the way they conduct experiments that neither of us realized would be an issue? Okay, I'll comm him."

35

MIRAI

OMOIKANE INITIATIVE

Dashiel walked into Nika's office wearing a speculative smile. The world had stopped being on fire long enough for her to claim a small room at the Initiative as her own personal space, and she was already regularly using it as a refuge from the madness.

She was coming around her desk to greet him when she noticed the enticing expression and stopped short. "What is it?"

He leaned against the desk and crossed his arms over his chest, then took a moment to enjoy the view. She looked gorgeous, as always, in a cream wrap-around dress and a jade necklace. Her hair was growing longer every day, too—more similar to how it used to be before the psyche-wipe.

"I just learned the most fascinating tidbit of information about kyoseil."

"Oh? Do tell."

"I'm serious. This could be huge, though I haven't figured out how yet. I don't even understand precisely what's happening. I wouldn't have believed it if I hadn't seen it with my own two eyes."

"So *do tell.*"

"Kyoseil only responds to us. To Asterions."

"What do you mean by 'responds'?"

"In this case, I mean shedding its Reor armor or adjusting the configuration of adiamene. Basically, responding to resonance wave functions in any manner. Kennedy Rossi wanted to try her hand at making adiaK, so I passed on all the details of the process we'd developed. Only it didn't work for her. So I took a quick trip over to Concord this morning.

"When I was in the room—when I set the frequency parameters and sent the wave myself—the Reor let loose of the kyoseil fibers exactly how it does here in our labs. So I left the premises, and she tried again. No response."

Nika stared at him, gleaming eyes growing wide. "That's…."

"A revolutionary discovery? Possibly, yes."

"I mean, we know it's intelligent. Sentient. We've speculated that it made the choice to bond with us all those millennia ago to create something greater than either form of life could achieve individually. But this would imply…and it was Concord's Reor, correct? The sample had never been in proximity to an Asterion before?"

"Correct."

The office wasn't large enough for her to pace much, so she made do with striding back and forth behind her chair. "Okay, I suppose this makes sense. It's all interconnected, right? While it's difficult to conceive of in practice, there's no scientific reason to believe their Reor isn't already aware of us."

"Are you auditioning for my job?"

"Stars, no." She smiled. "But I always listen when you talk."

"Oh." He…was he *blushing*? His cheeks felt warm with pride. "I'm glad. I realize I can wander off into the weeds sometimes."

"Nah." She fisted her hand at her chin. "What about Alex? She and the Reor have a kind of…relationship of sorts. She has a slab that allows her to read data stored in any other slab and, well, not read our thoughts, per se, but read certain things about us. She was able to see the giant hole in my mind where most of my memories should be."

The casual way she referenced her lost memories gave him some measure of comfort. He knew their absence still bothered her, but she was making progress. He'd like to think he was helping a little. "Interesting. How did she react to learning of their absence?"

"Oh, fine. Alex doesn't tend to get upset about much of anything unless it's in her way. Anyway, I'm curious whether the kyoseil will trigger for her."

"She and Caleb are checking out the Ourankeli system, aren't they? It will be a few days before she can visit the lab and try it out."

"Right. I had forgotten. It won't make much of a practical difference, anyway, if it does respond to her, though I would like to know. It might tell us something regarding what's at work here. Not sure what, but something." She sank against the desk beside him, letting their shoulders touch. "The ceraffin, the Plexes, now this? What is kyoseil, truly? What is it to *us*?"

"I can't say, but I have a distinct need to find out. Damn, I wish Magnus Forchelle was alive. I'm starting to suspect the files he kept around only began to scratch the surface of what he knew about kyoseil."

She fell silent, and he leaned in to kiss her ear. "What are you thinking?"

"I'm thinking that I wish this godsdamned war wasn't taking up so much of our time and mental bandwidth, because we need to find these answers."

He noted the glib, breezy tone of her voice. He'd known her for almost four thousand years, and very little slipped past him. He shifted around to look her in the eye. "I agree. But what are you really thinking?"

Her throat worked. "It's nothing."

"And now it's quickly becoming something. Tell me."

She sighed. "I just had the thought that Steven—your ancestor, Steven Olivaw—might have known the answers as well. He and Forchelle were colleagues, even friends. They must have worked together on the early kyoseil research."

Hearing the name still grated on his nerves; he hated the man for willingly giving up endless millennia at Nika's side. But it was long in the past, and he was his own person, not some ghost of a long-dead ancestor, so he worked to remove any acrimony from his voice. "And you think those answers are buried somewhere in my programming?"

"No, I don't. An R&R wipes out all historical information, and there were a lot of R&Rs between him and you. It was merely a fleeting, silly thought." She brought a hand to his cheek. "And it doesn't matter, because you'll figure it out. I have faith. And for now, the most important thing we've learned is that kyoseil *does* respond and adapt specifically for us. It wants to help us save ourselves."

36

CONCORD HQ
CINT

Malcolm wandered the bright corridors of HQ in a daze. His thoughts were parsecs away, fixated on the events on Pandora, and several times he barely managed to return the salute of a passing officer who recognized him despite his civilian attire.

Her eyes no longer shone jade, but silver. In truth, that rebuke had cut more deeply than her most vindictive words. Her altering their color simply because he'd fancied the jade had marked the beginning of their relationship fifteen years ago; did her reverting them mark the end of it now?

He'd lingered near her shop for almost two hours after their confrontation. Curious neighbors had soon arrived, followed by serious-looking men he assumed were local law enforcement. The two bodies were carted off, and everyone dispersed. She never emerged from the shop. Vanished, again.

He looked up to find himself standing at the entrance to CINT. Without stopping to second-guess his actions, he walked in and asked to see Director Navick.

Richard greeted him warmly as he showed Malcolm into his office. "It is so good to have you back safe and sound. I can't imagine what an ordeal you faced in captivity, but the important thing is, you're alive."

"Thank you." He settled uneasily into one of the guest chairs. "About that."

Richard hesitated halfway around his desk. "If you're here about Mia, let me say that I took no pleasure in—"

"No. I mean, I am here about her, sort of, but not in the way you're implying. If I thought I could pressure the powers that be into reducing or dropping the charges, I'd frankly try. But I realize it's out of your hands and up to the justice system now."

"Actually, I've put a plea deal on the table for her. The terms are...perhaps not ideal, but they're the best any of us could hope for. Crucially, the deal will keep her out of prison."

He exhaled in relief. "This is wonderful news. Does she know?"

"She does. I haven't spoken to her directly, but we've had back-channel communications regarding how to move forward. I'm optimistic that we'll be able to make it work."

Malcolm sank deeper into the chair. "I see. I would talk to her about it, but we're…"

"You broke my heart, dammit! You broke my world. You broke me—and there's no unbreaking any of it now." She wiped blood off her lips. "Leave."

"…not on the best terms at the moment."

Richard looked appropriately sympathetic. "I'm sorry to hear it. Your apparent death hit her quite hard—but this wasn't a surprise. Your return…I would have expected it to bring her joy, but I suppose life is sometimes complicated."

"You can say that again."

"I take it this means you've spoken with her—maybe even seen her. I won't put you in an untenable position by asking you to tell me where she is. As I said, I hope to have the matter resolved soon."

"I appreciate it." He fidgeted in the chair, trying to work out how to broach the topic banging away at the forefront of his mind. He counted Richard as a friend, but not necessarily a close one. And some topics were, if not off-limits, certainly not suitable for casual conversation.

Finally he decided to dive in. The worst he could do was offend the man. "Can I ask you something? Off the record, as a personal friend?"

"Of course you can."

"You're a believer, right?"

"A believer in…?"

"A higher power. A divine entity. God, whatever the title means for you."

Richard nodded slowly. "I am. I got the impression from the, um, funeral service that you are as well."

"I am. So my question to you is, do you have a 'no regenesis' clause in your will?"

"Oh." Richard sank back in his chair and clasped his hands in his lap. "I do not."

"Follow-up question: why not?" Malcolm immediately winced. "I apologize. That was rude. I only meant—"

"It wasn't rude. It's a valid question, and a…" Richard chuckled under his breath "…complicated one."

"Is it because of David? And now Miriam?"

"They're part of it, yes. I've watched them both struggle with the challenges of being reborn. And their struggles, more than anything else, convinced me they are the same people as they were before their deaths. Heart and soul."

"I haven't spent much time with Miriam since escaping from Savrak, but I readily concede that she appears to be utterly herself. And on a professional level, I'm not questioning it. It's not my place to judge the presence or absence of anyone else's soul. But for myself, I'm struggling. Are you saying you believe regenesis can return the soul to the body? How?"

Richard's hands rose to steeple at his chin. "You should ask a priest this question."

"I already know what a priest will say. I just need to talk about this out loud, and I'm interested in what you think."

"I'm afraid I haven't the slightest idea how, which brings us to the other reason I don't have a 'no regenesis' clause in my will. Who am I to question God's ways?"

Malcolm frowned. "I understand the sentiment, but...."

"My degrees are in history, so I've always viewed events through a particular lens. Trying to learn the lessons the past strives to teach us. Throughout history, whenever we've made a great medical or technological advance, there were those who insisted we were defying God's will. Medicine. Surgery. Blood transfusions. Ventilators. Synthetic organ replacement. Cybernetics. Cryogenic stasis. Prevos. Now, regenesis. What is the qualitative difference between the last one and all the ones to come before?"

"Well, with regenesis, the person was dead. Full-stop. Whatever regenesis creates is by definition something, or someone, new."

"A person who is revived via medical intervention after their heart or brain activity has ceased was dead, too. Sure, the body's the same in those cases, but the body's merely scenery when you're discussing a spiritual soul."

"It's...not a terrible point. But given what we understand about brain function in the minutes after death—"

"Absolutely. I don't have the logical *or* the spiritual answer, Malcolm. That's the point. Who am I to draw the line? If I were alive in the 1800s, would I have drawn it at anesthesia? In the early 2000s, at EPR? It seems beyond silly to do so now, but I bet it didn't to a lot of people then. Who knows? Maybe this line we're struggling to draw today will seem silly in another century.

"The point is this: I'm not privy to God's perspective, or their plan. I *think* they want us to grow and develop and reach ever outward as we struggle to become better people who are more worthy of their grace. They endowed us with these finicky brains for a reason, and on the whole we've made reasonably good use of them. What if regenesis is the next step in our guided evolution?"

"Then it would be a damn shame if we frustrated God's intentions by, for all intents and purposes, committing suicide by rejecting regenesis." Malcolm sighed. "It's a compelling argument, I admit. Thank you. You've given me a lot to think through."

"Listen, I'm not a theologian. I'm not even a particularly good believer. I've stumbled so many times that I've lost count. I just try to do what I think is right, for myself and my conscience. Every person's faith is their own, and this is a decision you have to make for yourself."

"I know it is." He pinched the bridge of his nose. "The truth is, I don't need to decide whether I believe regenesis can return my soul to a new body. I don't need to believe it will, because Mia believes it, and she's the one who'll have to accept this new...version of me. I only need to decide whether I'm committing a heresy in God's eyes sufficient to send my soul to Hell if I take the chance." He shook his head. "We shouldn't play God."

"We play God every day. People like you and me, at least twice a day. I, for one, hope it amuses them."

Malcolm couldn't help but laugh. "Valid point. Again I say, thank you. I don't know if I can follow the same path as you, but I'm glad it's there for me to consider." He stood and offered a hand across the desk.

Richard shook it, and Malcolm turned to go, then stopped and pivoted back. "What about all...this?" He gestured toward the viewport on the rear wall of Richard's office. "Amaranthe, pocket universes, aliens, primordial cosmic forces. A lot of people abandoned their faith after The Displacement."

"They did, but honestly, it only strengthened mine." Richard considered the scene outside the viewport, a speculative gleam in his eyes. "There are far more powerful beings in this universe than the Katasketousya or the Rasu, and I believe we've scarcely begun to meet them."

37

OURANKELI STELLAR SYSTEM

HALO RING

Caleb shuddered within the stifling confines of his heavily shielded environment suit. Stepping foot on a dead world—a dead artifact of a dead civilization—evoked primal emotions in him, some of which humans had yet to craft the proper words of expression for. The magnitude of the loss, of all the lives that would never be lived and the tremendous knowledge erased from the annals of the universe? Sorrow panged listlessly in his heart.

Akeso, however, conveyed only a vague curiosity. It recognized no life here, thus saw no potential connection to be explored. *Life once flourished here? I cannot conceive of it.*

It did. An organic species built all this as a magnificent monument to their intelligence and achievement. But now their achievements are gone, destroyed by the Rasu. And so are they.

Then I shall endeavor to mourn them, whatever they were.

After their time on Namino, he believed Akeso now identified the Rasu as a threat—to itself, to him, to all living things—but the devastation here served as a visceral reminder of what it meant in real terms. A day was going to come when he would have to face the Rasu again in bloody, violent battle, and when that happened he wanted Akeso on his side as an ally.

He expanded his lungs and breathed in the artificial air piping through his suit. Alex was meandering in slow circles, taking in the nearby crumbled structures, though her chin repeatedly lifted to bring her gaze to the star in the distance.

A pall had descended upon them both, and speaking felt like a violation. But if so, there was no one here to take offense. "For all the ruins, there are thousands of megameters of metal still standing. Why hasn't the radiation field disintegrated all these buildings? Any idea, Valkyrie?"

'Unknown. I can speculate that the Ourankeli took steps to shelter their own structures from the field's effects, but I do not yet know enough about the field or their technology to venture a guess as to how they accomplished it.'

Alex stretched out her left arm, a large scanner module grasped in her glove. "Let's take what readings we can capture, and we can try to piece together a theory." She gestured ahead. "After you."

Of course he would take point, because unlikely as it seemed, dangers may lurk in the shadows. "Are our shields holding up okay so far?"

'Yes. Nonetheless, I do not recommend spending longer than two hours out in the open without returning to the Siyane *to reset and refresh your shields.'*

"Noted." The ring stretched so wide in both directions that it fell away to the horizon before either edge came into view. It would take weeks to begin to scratch the surface of the habitat, so for now, Caleb simply went forward.

They ventured down what must have once been an avenue, or at a minimum a wide path cutting through buildings on both sides. Nothing but rubble remained on the left side, while on the right gutted structures stood in jagged sections up to around thirty meters in height. This suggested the damage in this area was caused by offensive weaponry rather than the ravages of the radiation field.

He reached down and picked up an ivory shard of metal and shifted it around in his palm. "This reminds me of the devastation on Ireltse after Tapertse retaliated for Pinchu's attack. The wreckage is metal instead of stone, but the destruction isn't so different."

"On Ireltse, there were still people to be saved."

"And we did save them." He reached out and squeezed her gloved hand, finding himself fighting to keep the melancholy at bay. This was supposed to be an adventure, dammit.

They walked for almost fifty minutes, taking readings and recording visuals. They passed countless demolished structures, as well as the wrecks of smaller objects that resembled vehicles of some kind. A few open areas were burnt down to a dusty soil. Perhaps they had once been parks?

'Another ten minutes and you should turn around. Or I can bring the ship to you.'

Caleb sighed; despite his best efforts, the endless dreariness of the dead landscape was taking its toll. "There do seem to be plenty of areas wide enough for you to land. Let's plan on moving the ship when we need to."

Ahead, brilliant sunlight poured through an enormous hole in the tallest standing structure they'd seen so far to fall in a wide beam upon the street. He couldn't say whether the Ourankeli's home had once been colorful, for even in the light, everything was cast in hues of gray—

Thrown into relief by the beam of light, a splotch of blackness stood out against the endless monotone. Caleb moved to the right and crept closer to it. As he drew near, he recognized it wasn't *blackness* as such, but rather a deep yet somehow faded purple.

Rasu.

"Alex, over here."

She hurried to his side, then pulled up short. Together they studied the tiny pool of liquid metal. No more than half a meter in diameter, it reminded him all too much of the pools of Rasu on Namino that had formed after his blades shredded their bipedal forms. Readying to rejoin together and rise up once again.

But nothing remained for this Rasu to rejoin with, and its ability to rise up had been stripped from it by the radiation field. He found he enjoyed the notion quite a lot. "What kind of readings are we getting off of it?"

Alex studied the scanner for a second. "The Rasu emission signature is there, but it's so weak it barely registers at all, though we're directly on top of it."

"Harmless, then."

"I'm not sure even an ounce of Rasu is harmless."

"Still." He took another step forward and crouched in front of the pool, peering at it with increasing curiosity. After another moment of contemplating it, he removed the glove from his left hand and reached out.

"What are you *doing?*"

"What I would have done on Namino if I'd been in my right mind." He extended his pointer finger and lowered his fingertip to the metal—

—a star system so clotted with Rasu they eclipse the star, churning and building and sending out their minions into the cosmos, mighty armadas tasked to search, find, study and consume everything in their path—

—searing heat/pain/disruption we are torn asunder where no response no guidance no order—

—cold desire need must reach must find must think must destroy where try again reach—

He yanked his hand back so hard he almost fell on his ass. He hurriedly checked the skin on his finger, half expecting to see dark molten metal seeping under his fingernail...but it was unmarred. He exhaled in relief and shoved the glove back on. His hand felt cold, numb; while his shielding had provided him some protection, the ravages of space had nonetheless been hard at work in the few brief seconds he'd exposed his skin.

Alex was kneeling beside him, a hand on his shoulder. "Dammit, Caleb! Are you okay?"

"Yeah. I, um...." He tried to scratch at his face, only to be blocked by his helmet. How had he sensed the Rasu's voice? Akeso was the obvious answer; if it could communicate with him, it stood to reason it could do so with other life forms. To his knowledge, in fifteen years Akeso had never done so, but the Rasu weren't like other forms of life, were they? "It's still alive. In the tiniest way, it's still thinking, still searching for a way to win this battle."

"It never got the message that they already won."

"No one won here." He stood, shivering.

This monstrous thing...it calls itself alive?

It is alien in a way few things we have encountered are, but yes. It is alive, and it is our enemy.

It is our enemy.

The remark took him by surprise. Had Akeso seen something yet darker than he had in their brief glimpse of the Rasu's mind?

He caught Alex studying him curiously, and he forced a laugh. "Before you suggest it, we are not taking this thing on our ship."

"No, I agree. Seeing it now, up close, I don't want it anywhere near the *Siyane*." He sensed her shudder through the environment suit. "What else did it show you?"

"I think I caught a glimpse of their home system."

"What was it like?"

He considered the molten pool for another second, then shrugged weakly and stood. "Rasu to every horizon. They're locusts."

"Locusts armed with planet- and species-killing weapons."

"That's not a very pleasant image."

She scoffed. "I didn't paint it, they did—" Behind the faceplate, her attention darted to a point in the distance behind him. "I just saw something. A shimmer."

He pivoted toward where she was looking, his hand instantly going to the Daemon on his belt. No protest erupted from Akeso as he unlatched it and brought it up in both hands. "Rasu?"

"I don't think so. Something else. It could have simply been a reflection of the shifting light."

"Let's take care nonetheless."

Alex armed herself as well, and they carefully approached an area that had been cleared of the larger chunks of debris, exposing a nearly smooth surface. Deliberately so?

Twenty meters into the open area, a faint shimmer wavered in the dancing starlight. It also obscured everything that resided beyond it. "This is functioning technology."

Alex glanced at him, then back to the shimmer. "Is something alive here? Something not Rasu? Valkyrie, I'm not picking up anything on the scanner."

'Nor am I. If this is Ourankeli technology, I do not possess the references to identify it.'

Caleb took another step forward, then froze as through the barrier emerged an alien. It was bipedal, at least for the moment, with four upper appendages encircling its body. Triple eyes floated in a wide band of gelatinous skin beneath a flat forehead and above a single oval orifice, and a barely detectable shimmer similar to the barrier it arrived through enclosed its head. Its torso and disproportionately long legs were almost entirely covered by a long frock that sparkled when it moved—or floated, which might be a more apt description. Everything about the form seemed to flow in constant motion, though the alien hardly advanced toward them at all.

It also didn't come out shooting or wielding any identifiable weapons, so Caleb holstered his Daemon and raised his hands in the air. Alex quickly did the same.

"Hello? We mean you no harm. Are you an Ourankeli?"

The alien vocalized a series of gentle, warbling sounds. They sounded almost like a chant delivered by several voices at once.

"Valkyrie, what are the odds for a translation program?"

'I have no Ourankeli broadcasts or texts to analyze. It will take a while.'

He could feel Alex rolling her eyes beside him, and a thought occurred to him. "Switch to Communis." He took a cautious step forward. "Hello. We come in peace. We didn't expect to find anyone alive, but we want to speak with you, if you'll allow it."

The alien's strange head lolled about in its helmet for several tense seconds. More warbles followed, then a pause. "You speak the language of one who visited us long ago."

The voice was tonally the same as the warbles. To all appearances it was speaking Communis without using a device to broadcast the translation. "Yes! Yes, we do. We've come at the behest of that man. He feared you were all dead and sent us to discover what happened here."

The alien regarded them for a long beat before sweeping an appendage out and motioning them forward. "Come. We will speak."

He and Alex looked at each other. She was grinning, all the melancholy of the setting washed away by the excitement of first contact. He smiled and took her hand, and they followed the alien.

It soon vanished through the barrier. When they reached it, he tested it with a gloved hand. The barrier gave way, and his hand passed beyond his sight. He nodded to Alex, and they stepped through.

Inside, every scrap of debris had been cleared away. A small, marble courtyard led to a two-story structure pieced together from large chunks of fallen façades. The alien continued on through an open archway into the structure, then stopped. Its eyes spun around to regard them without it turning its head, and one of its arm appendages again motioned them closer.

"In we go."

The first floor was filled with what he assumed were the trappings of an Ourankeli home, but few of the items were analogous to human fixtures. A long, cushioned slab along the right wall was identifiable as a couch or bed, and a tall enclosure on the back wall might be a refrigeration module or other type of storage unit.

The alien's translucent helmet melted away, revealing cameo skin that was *almost* translucent and three dark wells for irises.

"You may remove your helmets if you wish. The air is breathable by most organic species, and the Ymyrath Field does not penetrate the force field."

Alex's fingers fidgeted in his grasp. "The Ymyrath Field?"

'I can speculate that this is their term for the radiation field used to damage the Rasu.'

"A reasonable assumption. Valkyrie, why don't you join us?"

Caleb briefly considered dissuading her, but in truth it would make a lot of things easier. He checked the readings on his suit to confirm the alien's claim about the breathability of the air, then collapsed his helmet and inhaled. The air was slightly pungent, carrying a whiff of stale oranges and a stronger moldiness beneath it, but his eVi didn't ring out any alarms. By the time he turned to check on Alex, her helmet was already collapsed.

The alien stared at them, its 'expression,' to the extent it had one, giving nothing away. "You are organics. Good."

"We are."

Next to Alex, Valkyrie resolved into her virtual avatar, and the alien drew back. "But you are not. Is this trickery?"

Valkyrie's voice was smooth and conciliatory. "No. I am a synthetic intelligence, though I am bonded with Alex here." She gestured beside her. "Is this a problem?"

"Not as such. Synthetics are...complicated, but I am beyond harming now, in any event." The alien's numerous eyes settled on all of them at once. "Forgive my rudeness. It has been many cycles since I spoke with another living being. What do you want?"

Manners rarely translated naturally across species, so Caleb wasn't offended by the curtness. "Do you have a name? Something we can call you? I'm known as Caleb. This is Alex, and the synthetic is Valkyrie."

"My name does not translate into common phonetics, but you may refer to me as 'Wyddoniiet.'"

Alex perched against a ridged pillar on their left. "Thank you, Wyddoniiet. Do you know that there's a small alien outside, not far from your home?"

"Yes. It is my barometer. Should the Ymyrath Field begin to fail, its actions will alert me to this fact."

"Oh. That makes sense, I suppose. One more question: the man who visited your people—the one like us. His visit must have been…well, he didn't specify exactly how long ago it was, but it had to have been over three hundred thousand years ago. How do you still know his language? Do your people live so long?"

"Most do not, and I never met this individual. But we recorded his story and his language before he departed. This was all that was required."

It wasn't much of an answer, but it did imply some form of advanced data storage or memory sharing on the Ourankeli's part.

Caleb gestured back toward the entrance and the force field. "What happened here? To your people?"

"We were attacked by the…ah…I do not hold a reference to an appropriate word in your language."

"We didn't have a word for them until recently. Rasu. We call them Rasu."

"The Rasu happened. Ours was the greatest civilization in a score of galaxies, and they brought us to our knees, then ground us to dust beneath their metal forms."

"I'm so sorry. They are attacking our people now, and we're searching for ways to combat them. Did your…are you the only one of your species who survived?"

"Perhaps. I alone returned here, to wait."

Could other Ourankeli be alive out there somewhere? Caleb leaned forward intently. "To wait for what?"

"For many long cycles, I did not know. Salvation? A return of the enemy? My people are not immortal, but with proper care we can live for many thousands of cycles, so at times I believed I waited only for a long, slow death. But it appears I have now been granted a better answer. I was waiting for you."

Alex's lips twitched; the enigmatic ones always drove her nuts. To Caleb, however, this sounded like the best news he'd heard all day. He perched on the edge of the cushioned slab, motioning for Alex to join him. "And we're so glad to have found you. Will you tell us your story?"

The alien vacillated, literally, its skin giving the impression of melting and reforming; its legs lengthened until it was tall enough to sit upon the pillar. "I will recount what happened to my people, to the best of my ability. You can be the judge of whether the tale of our downfall aids you in any worthwhile manner."

38

HAELWYEUR

OURANKELI STELLAR SYSTEM

"They attacked our outermost settlements in the C14X galaxy first, a thousand kiloparsecs distant from our home here. We'd never encountered their kind in our explorations, and the assault arrived without warning. All our settlements maintained basic defenses strong enough to repel any conventional attack, but the Rasu completely overwhelmed those defenses. The first settlement to be hit simply vanished from our communications network. The second one managed to send a brief distress alert before falling silent.

"When our ships arrived to respond to the distress alert, they found both settlements—a series of orbital research stations surrounding two uninhabitable planets—in ruins. Likely the Ourankeli in residence were all dead, but our ships did not have the opportunity to find out before they were forced to engage the Rasu still pillaging the systems. In a matter of hours, they were destroyed by the far larger Rasu armadas. But the battles provided us with our first visuals and scientific analyses of this new enemy. When they attacked our third settlement in C14X a month later, we were ready for them. Or so we assumed.

"We were not a warring species, and maintaining a robust military was not a focal point of our government. However, recognizing the inherent dangers of both space and sentient life, we of course possessed weapons—tremendously powerful weapons. While most of these weapons were housed in massive and thus stationary batteries here at Haelwyeur, in our home system, we were able to send smaller versions with our fleet to the battle. Those weapons performed their jobs admirably and destroyed the Rasu vessels. But, as I suspect you are by now aware, doing so did not vanquish the enemy. While we licked our wounds, began repairs and compiled after-action reports, their ships reassembled themselves and attacked our fleet with renewed vigor.

"Though caught by surprise, our fleet succeeded in disabling the Rasu vessels a second time—but not a third. Only our command ship escaped to flee home and share its dark tale of the true nature of this strange and deadly new foe."

Wyddoniiet extended a fluid, almost rippling arm, and as they watched, it morphed into a spinning fan of flat blades below a flexible elbow joint. "See, we knew a great deal about transformation and regeneration, albeit from an organic perspective." The blades slowed to a stop, and in seconds their arm had regained its previous appearance. "Now properly respectful of these Rasu, we began to prepare a more appropriate response. We captured several small specimens and studied them, applying our in-depth knowledge to gain a fulsome understanding of our enemy. We reinforced our defenses, amplified our weapons and constructed a new fleet of formidable warships. And behind the scenes, we began to develop a weapon we hoped could fell the enemy with some finality.

"When they finally arrived here at Haelwyeur, we believed ourselves ready. We believed we understood the toll the coming battle would inflict upon us and were prepared to pay it. We were wrong, and it cost us everything.

"We mined our outer planets, moons and orbital settlements with antimatter bombs, willingly sacrificing them to thin the Rasu numbers at the start of the conflict. After all, orbitals could be rebuilt. Richer planets and moons could be claimed and harvested in other systems. We'd made hardly a dent in the attacking force, however, when they grew wise to our traps and avoided all structures and astronomical bodies in favor of striking directly at the heart of our civilization."

Wyddoniiet paused, all three eyes settling to gaze at the floor for a weighty moment. "The fleet they brought to bear on our home was beyond anything we had expected, or even believed possible. Tens of millions of vessels became hundreds of millions when it suited them. For every one we destroyed, three more soon arrived. We dared not risk antimatter explosions so close to our beloved Haelwyeur, so we blew the Rasu to pieces again and again and again. *And again.* Yet with each round, they inflicted more damage on our fleets and defenses, damage we could not repair quickly enough to keep pace with the enemy's destruction. The tide began to turn in their favor.

"But we had ruled Haelwyeur for a thousand thousand cycles, and we were not easily defeated. Our loss was a slow one, stretching over many periods, until suddenly we lost everything all at once.

"Protected by their millions of shapeshifting warships, a Rasu vessel of such size emerged through a wormhole...no words exist to adequately describe it. Its breadth stretched for a quarter the diameter of our stellar ring, and the vessel was devoted entirely to powering an array of weapons that carried the strength of stars. The behemoth concentrated all these mighty weapons on one section of Haelwyeur and...understand, multiple force fields protected the ring from the ravages of space and our sun and any enemy who dared to attack it. We had increased the strength and number of those force fields in preparation for this conflict. Beneath them, Haelwyeur had been constructed using the strongest materials in known existence.

"Yet one by one, the force fields fell to the onslaught of the behemoth. The defensive shields fell; the radiation shields fell; the atmosphere shields fell. The generators powering them fell, preventing us from safely sealing off other portions of the ring, and ten billion Ourankeli died in their next breath.

"Our forces could not penetrate the defenders protecting the behemoth. We were unable to damage it, even temporarily. Finally, Haelwyeur itself fell, sheared in two by hours upon hours of unrelenting assault. It was as if the universe itself had been wrent apart beneath our feet.

"We deployed our secret weapon, but by then it was far too late. We'd held it in reserve because its effects remained untested, and we feared in using it we would inflict the very damage to Haelwyeur the Rasu sought to exact. Until the end, we never believed Haelwyeur would actually fall, and in our hubris we ourselves allowed the impossible to happen.

"Only once we'd already lost did we salt the battlefield with the Ymyrath Field. A 'radiation bomb' would be the best way to describe it in simple terms. A bomb specifically crafted to create a subatomic chain reaction that interfered with the ability of the Rasu to take on new shapes and purposes, to join together and separate.

"The irony is, the weapon worked. Not in a single grand explosion, but rather like a cancer that spread from cell to cell, gradually weakening then crippling its hosts. When our remaining weapons fired on the Rasu vessels, they no longer reformed. Eventually, they began to break apart on their own. In the end those Rasu that remained intact fled our system. They had won the battle, but they would not survive to receive their reward."

Alex's voice broke the spell Wyddoniiet had woven like a clanging bell announcing the coming of the witching hour. "What about your people? Were you able to get anyone to safety?"

"We numbered tens of billions. In our arrogance, we did not consider evacuations until the attack was underway. Still, several million of our people managed to escape and flee to other settlements."

"Wonderful! Where are they now?"

Wyddoniiet's fluid skin seemed to sink in on itself. "Perhaps taking offense at our temerity to cripple their kin, other non-infected Rasu chased us down. With vengeance in their hearts? One must question if they feel such emotions. From system to system, wherever we took refuge, they arrived shortly thereafter to decimate our shelters. We possessed no portable version of our clever Ymyrath Field, and our wormhole drives were damaged in one of the early attacks, so we fled over and over again, each time in fewer numbers. When there were only hundreds of us left, we recognized that the next attack would bring our final extinction. We split up and sent scouts in every direction to search for a place where we might find permanent refuge. Find peace.

"Most of the scouts never reported back. To my knowledge, there now remains but a single settlement of Ourankeli. Several dozen, perhaps a hundred, of my people found refuge in the caverns of a moon in a system believed previously investigated and discarded by the Rasu. They hide there now, eking out what meager existence they can create for themselves, and wait to be discovered and annihilated by the enemy."

Alex's gaze, fixated on Wyddoniiet for the duration of his tale, now snapped to Caleb. Her eyes spoke a thousand silent words, as did his in return. They'd been here at this decision point many times before, and no discussion was needed.

They smiled at each other in the way only lovers do, and Caleb returned his attention to Wyddoniiet. "Let's go save them from that fate."

39

ARES

ANADEN HOME STELLAR SYSTEM
MILKY WAY GALAXY

The pale, mossy green-and-russet profile of Ares dominated the horizon as soon as the *Periplanos* exited superluminal fifty megameters distant. Terraforming the planet had taken their ancestors three thousand years, and even today the complex biosphere they'd created hung in a delicate balance that must be aggressively maintained—and it was. With Solum destroyed, Ares was now the crown jewel of the Anadens' displaced home stellar system, and it would not be allowed to fall to ruin.

As they exited the spaceport in Olympia, Nyx noted how the city seemed much more crowded than the last time she'd visited. She supposed it was likely many people who had called Solum home moved here after its destruction, and Ares had always hosted a diverse population drawing from every Anaden Dynasty. But for every additional person now present, it appeared there was an additional garden or nursery to counteract the negative effects of the greater population. The air still felt a little thin for her tastes, though it posed no danger to them.

She, Lontias and Ziton had wasted the last five days running down leads on Phoebe's possible location—in almost every instance the very thinnest of leads—but had come up empty. If Phoebe was alive, she'd deliberately vanished with a level of thoroughness that Nyx could only respect. Let her be.

It was comforting to walk the promenades of Ares with her brothers flanking her. The role of Inquisitor had always been a lonely calling, but maybe this no longer needed to be true. She was starting to get an inkling of what her grandfather had intended by sending her off to collect her surviving siblings. This sense of comradery, of…family was refreshing, arguably heartening. It made her feel stronger, which meant that together, they would strengthen him—and through him, all Anadens.

Corradeo and the would-be rebels had finally departed Epithero, and a new gathering of virtually all *elassons* from every Dynasty was convened at what used to be a vacation home of the Praesidis Primor. Did Corradeo own the place now? Estate regulations were sparse in Anaden society, since so few people ever permanently departed the mortal coil. Perhaps a traceable bloodline had won the day, or perhaps he had simply taken it for himself.

The residence was located outside of Olympia at a sprawling complex situated among the terraforming-friendly scrub brush. Several landing pads were being constructed to the east of the complex, and she made a note to land directly here next time. Beyond the landing pads sat an enormous and most unique spaceship: his command center when he'd led the anarchs.

Ziton arched an eyebrow in the direction of the impressive vessel. "What the hells is that?"

She shrugged mysteriously. "I'll let him explain."

Ziton grunted; he'd made it clear he was nearing the end of his indulgence for the secrecy routine. Which was fine. He wouldn't have to wait much longer for answers.

Several people walked in small groups along the cobblestone paths winding through the gardens that surrounded the cluster of buildings, and to a one they stopped and stared as she, Lontias and Ziton approached. She could practically hear the whispers. *The Praesidis Inquisitors are returning? I thought they were all dead?*

Not all of them.

Corradeo was waiting for them in a parlor off the east wing of the residence. His features brightened warmly when he saw her, and she hurried over to embrace him. After spending all her days with him for years, she'd missed him terribly these last several weeks.

"Nyx, my dear. I am so pleased to have you back."

Behind her, Ziton dropped to a knee in surprise. "Sir! It is my honor to see you again. We were told you were dead, murdered by the Humans and the anarchs."

Corradeo grimaced. "Please, Ziton, stand. No one kneels here."

Ziton stood, looking thoroughly confused, while behind him, Lontias watched on in reserved amusement. Of course, the Praesidis Primor had always demanded kneeling, even from his most favored children. "I don't understand, sir."

"I am not the man you take me to be—but neither was he." He motioned to two couches situated at the far end of the parlor. "Come and sit with me, all of you. I have a story to tell you. At its end, I will ask you to make a choice, and we will proceed from there."

RW

"You led the anarchs? But why didn't you reveal your true identity and demand your son step down?"

Corradeo's lips pinched together, and Nyx saw the strain behind his eyes. He'd patiently endured her own endless inquiries on this topic during their early travels, but he'd doubtless been berated with the same line of questioning hundreds of times since returning and surely must be growing quite tired of it.

But he quickly adopted an indulgent mien nonetheless. "By the time I could have done so, the Directorate had solidified such breadth of control that they would not have willingly given it up, even if they had learned Renato's true identity. Their rule had grown rotten from the inside out, and they had grown mad from power. No, the system required dismantling from the outside."

"So you had them killed." Ziton's voice hovered between a tenor of accusation and incredulity. She'd nearly forgotten, but he'd once been the Primor's most loyal servant of them all. Well, second-most loyal after her, back when she was foolish and blind.

"In the end, it was the only way to free our people while protecting the Humans, the Katasketousya and so many of our allies from annihilation. I mourn for the individuals the Primors once were—people I once called, well, not friends as such, but certainly colleagues and compatriots—but I will not mourn for the monsters they became." Corradeo regarded the three of them sagely, his gaze brimming with both warmth and steel. "So, what do you say? Will you stand at my side and, with me, build a new Anaden society?"

He already had her answer, so Nyx smiled and reached out to squeeze his hand. Lontias leaned back into the couch cushion, spreading his arms atop it, and contemplated the high ceiling. "I've tried to make what pitiful difference I could for the last decade, but I was a minnow in an ocean. Here, though? With all of us and your grand designs? What the hells. Yes, I want to do this. I'd be honored to do this."

"Wonderful." Corradeo stood and clasped Lontias on the shoulder. "Ziton?"

Ziton strode over to the low bar along the left wall and busied himself pouring a vodka tonic. Once he finished, he turned and rested against the bar, bringing the glass to his lips while he regarded Corradeo intently over the top of it.

"I'm still a little hung-up on how you killed my Primor. But I appreciate that, whatever he meant to me, he meant much more to you, so you must have believed you had no choice. And, having been there in the midst of the madness during those final days, I agree you probably didn't.

"I'll be honest. I liked the world the way it was before The Displacement. Then again, it's easy to enjoy the status quo when you're sitting pretty at the top of the food chain. I've seen the same things everyone else has these last fourteen years. Concord isn't so bad, though it might benefit from a firmer hand from time to time. Most of the citizens seem to be happier, which was something I never really considered one way or another back in the old days. But most of all, I've seen the reality that on a grand scale, our people are in trouble. They need you. They need us. I'm in."

40

ARES

Eren watched the steady stream of visitors emerge from the Caeles Prism originating at Concord HQ. Holed up at Corradeo's newly claimed estate outside Olympia, it was easy to get lulled into the sense that Ares existed in a bubble, albeit a high-pressure hydrogen bubble constantly on the verge of bursting from the roiling tensions of Anaden political gamesmanship.

But Ares had been one of the first worlds to receive a permanent Caeles Prism transit to and from Concord HQ (albeit in lieu of an absent Solum). A few steps and he could be right back at his old stomping ground of the CINT offices, as if he'd never left.

But every meeting room, every office and hallway and cafe on HQ reminded him of Cosime, so he thought it best to steer clear of it for a while longer.

He spotted Drae Shonen when his friend slipped easily between two bickering Erevnas to break free of the traffic and fade off to the left, like the well-trained CINT agent he was. Eren pushed off the wall and gave a slight wave to get Drae's attention. For half a second, Drae studied Eren sharply enough to make a lesser man squirm; then his friend smiled and jogged over.

"You look better."

"Thanks to you." He patted Drae on the back, and they fell in beside one another. "Have time for a bite to eat?"

"Sure."

"This way." Eren led them down a wide hallway to one of the delis set up to serve those traveling to and from other worlds, and they staked out a high pub table near the window. He ordered a citrus spritzer and some cheese chips, earning an arched eyebrow from Drae. He brushed past it before Drae added any color commentary. "Did you get my note?"

"You mean the one you left at HQ Medical? I got it. I'm miffed you skipped out on us, though."

"Sorry, mate, but I had to be alone for a while. Felzeor?"

"He saw the note also, and forgave you far quicker than I did."

"I'm glad. I thought you might bring him along today."

Drae rotated his glass a couple of times. "To be honest, I wasn't certain what state I'd find you in. If it wasn't a good one, I didn't want Felzeor to have to see you that way."

"Oh." Eren busied himself with slurping down the crushed ice in his spritzer. Shame fought its way past his defenses. He was reminded once again what amazing friends he had, and how shitty he'd treated damn near all of them in his grief. "Then thank you for looking out for him."

"It was never a question." The waiter bot arrived to set their chips on the table, which they both ignored. "So how *are* you doing? Are you okay?"

"No. Not really." The truth sounded unduly harsh to his ears, but Drae had seen him wither at the rock-bottom of the chasm leading to Tartarus. "But I am trying. Oh! And I got to rid the world of Torval, so that's helping."

"Until he shows up again."

"Nope. He has departed the firmament for the last time."

Drae whistled. "So you finally got proper vengeance. How did it feel?"

Eren shrugged. "What do you want me to say? That I got a perverse thrill out of blowing his brains out? I absolutely did. It was no less than he deserved. But his death didn't bring her back. I mean, I knew it wouldn't, obviously. Anyway, now I'm still here, and she's still gone. And I have to find another reason to continue drawing breath."

"Is that what you're doing here? On Ares?"

"Maybe." Eren finally grabbed a chip, studying Drae as he twirled it between his fingers. "Speaking of finding purpose in life, are you here to come back to work for the big guy?"

"Are you kidding? I have no desire to get within a hundred parsecs of the cesspit that is Anaden politics. I mean, for longer than a brief lunch. No, I merely wanted to stop by and, you know, say hello."

"You wanted to check on me."

"Well, after all the effort I put into keeping you alive, I think I'm entitled."

"You are." He almost said 'thank you' for the third time, but damn it was getting old. He spread his arms wide. "Satisfied?"

Again with the piercing gaze. "For now. I'm also supposed to express well-wishes from Director Navick, along with a gentle request for you to pass along any noteworthy information that hits your eyes or ears while you're at the Praesidis estate. In the spirit of intergovernmental cooperation, of course."

"Of course. It shouldn't be a problem. Corradeo is of a Concord-friendly mind."

"So things are going well with the conclave, then?"

"'Well' might be a slight exaggeration. Things are…in progress. Getting upwards of seventy *elassons* and a dozen *elas* to agree on so much as the color of the Ares sky is more of a pain in the ass than herding a brood of petaloúdas."

"Hence why I'm happy to stay at CINT."

"Eh, can't argue with you there." Eren scowled as a priority message arrived. "It seems I'm being summoned back to the estate." He rang up the deli account and deposited enough funds to cover the entire meal. "Lunch is on me, and anytime you want to reconvene, give me a shout."

"Will do."

Eren stood and placed a hand on Drae's shoulder. "Tell everyone I said hello, and that I'm doing well." He smiled a little sadly. "Lie for me."

RW

Eren passed two suspiciously Praesidis-looking men on the way to the parlor. He sighed to himself; nothing would dial up the fun and frivolity like a bunch of Inquisitors running around the estate. *Diati* or no, he didn't doubt they'd continue to lord their innate superiority over everyone they met, so he'd make a point to try not to meet them.

He walked into the parlor to find Corradeo talking intimately with a raven-haired woman. Praesidis—so much for his plan? When the door closed behind him, Corradeo gave him a casual nod. "Ah, there you are, Eren. Thank you for coming by so quickly."

As he spoke, the woman turned to inspect their new guest. As soon as he saw her face, he let out a pained groan. "*You.*"

Nyx elasson-Praesidis' mouth curled downward. "I could say the same. What are you…never mind. You were an anarch, and he was your boss. It makes sense."

Corradeo glanced between them. "You two know each other?"

"We've met. She once tried to kill me at Plousia. Also Cosime, Thelkt and Felzeor. Oh, and Caleb and Alex, too. Since we bested her, she had to settle for torturing one of my lady friends."

"I was simply doing my job."

"Whatever lets you sleep at night, sweetheart." Eren sat on the arm of one of the couches and threw his feet up on the seat cushion. "What do you need, sir?"

Corradeo frowned. "I had a mind to send you and Nyx on a mission together."

"Not a chance—"

"But Grandfather, I only just returned. I implore you, don't order me away again so soon."

Grandfather? Oh, fabulous. "See? She doesn't want to go. Whatever it is, I assure you, I can handle it."

"I prefer if the two of you work together to handle it. Nyx, I am indescribably happy to have you at my side once more. But the situation here is at a delicate stage, and I need your help to clean up the loose ends which I have let escape my grasp."

"What does that mean?" They both asked simultaneously.

A hint of a smile tugged at Corradeo's lips. "Before we left Epithero, our most troublesome *elasson*, Ferdinand, slipped away in the night. He's a coward, unfortunately, and he knew he'd lost this battle as well as any hope of gaining real power. But out there, away from my sight, he can still cause a great deal of trouble for us and for Concord."

Eren growled derisively. "You should have let me kill him that evening at dinner."

"As disruptive as his transgressions have been, they do not rise to a level warranting summary execution." Corradeo checked the closed door, as if to confirm the three of them were alone. "Also, I feared more bloodshed would have spooked the other *elassons* so early on in this...negotiation."

"I don't know. They were so shell-shocked after I blew Torval's brains out, they might not have noticed one more body on the floor. But I cede to your wisdom. What would you have us do with him now?"

"Concord wishes to imprison him, which is a suitable fate. If you instead bring him back here, I will see to doing the same, though additional precautions will need to be taken. In any event, I leave it to your—to both of your—discretion to determine the best course of action once you find him."

Eren squelched a smirk. Nyx was a killer as surely as he was, and he suspected she could be made to see the wisdom of his preference on the matter. Or he could kill Ferdinand without consulting her. He never had been one to seek permission.

Ugh, now he'd already accepted the reality that he was going to have to work with the Inquisitor. He hadn't meant to do any such thing.

She stared at him in haughty disdain for a moment, then seemed to reach the same conclusion. "Grandfather, tell me everything you know about Ferdinand's disappearance. I'll find him."

"*We'll* find him."

"*You'll* do as I say and not cause any trouble."

Eren just laughed.

RW

MENARIS

MILKY WAY GALAXY

Ferdinand crept uneasily through the late evening shadows toward the address he'd been given by his contact. The man living at said address could create a new identity for him, and with it, a new life for him to inhabit until he devised a way to reclaim his stolen power.

At this juncture, it appeared to be the only viable option available to him. His coalition was in ruins, his dreams of a new Anaden powerbase shattered. Concord wanted him in prison, and Corradeo Praesidis would demand his fealty then consign him to a back-room desk job at best. In the absence of his sworn allegiance, the man would give him over to his Idoni pet for entertainment or, more likely, instant, bloody and final death.

Right now, what Ferdinand wanted most of all was to feel safe. To be able to sleep at night without nightmares of Torval's head exploding all across the walls leaving him with cold chills in a sweat-soaked bed. To be able to walk the streets without checking over his shoulder every five seconds. He had plenty of money, so while he'd have to suffer the indignity of pretending to be an *ela* as part of this new identity, he wouldn't have to stoop to working for a living. He'd simply adopt his new persona, buy an apartment on a properly civilized world and settle into a life of relative luxury for a decade or so. It wasn't everything he longed for, but it would keep him alive and comfortable.

More aliens were wandering the streets of Menaris than the last time he'd visited the planet, as well as members of virtually every Dynasty. The standards here were clearly slipping. Of course, legally any person from a Concord Member or Allied species was *permitted* to visit Anaden-controlled planets, but the open borders were supposed to be a mere formality. No one ever actually did it—or they hadn't until now. His Primor would be aghast to see the rabble that traveled Kyvern streets these days, were she alive to witness it.

Ferdinand turned left at the next intersection, and the shadows grew darker. Menaris' capital city was reasonably clean and prosperous, but the address was located in a neighborhood that fell at the lowest end on both counts. Maybe he should return in the morning.

Out of an alley a few meters ahead, three people emerged. Two Anaden men, one Kyvern and one Diaplas, and a Barisan woman. The Barisan sneered toothily at him, but malevolence leaked in waves from all three of them.

Ferdinand shifted direction to cross the street and give them a wide berth—a clawed hand landed on his shoulder, halting his progress.

He spun around. "Excuse me?"

"Nice bracelet you've got there."

He glanced down at the woven platína chain adorning his left wrist. "Thank you. Now, if there will be nothing else, I'm late for an appointment."

The Diaplas man circled around behind him, eyeing him, or his jewelry and clothes, lustily. "You should give it to us."

"I…what?"

"Your bracelet. Give it to us."

Panic flooded his veins to muddle his thoughts. Were there no Vigil officers on patrol anywhere? Farther down the block, two Anaden men reversed course and disappeared around the corner. There was no one in sight to save him from this vulgar assault.

He'd owned the chain for twenty centuries; it was worth thousands of credits, but far more in sentimental value. Still, he valued nothing so much as his life.

"Okay, fine. Take it." He hurriedly forced the chain over his knuckles then chucked it into the man's chest. "There." He took two hurried steps out of their orbit.

"Oh, my! The gleam of the bracelet blinded me until now, but look at that shiny shirt you're wearing. It must be Novoloume silk." The Kyvern man elbowed the Diaplas man in the side. "You can't have one without the other."

"Carlen's right. We'll take your shirt, too."

"You can't have my shirt!"

The Barisan produced a long, curved blade from a belt hidden in her fur. "This says we can."

Ferdinand began backing away in horror. "I am an *elasson* of the Kyvern Dynasty, and I will not stand for this affront! You owe me your allegiance!"

The Kyvern man started laughing as he matched Ferdinand's retreat step for step. "Nobody cares about rank any longer, you poncy *elasson*. Didn't you hear? We're all free now. Free to take what we want for ourselves."

Ferdinand's back hit the façade of the building behind him. The Barisan growled and lurched forward, her foul breath wafting across Ferdinand's cheek. The tip of the blade dipped beneath the collar of his shirt. "What are you afraid of, *elasson*? Let us kill you and strip you, then you'll wake up in a cushy lab and can go buy some new expensive clothes."

"No, I won't!" He gasped air into convulsing lungs. "I'm not connected to a regenesis server—if you kill me, I'll die forever!"

The Diaplas man snorted. "Likely story, you smarmy little liar. You want to keep your shiny shirt that fucking bad?"

"No. No, I don't." Ferdinand hastily yanked the shirt over his head and thrust it out in front of him in a fisted bundle. "Take it. Just don't kill me."

"Awfully nice of you. This way, the shirt won't get messy from all the blood." The Diaplas man grabbed the shirt from Ferdinand's trembling hand, then nodded to the Barisan woman. The Kyvern man grabbed one of Ferdinand's hands and pressed his shoulder against the façade.

Light from a passing skycar glinted off the curve of the Barisan's blade as it darted out to slice like butter across Ferdinand's neck.

41

TOKI'TAKU

GENNISI GALAXY

The lush forest enveloped Nika with the scents of pine and sandalwood as the carriage sped through the thick canopy of trees toward the Alcazar.

This was her third time making the trip since returning to her Advisor duties, though intellectually she knew she'd made it hundreds of times in the past to meet with dozens of Elders. But surely few meetings had been as important as this one.

After ten hair-raising minutes of flight, the carriage arrived at its destination with everyone still in one piece. As before, an honor guard waited to escort her from the landing platform up the winding ramp that surrounded the vast and ancient tree.

Inside, a great deal of activity livened the meeting chamber. In typical fashion, everyone stood at their appointed station, their bearing guarded, but this time it appeared most of them hardly noticed Nika's arrival. She took in the scene with practiced eyes...the visuals flashing across the screens, the utilitarian dress of those present and their sharp demeanor as they conferred in small groups.

This was war planning. Good.

Elder Zhanre'khavet, however, greeted her displaying all customary grace and formality, bestowing upon her his most elegant bow. "Advisor Kirumase, welcome to our halls once again."

She sank low, until one knee nearly touched the ground, and crossed her arms in the traditional greeting, then rose. "Thank you, Elder. It is my honor. I come before you today bearing a gift for your people."

"Oh? I was led to understand we would be discussing developments in the Rasu threat."

"We are. My government fears that as part of their pillaging of our data stores on Namino, the Rasu learned the location of Toki'taku, much as they learned the locations of Chosek and all Asterion Dominion worlds. They are currently occupying themselves dismantling two of our Adjunct

Worlds, but it will not be long before they turn their attention here. In fact, I believe the only reason they have not done so already is because they have a certain...obsession with Asterions, or at least with our kyoseil. But while it could be today or it could be a month from now, each passing day makes a Rasu attack on Toki'taku more likely."

"My government does not disagree with your analysis."

This was a relief. Needing to convince them of the severity of the threat would've made her job so much more difficult. "I'm thankful you grasp the urgency of the matter. Given the strength of our mutual enemy and the risk they pose to your planet, we want to provide you with a technology we call a 'Rift Bubble.' It creates a barrier in your upper atmosphere that will send any vessel or object that crosses it through a rift in the space-time manifold and deposit it far away. We prefer to send them into the corona of a star to ensure they never return, but you are welcome to choose an equally suitable destination. Your ships will be provided with a broadcast code to enable them to pass through this barrier unharmed."

The Elder's feathered shoulders adjusted slightly. "This is not Asterion-developed technology." It wasn't posed as a question.

"No. Our new allies, the Katasketousya—you may have previously seen us refer to them as 'Sogain' in our intelligence reports—are building these devices. But we used one such device to expel the Rasu from Namino, and we're using them now to successfully protect our other Axis Worlds, as well as Chosek. The Rift Bubble represents a far superior defense mechanism to anything we or you can field at this time."

"Your worlds burn today beneath Rasu invasions, yet you are offering this precious technology to us?"

"Yes, we are. Those worlds were evacuated of people and valuables before the Rasu arrived. Only a few thousand residents remained when the attacks came, each of whom made their choice with a full understanding of the risks involved." The language of diplomacy rolled off her tongue with ease. "But now the Rasu threaten over a billion Taiyoks—the entirety of your species. We are friends to your people, and we do not wish to see such a fate befall you."

The Elder's copper compound eyes stared at her with shining intensity but gave away nothing. "Your words garner more appreciation than you know, and on behalf of all Taiyoks, I thank you for your generosity. But we know nothing of these 'Katasketousya' beyond a few glimpses of their grotesque ships during the Second Battle of Namino. We have no reason to trust them."

If her journals had taught her anything, it was that the Taiyoks were legendary for their slowness to trust. "Then trust *me*. I will vouch for the technology."

"Will you vouch for the Kataskeτousya?"

She opened her mouth…gods forgive her if she was wrong. "I will. They are on our side."

"On your side, perhaps. As I said, we know nothing of them." The Elder drew his wings in tight behind his back. "Thank you for the offer of this valuable gift, Advisor, but we must respectfully decline."

"You…" she couldn't have heard him correctly "…did you say you *decline*?"

"We cannot and will not stake our survival on technology we do not comprehend provided to us by ethereal strangers who fly ships dredged out of the underworld. We will instead defend ourselves."

"But Elder, with what?"

"We possess many defenses you have never seen. Nor should you have seen them, for you have never threatened our planetary security. Rest assured, we will be prepared for the Rasu when they arrive."

No. He had served as the leader of his people and the head of a planetary government for over two decades. He could *not* be this stupid. "Sir. Elder, please. Your military has fought this enemy. Your pilots have died at the hands of this enemy. You've witnessed the wholesale destruction the Rasu are capable of causing in a matter of minutes. We all need to do every single thing in our power to combat them and protect the lives of our citizens. I understand that your caution is rooted in the noblest of traditions, but your entire existence is now at risk. Doesn't the nature of the threat allow for an exception to be made?"

"I acknowledge your words, Advisor, but you have my answer."

MIRAI

RIDANI ENTERPRISES

"How can they *possibly* be prepared for the Rasu? No conventional weapons will touch this enemy—and they godsdamn know that!" Nika dragged a hand through her hair, still windblown and unbrushed from the visit to Toki'Taku, while pacing furiously across Dashiel's spacious office. "Infuriating aliens! Their overblown pride is going to get them all killed."

Dashiel came around his desk and laid a calming hand on her arm. "You've done everything you can. They are responsible for their own fate now."

"No. This cannot be the outcome. I refuse to watch the forests of Toki'taku burn."

"What else can you do? There is no higher authority in Taiyok society than the Elder. If he's rendered his judgment, isn't it the end of the matter?"

Her forehead dropped onto his shoulder. "There must be some way to make him see reason. Something I haven't thought of yet."

"What about the other External Relations Advisors? You're not alone in this."

"I'm afraid we have brainstormed until our brains ran dry." She sighed. "So I'm going to go talk to Xyche'ghael later today."

"Okay. Maybe he'll have insights into the Elder's reasoning."

"Oh, he'll definitely have insights. The trick will be manipulating him into sharing them with me." She stepped out of his embrace, though she kept hold of his hands. "Give me some good news. Have you had any luck cracking our new kyoseil mystery?"

"Which one? Why it only responds to Asterion signals, or why it's blocking us from accessing sidespace and opening wormholes?"

"Selfishly, I meant the second one."

"Sorry, none whatsoever. But it continues to happily respond to our every signal, so for now I'm contenting myself with building a voluminous number of indestructible and adaptive warships using it."

"It's incredible work you're doing." She kissed him softly, trying to lighten her demeanor, for his sake and her own sanity. "Soon, we won't be defenseless any longer. And in the end, that's not going to be because of the Kats, but because of you."

42

KIYORA

KIYORA TWO

The Administration Division had set up a Taiyok refugee center on Kiyora for those who had escaped the Namino siege, as well as for the fifty or so Taiyoks who had been living on Adjunct Worlds. The Kiyora climate most closely matched that of Toki'taku, so the thought was they'd be more comfortable there.

Gemina Kail said the refugees had simply brought along their meager belongings and settled in without commentary, so it was difficult to tell if they'd judged the situation correctly. Then again, Gemina wasn't exactly someone the Taiyoks were likely to open up to, pour out their feelings and hug for comfort. Kiyora seriously needed a new, permanent Administration Advisor, but filling the position was currently hanging around #300 on the Advisor Committee's list of to-do items.

The long, low-rise building in a quiet neighborhood of Kiyora Two was sparsely occupied, the majority of its suites empty and untouched. Whether Asterion or Taiyok, it was a stark reminder of how few had survived the Namino invasion. Nika's heart ached as she strode through the wide, silent halls. If only she'd worked out how to get to Namino and destroy the quantum block sooner, she could've saved more lives.

Xyche'ghael's door was open when she arrived, and she found him inside doing the only thing she'd ever observed him do with any regularity: fiddling with photal fibers and small metal alloy modules. "Setting up shop here already?"

He didn't look up from his work. "No, but when I do, the next shop will need inventory. So I prepare."

"It's good you're looking toward the future. Let me know if I can help in any way with the new shop."

"Your assistance should not be necessary, but I do appreciate the offer."

"I'll keep it open in case you change your mind." She gazed around the spartan suite; other than several open boxes of supplies, she discerned no sign that someone was actually living here. "Do you and the others have everything you need? Did we unknowingly screw up some basic necessity of Taiyok daily life?"

"Only a few non-essential ones. We are doing fine." He finally set aside his soldering iron and turned to her. "I have not properly thanked you for saving my life."

"What?"

"On Namino. I recognize my life was not the focus of your efforts, but I have you to thank for it all the same. Name your boon."

She leaned against the wall by the open door. "I am so glad you were one of those I was able to help save." Her lips pursed. She liked to think they were friends now, but being friends with a Taiyok was a delicate affair. "I'm also glad you said what you did, because a favor is why I'm here. Do you know about the Rift Bubble technology?"

"The device you used to insulate Namino from further Rasu incursions, yes? I believe there is now one installed at a secret location here on Kiyora as well."

"There is. The Rasu tried to attack Kiyora two weeks ago, and the device prevented their incursion. It's tremendous technology that is currently saving all of our lives. For this reason, I offered the newest Rift Bubble to Elder Zhanre'khavet, because Toki'taku is without question on the Rasu's shortlist of places to strike. When they tire of pillaging our Adjunct Worlds, they *will* head for Toki'taku."

"You are kind and generous to think of my people's safety, when you have so many of your own people to protect."

"Of course I want to protect the Taiyoks from the Rasu. You are our allies, and your people have fought and died to protect Asterions. But here's the thing: the Elder refused it. He said he could not trust the Katasketousya and, as such, the Taiyoks chose to protect themselves. Now, I *realize* how Taiyoks take a lot of pride in their own technology and institutions, but they can't stand up to a Rasu invasion without the help of something like this device. As of right now, no one can."

"What you call pride, we call a form of honor—*malu'oel* in our language. It is not a sentiment or a personality trait, but rather a way of existing. Did you ever notice that while we are happy to share our technology with Asterions, we have not integrated any of your technology into our own society?"

"Well, 'happy to' might be a bit of a stretch, but..." she frowned "...no, I hadn't really thought about it. Surely there is some Asterion technology in use on Toki'taku."

"Only that which you bring to your embassy, and it is for you alone to use."

"I don't understand. Is your government afraid our tech will somehow pollute your culture or…?"

"Not as such. We consider you allies and, in our own way, friends. We harbor no ill will toward Asterions or the wonders you produce. We are simply…as we are, and we will have it no other way. If we live, it will be by our own means. If we die, it will be by the same, and we will do so with *malu'oel.*"

She shook her head in growing frustration. "I can't accept that as an answer, not when we're talking about the survival of an entire species. Listen, you've intimated in the past that you know the Elder personally, or have some history with him. So here's my boon: go to Toki'taku and speak to him. Try to convince him he must allow this one exception to the *malu'oel* and use the gift we are begging him to accept to save his people."

In a rare—possibly singular—display of physical affection, Xyche came over and grasped her hands with surprising gentleness. "Ask anything else of me. For this, I cannot do."

She groaned and yanked her hands away. "Why not? Do you not believe the Rift Bubble will prevent a Rasu invasion of Toki'taku?"

"On the contrary, I have seen its magic work. Were it up to me, I would instruct my people to deploy this gift with humility and thanks."

"Then help me convince them to do so!"

"This is beyond my ability. You see, I can never go home. And even from here, any message I were to send to Zhanre'khavet would go unopened."

"Why? I thought you knew each other?"

"Oh, we do. Or did. See…" Xyche eased back onto his stool "…I killed the Elder's brother."

Flabbergasted, his statement rendered her speechless for a few seconds. The hells? Xyche, a murderer? It went against everything she'd ever known or judged about him. Finally she stuttered out a weak, "What happened?"

"The details would bore anyone not immersed in Taiyok culture. I shall merely say that the crossroads of honor, love and betrayal resulted in a duel. Though technically legal under Toki'taku law, they have long been deemed a disfavored, archaic manner of resolving disputes and are frowned upon by all in polite society.

"I won the duel, but in order to save my own life, I struck the killing blow using trickery and deception. To fell a member of the royal family in such a scorned practice meant public shame for me in any event, but to not honor the ancient rules of the duel? The family demanded the legal protection of the duel be revoked and I be punished as a murderer.

"The Elder performed his duty to our people and his family and revoked those protections. Still, he granted me a mercy. I could have swung from the highest branch of the Alcazar, but instead he imposed exile upon me. For life.

"So now you know my tale of woe. I can never return home, never feel the warmth of the sun or the flutter of the breeze upon my feathers. I can never break bread and sip spirits with those who I once counted as closer than family. I apologize, Nika, I do, but I cannot help you."

She wanted to ask him what he meant by 'honor, love and betrayal,' for she'd frankly take comfort from the notion of love making Taiyoks do stupid things, too, just as it did Asterions. But she recognized from his body language how much sharing even these small details had distressed him. As he *was* a friend, she didn't want to cause him further anguish.

"I'm sorry, Xyche. I didn't know, and I didn't mean to make you relive painful memories."

"How could you have known, when I have not told you until now? It is what it is, and I long ago made my peace with it."

"I'm glad for this, at least. Then...can you tell me anything that might persuade the Elder to change his mind? Some unexplored argument I can try that will allow him to preserve *malu'oel* while still using a Rift Bubble?"

"He is a principled man steeped in tradition, but he is not suicidal, and he values the welfare of his people above all. He has seen the power of the Rasu through the reports of the military officers who fought them at their stronghold and again at Namino. Our belief in *malu'oel* is deeply rooted indeed, but I doubt he would have refused this technology if he did not sincerely believe he was capable of defending Toki'taku from the Rasu."

"I don't see how he can be right. They are too strong and too many."

"Perhaps, perhaps not. There is much you have never seen from us."

"He basically said the same thing to me."

"Then I can only advise you to take him at his word."

She dragged a hand down her face. "I'm sorry, Xyche, but I can't do that. Reality trumps honor every damn time, and if things remain as they are, it will mean the death of your people."

43

MIRAI

NIKA'S FLAT

Dashiel watched as Nika wove frenetic figure-eights across her living room. She'd been carving a path in the flooring when he'd arrived, and in fifteen minutes she'd yet to stop. She'd muttered enough about her meeting with Xyche'ghael for him to deduce that the Taiyok hadn't provided her with any easy solutions, but little else.

"There must be a way to convince the Elder to use a Rift Bubble. I'm simply not seeing it. Maybe I need to take a step back and consider everything again."

"Literally?"

She shot him a squirrelly glance on her latest pass around the room. "What do you mean?"

"It's just that you're already taking a lot of steps as it is."

"What…oh." She stopped cold and started laughing. "Sorry. I'm being a high-maintenance mess, aren't I?"

"No." He went over and grasped her shoulders. "I want to help you figure this out. All those ships I'm building? I recognize full well they won't be enough to defeat a major Rasu attack. We need something else, some magic trick. The Rift Bubbles have so far been the 'something else,' for us, but if they're off the table for the Taiyoks…." His voice drifted off, and he dropped his hands to go to the window and stare out at the encroaching night. "What if you're asking the wrong question?"

"I don't follow."

"Assume you have no choice but to take the Elder at his word, and a Kat Rift Bubble is off the table. Then the question becomes this: given the restrictions the Elder has laid out regarding what he will and won't accept, how *can* we help them properly defend against a Rasu attack?"

She resumed pacing, but in a slower, more methodical manner. "You're saying a Rift Bubble isn't the only way. Of course it isn't. They're going to let us send our fleet, much as they sent theirs to aid us. I think they're even going to let Concord ships enter their stellar system when the time comes.

But without a Rift Bubble to keep the Rasu off the ground, it's still a war of attrition at best, and in that situation the Rasu will always have the advantage. They'll keep sending additional ships until they overwhelm our blockade."

"I'm not sure you're correct. The Rasu have demonstrated they *will* retreat once they know they can't win the day. So how do we show them they can't win the day?"

"With a Rift Bubble."

He stepped into her path to draw her into his arms and kiss her on the forehead. "You're stuck, Nika. And I get it, because those devices have been a godsend. They've saved millions of Asterion lives and will save millions more. But they won't win this war for us."

"That's what Miriam Solovy says."

"She's right. But every day, we and Concord are developing more and better weapons and tactics to destroy the Rasu. What if we can devise a weapon, or a defense, that incorporates Taiyok technology? If it also includes Asterion or Kat tech, do you think the Elder will accept the compromise?"

"He took a rather hard line against Kat tech. According to Xyche, the Taiyoks don't care for using Asterion tech either, but I think once his world is burning, the Elder might be willing to bend the rules, given how we're allies. What do you have in mind?"

"Can we start with the Rift Bubble, deconstruct it and build something new from it? Something Asterion in design?"

A new intensity in her expression suggested he had her on the hook. "It can't hurt to try. We have to try something…" she smiled a little "…because pacing isn't getting it done."

"That's the spirit." He nudged her over to the couch, sat and drew her down beside him. "Let's get Hoya Isao, Parc and a few others on a ceraff and see what we can create."

RW

Parc: "This Rift Bubble code is insane. Nika, why didn't you show it to me before now?"

Nika: "You've been busy, and I've been noodling over it, trying to make sense of it on my own."

Parc: "I'm not that busy. Plus, there are two of me. You're a decent enough deriver, don't get me wrong, but you should've brought it to me."

Beside Dashiel on the couch, Nika rolled her eyes. *"I've brought it to you now."*

Parc: "Right. Thanks." Silence fell for a few seconds. *"Where have all these dimensions been my whole life?"*

Dashiel: "Right beneath our feet this entire time, apparently."

Parc: "And above our heads and dancing around in our skin. Damn. I need a minute with this."

Nika: "If it helps, Alex sent me a copy of the code for Concord's Dimensional Rifter shielding. It's based on the Rift Bubble code." She situated it in a new column beside the first program.

Parc: "Oh!"

Nika: "Oh, what?"

Parc: "I'm an idiot, but Alex isn't. Now I see how to fold and unfold the dimensions. Like so."

New quantum functions spun out and spiralized across their virtual headspace. Dashiel tried to concentrate on the logic flows. After a minute he was able to follow what Parc was doing, but only barely.

Nika: "Fantastic. This is similar to what I was starting to explore earlier for...it's not important for now."

Parc: "My mind is exploding with ideas on how we can modify this design to fuck some Rasu shit up."

Dashiel sighed. That was the goal....

Dashiel: "Can we do it in reverse? Turn the bubble inside out?"

Parc: "With infinite dimensions available, I'm not convinced 'reverse' has any practical meaning."

Dashiel: "I only mean—"

Parc: "No, I get you. What if—"

Hoya: "What if we made the devices tiny?"

Nika: "I assume they'll pull whatever crosses their threshold into the dimensional folds then spit it back out somewhere else. But unless they act like a black hole and actively suck in everything in the vicinity, if they're too small they won't do much damage."

Hoya: "True, but if we—"

Parc: "Everyone shut up. Give me ten seconds."

Ceraffin were a much less disorienting experience if you closed your eyes, but in the lull, Dashiel peeked over at Nika beside him. She'd dropped her head against the cushion and was pinching the bridge of her nose, her lips drawn tight. Still insisting on carrying the weight of the universe on her shoulders. He squeezed her hand and was rewarded with a slight upward curl of her lips.

Parc: "I am the smartest man in the universe."

Nika: "No one is disputing this. What do you have?"

Parc: "We make it tiny, and we turn the mechanism inside out. Great ideas, both of you."

Dashiel: "Thanks, but what does doing so get us?"

Parc: "If I understand these gems of equations correctly, the size of the device will constrain the reach of the rift. But considering one five-meter-wide device can protect an entire planet, a finger-sized one should be able to consume a Rasu leviathan. Yes, that's as wild as it sounds.

"So, say a tiny one impacts a leviathan. The dimensional mechanism is activated, and the rift explodes outward like a supernova to its maximum circumference. Then it collapses in on itself, all the way until the device falls into the rift as well, and the rift is sealed."

Dashiel: "But that's not much different from how negative energy weapons function. We already have those."

Parc: "True, but we won't need big ships to fire these. Also, we can't use negative energy weapons of any measurable size groundside, or in the atmosphere, or anywhere near anything we want to survive."

Dashiel: "And this we can?"

Parc: "It's completely self-contained, and it cleans up after itself. We'll want to keep the impact zones well above the tree lines and a few kilometers away from any buildings, but otherwise it should be safe to use groundside. Safe for us and the Taiyoks, not for the Rasu."

Nika: "This brings up another problem. The Kats have programmed all the Rift Bubbles so far to dump out their captures into the center of the closest star. This works because the device is stationary, so the output calculation remains static. But the Dimensional Rifters have a lot of trouble with the inherently dynamic nature of the exit rift, which is why they can't be used close to planets or stations, either."

Parc: "I'm looking, I'm looking...yeah, the Humans are dumb. I can fix it."

Nika: "I thought you said they were smart?"

Parc: "No, I said Alex *was smart. Fine, maybe not 'dumb' exactly, but I can fix it. Well, not 'fix it' per se, but I think I can wedge a static destination point into the code for the tiny versions. It'll only be applicable for Toki'taku, though. If we want to use them anywhere else, we'll need to tweak the parameters, but it won't be too much trouble. With a bit of work, this tweak might even help narrow the Dimensional Rifter problem, too. I'll talk to Devon Reynolds later."*

Nika: "Okay, taking you at your word for now, what does this mean? We can create little rift supernova grenades that will destroy Rasu?"

Parc: "They won't really be grenades when we shoot them out of rocket launchers. More like pellets of doom."

Nika: "Pellets of doom."

Parc: "Yep."

Dashiel: "Dreadful naming conventions aside, this is a genuinely good idea. At a minimum, we'll now have one more tool in our arsenal. But will the Taiyoks accept it?"

Nika: "I think I can position it as Asterion tech. We've done precisely what you suggested, Dashiel. We deconstructed the Kat tech, built it back up and made it our own. But I'm honestly not certain it will be enough."

Parc: "I bet it will be enough if we conceal the Pellets of Doom using a Taiyok stealth wrapper. They have the best stealth mechanism I've ever seen."

Dashiel: "Nika?"

Nika: "Depending on how dire things get on Toki'taku, it could give the Elder enough leeway to both save face and save his planet. Director Isao, can you build these?"

Hoya: "If Parc gets his ass back to the lab and gives me actualized code I can implement? I can build them."

Nika: "Parc, this is all very impressive in theory, but can you really just create working code out of all this?"

Parc: "Not 'just,' no. It'll take me—both of me—at least ten hours of intensive work, and I'll probably need to borrow some people from the Conceptual Research ceraff to help map out every possible branching function. But Director Hoya will have his actualized code by tomorrow morning."

Dashiel: "Do it. Every expense is authorized. Whatever it takes."

44

MIRAI

MIRAI ONE

Parc wandered dejectedly around the spacious warehouse apartment. It was packed with servers and gadgets and his command center and Ryan's machines, but it felt empty. Desolate.

Or maybe he was simply exhausted. The promised ten hours of intensive coding—more 'weaving magic straight out of the ether' than 'coding'—had taken almost fourteen hours, plus another two hours reviewing the code flow and manufacturing schematics with Director Hoya. But custom assembly lines were now rolling, producing the first run of their newest weapons to combat the Rasu. They hadn't named the weapon yet, since 'Pellets of Doom' had been unanimously voted down….

He realized he was standing in front of IkeBot 2.0, and he smiled without meaning to do so. Every day he came home and the mech was still standing here, secure in its rack, was a day that Ryan hadn't irrevocably given up on them.

The smile drifted down toward a frown when he noticed the dyne's chassis was sporting a new, reinforced cover. It hadn't been there…he'd been gone for most of the last forty hours, but it definitely hadn't been there a few days ago.

Which meant Ryan had been coming by to do work on the dyne when Parc wasn't here. He wasn't sure how to feel about this.

He ran a hand along the smooth metal of the dyne's torso up to its neck and around the back—

—abruptly two ocular orbs and a ring on its torso lit up in a cool green hue. He leapt away in surprise, but the dyne remained otherwise docile in its rack. His fingers must have slid past an 'on' toggle. He was getting sloppy in his weariness.

He patted the dyne on the shoulder and left it behind as his duplicate retrieved two beers from the refrigeration unit and tossed him one. They collapsed on opposite couches facing one another and simultaneously cracked the beers open. "What am I going to do?"

"Well, let's review the situation and how I got here. My insistence on leaping headlong into every new hijinks to cross my awareness got me infected with a virutox, arrested, tortured by the Rasu and finally, mercifully killed. It then got the next incarnation of me gravely injured and trapped in the middle of a planet-wide Rasu invasion. It cost me the best relationship I've had in years. Hells, centuries. Not such a great track record this last year."

"*But*, it hasn't all been bad. My hijinks also led me to discover how kyoseil connects all Asterions, thus paving the way for the ceraffin, Plexes, cocooning ships and all sorts of other technological advances. They helped me to rescue Perrin's sweetheart and capture a sadistic madman. They enabled Nika to find out people were alive on Namino, reach them in one piece and ultimately save the planet from the Rasu. All good things."

"True. Call it a mixed performance. So...what am I going to do? Can I give it up for Ryan? Not the hijinxing, though I can certainly try to rein it in to a reasonable level. The Plexing."

"He's worth it, isn't he? And, in all honesty, two of me might be more than this world can handle right now."

"There I go again, deflecting uncomfortable, serious questions with an arrogant wisecrack."

"It's one of my best skills."

"But maybe it shouldn't always be."

They paused, staring at each other for a moment. "Maybe not."

"I'm grumpy, I'm lonely—no offense, but I'm not much company for myself—and I'm frustrated. I'm...sad. Being the coolest guy in the city isn't any fun if I'm all alone. So what do I do?"

"You clasp your hand over your heart, tell Ryan how much you love him and need him in your life, and beg for his forgiveness."

Both of him leapt to their feet at the sound of IkeBot's electronic, affectless voice. "What the hells?" He/they ran over to the dyne, which otherwise continued to stand placidly in its rack, though the green lights remained on. Parc scrutinized the chassis and the head casing. "Why did you say that, IkeBot? Have you been listening to me?"

"Only since you turned it on."

Parc whipped around to see Ryan standing in the entry doorway, arms and ankles crossed. "That was you? I mean of course it was you." As thrilled as he was to see the man here, he scowled nonetheless. "Did you set IkeBot up to record me while I was here?"

"No, you idiot. You're the one who activated it. The last time I was here, I ran a diagnostic routine on its sensor functions, and I must have forgotten to toggle off the routine before I shut it down."

Parc glanced back and forth between IkeBot, Ryan and himself. "When I turned it on, it started recording and sent you the stream."

"More or less."

He/they smirked; they couldn't help it. "And what you heard spurred you to sprint several kilometers across the city to get here as fast as you could?"

"Actually, I was down the street at the noodle shop, but…more or less." Ryan sighed heavily and shook his head. "I'm sick of pouting like a whiny little bitch. I'm not having any fun, either, you know. And you got a couple of things right in your migraine-inducing debate with yourself. Your multiple versions have been straight-up heroes lately. If there weren't two of you running around, a lot of people would have died in a lot of places over the last few months. I can't in good conscience demand to trade my psychological comfort for the lives you saved."

This was starting to sound like a reconciliation. He joined his duplicate in propping against the server stack closest to the door. "I don't know if you've heard, but Plexes are legal now. So if that's what was holding you back…?"

"I heard, and it wasn't. I don't have any interest in being two of me. But I understand why you do. I just need to know that you spare half a nanosecond of thought to care every now and then—"

"Not every now and then. All the time. Listen, even two of me are boring without you at my side. I want to go on adventures and kick up trouble with you. I want to collaborate and invent outlandish new mechs and drones and attack routines. I want to sit on the couch and watch stupid vids ironically with you. I—"

He/they went up to Ryan and palmed their left hands over their hearts. "I love you, and I need you in my life."

Ryan's cheeks flushed bright red. "Gods, Parc, I didn't mean—it wasn't an order or an ultimatum."

"But it was a great suggestion, I believe. Please forgive me for being a thoughtless, selfish ass."

"We're all selfish, Parc. But isn't it better to be selfish about each other?"

"Yes! Let's do that." He/they took one more step, each placing a hand on

Ryan's shoulders. Their voices dropped to a murmur. "Can we do that?"

Ryan's gaze drifted from one of them to the other. "This is still weird."

"Good weird, though, don't you think?" Parc's lips hovered centimeters away—from Ryan's twitching mouth, and from the curve of his neck.

"I could...with some practice...probably find a way to get used to it."

"Excellent. Let's start practicing now."

45

SAVRAK

SITE 2A

Ghorek was checking the perimeter defenses of their hidden camp when a breeze rushed past him. The air was otherwise hot, humid and most of all *still*, so he drew up short, instantly on alert.

Ahead of him, a wave of starlight danced amidst the jungle flora and coalesced into the translucent form of a towering Savrakath.

We must speak, Ghorek.

There was no sound; the voice whispered in his head, yet was distinct from his own thoughts. His heart pounded in his chest, but he forced his stance to remain tall and proud. Many years ago, Jhountar had once told Ghorek that the gods spoke to him. Ghorek had ascribed the absurd declaration to Jhountar's continuing attempts to amplify his image and stature. He might have been wrong on that point.

"Who are you?"

Your people have long called me Galakharno. I come to you now, in your time of greatest need, with counsel.

The being's commanding presence shook Ghorek's composure, though he continued to do his best not to let it show. He was the leader of his people now, and this being clearly recognized his status. But he'd never been a religious person, and if any crumbs of faith had once clung to his psyche, the sea of death and destruction he'd witnessed these last weeks had swept them away. "Whatever you believe yourself to be, Galakharno, the old gods are dead. We have forged our own destiny without them, and we have no need of them now."

You exist only at my pleasure, and you must heed my tidings if you wish to survive this trial and rebuild your world.

"Must I? If you are in fact all-powerful, why haven't you protected us from Concord's vicious attacks?"

Your people provoked Concord into war, and you continue to misapprehend their intentions now. The blame does not fall on you personally, Ghorek, for your voice was not the one giving the orders that ignited this war. But the deaths still to come will fall at your feet if you do not end the conflict now.

"End it? Concord wants to annihilate us. I will do what is required to make them pay for their transgressions." He'd received a message from Concord Command the day before expressing regret for the most recent attack and blaming it on 'rogue elements,' but he'd deleted the message without replying. His people were dead by the hundreds of thousands, and the time for empty excuses was long past.

Do not. This is your last opportunity to save your people, and time grows short. Stand down. Make peace. Your future depends upon it.

Feeling emboldened, Ghorek thrust a hand into the ethereal shape. His skin felt nothing—no resistance, no tangibility. This being wasn't Savrakath; it wasn't even real. He took a step back and snarled. "Peace? How can there be peace when all around me there is only death? Begone, spirit, and leave me to my mission."

The shape quavered for a moment, then lost definition and faded away on a closing breeze.

Ghorek breathed out through clenched teeth. Had he just intimidated a god into submission? No, he assured himself. Whatever remnant or spirit had visited him, it was no god. The old gods were dead.

His communicator burst to life in his ear, shattering the eerie spell the being had left behind. *"Sir, the tactical squad has returned from their mission."*

He pivoted, eager to leave the jungle and its spirits behind. *"I'll be right there."*

RW

The foul creature lying prone on the cot in the medical tent began to stir awake. It was a gangly looking alien, with coarse fur the color of molasses covering a skinny frame and long limbs. A pitiful excuse for carnassials poked out of a muzzled mouth, and two triangular ears jutted out of the top of its small head.

Concord included in its ranks many species of aliens, and for the most part Ghorek had never bothered to distinguish one from the other. This was one of the furry variations, obviously.

The tactical squad had returned an hour earlier, Concord merchant vessel in tow. As ordered, they had spaced the vessel's crew, save one member. The leader of the tactical squad and the captain of the warship both insisted that they had not been detected. After some translation issues, the squad's technical officer had managed to fly the alien vessel back to Savrak without crashing it into any planets or other celestial bodies.

The alien's teardrop-shaped eyes fluttered open to reveal golden panthera irises. The next second it tried to leap into action, only to find itself restrained quite securely. It let out a guttural snarl as it tugged ineffectually at the restraints securing its wrists, ankles and torso.

Ghorek leaned in closer to the alien, answering the snarl with a hiss. "What is your name and species?"

The alien frothed at the mouth, shooting saliva outward to land on Ghorek's collar. He grabbed the alien by the throat and bared his teeth. "Answer me, or die now."

A thin tongue darted out, but the alien sagged in Ghorek's grasp. He loosed his grip on the alien's neck. "Yes?"

"Hohlaak Ponla-min, of the mighty race of Barisans."

"Listen to me carefully, Hohlaak Ponla-min. We have placed a bomb in the lining of your stomach. It is linked to a detonator I control. Unless you do exactly as I instruct, I will detonate it without hesitation, and you will die in a messy and unpleasant manner. Do you understand what I have told you?"

The alien's pupils dilated, and it nodded weakly.

"Good. Here are your instructions: you are going to fly your vessel to Concord Headquarters. One of my men will accompany you to ensure you reach your destination and do not attempt to flee. Once there, you will do everything necessary to see to it that a specific cargo container in your hold reaches the innermost region of the station, where its power is generated, without detection by Concord authorities. You will then take your vessel and depart, returning here to this location. Once you land, we will deactivate the bomb inside of you, free you and allow you to go on your way."

It was a lie, of course—the last part of it, anyway. There *was* a bomb in the alien's stomach, but the alien would never leave Concord Headquarters. Like all sentient beings, however, belief in a chance of salvation at the other end of this trial was what would drive the alien to follow Ghorek's orders and execute on the mission.

"Do you understand these instructions?"

The alien glared at Ghorek, a hatred shining in its eyes that transcended species. "I understand. I have your word that you'll remove the bomb and set me free if I do as you ask?"

"On my honor as a Savrakath military officer."

"And how much honor is that?"

Ghorek bristled. "Honor enough for your purposes."

RW

Dr. Khalik had insisted on setting up a fully functioning lab in the far west corner of the site—or as close as they were able to conjure to one. An impermeable force field surrounded the lab, its sole purpose keeping out microbes and other contaminants. Ghorek was forced to don a clean suit before entering, which seemed far too much pomp and protocol for a single improvised explosive. But he complied, because without Khalik's work, his plan could not succeed.

Inside the lab tent, the missile casings now sat empty. Their contents had been temporarily transferred to a sterile box and the box enveloped in another force field. In the center of the tent, a two-meter-high, circular container with a flat top and bottom sat open. The ceramic composite material gleamed faintly from a new coat of polish, and a glass lid hung from the ceiling above it.

Khalik busied about at a long table stretching nearly the length of the tent, while two assistants scurried in his wake, adjusting settings on portable control panels and double-checking one another's work.

Ghorek finally grew tired of waiting to be noticed and let out a snarl. "Dr. Khalik! We have acquired our delivery mechanism and are ready to proceed. How long until the bomb will be complete?"

"Ah…" Khalik glanced distractedly over his shoulder, displaying far too little respect for Ghorek's authority "…another twelve hours. Perhaps fourteen."

He'd known two days to finish the project was unrealistic from the start, but impossible deadlines kept people working to the limits of their ability and stamina. Nonetheless, he had to refrain from stepping outside and peering up into the sky above in search of the encroaching shadows of Concord warships. The false god was right about one thing: time was surely growing short for them.

"Work faster. I will not ask again."

46

SOGAIN STELLAR SYSTEM

GENNISI GALAXY

The orbital platform spun so rapidly its features blurred away as it sent a barrage of ultra-high-density graviton orbs shooting scattershot into the star on every revolution. Though preparations for this eventuality had begun weeks earlier, urgency now gave purpose to the platform's operation.

The Rasu would be arriving soon.

Watching the endless revolutions of the platform had lulled me into a mild trance, but my awareness stirred as Lakhes swept in from the ether beyond to join me in my observation of the coming gambit.

"Mnemosyne."

I drew myself into a proper presentation and redirected the bulk of my attention away from the platform and toward Lakhes. "How goes it on Savrak?"

"Ill. I fear there remain no sane Savrakaths with whom to entreaty. It may well be time to admit failure and end the experiment before they wreck something truly essential."

"The *experiment* ended fourteen years ago, Lakhes. Savrak is no longer tucked away in an isolated enisle in a secure universe where we can tinker with its inhabitants at our leisure. It exists out in the world now."

"All the more reason to end it. The Savrakaths are our responsibility, and we cannot allow them to damage Concord in any meaningful way. Not now of all times, when so much depends on Concord's strength."

"Miriam Solovy will not allow you to eradicate the Savrakaths."

"Miriam Solovy is not my superior." Lakhes paused. "Still, there might be another way. A way to protect Concord as well as preserve the Savrakaths as a species. I am investigating the matter. Now to you: how goes it in the Dominion?"

I cast my perception out toward the fringes of the stellar system. The enemy shouldn't be long now. "The Asterions have shaken off the blow they suffered at Namino and are, I daresay, rising to the occasion once more. As we speak, they are spinning out new modifications and uses for the Rift Bubble technology."

"They understand how it works?"

"Alex showed Nika how to delve the programming of the Rift Bubble we delivered to Namino."

Lakhes drew into itself in surprise. "You didn't stop her?"

"I voiced minor consternation, as I would be expected to do so, but I allowed it."

"Isn't it too soon?"

"The Asterions need to be able to defend themselves, and it is deeply important to them to do so on their own terms rather than depend upon others for protection. If they can invent yet better uses of the dimensional rifts than we have deployed, we should not stand in their way. Besides, time and again, Alex has been the one to push everyone—us, the Humans, the anarchs, now the Asterions—forward into their next evolution. I have learned to trust her judgment on these matters."

"Nonetheless, it's a risky proposition to do so."

The platform's energetic work faded into the periphery of my awareness as I focused sharply on Lakhes. "Everything we have done from the start of this endeavor has been risky. Is the goal not worth any risk?"

"It is, of course. I only...how have you lived with such burdensome knowledge all these millennia?"

"Stoically."

Lakhes rippled in amusement. "It must have been terribly lonely for you."

"All of our work is lonely. You, perhaps more than any of us, appreciate this."

"Yes, but that is not what I meant."

"I know it isn't. Thank you for your concern, but the past no longer matters. Only the future." A warning tickled at the fringes of my perception. "They approach."

The shadow of a Rasu scouting party broke across the spilling light of the star as the vessels accelerated directly toward the platform. Since being forcibly removed from Namino, the Rasu had been systematically investigating and, where allowed to do so, dismantling every settlement of sentient life they had uncovered in the Dominion's databanks. In a small stroke of luck, solely the most basic of information about Concord had been memorialized in the servers at Namino Tower and DAF Command. For now, its location remained secret, if not its existence. But every Axis and Adjunct World, every asteroid and moon worthy of mining, had now received visits from the Rasu. Today, it was our turn.

And today, the Rasu were in for a rude surprise.

The nearby ether gained greater substance as Tyche manifested beside them. "I have completed my work."

Lakhes greeted their new arrival. "Is there time?"

"Yes. In fact, the chain reaction has already begun. If the Rasu had arrived a few hours later, they would have found nothing but an expanding supernova remnant."

"Come then. Let us retreat to a safer distance, where we will observe our efforts to wreak what havoc upon them as we can."

We regathered another five hundred megameters distant from the star, though shortly even here would no longer be safe. The platform spun faster and faster now, emptying itself of everything it could produce in its final minutes.

When the first Rasu laser tore into the platform's structure, it put up no fight. The metal comprising it was strong, but the structure was built to withstand the vagaries of its stellar companion, not an attack by offensive weapons. Without a solid outer hull, the onslaught quickly destroyed the platform's intricate inner workings, and its barrage of the star ceased. The tremendous cosmic energies generated by the engine at the platform's core exploded outward in a blast that cascaded across over a dozen dimensions.

The two closest Rasu vessels were disintegrated by the combustion, and the cascading force of it sent a third careening off toward the star.

Whether cowed into caution by the blast or obsessed with destroying any pieces of technology that remained and collecting them for study, the surviving vessels appeared to take no notice of the increasingly dangerous agitations of the system's star in the minutes that followed.

"It is time to go, Mnemosyne."

"You go. I will follow."

I sensed Lakhes' hesitation, but after a microsecond both Lakhes and Tyche dissipated, and I was again alone.

Still I lingered until the last possible moment, when the supernova ignited and the shockwave swallowed every Rasu in the system beneath its swelling wave. An avalanche of cosmic forces pressed upon me—another second and I would be ripped apart—and I vanished.

47

CONCORD HQ
CINT

Richard greeted Mia with a great deal more warmth than at their last meeting. "Ms. Requelme, thank you for coming today."

She gave him a reserved smile, as a brighter one seemed in poor taste given the setting. "I won't say it's my pleasure, but I am grateful to you for arranging this opportunity for me."

"I'm relieved to be able to bring these difficulties to a favorable conclusion." He gestured toward the conference table, where a man and a woman, each stern and dour in their own way, sat wearing tailored suits and stiff bearings. "This is Concord Justice General Absolohl Perralle and AEGIS Judge Barush Sarna. They'll be overseeing the proceeding today."

Richard had clearly gone to fairly significant lengths to ensure the 'proceeding' was as informal, private and painless as possible, and she made a note to thank him personally later, once the documentation was signed and the judges were gone.

She nodded politely to both officials and took a seat opposite them at the table. She wore an appropriately severe black pantsuit with a pearl necklace, and her Caeles Prism was tucked discreetly away beneath her white silk blouse. Though she'd reclaimed her name by coming here today, she was keeping the hair for now; it made her feel…free, somehow. And once this proceeding concluded, she *would* be free, albeit with a few weighty strings attached. As for her eyes, well…one decision at a time.

The Justice General opened an aural and slid it across the table until it rested in front of her. "Ms. Requelme, please review your confession and inform us of any inaccuracies or corrections you wish to make."

She forced herself to read it from beginning to end, and in doing so, to acknowledge and internalize what she'd done. The mistakes she'd made. Funny, they still felt like the right mistakes, given the circumstances. Hopefully they wouldn't ask her if she felt any remorse for her actions, because she'd have no idea how to answer.

"This is correct."

The Justice General's grim countenance didn't soften. "Then if you will affix your signature to it, we can move on to the pronouncement of sentencing."

She drew in a deep breath and complied. Informal and private, perhaps, but not completely painless.

"Judge Sarna will now announce your sentence."

Mia lifted her chin—not proudly but rather solemnly—as the sentence was read. It contained no surprises. She'd pay the fine before she left HQ, and this morning she'd made arrangements to begin her community service time working with the Godjan refugees. The lifetime ban on government positions…it was what it was. No going back.

"Failure to comply with the requirements of your sentence will result in additional fines as well as imprisonment. Do you understand your obligations?"

"I do."

The Justice General closed all the files with a swipe of his hand. "This concludes our proceeding today." He stood and extended a hand across the table. "Thank you for your cooperation."

Startled, she hurriedly accepted his hand and shook it, then did the same for Judge Sarna.

Richard saw them out; once the door had closed, he turned to her with a full-bodied sigh. "I don't imagine that was pleasant for you, but at least it's done. Can I get you some coffee or tea?"

"Coffee, please."

He brought her a cup and sat back down at the conference table. "How are you doing?"

"Better now. Thank you for making that as painless as possible. After the way I behaved at our last meeting, you didn't have to be charitable to me. I would have understood."

"It seemed the least I could do under the circumstances. You've, um, seen Malcolm?"

She cleared a sudden lump in her throat. "Once. We have some issues to work out."

He merely nodded like some wise elder sage, and she couldn't help but frown. "You don't seem surprised."

"He came to see me the other day. He didn't share any details of your situation, of course. He wanted to talk about a personal matter. But I gathered from what wasn't said…. Anyway, it's none of my business. But I do wish you both well. The Savrakaths wreaked a lot of destruction with their thoughtless actions, but none so unfortunate as what they did to the two of you."

"You're not wrong." A pang of sorrow echoed through her chest, and she breathed in deliberately until it faded to the background. Then she reached into the bag she'd set on the floor, retrieved a tiny quantum cube and slid it over to him. "This is for you."

"What's on it?"

"Aiden Trieneri had a son he kept secret. I assume Olivia Montegreu didn't know about him, or else she'd have killed him not long after she killed his father. The boy was only around nine years old at the time of his father's death. Now, he goes by the name Enzio Vilane. His public business is as a real estate mogul on Pandora and, to a lesser extent, several other colonies, where he owns dozens of apartment complexes and retail and restaurant space. Behind the scenes, however, he's building a new criminal organization, informally known as the Rivinchi cartel.

"They already have a stranglehold on the retail business sector in The Approach, and presumably in other neighborhoods as well. I expect their reach also extends into other criminal arenas, but I don't have definitive knowledge or proof of it. Though he's personally charming, he's not averse to using extreme violence to achieve his ends, whatever they may be. Oh, and he's also a Prevo, as are many of the Rivinchi cartel members. That cube contains all the information Meno and I were able to gather on him and his activities. I thought you could put it to good use."

"I admit, this is news to me. How is it possible we never knew of his existence?"

"No official records tie Vilane to Trieneri, only a labyrinthine trail of money for his education. But he effectively confirmed his heritage to me when I challenged him on it."

Richard leaned forward, concern darkening his features. "What sort of interactions did you have with this man?"

"Pleasant ones, at first. Then, not so much."

"I see. I can't pretend to be surprised you survived those encounters with the upper hand, but people of this ilk aren't to be trifled with."

"Believe me, I understand that. It's only one reason I'm glad to be rid of Pandora."

"Well, I can definitely put this information to good use. Do you know who his mother is?"

"There's none on record, nor was there any trail that might lead to one."

"Interesting. Do you think he's a vanity baby?"

She considered the question. "People can alter their appearances a fair amount these days. But while he favors Aiden Trieneri, he doesn't look like a clone. Fairer complexion, slighter build."

"Trieneri probably used an anonymous DNA donor." Richard stared at the cube, then at her. "Listen, if your information pans out, this could warrant a partial commutation of your sentence. A reduction in the amount of the fine and number of hours of community service, at a minimum."

"But not a weakening of the ban on holding government positions?"

He shook his head. "I'm sorry. Both governments have indicated their intransigence on that point."

"I figured."

"Do you want me to get Justice General Perralle and Judge Sarna back in here to review—?"

"No, it's not necessary. I wasn't trying to negotiate…the information is yours to use as you see fit."

"All right. If you're sure." He set the cube to the side. "What are you going to do now? If you don't mind me asking."

Her gaze drifted to the tableau outside the viewport. It was good to be back at HQ. The sentencing was done, the ordeal endured, and she was still on her feet. It was time to move forward.

"I'm a survivor, but it appears I have some lessons to learn about navigating this world the proper way. I'm going to go piece my life back together and see if I can make something new of it. Speaking of which, is your husband available to chat for a few minutes?"

Richard blinked. "You want to talk to Will?"

"If it's permissible."

"Of course—I mean, it's absolutely permissible. You merely caught me by surprise. Um…given the nature of today's meeting, can I ask what it's regarding?"

"Nothing involving law enforcement, past or future crimes or prison sentences, I promise. I only want to float the idea of a little side project by him and see if he might be willing to help me with it."

RW

After Will arrived and escorted Mia off to discuss her 'side project,' Richard considered the tiny cube sitting at his fingertips. The ghosts of the past never stayed dead for too long, did they?

Without thinking overly hard about it, he sent a livecomm request.

Graham Delavasi answered it from his boat, a beer in one hand and a fishing pole in the other. The forested mountains swayed like shamrocks behind him amid a clear midday sky.

"Richard! Are you comming me to arrange another visit?"

"I wish. Soon, if I have my druthers. First, though, I've got a tip I'd appreciate your help with in running to ground."

"But I'm—"

"Fishing. I know. But trust me, my friend, you want in on this one."

48

SIYANE

BEYOND THE BOUNDARIES OF CONCORD SPACE

Wyddoniiet glided around the cabin of the *Siyane* like a specter given physical form. Rotating eyes took in machinery and furniture that must look as strange to them as theirs had to her and Caleb. After a full visual tour, they dismissed their surroundings to drift toward the cockpit.

The alien wasn't so incomprehensible as the average Efkam, but they were damn close. Of course, Alex had no reason to believe Wyddoniiet was a good representation of the Ourankeli species. The psychological trauma of seeing your civilization destroyed, followed by centuries of running in constant fear, followed by yet more centuries of forced isolation, would damage any sentient being's psyche, and possibly their sanity.

"Your synthetic companion. Where has it gone?"

'I am in the ship now.'

Much as every visitor before them, upon hearing Valkyrie's disembodied voice emerge from the ship for the first time, Wyddoniiet's multi-faceted gaze flitted to the ceiling and swept across the walls. "Strange."

Alex shrugged as she checked over the system readouts to triple-confirm the *Siyane* hadn't suffered any damage from the Ymyrath Field. "In many ways, Valkyrie *is* the ship. A copy of her hardware resides within its hull. But she's also much, much more than the ship."

"Your people coexist peacefully with synthetics, then?"

"We do."

"Interesting. Not many species reach such an advanced stage of evolution."

How many species had the Ourankeli watched rise and fall across the millennia? She'd never thought of accepting synthetics as a matter of evolution, but rather one of refined societal advancement. But if it was a stage virtually every species encountered, then perhaps the description wasn't far off. She found she liked the idea, if only because it put them further ahead in the evolution game than their elder Anaden cousins. Also, she took no small pleasure from impressing their reticent alien guest.

His own checks complete, Caleb spun his chair around to direct his attention to Wyddoniiet. "You said your people are hiding in a system they believe the Rasu have already pillaged and moved on from?"

"Yes. After fleeing for so long, this group elected to circle back. Rasu clog our galaxy cluster now, but they are not everywhere. As they are fundamentally scavengers, not every stellar system holds resources worth dismantling and confiscating."

Alex frowned. "I've never thought of them as scavengers."

"They take what belongs to others and repurpose it to their needs."

"But they're not going through people's *garbage.* They're razing entire civilizations, then stripping away everything the civilization had built. That's not scavenging, it's...marauding?"

Wyddoniiet waved an appendage toward the viewport. "A matter of semantics, one supposes."

She shot Caleb a squirrelly look. She really should be used to even the quirkiest aliens by now; she'd spent plenty of time around her fair share of them.

'Based on the information Wyddoniiet provided, I have identified the stellar system in question with a ninety-two percent likelihood.'

"Good job, Valkyrie. Are we ready to wormhole in?"

Wyddoniiet's face drew in tight. "I do not know what we will find when we arrive. It has been almost two centuries since I last made contact with those who settled there."

Caleb projected a confident demeanor for their guest. "We'll stealth as soon as we exit the wormhole."

"What makes you believe your stealth technology will defeat the Rasu's scanners?"

"Oh, we've tested it quite thoroughly against them. It'll hold, and we'll be able to assess the situation in relative safety."

"Safety is not a concept that has meaning for my people any longer."

Melodramatic much? At least she turned away before she rolled her eyes. "Let's just see what we find when we get there. Valkyrie, whenever you're ready."

'Prepare for wormhole traversal.'

The Caeles Prism burned out a tear in space in front of the *Siyane.* The Ourankeli might have been impressed for the second time in five minutes, judging by the quiet noise that escaped their constantly shifting mouth. Or maybe not.

The system they exited into hosted a K1 IV star and little else. A roasting tidally locked planet orbiting at a snug 0.05 AU, a captured gas giant at 2.6 AU, and a rocky planetoid devoid of any atmosphere at 0.7 AU. The last one was their destination.

Alarms began ringing when they were fifty megameters out from the planetoid. 'Rasu signatures detected in the area.'

"Goddammit!" Alex stood and slipped past the hovering Ourankeli to pace in agitation through the cabin. "What are the odds of them showing up here at this moment, right the fuck when we arrive?"

The Ourankeli's fluid body seemed to deflate, shrinking in on itself. "They have pursued us across the stars for centuries. It was always inevitable that they would find us yet again. The only question is whether we have arrived at the end of their massacre, or the beginning."

RW

Four Rasu cruiser-style vessels circled the planetoid, firing their violet beams at the surface in a systematic pattern. It appeared they intended to burn through the exposed crust until they reached the Ourankeli hiding beneath the surface.

Alex glanced over her shoulder to find Wyddoniiet vibrating behind her chair. "What kind of protection do they have in there?"

"The settlement is almost wholly self-contained. Small vents chiseled through the crust to the surface expel what gases and refuse they cannot recycle. A single hidden entry exists, in the form of a door crafted out of the bedrock itself. It is controllable only from the inside. The Rasu have not detected it, else they would have concentrated all their fire on its location, burned the door away and entered the settlement with all due speed."

Caleb nodded grimly, though his eyes danced with intensity. "Then we can still save your people."

"You are a single, tiny ship facing untold megatons of Rasu weaponry."

Alex snorted. "A single tiny ship with four 7,000-kilotonne equivalent negative energy missiles ready to launch. Four missiles, four Rasu cruisers."

Despite her bravado, Caleb winced. He wasn't convinced, either. "The damage spread from a single missile isn't wide enough to completely destroy one of those ships, is it?"

Alex glared out the viewport and let Valkyrie answer.

'If the Rasu vessels maintain the approximate size and shape they currently display, I estimate detonation by all four missiles will result in seventy-three percent destruction of Rasu material.'

"And the remaining twenty-seven percent will then reform and continue shooting." Alex gave up pouting, conceded the point and started studying the incoming scans of the vessels. "If we aim the missiles at their weapons assemblies, whatever Rasu material that's left won't be able to shoot. Remember, those crystal weapons of theirs aren't Rasu."

"True. But as soon as that door opens to let us in, they can still transform and flood the settlement."

For a second, she almost wished Caleb would return to being detached and distracted, but she hurriedly banished the thought. Hopefully the shame she felt at having entertained it didn't show on her face. It was beyond wonderful to have him back—really back. Besides, he was right, and in her world reality always won out.

She offered him a chagrined smile. "Good point. Give me a minute to work on this."

But it didn't take nearly so long, as inspiration flared and took shape in her mind. "Wyddoniiet, do you know how to recreate the radiation bomb your people used on the Rasu? The Ymyrath Field?"

"I know the formula underlying its design, but building it took us months and thousands of workers."

"We don't need a big one. Merely one powerful enough to disrupt the functionality of these four Rasu for, say, a few hours."

"You will not have on hand the materials required."

Yep, the arrogant ones still annoyed the hell out of her. "You might be surprised. Caleb, what do you think?"

"You want to pull something like what we did to the superdreadnought factory in the portal space, don't you?"

She flashed him a grin; she adored how he never needed for her to explain what she was thinking. "If Wyddoniiet can tell us how to recreate the bomb, can you rig one of our probes to deliver it?"

His grin was far closer to a smirk, of course. "You know I can."

"I do. Valkyrie, pull us back another twenty megameters to be safe, so we can work without worrying about catching errant fire." She stood and went to the data center table, where she opened a new file. "Tell us about the radiation bomb."

"In the simplest terms, it was similar to a neutron bomb."

"That's not very high tech."

The alien fixed three eyes on her. Oh no, were they offended? Turnabout was fair play. "The more advanced and comfortable a civilization becomes, the more likely it is to neglect the most basic rules of chemistry. Of physics. Of existence. The concept behind the Ymyrath Field relies on those basic concepts. The design and delivery, however, were most elegant."

"I'm sure they were, but today I don't care about elegance. Why a neutron bomb?"

"I stated it was *similar* to a neutron bomb. The details of the device were extremely complicated."

"In addition to being elegant? Sounds like quite a weapon indeed." Caleb choked off a laugh, but her sarcasm was lost on their guest, who simply stared at her. Did they have eyelids? They never seemed to blink. "Okay, why something *similar* to a neutron bomb?"

"It was deemed the most effective way to create rapid but subtle—thus possibly unnoticed—radiation damage across the largest region of material. In particular, the radiation damage it caused was deliberately potent in increasing the number of dislocation loops in the Rasu's atomic makeup, thereby disrupting their resonance hybrid structures—"

"Resonance? Oh, never mind, you mean *chemical* resonance. Go on."

"A sufficient concentration—"

"Wait a minute. The Rasu operate almost entirely in space, so far as we've seen. They must have protective measures to deal with all manner of ionizing radiation."

"Indeed they must. But neutron-based radiation would not be high on their list of threats, so long as they stayed outside of a star's corona and didn't attack a nuclear-capable civilization prepared to destroy its own world in order to defeat the enemy. We played the odds."

"Fair enough. Please continue."

Did the alien sigh? It looked like they sighed. "As I was saying, a sufficient concentration of dislocation loops induced radical plasticity in the Rasu. Once deformed, they could not reform." Wyddoniiet's eyes swirled around. "Now that I have informed you of the bomb's nature, I assume you cannot manufacture such a device on this ship in the next hour."

Valkyrie?

I am intensely curious about the details, but the science is theoretically sound.

We get these people rescued, and I guarantee one of them can give us a full download on the weapon. But seeing as we don't have those details at the moment, what do you think? Will a basic neutron bomb accomplish the same result?

For a short period—several hours, perhaps as long as a day—I believe it should.

'Should' wasn't an overly strong endorsement from Valkyrie, but it was what they had. "Oh, but we can." She spun to Caleb. "The old He3 LEN fusion reactor that used to power the ship's internal systems. We retired it when we installed the Zero Drive, but I kept it in storage in case the Zero Drive didn't live up to expectations.

"If we strip off the protective enclosure, which we'll need to do to allow the neutron radiation to escape, I think we can fit it inside one of the probe casings, then wire it to turn on remotely. It'll be sloppy and I'm *sure* a pale imitation of the Ourankeli's Ymyrath Field..." she arched an eyebrow, but Wyddoniiet remained oblivious "...but I bet it will get the job done for long enough for us to get everyone out and escape."

Caleb nodded sharply. "I'm on it. Any other special rewiring I'll need to do?"

"Almost certainly, but Valkyrie will walk you through it. I'm going to work out the logistics of our little staged battle here."

RW

Caleb emerged from the engineering well coated in a layer of sweat from working in an environment suit for safety reasons, his hair a rumpled mess. But he looked inordinately pleased with himself and all the more handsome for it. "Done and loaded into a launch bay. We'll have to reload one of the negative energy missiles once we fire the probe."

"We'll have time to reload, as we'll want to give the bomb a few minutes to do its work before we start firing." When he got to the cockpit, she reached up and wiped a smudge of grease off his cheek. "Thank you."

"Always." He collapsed into his chair and took a swig of the water he'd grabbed on the way. "Are we ready? We should get it launched quickly, before it irradiates the ship."

She shuddered at the thought. "Closing to four megameters from the planetoid's surface."

The Ourankeli agitated behind them. "When your makeshift bomb detonates, won't the radiation degrade the hull of your ship as well?"

"It will not. I'm skeptical that it would affect adiamene—the extraordinary metal comprising our hull—but in any event, the Dimensional Rifter will collect any radiation to blow our way."

"You are so confident in your technological marvels. We were like you once."

Caleb's hand landed on her knee before she could voice the retort that was priming on her lips. She gritted her teeth instead. "We'll be fine."

The ship slowed to drift above the pock-marked remains of the planetoid, and the Rasu attackers came into full view to their starboard. "No time to waste. Launching the probe in 3…2…1…launch."

The tiny probe shot out from beneath the *Siyane* and sped to its targeted location dead center of the four Rasu vessels. It was too small to draw any attention, and it reached its target and exploded without fanfare.

The explosion was hardly big enough for the Rasu to notice, either, and they seemed to pay it no mind. "Valkyrie, confirm detonation of the payload."

'Scanning. Confirmed. I am detecting drastically increased levels of neutron radiation in the area.'

Caleb leapt up and headed back downstairs. "Give me two minutes to reload the bay."

The Rasu abruptly stopped firing on the planetoid. All four vessels pivoted and spread their formation out. They, too, had detected the increase in radiation. She shouted over her shoulder. "Better make it ninety seconds. They're getting twitchy already."

He vaulted back up the stairs eighty seconds later. "Go."

Unfortunately, in the intervening time the Rasu had spread out enough that this wasn't going to be the straightforward 'aim and fire' scenario she'd mocked up. As soon as one of her missiles hit the first ship, they would realize an armed enemy was in the immediate vicinity. The *Siyane* should be invisible to their scans, but the Rasu could reverse-calculate trajectories as well as anyone, so she'd need to move fast.

In her head, Valkyrie supplied an ideal trajectory from one target to the next. It might even work.

She positioned the *Siyane* as close to the first Rasu as she dared, barely staying outside the projected blast radius. "Firing the first missile."

Two seconds later, a frothing globule of pure void ballooned out from the crystal weapons assembly, obliterating the center mass of the Rasu vessel and sending the rest careening away.

Right on cue, the other three vessels instantly moved into a defensive formation. They shifted in three different directions, each adopting a frankly ingenious spin that made the weapons assemblies almost impossible to hit.

Only almost.

She chuckled under her breath. The wafer-thin line between her and Valkyrie blurred and vanished as together they maneuvered, aimed and fired. The weapons assembly on the second Rasu slid into the crosshairs, and she fired. Perfect strike. Five seconds later, the core of the third Rasu crumbled as well.

A violet beam shot toward them; the *Siyane* lurched to port and dove at a thirty-degree angle under their combined, instantaneous control, and the beam missed by an easy hundred meters.

The final vessel fired a second time, which they more easily evaded, then made to flee. She was tempted to let it go….

Caleb shook his head in her peripheral vision. "We can't risk it returning while we're evacuating the settlement."

"Right. Impulse power it is." The modified Zero Drive meant full impulse power was fast, and the Rasu vessel wasn't fleeing at full speed. Instead, space in front of the alien ship began to contort. It churned in on itself until a bright vortex swirled around an *absence* of space, falling into it like water circling a drain, yet never dissipating.

"And we *definitely* don't want it reporting back home."

"No, we do not." She fired. The center of the vessel disintegrated, and the forming wormhole petered out and died.

Chunks of Rasu now littered the region above the planetoid, drifting and powerless. A few pieces tried to stretch and morph, only to fail. Assuming their improvised bomb had done its job well enough, they wouldn't be reforming for several hours.

"Nice weapon you've got there, Wyddoniiet. Now, how do we get this hidden door open?"

PART IV

...NOW IS FOUND

49

MIRAI

OMOIKANE INITIATIVE

Thanks to the placement of sensitive long-range scanners along the outer reaches of every system in the Gennisi galaxy that held valuable allies or assets, Lance Palmer knew the Rasu were incoming to Toki'taku before the Taiyoks did.

The constant and relentless Rasu probing of their defenses had set everyone's nerves on permanent edge, and when an alarm rang out in the DAF suite at the Initiative, in seconds a cadre of Advisors and military officers came running. Frantic questions from the Advisors overlapped with orders from the officers, and chaos took hold.

Lance shouted over the sudden clamor. "Everyone, shut it for five seconds! The situation is this: a Rasu armada is on approach to Toki'taku. We've been expecting this eventuality, and we have prepared for it. I'm issuing an order now to implement Scenario 2B. Brigadier Johansson, you have command of DAF operations at the Initiative. Advisors, direct your questions to Johansson." His gaze swept across his lieutenants, his expression grim. "Everyone else, to your ships. Now."

Today, the Rasu weren't coming for them. But they were coming for the Taiyoks, and in these games of war, the military distinction was irrelevant. He passed on the warning to Elder Zhanre'khavet on his way out of the suite, then ordered the DAF fleet to the Toki'taku system before receiving a formal request for assistance.

Next, he stopped by the top floor long enough to confirm that Nika was nowhere in sight. Last he'd heard, she was working on some sort of plan to save the Taiyoks from their own stubbornness, so he sent her a message alerting her to the fact that the battle was about to be joined. Then he strode through the d-gate to the DAF orbital docks and headed for the *Dauntless*.

RW

ADV DAUNTLESS

TOKI'TAKU STELLAR SYSTEM

The Asterion fleet dropped out of superluminal above Toki'taku a scant few seconds before a menacing wave of Rasu ships closed in on the planet. The sight of so many of the metal shapeshifters arrayed in a purposeful attack formation sent a chill through Lance's bones. Considering they'd already killed him once, it probably always would.

He drew in a sharp breath and immediately went to work.

Commander Palmer (TT Mission Channel): "All DAF vessels, execute on Scenario 2B, extra-planetary engagement only. Fire at will."

As the viewport exploded in laser fire and shadowy missile trails, he sent a private communication.

Commandant Solovy, you and your fleets are cordially invited to a Rasu engagement in the Gennisi galaxy, Toki'taku stellar system.

The response arrived promptly, as was her way. *The Taiyok planet? Are they amenable to our assistance?*

If they aren't now, they will be by the time you get here. Just keep your ships in space. Trust me, they'll have plenty to do there.

Understood. First wave ETA is...fifty-two minutes.

This was the first real battle test for Lance's new and improved fleet, and now they had a clear goal: keep the Rasu off the planet below for fifty-two minutes.

His ships had barely begun to engage the enemy when a full brigade of Taiyok warships breached the outer atmosphere, weapons firing. So they'd have some help. The Taiyok vessels were light, fast and incredibly agile, but they were not indestructible and their crews were not immortal.

The Taiyoks did not lack for bravery, however, and they comprehended the mission, the risks and the consequences if they failed. So Lance needed to let the Taiyoks do their thing and focus on his fleet's performance—including his own new ship. As command vessels went, it would be dwarfed by the Concord dreadnoughts when they arrived, but unlike them, his ship didn't need a crew of thousands to operate it. To do his job, he merely needed an impervious and fluid hull surrounding him, a finely tuned advanced warfare system at his fingertips, and lots and lots of weapons. And those, he had.

A large salvo of negative energy missiles fired from a squadron of his fast-attack frigates wiped out the enemy's rear flank in a matter of minutes. He'd have smiled, but the truth was, despite their imposing profile and intimidating numbers, what they were currently fighting was little more than a scouting party. Once the Rasu determined the planet was not protected by a Rift Bubble, the real fleet was going to arrive, and things were certain to get a lot dicier.

Still, the longer they kept the Rasu engaged away from the planet, the better. The longer it took them to parse the situation, the longer it would take for enemy reinforcements to show up once they did identify the planet's vulnerability, and the more Concord ships would be in place when they did.

Lance studied the evolving tactical map, letting the frenetics of the battle outside fade away from his active perception. Something about what he was seeing wasn't right; the engagements, the ship movements, the ebb and flow of the combat felt…off. Unfamiliar.

He frowned, struggling to put his finger on the nature of the problem….

Suddenly he realized what it was. None of the Asterion ships were dropping off the map, because none of them were getting disabled or destroyed. The scrolling feed on the right side of the map displayed literally zero damage reports or pilot rescue requests.

He chuckled to himself. *What a fine invention you are, adiaK.* Give him another hundred thousand of these indestructible, impenetrable warships, and he'd daresay he could change the world. Or at least warfare.

But he didn't have a hundred thousand of them today, and even this relatively small Rasu force was putting up a brutal fight. The Taiyok fleet was not faring quite so well as his—how could it—and the viewport splashed with multiple explosions across the edges of the planetary atmosphere.

Those explosions were abruptly drowned out as the battlefield was bathed in flares of blinding light. He blinked away halos and adjusted the filters on the viewport. What the hells was going out there?

The filters kicked in to dim what turned out to be sunlight bouncing off a vast array of orbital weapons batteries. They had materialized out of nowhere and…he checked the sensors…appeared to encircle the planet.

The array had been there all along, hidden and silent, until it was needed. Unmatched Taiyok stealth at work, indeed. Lance mused briefly that he was glad they'd never made enemies of their allies.

Thousands of lasers erupted from the batteries at once to target the front line of Rasu vessels with shocking firepower. On contact, they ripped the attackers apart from end to end in one of the most dramatic acts of sheer destruction Lance had ever seen. He made a note to congratulate the Taiyok military leadership on the feat, assuming they survived the battle.

Because as stunning and impressive as the feat was, it wasn't going to be enough to win the day. The destruction the array had wreaked wasn't permanent. As imposing as these new weapons the Taiyoks wielded were, they were conventional in nature, and they'd only slow the enemy down for a time.

Commander Palmer (TT Mission Channel): "All fast-attack craft, concentrate your negative energy fire on the scattered pieces of Rasu the planetary array just littered the battlefield with. Let's prevent them from regrouping and getting back in the fight."

Hundreds of Asterion ships swarmed into the Rasu debris, but Lance watched the gambit unfold in growing frustration. His ship captains were doing everything in their power to target the chunks of Rasu already drifting back toward one another, unleashing their negative energy missiles before the Rasu could reform. But his fleet was still too small and the Rasu still too godsdamn many.

The array weapons continued firing, and in minutes they'd made a proper mess out of the battlespace. Clumps of Rasu the size of fighters raced to regroup while actual fighters chased them. Chaos intensified.

Commander Palmer (TT Mission Channel): "Remember, your first priority is to keep the Rasu away from the planet for as long as possible. Make them chase you if you must. Your ships can take the abuse now."

The mental leap required to accept and internalize the fact that one's ship was simply *not* going to disintegrate under even the most sustained fire was a difficult one to make, no question. Perhaps a little easier for Asterions than most, who had long ago internalized the reality of eternal survival about themselves, but nonetheless difficult.

To underscore the necessity—and despite herculean efforts, the increasing failure—of his strategy, a wide violet Rasu beam sliced through the chaos, aimed directly at the surface of the planet. He sighed; thus brought an end to their charade.

To Lance's astonishment, though, the beam impacted something far short of the surface and was reflected cleanly back to burn into the very Rasu leviathan that had fired it, cleaving the massive vessel in two.

He quickly reviewed the footage of the incident…and still wasn't entirely sure what he was looking at. Some manner of responsive defensive mirrors hidden between the array batteries, maybe? Nika had said the Elder insisted they had ways to defend their planet, and it seemed the Taiyok leader hadn't been lying. Hidden orbital arrays, now massive mirror defenses. What else did the Taiyoks have secreted away beneath their reticent feathers?

Encouraged anew, he checked the time. *Come on, Solovy. Get your ass here, and if we're lucky we can finish off Round 1 before Round 2 arrives.*

50

PERIPLANOS

MILKY WAY GALAXY

Eren strolled around the main cabin of the *Periplanos,* running his hands along the furniture and fiddling with every control panel he came across. "Nice little ship you've got here."

Nyx glanced away from studying the HUD readings long enough to shoot him an annoyed frown. "It's served us well."

"And by 'us,' you mean you and Nisi—I mean Corradeo. Your grandfather."

"Yes." She handled their departure from Ares with quick, skilled economy of motion, and they were soon in the stars.

He went into the cockpit and sprawled in the passenger seat, throwing one leg over an arm of the chair. "He's not literally your *grandfather,* though, right?"

"Actually, he is—or rather, he believes he is, and I have no reason to doubt him. According to him, I was the daughter of his daughter."

"From before."

"Before what?"

Eren gestured toward the black outside the viewport. "Before...everything. Before his son tried to kill him. Before the Dynasties took control of the government. Before the integrals turned everyone into slaves."

Her lips pursed into a thin line. "Yes. From before all of those things."

"But you don't remember that time. You don't remember your mother, do you?"

"Obviously I don't." She groaned and pivoted her chair to face him. "If you insist on talking, then we should talk about the mission. Ferdinand will be wanting to change his identity so he can fade away into the masses. There are a number of places he can go to accomplish this—"

"I'd go to Lethe. In fact, I did go to Lethe."

"Ferdinand would not be caught dead in a slum of Lethe's caliber. He's far too cultured—"

"Prissy."

"Cultured. He's far too *cultured* for Lethe. No, he'll go to Boeno or Menaris. He's got the money and the connections to pay for a high-quality identity transfer."

"Whatever you say, sweetheart."

She shot him a renewed glare as she entered new coordinates. "I've distributed a request to the Vigil *elas* on Boeno and Menaris to be on the lookout for Ferdinand. If one of the officers spots him, we'll know in minutes."

"Ever the Inquisitor, aren't you?"

"Not any longer. Grandfather is doing away with the title. He says it sounds too ominous and threatening, and there's too much negative history associated with it."

"He's not wrong. But have you undergone any adjustments to your genetic profile during a regenesis in the last fourteen years?"

"No. Why would I have done any such thing?"

"So many reasons. But it means you're still an Inquisitor where it counts: in your own mind."

She shrugged, not disagreeing. "This is what I do. It's who I am."

"This is all I'm saying, sweetheart."

"Stop calling me that. It's insulting."

He grinned wolfishly. "I know."

"You are terribly arrogant for an *asi*."

"I haven't played the role of a proper *asi* since I severed my integral connection one hundred fourteen years ago—in a far more painful and grueling manner than what Corradeo used on the recalcitrant *elassons*, by the way."

"Is that intended to be some sort of badge of honor?"

"Nah. I'm merely saying, they got off easy."

"They'd likely disagree." Her expression darkened. "It was a bold move on his part, but I hope he's being careful. Some of the *elassons* might want retribution for their perceived affront."

Eren dropped his chin into his hand. "You're worried about him?"

"Of course I am. He's playing a very dangerous game—no, not a game. A gambit for the future of our people, but a dangerous one."

"He's literally a *million* years old. He's survived countless wars, revolutions, multiple assassination attempts and a couple hundred thousand years of wandering around the cosmos. I think he can take care of himself."

"Which does nothing to stop me from wanting to take care of him—" She cut herself off. "I've received a report of a man matching Ferdinand's description seen on Menaris."

"Damn, that was fast."

"My connections are quite extensive."

"And the order of an Inquisitor makes people jump like their pants are on fire."

A corner of her mouth curled up briefly. "I suppose it does."

MENARIS

A police barrier shimmered across the entrance to an alley off the main thoroughfare. The surrounding buildings were all shades of brown, varying only from yellowish-brown to reddish-brown. Menaris was not an attractive planet to begin with, and the local architects had done nothing to improve its presentation. Were she here, Cosime would be burning Eren's ears with colorful complaints about the environs....

A small crowd of interested onlookers milled around in the street near the barrier. Nyx moved through them with such smoothness it was as if the waters had parted for her, while those gathered jostled Eren rudely as he tried to follow her through. As soon as she'd cleared the crowd, she strode up to the Vigil officer guarding the barrier matter-of-factly. "Nyx elasson-Praesidis. Let us pass."

The guard's eyes widened, and he stammered out a, "Yes, ma'am." He entered a code on his handheld module, and the force field vanished long enough for them to walk through.

Once they were on the other side, a Praesidis man dressed in a drab—wait for it—*brown* suit hurried up to them. "Inquisitor?"

"I..." Nyx sighed "...yes. Are you Investigator Caban?"

"I am. We've left the crime scene untouched, as you requested."

"Stay nearby, and I'll inform you if I need your assistance."

Damn, she was hardcore cold. Eren shook his head as they picked their way toward a body lying prone in the rear of the alley. A thick trail of blood began outside the alley entrance and painted a viscous path to its source. It didn't take an Inquisitor to deduce that the person was killed in the street then dragged down the alley in a half-assed attempt to conceal the body.

The pasty, ashen, frozen face of Ferdinand elasson-Kyvern stared up at them from the concrete. He'd been stripped of clothing except for his briefs and socks, and no personal effects littered the area.

Eren groaned and cast his gaze to the dull evening sky. "And now I've got blue balls again. This is just great."

Nyx's eyes cut over to him, narrowed. "You were planning to kill him when we found him?"

"Fuck yes, I was."

"But Grandfather told us to take him into custody and either turn him over to Concord Security or bring him back to Ares."

"And do you always do what you're told?"

"When he's the one doing the telling, yes. I owe him my loyal allegiance."

Eren sank against the alley wall, careful to avoid the blood trail, and crossed his arms over his chest. "That's nice. Listen, sweetheart, there's something you need to understand about me. I like your grandfather. I think he's a good man and an inspiring leader, and I was honored to play a small role in helping him take down the Directorate. I fancy the notion that I was a damn good anarch agent who furthered his cause in a thousand ways through the years. But unlike you, I don't always do what I'm told, no matter who's doing the telling. And your grandfather knows this perfectly well."

"Then why did he keep you on as an anarch agent if you routinely disobeyed orders? Why is he allowing you to help him now?"

"Because things usually turn out better for the good guys when I *don't* follow orders and instead do things my own way."

"Forgive me if I'm skeptical of your claim." She knelt beside the body and placed a small scanner over a locked-open left eye. "Scan confirms it's him."

"You were thinking he could have gotten someone else to wear his face, then killed the imposter?"

"It would have been the smart thing to do if he legitimately wanted to disappear. But this scene…the temptation is to assign some nefarious scheme to it, but I suspect this was simply a robbery gone bad."

"Ferdinand would not have been polite to any would-be robbers, entitled tosser that he was."

She didn't argue this time, keeping her attention on the readout of the scanner. "Brain activity has ceased, but I'm not seeing any evidence of an integral connection. I'll order an autopsy of his brain to make certain, but I don't think he had time to find a way to reconnect to a regenesis server."

"Good riddance. I'll let Richard know what's happened."

"Who?"

"Director Richard Navick? Head of Concord Intelligence?"

Surprise flickered across her features. "You consort with some powerful people, it seems."

"For my 'station' as an *asi*, you mean? I sure do. You'll find I am just full of surprises."

"And I'd prefer it if you kept them to yourself." She nodded perfunctorily and stood. "We're done here." Her voice raised a notch. "Investigator Caban, you can process the scene now. Autopsy his brain to confirm the absence of an integral connection and inform me if your investigation uncovers anything unusual. I don't expect there to be anything, but treat this case with the utmost care and attention."

"Yes, ma'am. We won't let you down." Caban was practically slobbering in his eagerness to obey her.

Eren grumbled in annoyance at the officer's ridiculous fawning and pushed off the alley wall. "Back to Ares, then?"

Nyx didn't answer him immediately. Instead, she pivoted on a heel and strode out of the alley and back onto the street, forcing Eren to scramble to catch up to her. Only once they were clear of the crime scene did she stop and turn to him. The all-business Inquisitor's mien she'd worn for the Vigil officers cracked a smidge to reveal something…darker.

"No. As much as it pains me to say this, I need your help on one more mission."

51

CAF AURORA

TOKI'TAKU STELLAR SYSTEM

The *CAF Aurora* arrived in the midst of a veritable ocean of Rasu vessels. Frowning, Miriam sent out the initial orders to the battle groups then messaged Commander Palmer.

The first deployment of Concord vessels is now on the field, and we can expect reinforcements in another thirty-six minutes. You indicated the attacking force was of a manageable size. Perhaps we have different definitions of 'manageable'?

The attacking force WAS of a manageable size. Five minutes ago, another fifty million of them showed up.

I see. I'll activate an additional battalion.

Palmer was exaggerating, but not by enough to make her comfortable. It took only a quick check of the tactical map to determine the Taiyoks and Asterions now found themselves vastly outnumbered. And unlike at Namino, here no Rift Bubble was en route to save the day.

Miriam had spent the last fourteen years managing the often peculiar sensibilities of a variety of alien species. While she'd take great pleasure in finding the Taiyok leader and shaking some sense into them, she knew only hard-earned experience could change ancient ways.

Today, they'd have to defeat the Rasu fair and square. Not that she expected the Rasu to appreciate such a concept.

While the ships she oversaw maneuvered into position and she readied to take command of the battlefield—the sheer numbers of the Concord fleet allowed for no other eventuality—her gaze took in the expanse of shadowy creatures amassed before her. The quiet flutter in her chest the sight induced was so minor this time that it might have passed unnoticed if she hadn't been waiting for it. But her nightmares were banished, and so too should be the deep terror elicited by the presence of these metal monstrosities.

"Thomas, let's take some of this heat off of the defenders. Let the Rasu know we're here."

'With pleasure, ma'am.'

*Commandant Solovy (*CAF Aurora*)(Concord Command Channel): "Fleet Admiral Bastian, take command of Battle Groups #2 and #3 and execute on TP-Epsilon 4B. Pointe-Amiral Thisiame, assist DAF's Fast Attack Squadrons in engaging the smaller and splintered Rasu vessels. Tokahe Naataan, initiate TP-Gamma 1A, as we previously discussed."*

*Fleet Admiral Bastian (*AFS Leonidas*)(Concord Command Channel): "Commandant, wouldn't TP-Epsilon 5A be more appropriate here? I can deploy a squadron of Sabres on two flanks and snare—"*

*Commandant Solovy (*CAF Aurora*)(Concord Command Channel): "You have your orders, Fleet Admiral."*

The response took far too long. *"Acknowledged."*

She sighed quietly, then sent a pulse.

Fleet Admiral, the time to disagree with our tactical combat scenarios is before the combat has begun. Nonetheless, if you take umbrage with my orders in the future, raise your concerns in private, not on an open channel.

But it was the Command Channel—

To the battle, Fleet Admiral.

He didn't argue further, but she kept a close eye on Battle Groups #2 and #3 until it was evident they were following her initial orders. She'd learned to manage Bastian's insistence on playing devil's advocate against her every decision during strategy sessions, but she'd believed him too professional to engage in it on the battlefield. Her thoughts drifted to Malcolm and whether his leave of absence might be nearing an end, though she recognized that his return to active duty would only complicate matters.

Commander Palmer (TT Mission Channel): "To all the new arrivals, watch out for the Taiyoks' planetary defense weapons. They are surprisingly robust."

Commandant Solovy (TT Mission Channel): "Duly noted."

It didn't take long to see what Palmer was referencing. A planet-wide array fired repeaters into clusters of Rasu from every vantage, but a few gaps were appearing in their coverage; the batteries were beginning to take damage. Beyond the weapons array, reflective plates deflected a full half of the Rasu fire that made it past the fleets. She made a mental note to recommend AEGIS investigate similar tools to augment their own planetary defenses, as new ideas were always welcome.

Commandant Solovy, permission to join the Command Channel?"

She almost stumbled off the overlook in surprise. *Casmir?*

Yes, ma'am. Corradeo Praesidis sends his regards. At his behest, I and three brigades of Machim warships would like to assist you in your battle against this enemy.

Three Machim brigades constituted *a lot* of ships, so she'd worry about how the Anadens had known about the battle and its location later. *Convey my thanks to him. You are clear on who the enemy is here, yes?*

The soulless shapeshifting metal contraptions clogging this star system.

Correct. I'm glad to have you at my side, Casmir. I'm sending you the combat briefing package on the Rasu. I hope you read fast.

Already on it, ma'am.

She shook her head, smiling—then realized she should make sure no one mistook the Machim ships for traitorous enemies and started shooting at them.

*Commandant Solovy (*CAF Aurora*)(Concord Command Channel): "Navarchos Casmir, I believe Pointe-Amiral Thisiame's ships could benefit from some tanks taking a few of the blows for them, the better for their shots to strike true."*

*Navarchos Casmir (*AMF Imperium Alpha*)(Concord Command Channel): "Understood, Commandant. Pointe-Amiral, let us provide you some cover."*

Did this mean the Anaden pseudo-rebellion was over? Had Corradeo Praesidis succeeded in bringing the recalcitrant *elassons* into line, and on the right side of the conflict? Few things were ever quite so simple or straightforward, but she would take Casmir's arrival as a positive sign and hope for more such signs to come.

And the Anadens' arrival was none too soon. The long-range radar flashed red as a new slate of Rasu poured out of wormholes on the fringes of the stellar system. Word was out: Toki'taku was defended, but it was also vulnerable.

RW

An hour and two rounds of additional Rasu reinforcements later, a question rattled around in Miriam's head: was there no end to the enemy's supply of warships?

It appeared to be a rhetorical question, for the answer was thus far 'no.' There was not an end to them. After being rebuffed at all Asterion Dominion worlds of consequence and getting embarrassed by the Kats, they wanted this planet badly.

Miriam was not inclined to give it to them, and Commander Palmer had certainly made it obvious that he was also not so inclined. The DAF fleet was holding up considerably better this time around. They'd taken their under-the-table adiamene gift and promptly improved upon it to make the perfect metal somehow yet more perfect. She couldn't help but be impressed.

Kennedy Rossi was most perturbed at the failure of the kyoseil to perform for her, and rightly so. It was apparent the Asterions and the kyoseil enjoyed a...special relationship, as it were, even if the exact contours of that relationship remained mysterious.

But Miriam had her impervious double-shielding, which was a less complicated if less elegant solution. Thirty-eight percent of the AEGIS cruisers now fielded the shielding as well, along with around twenty percent of the Novoloume and Khokteh ships. This still left many vessels unprotected from a Rasu boarding incursion, but they'd also developed new contingency plans to come to the rescue of any such threatened ships. Those plans had been successfully called into action almost a dozen times so far today.

Despite their best efforts to keep the battle well clear of the planet below, the Rasu were slowly but surely dragging the fighting inexorably closer to Toki'Taku itself. As they did so, her fleet's ability to utilize Dimensional Rifters and negative energy weapons became increasingly constrained. She thought perhaps the Rasu were beginning to notice this little detail, which, if true, stood to make future engagements that much more difficult. Their enemy was brutal and callous, but they were also smart, observant and swift to take advantage of any weaknesses once they were uncovered.

As the Rasu numbers grew and Miriam's available strategies dwindled, the Taiyok's impressive orbital weapons array began falling to overwhelming Rasu firepower. One by one, their batteries fell silent and their defensive mirrors were shattered.

When a sizeable gap in the defenses finally opened the planet itself to attack, a massive violet beam fired by a Rasu leviathan streaked toward the surface—and an even more massive bronze beam streaked up from somewhere on the planet to impact the leviathan, shredding it into pieces in a matter of seconds. It seemed the Taiyoks were not out of tricks just yet.

Still, the Rasu weapon found its mark, lighting a conflagration on the forested surface below.

Miriam ordered another four AEGIS Assault Divisions to report to the battle with all due speed, then gritted her teeth and glared at the tactical map. How were they going to stop the planet from burning?

52

FICENTI

The vile smells and screeching noises of the Mikro-Teln district had not improved in Nyx's short time away. For this visit she was prepared, though, and fine-tuned her senses before they departed the spaceport to explicitly filter out what displeased her and hone only what she needed to monitor.

She hadn't warned her companion about the particulars of their destination, and Eren made a string of increasingly foul faces as they neared the district. His reaction evoked a perverse sense of satisfaction, which she quickly squelched, for it was petty and frivolous of her. After chastising herself, she stopped and touched his arm. "It only gets worse from here. You might want to filter out what you can."

"Thanks for the belated warning." He scowled at her, but after a few seconds his nose uncrinkled and his eyes uncreased, which she took to mean he'd followed her suggestion.

She didn't like him. Every aspect of his cavalier attitude and reckless behavior made her deeply uncomfortable. He did everything the wrong way, openly flouting every rule and tradition he encountered. And worse, he appeared to take unashamed enjoyment in doing so. Why did her grandfather trust an Idoni *asi* at all? Obviously they had a history together, but she couldn't imagine how the relationship had managed to go so favorably for her companion.

She would follow her grandfather across the Styx and into the depths of Tartarus without hesitation. He was her blood and her liege. But centuries of hunting—and often killing—anarchs had embedded in her a deep sense of loathing for them. They were violent, aggressive and disruptive. Criminals and saboteurs.

A voice in the back of her mind demanded she recognize that they had also been *right.* But ingrained prejudices demanded equally loudly that anarchs were beneath her. Miscreants to be corralled, imprisoned and reconditioned.

The contradiction meant she had some more adapting to do if she wanted to thrive in her grandfather's new empire. She'd work on it.

Her thumb fiddled with the Veil module Eren had given her when they'd departed the *Periplanos*. She'd never needed a stealth device before. For millennia the *diati* had hidden her whenever she required it, and she'd had no cause to hide these last fourteen years. But, she admitted, it should come in handy tonight.

When they reached the final block before the arena, she laid a hand on Eren's shoulder to stop him a second time. "Let's go over the plan again. When we're close enough, I'll de-stealth and distract Kolgo while you poison his drink. Where is the *apomono?*"

He fished the vial out of his pocket and held it aloft on his palm. His gaze unfocused as he fixated on the small object and its clay-hued contents; a muscle in his left temple twitched.

"Eren?"

He didn't answer.

"What's wrong?"

"Just playing chicken with my darker impulses." He blinked, seemingly shook off the spell and pocketed the vial.

Was he suicidal? She opened her mouth to probe the ragged edges of his psyche, then thought better of it. She didn't care. "If you're planning to permanently shake off this mortal coil, kindly do it after the mission is complete."

He gave her a blasé look. "Not to worry. I'll message you once the poison's in place, then you—are you certain you don't want me to shoot this guy? Truly, I'm happy to do it."

"I'm sure you are, but no. It's my responsibility."

"Fine. But after we've gone to all this trouble, take care to do it properly."

Nyx bristled at the insinuation that she wasn't capable of effecting a proper assassination. Still, a twinge of dread snaked through her chest. She didn't want to kill her brother, no matter what he had become. But what he had become was a monster, and she couldn't in good conscience let him continue his reign of terror. He stood in the way of what her grandfather wanted to accomplish, and in her heart she knew that Kolgo was beyond redemption.

"Activate your Veil. Let's move."

Eren vanished from her sight, and she slipped into the crowd moving toward the arena. If he ran into trouble, he'd promised to message her, but otherwise she needed to trust that he'd make it to the far platform in a reasonable amount of time. In reality, she didn't trust him to so much as fetch breakfast, but if she expected to get this done, she had little choice but to rely on his assistance.

She cringed as she passed two Anadens beating up a malnourished waif of a Naraida woman…then realized she wasn't able to determine their Dynasties, even at a hard glance. The rigid lines that had structured their society for millennia genuinely were breaking down, weren't they? She wanted to stop and help the woman—another unfamiliar sensation—but she couldn't afford to draw any attention to herself until she was on the platform. Besides, if she succeeded here tonight, far more people than a single Naraida would be saved.

Her path took her close to the animal cages, and her most stringent olfactory controls didn't mask the predatory, bloodthirsty pheromones coming off the strange creatures in waves. Whether bred, trained or tortured for the task, these animals now existed for a single purpose: to kill.

A roar erupted out of the arena below, and she turned toward it in time to see a spray of gore decorate the high, curving wall. She didn't peer into the arena to determine if it belonged to man or beast.

I've reached the platform, far right side. Mr. Sultan's drinking a giant mug of something. This will be as easy as pie.

Wait until I've revealed myself. You can't risk being noticed.

Whatever you say, sweetheart.

Now that Eren had reached the platform, she zeroed in on her destination. Kolgo had surrounded himself with a new cadre of naked women, as well as six identifiable guards. There were likely another two or three blending in with the supplicants.

She watched the movement of people around the ramp leading up to the platform for several beats, getting a feel for the ebb and flow pulling at them. Then she joined it, writhing delicately through the throng. It was crowded enough that the two times she brushed up against someone, it could have been anyone who did so, and she'd moved on before they'd begun to hunt around for a culprit.

But now four of the guards blocked her final access to the platform.

Eren, get ready.

Nyx maneuvered to the outside of the leftmost guard. Breathed in and palm-chopped him beneath the chin, sending him sprawling into the crowd at the top of the ramp. Then she launched off her left foot and swung her right around to deliver a roundhouse kick into the crotch of the middle guard.

The third guard dropped into a defensive stance. "Kolgo, trouble!"

The guard swung blindly for his invisible attacker, but she ducked down and to the side as Kolgo turned his head toward the shout. When she stood tall, deactivated the Veil and stepped forward, recognition dawned in his hypnol-and-spirit addled eyes. "Stand down, Dmitri. Nyx, this is a surprise. I thought you were dead."

"It seems everyone did, but I was merely on an extended journey. What *is* all this, Kolgo?"

He smiled malevolently. "My kingdom, of course. Don't you like it?"

"It's not to my taste." Behind him, a servant refilled his mug out of a bell-shaped beaker. "This is beneath you, brother."

"That's what makes it so enjoyable, *sister*."

Poison applied. Your turn.

"I don't understand. We're supposed to be enforcers of order, peace and the rule of law. What you're doing here is madness."

"Isn't it, though? I assure you, I have gone quite mad indeed." He picked up the mug and took a long sip—then flung it across the platform. "This is swill! Get me a new bottle!"

She only hoped he'd ingested enough.

His mouth curled down, and he rubbed at his temples. The *apomono* worked swiftly, but its speed brought with it noticeable side effects. "Why are you bothering me, Nyx? If you've come all this way just to deliver a disapproving lecture, I'm not in the mood. As a courtesy, I'll have you escorted out unharmed. But don't come back, or you may find yourself part of the show." His head tilted meaningfully toward the arena pit, but the threatening countenance was interrupted by him frowning and clutching his stomach.

"I can't let you continue on this path. You're a criminal, a depraved torturer and a despot."

"Oh, I am so much worse than any of those things."

"Come with me, Kolgo. Leave all this behind, and I can help you."

DO IT ALREADY, INQUISITOR!

She gritted her teeth. But it was overly sentimental of her to imagine that she could talk Kolgo down and lead him into some light of righteousness.

"Never. Last chance to leave under your own power, sister."

"I am so sorry, brother." She whipped the gun out from beneath her coat and shot him between the eyes.

In the second that followed, when the occupants of the platform were stunned into inaction, she reactivated her Veil and leapt off the platform to the narrow passage ringing the arena below.

Then everyone was screaming. In the periphery of her vision, she saw the guards fan out through the crowd, searching for the shooter.

Someone bumped into her from behind, and she leapt to the side—only to have a hand grab her wrist and drag her in the other direction.

This way. With me.

How had Eren found her in the chaos, while she was invisible? It didn't matter. She scanned the area in front of them and instantly saw the path he had in mind, even as he started towing her along it. The pandemonium grew in their wake, and as they reached the street, they were shoved and jostled by people who didn't know whether to rush to the platform or flee in panic.

Her body felt battered and bruised by the time the crowd began thinning and they stumbled out of the Mikro-Teln district.

"Don't deactivate your Veil yet. We don't know the reach of his control."

She nodded, then realized he couldn't see it, then realized she was supposed to be the one giving orders. But it was a smart precaution, and now was not the time to pick a fight. They wound carefully to the east, then north, then east again, until finally the rundown spaceport was in sight.

She de-stealthed and sank against a pillar for half a breath.

Eren materialized in front of her; blood trickled down his nose from a cut on his forehead, his hair was tangled into knots and sweat glistened above his upper lip. "Are you all right?"

Did she look as much of a wreck as he did? She nodded, visibly this time. "I'm fine. Let's get back to the *Periplanos.* We can treat your wounds there."

"What?" His hand came to his forehead. "Oh. Huh."

She strode off for the spaceport, assuming he would follow. As she did, she sent a message to the head of the local Vigil office.

The Sultan of Ficenti has been permanently neutralized. I suggest you take a battalion of well-armed officers into the Mikro-Teln district and clean the place out before one of his lackeys decides to step into his shoes.

53

HAAFAN

BEYOND THE BOUNDARIES OF CONCORD SPACE

A hundred-meter section of bedrock detached in clean lines from the surrounding crust, jutted outward and slid to the side, revealing a modest hangar bay carved into the planetoid. Two fat, squatty ships constructed of a milky gray metal resembling opaque glass sat docked in secured berths on the left section of the bay. A smaller, thinner needle ship was docked on the right side, leaving one open slot.

As Alex maneuvered into the berth, a blast door at the far end of the hangar bay opened, and several Ourankeli emerged.

Caleb studied Wyddoniiet. "Our welcome is going to be a friendly one, correct?"

"They know I accompany you."

"That doesn't answer my question."

"They will be cautious, but you will not be restrained without provocation."

"I see." It was a somewhat less than reassuring answer, so Caleb went to the cabinet beside the data center table and retrieved his Daemon and plasma blade. Only after he'd latched both of them to his tactical belt did he realize that Akeso hadn't uttered so much as a displeased murmur at his actions.

You must defend yourself from those who are not peaceful. I accept this.

Acceptance was a huge step. *My hope is these strangers will be the peaceful sort. I'm merely taking precautions in case they are not.*

To be able to determine their intentions from afar would be most beneficial. Through pheromones, perhaps, or phototransduction.

Caleb shook his head wryly. The way Akeso pulled ideas from his mind and fit them into its own milieu still astonished him. *I wish people were that simple. But I need to observe them, read their body language and ideally speak to them in order to judge their intentions. Hence the weapons.*

This comports with our previous experiences.

He glanced back at Wyddoniiet. "Atmosphere?"

"It will be as breathable as my home on Haelwyeur."

"Thank you." He went back to the cockpit and leaned in close to Alex's ear. "Let's take our breather masks, just in case."

Her gaze immediately dropped to his waist. "And weapons?"

"Just in case."

She shut down the engines. "Valkyrie, keep your primary consciousness in the ship...just in case. We don't know when those pieces of Rasu outside are going to wake up. Among other things we don't know. I promise you'll be able to see everything through my eyes."

'I will maintain the ship in a ready state.'

They'd deployed a small sensor probe before entering the hanger bay, so they should get at least a few minutes' warning if the Rasu started getting frisky. But depending on how large the settlement was, a few minutes might not give them much leeway. "Thank you, Valkyrie."

While Alex stood and disappeared into the main cabin, Caleb mentally checked himself, as he always did before walking into an unfamiliar situation. They were being overly cautious. If the rest of the Ourankeli were anything like Wyddoniiet, they would be stared at and challenged with curious questions, but ultimately tolerated if not effusively welcomed. These aliens had been on the run for centuries, cowering in fear from their enemy, and were not likely to attack newcomers who arrived offering aid. Still, an abundance of caution had saved them more than once.

Alex returned to his side with her breather mask draped around her neck and a Daemon on her hip. "Are we ready?"

He ticked off the last few items in his head, then nodded. "Wyddoniiet, you should exit the ship first. We will defer to you on introductions and our movements until everyone is comfortable with our presence."

"Yes."

The airlock opened, the ramp extended and new air wafted in. Much as at the alien's home on the halo ring, it carried a faint musty odor, but it was acceptably breathable.

Wyddoniiet glided down the ramp, their feet barely skimming the surface. When they reached the bottom, they approached the growing crowd at the blast door and began speaking in a convoluted series of echoing trills and deep-throated rumblings.

One of the gathered Ourankeli rushed forward and met Wyddoniiet halfway. Their arm appendages reached out to caress one another as they spun in a slow circle, almost like a dance. Family? Old lovers?

Finally two of Wyddoniiet's eyes spun toward the ship, where Caleb and

Alex waited at the airlock, and they extended one appendage. "You may join us."

He and Alex descended the ramp, him one step in front. He didn't need to remind Alex of the standard operating procedure in this situation: approach deliberately, hands in full view, no sudden moves, present as non-threatening while staying on constant guard. Their track record in these encounters was around eighty/twenty in their favor, but the twenty percent had left their mark.

Wyddoniiet continued to speak in their lyrical, convoluted tongue until he and Alex drew alongside them, then switched to Communis, which apparently everyone understood. They had learned next to nothing about the technology and practices of the Ourankeli, but it appeared the aliens' knowledge stores were vast and far-reaching.

"My companions, known as Caleb and Alex, have used their Valkyrie synthetic ship to disable the Rasu vessels that were bombarding Haafan. You are safe, but only for a short time. They have offered us permanent refuge in their civilization."

Rolling, trilling murmurs broke out among those gathered. Wyddoniiet listened for a time, then made a wavelike gesture with two of their appendages, and everyone quieted. "We will confer on this question. Cyfeill, will you guide Caleb and Alex on a tour of Haafan while we do so?"

An Ourankeli with pale azalea skin emerged from the group. They went first to Wyddoniiet, and light touching of the appendages occurred for several seconds. Then they rotated toward him and Alex, eyes first. "You are guests. Come."

RW

Caleb expected the space beyond the blast door to be similar in many respects to Taenarin Aris. After all, like the Taenarin, the Ourankeli had carved a home out of the bedrock of a planetary body, if a small, dead one. But his preconceived notions were instantly proved wrong.

As soon as they traversed the door, a world of light and glass opened up before them. The rocky ceiling high above was subsumed almost completely by pervasive blue-white light. The inhabited space resembled a giant dome, only beneath instead of above.

Along the outermost band of the dome, a series of large structures stretched one after another, with narrow pathways cutting between them. The utilitarian design suggested they served as factories or warehouses. A middle band consisted of numerous more ornate but smaller buildings placed along a wide, curving walkway of polished stone. The innermost band was filled with several dozen small structures in all shapes, sizes and heights, many of them sporting adjacent patios or rooftop verandas. Homes, perhaps?

Occupying the center of the habitat was a collection of mini-domes built of translucent glass. Within them, colorful flora bloomed in expansive arcs or climbed up vertical trellises. Several Ourankeli could be seen through the glass tending machines that tended the plants.

"As you can see, we have constructed a completely self-sufficient biome here. We create and recycle our air and water, and the greenhouses provide renewable nourishment."

"This is most impressive. How many of you are there?"

"Sixty-two."

Alex looked over at their guide in surprise. "All of this for only sixty-two Ourankeli?"

"Is every life not precious? Not worthy of fulfillment in all things?"

Alex's eyebrows twitched in amusement. "Of course it is. I wasn't being judgmental. It's all quite inspiring. I merely…Wyddoniiet led us to understand that you were refugees."

"We are. Does our status mean we should not strive for both achievement and contentment in whatever circumstances we happen to occupy?"

"Nope!" Alex pursed her lips shut.

Caleb swallowed a chuckle. "It's very bright in here. Do you have a day/night cycle?"

"A what?"

"Do the lights dim on a regular schedule? To aid in your sleep in accordance with a circadian rhythm?"

"We do not require the dark to sleep. We never have."

Alex's lips quirked around; she never could stay silent for long. "The halo ring—Haelwyeur—faced the sun, so you wouldn't have had nights there unless you artificially created them. But what about before? Didn't you live on a planet before you built the ring? Serencaar, I think Wyddoniiet said your homeworld was called?"

"Ah. Yes. Our ancestors evolved on Serencaar, a planet in a nearby system to Haelwyeur. Triple suns meant we experienced only a few hours of dark every year. We have always lived in the light."

Alex smiled. "It sounds lovely. Why did you leave?"

"The interplay between our stars grew increasingly unstable. Our scientists posited that one of the stars would eventually be radically ejected from the system, rendering our planet's orbit fatally damaged. Our engineers spent ten thousand years constructing Haelwyeur to be our new home." Cyfeill's eyes swirled through a complete orbit. "In comparison, building this refuge was not so great a task."

"No, I suppose not."

Cyfeill had been leading them on a ponderous circuit of the habitat, but now they abruptly turned around. Caleb and Alex followed suit, to see Wyddoniiet approaching them. "It is settled. I have convinced the others that this haven will not remain so for much longer. They are sad to do so, but they have agreed to accompany you to your 'Concord.'"

"What? Leave Haafan?" Cyfeill's finger digits wound together in agitation. "But we—"

"Will not be safe here. The damaged Rasu outside will reform. More Rasu will answer their call for assistance, and soon."

Cyfeill deflated—literally—but didn't argue further. "Then I need to attend to my things. Excuse me." The Ourankeli dragged off toward one of the homes situated along the inner circle.

Alex sighed dramatically and shot Caleb a grimace. "I guess the *Siyane* gets to be a refugee ship again."

He tried not to laugh at her obvious displeasure, but only partially succeeded. "It'll be fine. We can patch up any damage they inflict."

"*Again.*"

Wyddoniiet appeared to understand the gist of their conversation, though they missed the nuance. "I and two companions will join you on your Valkyrie ship. The vessels in the hangar bay will be sufficient to carry the rest of our people and supplies."

"Oh. Good. I mean, they'll be more comfortable on their own ships." Alex frowned. "But didn't you say their wormhole drives were damaged? Concord space is a great distance from here. It will take you centuries to reach it at superluminal speeds. And the Rasu may be able to chase you there, which we do not want to happen."

"It is true that the wormhole drives on the docked vessels are nonfunctional."

Alex spread her arms wide. "Well, what's the state of the repairs? I guarantee I can help speed them along."

"You misunderstand. If they were easily repaired, we would have done so years ago and fled a far greater distance, to a place beyond the Rasu's reach. Unfortunately, we have been unable to locate the rare materials necessary to return them to functionality." Wyddoniiet gestured with an extended arm to the outer row of buildings. "A portion of these foundries are dedicated to recreating the required materials, but as yet they have not succeeded."

"Then we're going to need a bigger wormhole than the *Siyane* can produce to evacuate your ships. Give me a minute."

Her gaze unfocused for a moment, and her expression morphed through mild surprise to consternation. A blink and she refocused on Wyddoniiet. "How long do you think it will take to prepare the evacuation?"

"Three of your standard hours."

Caleb grimaced. "That long? I'm sure we don't have to impress upon you how much time is of the essence. You're the one who voiced doubts about how effective the improvised neutron bomb was going to be—and you're right. We don't know how long the Rasu will be hobbled, but every second we spend here brings them closer to functionality."

"We will endeavor for speed. We have done so before." Wyddoniiet glided off to hopefully start issuing orders, leaving the two of them unattended. They must have passed whatever tests they were being measured by.

"What's the story?"

Alex rubbed at her eyes; her energy for dealing with recalcitrant aliens had always been finite. "Mom is currently engaging a Rasu armada over at the Taiyok homeworld, but she promised to send a spare ship with a Caeles Prism to us soon."

"How's the battle going?"

"She said 'strangely.' I'm not entirely sure what that means. Anyway, now I don't know who to comm about preparing for the Ourankeli's arrival. Mom doesn't have the bandwidth to deal with refugee issues while she's fighting Rasu in the Gennisi galaxy. Dad's stopped issuing orders now that Mom's back on top of Concord matters, and Mia's no longer at the Consulate. I guess I could comm Veshnael, but I don't know him well."

"Comm Marlee. It'll make her week. And she's actually proved to be rather skilled at refugee resettlement."

"The Godjans and whatnot. Good point. Do you want to do the honors? It'll show her how much you've come to trust her."

He smiled, because she was right. "I will. It should present a new challenge for her, which she claims to want to tackle whenever possible. These aren't exactly Godjans."

"No. No, they are not."

Hey, Marlee, is the Consulate ready for a new influx of refugees?

Where did you find more Godjans?

Not Godjans. Ourankeli.

Who? Oh, the species Corradeo Praesidis met a gazillion and a half years ago.

And how do you know that?

Don't be silly. I know everything that happens at Concord HQ.

This, he believed. *Do me a favor and don't tell me how. We've got sixty-three Ourankeli who need a new and eventually permanent home.*

So few? The poor souls! It won't be a problem. We can simply stick them in a hotel until they tell us what they need, then what they want.

He took in the habitat, where dozens of Ourankeli now hurried about. A new urgency gave purpose to their hastened actions, but each one remained utterly composed, calm and dignified. *Better make it a nice hotel. The Ourankeli make the Novoloume look like slum-dwellers.*

They sound fantastic. I can't wait to meet them.

54

EARTH

VANCOUVER

Malcolm strolled along the shore path in Stanley Park, hands stuffed in his pockets and his collar pulled up high to fend off a gusting wind. Ahead, waves crashed into the pillar bases of Lions Gate Bridge, and his gaze drifted up toward the foothills. Their home was less than a kilometer away across the bridge, and he'd spent a miserable morning there before seeking the refuge of the outdoors.

One thing had remained true for all these years: he still preferred the sensation of soil beneath his feet and wind in his hair. He preferred what was solid and real, where if you could see it you could touch it, feel its texture between the tips of your fingers.

Today, the violently brisk air and enthusiastic sea-spray were like continual slaps in the face, which was definitely what he needed. He'd taken Richard's advice and talked to a priest after their conversation, but the father had been about as much help as he'd expected, which wasn't much at all. He understood, for the priest was bound by doctrine and Papal directive. But it meant a meaningful resolution of this overdrawn soul-searching continued to elude him.

He'd never pretend to consider himself a deep thinker; he was a doer, a man of action. But he'd 'actioned' himself directly into captivity, a trial run of his death and a pseudo-rebirth. Now, out the backside awaited a semblance of a new life for him. It wasn't the one he wanted, but it increasingly looked like he wasn't getting the old one back.

"You broke my world. You broke me—and there's no unbreaking any of it now."

Only, since her world was his world, he'd broken his own in the process. So where did he go from here?

A Concord Command alert flashed in his virtual vision, drawing his attention. Even during his leave of absence, the concept of cutting himself off from critical events was unthinkable.

ACTIVATION ORDER:

Mission: Rasu Engagement Alpha Three, Gennisi galaxy, planet designation 'Toki'Taku'

Instructions: All Battle Groups cleared for Rasu action and not previously activated are ordered to report to your assigned staging points by 1425 GST, where you will receive deployment orders.

He wasn't so arrogant as to believe God responded to his personal pleas on command, but the coincidence was notable enough that he should probably take the hint?

Without making a conscious decision to do so, his feet were carrying him up one of the cut-through paths toward the skycar station. He'd never make it in time, if for no other reason than he wasn't on active duty and the *Denali* was in dry dock and crewless at the Presidio. But a powerful need to *try* propelled him forward.

He broke into a jog as he filed a Resumption of Active Duty Notification with AEGIS Operations, then immediately followed it up with a request for all personnel not on reassignment to report to the *Denali* ASAP.

He didn't want for any of this to have happened. He *wanted* to wrap himself up in Mia's arms and kiss her forever. But he, somewhat unexpectedly, found he now knew one thing with a reassuring clarity. He *needed* to be on the bridge of his dreadnought.

RW

AFS DENALI

THE PRESIDIO

One hour and twenty minutes later, Malcolm stood on the bridge of the *AFS Denali.* He hadn't set foot on it in months, but the ship welcomed him back nonetheless.

For so long, he'd hated serving on ships in the void of space. But he'd turned out to excel at it, so in time he'd accepted the necessity of doing so, and that decision had carried him to the rarefied heights of his profession. Then he'd run from the obligation and nearly gotten himself killed and lost Mia for his effort.

Now, standing here on a bridge bustling with activity as crew members reported in and flight preparations began in earnest, with the adiamene hull, bright lights and virtual screens surrounding him...it felt right. He'd missed it. The skid-resistant flooring wasn't soil, and the atmospheric recycling system wasn't a fresh breeze, but...he ran his hand along the railing...this was solid and real enough. And until he stumbled his way out the other side of this crisis of faith and love, maybe he could again find purpose in duty.

He'd somehow yet to face the Rasu in battle, which shamed him. With nothing else to do but brood, he'd stayed up late the last two nights studying battle footage from every encounter so far, watching and learning until he had a reasonable feel for their battlefield tactics. He was ready.

He reviewed the staff report. The *Denali* was only sixty-eight percent crewed due to reassignments and leave, but its Prevo pair could pick up the slack and cover any unmanned stations. If asked, he'd opine that AEGIS warships were now chronically overstaffed in light of the many technological advances of recent years. In fact, as the fleet admiral, he'd asserted precisely that opinion several times to the various committees which oversaw such matters. But military bureaucracies were slow to change unless shoved off a cliff and forced to do so.

He considered the bridge again, reviewed the newest ship readiness update as soon as it came in, then sent a message.

Commandant Solovy,

The AFS Denali *stands ready to assist in the Toki'taku battle in whatever manner you can best use us. We await your instructions.*

—Admiral Malcolm Jenner

He busied himself with last-minute flurries of arriving crew and tactical scenario updates until a response arrived in a more personal pulse.

Malcolm, welcome back. As much as I would value your assistance at Toki'taku, we are thus far managing passably well. Instead, I have another mission for you.

55

CONCORD HQ
CINT

Richard studied the recorded Ghost footage from Savrak with a mixture of disgust and growing dread. The Savrakaths were not merely resilient, but as stubborn as mules. He'd grudgingly admire them, if only their stubbornness wasn't directed at trying to murder as many Concord citizens as possible.

In the overly crisp images of an enhanced long-range capture, he watched as a team unloaded antimatter missiles from the lone warship docked at a secret encampment deep in the jungle far to the northwest of the capital city. The team trudged it to a long, fully enclosed tent erected nearby. A makeshift cleanroom?

The imagery transitioned to washed-out infrared to penetrate the tent. A lone Savrakath opened up a missile and removed a package from its interior. Surely the antimatter casing itself. The package was transferred to a smaller box on an adjacent table. The Savrakath then moved to a tall, circular container situated on a second table. The visual wasn't good enough for Richard to make out the details of the alien's work, but according to the log, they continued their work for almost an hour. Richard sped up the video until the Savrakath closed up the open materials and left the tent.

Intel estimated with sixty-eight percent certainty that the Savrakath scientist Dr. Khalik was on site at the camp, which made him the one performing surgery on the lethal antimatter. The size of the circular container, around two meters by three, combined with the material extracted from the missile, suggested only one reasonable possibility. They were making an antimatter bomb, one that could be easily transported anywhere.

While he kept one eye on the video feed, he sent Miriam a message. Yes, she was currently spearheading a battle against the Rasu five megaparsecs away, but this was legitimately important.

We need to increase the alert level for Savrakath incursions. They're trying to make a small-payload antimatter bomb.

Considering her current state, the reply arrived quickly. *The alert level can go no higher than Red Flag. Any Savrakath vessel will be shot down the instant they are caught in Concord space.*

I know. I'm simply saying we need to be on the lookout, now more than ever.

Then implement whatever measures you believe are appropriate to ensure we're doing so.

She was right—the Savrakaths would never get a ship close enough to fire a missile at a Concord target...but they were no longer trying to fire a missile. They were trying to plant a bomb.

The video again drew his full attention as Dr. Khalik returned to the tent. He and two assistants transferred the contents of the box to the circular container and, after much fiddling, closed it up. The container—now a bomb—was trolleyed out of the tent and loaded onto a small transport-type vessel. It didn't display the usual Savrakath design sensibilities; in fact, the ship more closely resembled a Dankath or Barisan design. The vessel lifted off and vanished into the sky.

The Ghost was tasked with surveilling the secret encampment, so it didn't follow the vessel when it departed. And this footage was six hours old, having first passed through Cliff's algorithms then directed to Analysis for greater scrutiny by CINT analysts, before finally being cleared to land on his desk.

Dammit! What was that ship, and where had it taken the bomb?

The Savrakath's strike options were pitifully limited. No Savrakath vessel would be permitted to dock at any Concord station or land on any Concord world. But this wasn't a Savrakath vessel!

He sat bolt upright in his chair, fingers flying over his control panel in search of a file. He'd seen something this morning, one of hundreds of data points to pass across his awareness. Something in the daily briefing materials. A tiny thing—there.

A Barisan merchant vessel had been reported missing yesterday by its owner, Manu Provisions. Normally such a report never would have been elevated to inclusion in the daily briefing, but the last known location of the vessel was Antlia Merchant Waypoint #3, the closest facility to the Savrak stellar system that Concord operated. As such, the Waypoint was under heightened alert and any anomalies were flagged for review.

"Cliff, initiate a system-wide search for any information on Barisan merchant vessel #BSA-4162-dd6a."

'Acknowledged.'

Richard sent a comm request to the reporting party at Manu Provisions.

"Director Navick? This is a surprise and an honor. What can I do for you?"

"I wanted to check on the status of the ship you reported missing. Do you have any updates, or have you heard from any of the crew?"

"Unfortunately, no. Messages to the crewmembers bounce back as undeliverable, so I fear the worst for them."

"I'm sorry to hear it. We're investigating the ship's disappearance, and I'll update you when we have any information."

When the comm ended, he rocked his chair back and steepled his hands at his chin. Either the crew had collectively gone rogue to join some pirate group or other, or they were dead. Space was dangerous; ships were lost all the time, and because space was also vast, most of the time the wreckage was never found.

'Director, the vessel in question has not interacted with any Concord facilities since it was reported missing. However, I have detected an anomaly.'

"Oh? What is it?"

'A merchant vessel belonging to Manu Provisions with the ID #BSA-4162-dd6b docked briefly at Concord HQ forty minutes ago. However, a vessel with that same ID is also currently docked at Andromeda Merchant Waypoint #2.'

Richard's pulse ticked up a notch. "Could the crew have altered the transponder code on the missing ship?"

'Not legally, but someone with the necessary technical knowledge likely could have made such an alteration, yes.'

"Show me the details on the vessel that docked at HQ."

A series of log entries appeared a screen. 'I have also attached the visuals captured as part of the regular docking procedures.'

He leapt up, sending his chair skidding into the wall. He hardly had to glance at the visual to confirm what he already knew—that it was the ship from the Savrakath encampment. "Where is it now?"

'Records indicate its cargo was unloaded and sent to processing. As soon as the unloading was complete, the vessel departed again, approximately twelve minutes ago.'

"Track every container transferred off the ship, highest priority. I need to know where that cargo is right now." As CINT's official Artificial, Cliff's quantum fingers extended into every system on Concord HQ. If anyone could find the cargo, it was Cliff.

Richard forced himself to pause for a single moment. Was he overreacting? He had no hard proof, only a hunch based on logical lines he'd drawn from one event to the next.

'Here are the current locations of all tagged cargo containers originating from the merchant vessel, with one exception. The container tagged #BSA-C859-fk24 never made it to its designated slot in Warehouse 3C.'

Not a hunch any longer. He accessed the top security layer and activated a silent, Tier IV emergency protocol ordering Security to begin a quiet, orderly evacuation of Concord HQ. With more than ten thousand people on the station, it was going to take hours, but making a public announcement would not speed up the process and would only cause a panic.

'I have also acquired a visual of a single individual departing Vessel #BSA-4162-dd6b with the cargo containers. Analysis of the Security footage indicates the individual did not reboard the vessel prior to its departure.'

"Send me the visual, along with anything else you flag as related to the ship or its cargo. And issue an order halting the movement of all cargo containers on the station." He latched his Daemon to his belt and headed for the door—where he ran smack into Will.

His husband grabbed his shoulder. "What's going on? I just saw the alert."

"I think the Savrakaths have sneaked an antimatter bomb onto the station. Will, I need you to go home."

"Home? No. I need to oversee the implementation of CINT emergency protocols and assist Security with the evacuation procedures, none of which can happen from home."

"Please. I'm going to find the bomb, but I won't be able to properly concentrate and do my job if I'm worried about what will happen to you should I fail."

Will nudged him backward, over the threshold of his office, and closed the door behind them. He brought both hands to Richard's face. "I love you for being afraid for me and wanting to protect me. You know I do. But I can't shirk my responsibilities any more than you can. I trust you to find and disarm the bomb. I need you to trust me to do my job."

Richard opened his mouth to retort, but he had no response that wasn't based on pure emotion. So instead he drew Will into his arms and kissed him, long and slow, then whispered against his lips. "The instant you can leave, do it. I'll see you soon."

He reached around and opened the door, and they both took off in opposite directions.

"Cliff, anything?"

'Nothing so far. The container has not been scanned into any new sectors. A comprehensive threat scan is underway, but thus far no traces of antimatter have been detected.'

This was why Dr. Khalik had handled the transfer. Any moderately trained Savrakath military officer could move an antimatter casing from one container to another. Khalik had been called upon to build a shield around the casing, one designed to insulate it from most standard scans.

Richard didn't stop to check in with any of the CINT departments. Those who could meaningfully contribute to tracking down the bomb or the missing crewmember or helping to effect the evacuation had their orders, and everyone else was being sent home. Him, though? He had to find that bomb.

He finally reached the CINT entrance and headed out into the open atrium, toward the nearest levtram station. He'd start at the last tagged location of the container, then work from there—

"Richard!"

He turned at hearing his name to see David jogging over to him from one of the levtram platforms. "Is something up? My class at SWTC got evacuated by several very terse Security officers."

His gaze darted between the levtram platform and David for several seconds. They had not mended their relationship, but now was not the time to worry about interpersonal conflicts. David Solovy was a faster and more creative thinker than any person he knew, and doubly so in the midst of a crisis. He should send the man off the station, because whatever their current differences, he did want his friend to be safe. But he also needed him.

He grabbed David by the upper arm. "Come with me."

"Of course. Where are we going?"

"I'll let you know as soon as I figure it out."

56

ADV DAUNTLESS

TOKI'TAKU STELLAR SYSTEM

Lance gripped the railing until his knuckles turned white as the *Dauntless* dropped into an eighty-degree plunge toward the planet's mesosphere. The thickening air fought back, and the hull shuddered as they pulled up out of the dive and skidded along the buffeting atmosphere.

A powerful laser strike impacted their port side, and the force of the strike drove the ship down toward the planet once again. If this were the previous incarnation of the *Dauntless*, they'd all be dead now. But this was a new ship constructed under a new set of rules, and his ace navigator skillfully maneuvered them up out of the atmosphere, then promptly flipped their heading to target the firing Rasu.

From this vantage, with the planet at his back, Lance had a brief opportunity to survey a wide swath of the battlefield. The space between here and Toki'taku's small moon was thick with Concord vessels—Commandant Solovy had not skimped on this battle—but it remained even thicker with Rasu. His gut told him how the rest of the battle was going to play out, and it boiled down to the Rasu sending ever more forces until they could simply bulldoze their way through the defenders and descend upon the planet.

He was doing his damnedest to keep the Rasu in space, but despite a fleet of indestructible, state-of-the-art warships, he was giving ground every minute. They all were.

On the far edge of the tactical map, multiple red blips flashed into existence, only for many of them to vanish again seconds later. Three stealth squadrons were responding to new Rasu arrivals, greeting them with a barrage of negative energy missiles even before they finished emerging from their wormholes. But some always slipped through—

—the bridge whipped around beneath his feet, as if it had been spun like a top. "Report!"

"We're losing impulse control! The engine is firing, but it's not doing any good!"

As the ship cavorted helplessly, the viewport showed flashes of a blinding vortex on every spin. Lance fought past nausea to try to focus. Had the Rasu really dared to open a wormhole right at the edge of the atmosphere? The defenders didn't dare use negative energy weapons en masse so close to the planet…and the Rasu knew it.

"We're trapped in the gravitation pull of a wormhole vortex. All engines reverse full. Whatever we've got, use it!"

The hull would hold; it had taken enough of a beating today already to convince Lance of this. But the last thing he wanted was to be sucked through a hole in space and deposited in the middle of Rasu Central untold megaparsecs away. His battle was *here,* and he'd be damned if he was going to be forced into abandoning it.

The swirling light of the vortex was blotted out by the encroaching shadows of several massive Rasu emerging from it, and abruptly the cosmic forces tearing at them faded away as the vortex dissipated.

"Get us some room so we can tally up what that wormhole brought down upon us."

"Yes, sir." The navigator's voice shook, but he'd performed above and beyond when it counted.

Steering control regained, they banked up and away from the planet before swinging around…Lance's heart sank. Several dozen Rasu of varying sizes had exited their vortex and immediately accelerated into the atmosphere below. Agile attack craft pursued them, but mid-atmosphere dogfights were not particularly accurate or productive—and soon they'd be fighting only a few kilometers above the surface.

They needed a new strategy, but hells if he knew what it might be. Nothing in his past had prepared him for this manner of enemy.

As if on cue, Commandant Solovy called an impromptu conference with the battlefield commanders. Before Lance joined it, he sent Nika a message.

MIRAI

OMOIKANE INITIATIVE

A group of oversized Rasu vessels are starting to break through the blockade and enter the atmosphere. If we've got some trick stashed up our sleeve, we need to play it now.

Nika closed her eyes and pressed her fingertips to her temples, breathing in a final moment of calm.

Understood.

She pivoted to Dashiel. "Get to the DAF Military Services Center and be ready to offload our entire supply of Rima Grenades as soon as I give the word."

He reached out and drew her into his arms for a brief embrace. "Good luck."

"Thank you. I need it." With tense smiles they parted ways, and she grabbed the large, heavy bag she'd stashed in a corner then headed up to the roof.

When the battle had begun, she'd considered traveling to the Dominion Embassy on Toki'taku to better be in a position to act quickly. But it meant leaving the Initiative in the midst of a crisis, and there was no guarantee the Elder would authorize an official visit on her part while he was busy managing the planetary defense. So she'd remained at the Initiative until the last possible minute—and now she needed to get herself in front of the Elder with a snap of her fingers.

Atop the Mirai One Pavilion, enclosed in a protective force field, sat a modified Sukasu Gate. Given her continued failure to decipher how to open wormholes using her mind alone, the device constituted the only way they had to create a wormhole with a dynamic destination point. The technology worked—she'd proved that by hop-skipping the *Wayfarer* across five megaparsecs of space in a few weeks to reach the Milky Way. But in practice it was bulky, delicate and required a great deal of power, hence its location on the roof instead of inside with the more traditional d-gates.

Because she'd alerted the staff that it would likely be called into use today, a DAF officer waited beside the force field in addition to the usual dyne security detail. He nodded sharply as she approached. "Advisor."

"Good evening, officer. Please deactivate the force field."

"Yes, ma'am." He punched a code into the control pane, and the field sizzled briefly then flickered off. "What's your destination?"

"Toki'taku. The Alcazar."

"We don't have authorization to open a wormhole on Toki'taku, except for inside our embassy grounds."

"I realize that, but the exigent circumstances require it. Please...Lieutenant, is it? I take full responsibility for any negative consequences that may result from my actions."

"It's not about—"

"I'm filing a report this instant with Commander Palmer and DAF Command absolving you of any and all blame related to my use of the Sukasu Gate."

"Yes, ma'am. The Alcazar, coming up." He entered a series of instructions into the large module to the left of the device, and a wave of electricity rushed over her skin as the d-gate shimmered to life. "Will you be needing a return trip as well?"

"Honestly, I might. Shut it down once I'm out the other side, and I'll send you a message if or when I need a pickup."

"As you wish." The officer studied the readout for a second. "You're good to traverse."

"Thank you." She squared her shoulders and stepped through the d-gate.

TOKI'TAKU

ALCAZAR

The deadly end of four Taiyok rifles greeted Nika on her arrival in the Alcazar main chamber. She raised both hands in surrender, though she didn't drop the bag, as the tickling energy of the d-gate faded away and the wormhole behind her closed. "Please lower your weapons. You know me as Asterion Dominion Advisor Nika Kirumase. I need to speak to the Elder right away."

Behind the armed guards, Taiyoks rushed in every direction. The scene was teeming with activity, but it wasn't as panicked or chaotic as she'd expected. Did the Taiyoks never lose their cool? Even the guard who seemed to be in charge studied her wearing a hooded expression; his feathers hadn't so much as fluttered once. "The Elder is occupied with the invasion resistance."

At least they called it what it was. "I realize he is. This is why it is vitally important that I speak to him immediately."

The guard dipped his head toward her left hand. "What's in the bag?"

"A way to save your people and your planet."

"Put it on the floor and step away."

She choked off an impatient groan as she complied with the order. She'd been traveling to Toki'taku and meeting with Taiyok leaders for *thirteen thousand years*, and now she had no time!

The guard kept one reflective eye on her as he crouched in front of the bag, opened it and peered inside. "This looks like a weapon."

"Yes, a weapon that can stop the Rasu cold. Please."

He stood and glared at her for a moment—then he blinked, and his demeanor shifted. "The Elder says he will see you. I will maintain possession of the bag and its contents while I accompany you inside."

"That's fine, so long as the bag accompanies us both. Thank you."

The other three rifles finally lowered. The head guard closed up the bag and draped it over his shoulder, then used the rifle to motion her forward. "This way."

He led her through a discreet door in the back of what she had always thought of as the main chamber. It opened up into a space she'd never seen before—or not one she remembered visiting.

The architecture was classic Taiyok, all wood and stone and subtlety. But in a striking departure from most facilities, the tech at work was on full display here. Conductive metal frames powered an array of giant screens; several displayed the battle underway above the planet, and others tracked the movements of Rasu vessels encroaching upon the surface. Officers dressed in full military regalia worked at three-paneled, arcing stations attached to stacks of quantum servers.

The Elder stood near the center of the room, deep in discussion with two officers while war chatter scrolled frenetically on a screen beside him. Perhaps sensing their arrival, he made a cutting motion with one hand and spun toward them.

"Advisor Kirumase. You bring news of import, I hope?"

"Your world is burning—but you already know this. I bring a weapon you can use to not only keep Rasu ships from landing on Toki'taku soil, but to permanently remove them from your skies altogether."

The Elder's wings twitched, but he held them rigidly high. "Advisor, you have our deepest appreciation for all you've done to aid us, including for your ships fighting to protect us as we speak. But we have discussed this matter before, and at its root, my position has not changed. We will survive or fall by our own devices."

"I respect your position, and my scientists have striven to comply with your wishes as closely as possible. If I may retrieve something from my bag, I can demonstrate for you."

The officer who had accompanied her made a grumbling noise. "Elder, her bag contains what I believe to be a weapon. I recommend caution."

"It's all right, Lieutenant. I don't believe the Advisor has traveled all this way to assassinate me."

"I assure you, I mean no one in the Alcazar any harm. The opposite, in fact."

The Elder nodded, and she knelt in front of the bag. Tucked inside at one end was a much smaller compartment, and she opened it up. As her hand wrapped around one of the small objects it held, she activated the recessed button in the shell.

She stood and extended her hand, palm open, in the direction of the Elder.

"I do not have time for trickery or amusement, Advisor."

"Can you not see through your own stealth technology, Elder?"

His copper eyes flickered brightly. "You have made your point. Now show me."

"Of course." Her thumb pressed the button again, and a tiny orb two centimeters in diameter materialized in her palm. It was encased in a mesh shell, which included retractable fins, a microscopic power source and enough drone code to guide the orb to its selected destination.

"We call it a Rima Grenade. When fired from a launcher, it will draw any object it impacts, up to three kilometers in length and breadth, into a type of singularity, then eject the object directly into your sun's corona."

The Elder's gaze was riveted on the orb resting in her palm. "If true, this is a most impressive weapon. But it sounds similar to the Rift Bubbles. This is Katasketousya technology."

"It originates from the engineering that drives the Rift Bubbles, yes. But we have stripped the engineering down, all the way to its base operating code, and used it to build something new. Something I'm proud to call an Asterion invention. Then we wrapped it in Taiyok stealth technology." She toggled the button, and the orb vanished. "The enemy will never see it coming. And what they can't see, they can't destroy."

The Elder stared at her seemingly empty palm, coming closer to peer at it from various angles. "The concealment is effective enough that I concede it must be of our own design." His gaze rose to meet hers. "Nonetheless, you are, as one says, splitting some very fine feathers indeed here."

She held his piercing, recondite stare; if she flinched now, all was lost. "On the contrary, Elder, I am presenting you with a solution that allows you to uphold *malu'oel*—" his narrow chin flinched in surprise at the native word rolling off her tongue "—while still defending your people and your world. Please, Elder, in the spirit of our long and fruitful alliance, accept this gift."

His attention finally diverted to the open bag beside her. "Show me how it works."

RW

Nika gasped in horror when they stepped onto the platform outside the main chamber. The Sukasu Gate had deposited her directly inside, so she hadn't gotten a look at the surrounding area until now.

The sky glowed the same copper as the Elder's eyes. In the distance to the east, a torrent of flames wrent the forest apart, sending embers shooting into the sky like fireflies. High above the conflagration, wide, violet beams streaked out from the bellies of two cruiser-sized Rasu vessels to expand the reach of the flames by what appeared to be dozens of meters every second. Hundreds of Taiyok fighters buzzed around the Rasu, shooting and being shot at in return but doing little to slow down the destruction.

"Elder, don't you need to evacuate the Alcazar?"

"Not until there is no other option. Show me."

She retrieved the specially designed launcher from the bag, slotted three of the Rima Grenades into the chamber and started to lift it up onto her shoulder—then held it out to the Elder instead. "Would you like to do the honors, sir? Perhaps you will feel more comfortable with the technology if you operate it yourself."

"I am not a soldier…but I can aim a reticle." He accepted the launcher from her, then passed it from one hand to the other, as if evaluating the heft of it.

"Simply brace it on your shoulder, and the guidance reticle will pop out. Use it to lock onto the desired target, then press the trigger. Everything else will take care of itself."

He did as instructed, adjusting it once before settling into peering at the pop-out screen. "What is the range?"

"Up to one hundred kilometers—and we don't recommend targeting anything closer than five kilometers to you or vital structures."

"That is acceptable." Without fanfare, his finger lightly pressed the trigger.

Other than a slight air compression sound, it looked as if nothing happened. The Elder lowered the launcher and let it dangle from his hand, his eyes locked on the burning horizon.

Abruptly the air around the closer of the two Rasu cruisers flared in a starburst of light for an instant. Then the light and the cruiser were simply…gone.

The Elder breathed in deeply. "Our sun's corona, you say?"

"For the nanosecond it lasted there before being atomized by the 6,000 K temperature and relentless nuclear reactions."

He jerked the launcher back up onto his shoulder, aimed and fired again. The second Rasu cruiser vanished in a burst of radiant light. When it was gone, he handed the launcher back to her. "How many do you have?"

She tried to keep her smile polite and respectful, but her skin flushed from a deluge of relief. "2,240 Rima Grenades, with thirty additional ones being completed every hour, as well as forty launchers. Tell me where to send them and authorize us to open wormholes at those locations, and your soldiers can be wielding the launchers inside ten minutes."

MIRAI

DAF MILITARY SERVICES CENTER

"Two hundred Rima Grenades plus three launchers." Dashiel made a circling motion with one arm. "Get them loaded onto the trolley and through the wormhole—go!"

The two DAF officers stacked the deadly little grenades onto the rack as fast as the warehouse dynes delivered them. The orbs were inert until activated by the launching mechanism, which was a good thing, as they didn't have time to observe much in the way of safety measures. One officer tossed the launchers one by one to the other, who hooked them onto the sides of the rack then guided the trolley through the dynamically generated d-gate.

No time to rest. "As soon as he returns with the trolley, we've got a new destination southeast of the capital city. Let's get everything queued up." Everyone scrambled in response, almost as if Dashiel were a military officer legitimately authorized to order them around, which he was not.

The officer reemerged with the empty trolley a minute later, and the staff loaded up a new rack while the Sukasu Gate located at Military Services was reconfigured for the next destination.

Dashiel considered the rows upon rows of shelves that had been converted into Rima Grenade storage. Their supply was already running low. It appeared that once convinced, the Elder was all in. Good, as nothing less would rid the Toki'taku surface of Rasu and keep them gone.

The newly full trolley again vanished through the Sukasu Gate, and he checked the updating list of instructions. "Interesting. The Alcazar is asking for a resupply of two dozen Rima Grenades. They've got a launcher." He glanced around the open area at the front of the warehouse. "Let's box them up and carry them through by hand."

He started queuing up the next several deliveries—only four remained for now—while the Sukasu Gate was reconfigured yet again. The machine was a scandalous power hog, but it was a most useful one nonetheless.

One of the officers carried the box of Rima Grenades through the d-gate to the Alcazar, then returned thirty seconds later without the box but with a companion.

"Nika!" She'd barely cleared the d-gate when he swept her up into his arms and spun her around. "You did it."

She sighed into his neck. "I did. And none too soon. Rasu cruisers were advancing on the Alcazar, burning the forest as they moved."

"And now?"

She kissed the corner of his mouth before stepping out of his embrace. "The Elder himself took great pleasure in dispatching those Rasu cruisers, then decided he wanted a small stash of the Rima Grenades in case more show up."

"Understandable." He smiled wearily. She looked as exhausted as he felt, but the adrenaline surge from making a godsdamned difference in this war fueled them both onward.

"How goes the main battle?"

"I can't say. I've been consumed with getting these weapons where they needed to be."

"And I adore you for it." Her gaze drifted toward the door. "I think I'll run next door and peek over Colonel Rogers' shoulder to see if I can get a feel for the situation. Want to come with me?"

He peered behind him, where the trolley was being stacked anew with a full loadout, then shook his head. The staff here could assuredly manage the remaining orders now that the process had been perfected, but he didn't dare risk stepping away at this crucial juncture. "I owe the Taiyoks four more deliveries first. I'll catch up with you."

57

CONCORD HQ

"The last official record of the cargo container shows it being scanned through this location."

While Richard waited for the Security officer to check his panel, David took in the lengthy warehouse stretching into the distance behind the man. An antimatter bomb, here. A death sentence for thousands of people and fourteen years of hard work was hiding somewhere in the deep labyrinths of the station. His blood rushed with anticipation of the chase, but dread at what would happen if they didn't find it in time darkened his thoughts. He'd never imagined the pitched throes of combat against the Rasu would be the safer location, but he found himself glad that Miri was currently galaxies away.

Richard instantiated an aural and spun it toward the officer. "Do you remember this Barisan accompanying the container into storage? He'd have been here within the last hour."

The officer studied the vid. "I think I do recall checking him in."

"Was he acting strangely?"

The officer shrugged. "No more strangely than most Barisans. Sorry, sir, but I don't have their body language down yet. Our stocker was busy situating a shipment of industrial-grade photal fibers, so the Barisan offered to slot the container himself. I'm supposed to stay at this post, so I let him. Did I make a mistake?"

Any CINT agent could tell you the signs of stress, panic or fear in the demeanor of every Concord Member and Allied species, but Security officers hadn't yet received such in-depth training. David made a note to see to it that such training was added to the curriculum, though Richard was likely making the same note. "Ideally, you should have called another officer here to accompany him, but I'll concede we might have a gap in the protocols. Do you remember when he checked back out?"

"No, sir. Officer Sandal relieved me for my regular break, so I assume it happened while I was gone. But..." he frowned at his screen "...it doesn't appear he ever returned to check out at all. Do I need to institute a Security alert, sir?"

"That won't be necessary. The warehouses are now closed due to the evacuation order, but I need you to stay at your station and keep an eye out for this individual. If he does return, please detain him and notify me immediately."

"You, personally? I mean...yes, sir, Director."

Richard motioned for David to follow him, and they plunged into the depths of the warehouse. Richard set a brisk pace as they wound through the endless shelves, refrigeration units and shielded rooms. His friend didn't speak, and David recognized this was not the moment for lighthearted banter.

He wanted to ask if Miri had been informed of the threat, but he refrained from doing that, too. She was waging a battle five megaparsecs away, and she trusted Richard to handle Concord affairs in her absence. So did he. He did, however, compose a brief message to her, sent it to a remote server on Earth, and queued it to be delivered in two hours in the event that he and Richard blew themselves up today.

Having suffered through such a calamity recently himself, his heart seized up at the thought of leaving her alone for even a day. But at least this time, it wouldn't be for a quarter-century.

As the towering shelves and corridors began to blend together, David's mind drifted to idle curiosity at what his regenesis would involve. He'd inhabited this body for more than fourteen years now, but it remained unique. Whenever he went in for his regular backup appointment, the techs at Medical insisted they were capturing a typical neural imprint from his brain function, one fully capable of supporting regenesis. But this would be regenesis into a standard human body, not the Anaden-human-synthetic hybrid one he currently inhabited. Would it feel different?

"Here." Richard skidded to a stop halfway down one of the endless rows, but his chin dropped to his chest. The slot along the bottom row where the container should be located sat empty. "Dammit!"

The tension ratcheted up, tightening its grip on David's chest. But he'd been in these situations before. Sort of. "How do we find a rogue cargo container?"

"Cliff, I need the closest Security footage to Grid 6 in Warehouse 3C." Richard instantiated an aural so David could see the footage as well. The cam was situated some distance away, but it showed a Barisan pushing the dolly holding the container along this row. He stopped at the empty slot, peered furtively around, then hurriedly continued on, taking the next right and vanishing.

Richard took off at a brisk jog down the aisle, and David hastened to catch up. Two turns later, they came to a maintenance door. A female Anaden in a Security uniform lay sprawled on the floor by the door, which was held ajar by a shock stick jammed into the opening.

David dropped to his knees by the woman. An ugly gash on her forehead dribbled blood onto the floor, but she had a pulse. "She's unconscious but still breathing. Steady pulse."

Richard nodded. "Cliff, I need an armed Security squad with a medical detachment at Maintenance Door 3C-6E. We've got a Security officer in need of urgent medical attention at this location." Next he entered a code on the panel, and the door slid the rest of the way open. "Down we go."

Normally they'd never abandon an injured person, but the Security squad would reach her in less than five minutes, and the rest of the people on the station might not have five minutes. David climbed to his feet and followed Richard through the door, which led directly to a lift. As soon as they stepped foot on it, it began descending into the maintenance levels. Ten interminable seconds later, it slowed to a stop at a floor labeled 'Maintenance 4.' Hallways forked out in three directions.

David rubbed at his jaw. "Any chance we've got Security footage from this area?"

Richard held up a finger, and David waited. "The Barisan took the left hallway, but then he started spotting the cams and shooting them out."

David peered down the left hallway. "Can you pull up the floor plan for everything from here? Maintenance, engineering, power?"

"All twenty-two square kilometers of it?"

David shrugged.

"Right. One second...here we go." An aural appeared between them displaying a complex sketch of multiple interlocking levels.

David pointed to a spot near the top left. "We're here?"

"Approximately."

"And our suspect went left, then we lost him."

"Correct."

He studied the schematic, his eyes running along several potential paths like he was trying to solve a maze puzzle.

"David, we need to keep moving."

"Not until we know where we're moving to."

"But we—"

David glanced at Richard through the glow of the schematic aural. "How much antimatter would you say is in the bomb?"

"Based on the Ghost footage? Two, maybe three kilograms."

"Enough to blow a giant hole through warehousing and maintenance, but this far from the outer hull, not enough to breach the exterior of the station—unless it detonates in proximity to Power Generation."

Richard considered the floor plan for half a second. "*Shit.* Let's go."

They sprinted down winding hallways and vibrated through four lift descents. They passed only two Security officers during the journey, as regular maintenance staff had been ordered to evacuate. Their path led them through Engineering…David briefly considered stopping for a quick search there, because if placed at certain locations, a detonation in Engineering would have nearly as devastating of an effect on the station. But this Barisan was a merchant, not an experienced terrorist or an engineer, and the Savrakaths calling the shots didn't know the details of HQ's design. They'd go for the power center, because there would be a sure thing.

Finally they reached the entrance to Power Generation. The wide blast doors were stuck in the open position and, as before, a guard lay prone on the floor beside them. This one was human, and he'd fared worse than the first guard. His throat had been sliced opened by multiple gashes.

"Barisan claws."

David shook his head roughly, fighting back the bile rising in his throat. "Not a pleasant way to go."

Richard studied the panel controlling the doors. "Our suspect must have used the guard's retina and ID scan to get the doors open."

They skirted the pool of blood surrounding the guard and stepped through the open blast doors onto the top gangway ringing the power station.

David's skin felt as if it had been set afire. Beyond a protective double force field, the first of five massive Zero Engines churned like a captured sun. Though the force fields dimmed the light enough to protect them from being blinded simply by walking in, he had to adjust his ocular implant to filter out much of the blazing inferno.

He peered over the railing, but the fiery light obscured the details of the second Zero Engine situated far below, and he made out only hints of the three additional ones stacked all the way to the 'bottom' of the station.

"Our guy might have figured this was good enough—which it surely must be. We should search the ring."

"You go left, I'll go right."

David nodded and took off along the translucent gangway that arced around the towering Zero Engine.

RW

SAVRAK

SITE 2A

Ghorek paced in agitation across the command tent. They should have stitched a cam to the Barisan in addition to the bomb and the transmitter. As it was, he felt blind.

The Barisan's raspy, heaving voice came over the comm. *"Okay, I've reached the power generation section. Gods below, this engine is huge."*

Ghorek tapped his comm. "Good, then it will serve our purpose. Can you take the container any deeper into the room?"

"Room? This isn't a room—it's an entire bloody station all its own. And no. I'm on a circular gangway, and...I see a ladder farther around to the right that leads to a lower-level gangway, but I can't maneuver the container down a ladder. Please, sir. This is all I can do."

The location transmitter indicated the Barisan had proceeded into the interior of Concord HQ, but they lacked a more detailed map upon which to pin the alien's location with any greater accuracy. Curses that Ghorek hadn't been able to send one of his own men on the mission, but any Savrakath would have been shot on sight.

This had to be good enough. "I'm activating the timer on the container now. It's set to go off in twenty minutes, so if you hurry you can make it back to the ship and get off the station in time." It was a lie, of course; the timer was set for five minutes, the ship was long gone, and the alien was never getting off the station.

"Twenty minutes? It took me half an hour to get here—wait, I hear something. Someone's coming."

Kankii! Ghorek lunged for the detonator linked to the device implanted inside the alien and slammed a claw down upon it.

One problem disposed of. Now deaf as well as blind, he could only watch the countdown tied to the antimatter bomb.

4:50

4:49

4:48

RW

CONCORD HQ

POWER GENERATION

A shout followed by a muffled gurgling noise echoed off the smooth walls of Power Generation, and David spun and sprinted back the way he'd come, then kept going. He found Richard in one piece near a large circular container, thankfully, staring at a righteous mess of blood and gore. It decorated the gangway and the wall, and droplets sparked against the force field as they dribbled down it.

"*Bozhe moy*! What happened?"

"This was our guy. I saw him and started shouting for him to step away from the device. He glanced up at me, stumbled backward and blew up, as if from the inside out."

"Goddamn. The Savrakaths booby-trapped him."

"Looks like."

"It also means they were watching or listening through him, and now they're blind."

"Unless there's a cam on the container."

"If there is, we're already dead."

"Good point." Richard stepped around a blotch of blood on the floor with wiry hairs sticking out of it. "The question is, did he arm the bomb before we got here, or did I interrupt him?"

"We can't take the chance that you didn't." David picked his way past the carnage and knelt in front of the circular container. "We need to get this thing open."

Richard produced a multitool from his belt, pressed a button, and a chisel snapped out. "There's a seam along the edge of the top here."

Thank god for inferior Savrakath construction; if this had been a Concord device, it would have been impenetrable.

Richard jimmied the flat edge of the chisel into the tiny seam and leaned into it as best he could given the top of the container was almost as tall as he was. Nothing happened. "A little help?"

David stood and wrapped his hands around Richard's, and together they threw their entire combined weight into it.

A tiny crack appeared in the top, less than a centimeter wide.

Richard exhaled and moved the chisel farther along the seam, and they repeated the process. Finally, when they'd worked a quarter of the top loose, on their next attempt the lid went flying up into the air, bounced off the force field with an angry sizzle and clattered to the gangway.

They both leaned over to peer inside the container. Suspended by five metal braces halfway down was an opaque, heavily shielded orb.

Richard let out a tense breath. "Ever seen anything like this?"

"Not since those eight hours of bomb identification training fifty years ago."

"Yeah...I seem to recall the trainers saying something to the effect of, 'Identify what you can, then call in a hazmat team and let them handle it.'"

"Go ahead and give them a comm so they can start heading this way. But we don't know how long we have, so we can't wait around twiddling our thumbs."

"Nope. They're on the way. Now, what can we do?"

David had been studying the various components situated inside the container as much as he could from this vantage. The design and materials were all unfamiliar, but the rules of physics and engineering were universal, and there were only so many ways to craft working circuits. "Does this remind you of the mission on Radavi where we first met?"

"What? No, not at all. Does it to you?"

"A little bit." He pointed to a blocky gray module stuck on the inner wall, near the top of the container. "This is the only possible control mechanism I can see. Everything else is padding and shielding or the antimatter core."

"Agreed. But is it acting as a timer, a remote detonation receiver, or a catch?"

"I doubt the Savrakaths expected the bomb to be discovered and disarming attempted. It's either a timer or a receiver. If it's the latter, this thing could go off any second..." David shook his head "...no, it's a timer. Otherwise it would have already gone off."

"Why do you say that?"

"Imagine this scenario. Some Savrakath is talking the Barisan through placing the bomb. The Barisan hears you coming and says, 'someone's approaching.' The Savrakath recognizes this is the end of the road and blows up this poor sodding soul. If they had the capability to do so, I cannot think of a reason for them not to immediately detonate the bomb as well."

Richard didn't argue. "So it's a timer. I don't see anything so helpful as a countdown clock to give us a clue on how much time we have, so we'll assume it's not long." He peered deeper inside. "I also don't see any nanowires connecting the module to the orb."

"They could be built into the containment walls and threaded through the braces." David activated his plasma blade and climbed on top of the container.

"David!"

"I am open to other suggestions." He grunted, maneuvered around until his arm wasn't at an impossible angle, then gingerly brought the edge of the blade closer to the module.

"I don't have any."

"Neither do I." He paused, the blade two centimeters away from the edge of the module. "If I fuck this up…well, I know we'll wake back up in a few days and see each other again. But it still feels like dying, so I want you to know how sorry I am about what happened with the Ghost. Genuinely, truly, sorry. If I've ruined our friendship, I will regret it for the rest of my days."

"David, now is not the time."

"I know it isn't." He squinted, winced and slipped the blade into the tiny gap behind the module, then worked it around. The module was secured in the same manner as the container top had been, and after a few wrenches it came loose and dropped into his hand.

He fell off the casing, module lifted triumphantly above his head. "How about now? Is this a better time?"

Richard shot him an incredulous look, grabbed the module from him, and took off running. "It could be wireless!"

Oh, right. Good point. He sucked in air to burning lungs and sprinted along the gangway after Richard.

Richard lurched to a stop fifty meters around the ring, knelt on the gangway and placed the module in front of him. "I'd throw it into the Zero Engine, but I don't have the code to open an entrance in the force field. Shooting anything in here seems like a profoundly terrible idea. So…." He produced his own blade, hesitated for half a second, then started stabbing the module over and over.

Sparks flew out of the object as it splintered into pieces, but any ozone that might have accompanied the sparks was subsumed by the natural ionization from the Zero Engine. Not satisfied, Richard picked up the pieces and tossed them over the edge of the railing. The 'bottom' of Power Generation was more than a kilometer below them; they'd never hear it when the tiny pieces finally landed.

Richard sank down to the gangway and dropped his head against the curving wall. "That had to have done it. Right?"

David collapsed next to him. "If it didn't, I've got no more suggestions. I mean, other than how we should definitely get this antimatter far away from here as soon as possible."

Richard nodded wearily. "The hazmat team is forty seconds out. I say we let them handle it."

"Good idea."

Richard's gaze cut sideways to him. "So, about that apology?"

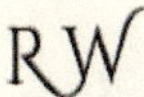

SAVRAK

SITE 2A

0:03

0:02

0:01

—

Was it done? Ghorek activated the comm channel to his man situated on the merchant vessel, who he'd ordered to retreat to twenty megameters away from the station after undocking, then wait.

"Officer Khonarg, report. Has the station suffered any damage?"

"Um...no, sir. I'm some distance away, but I'm not detecting any signs of explosions or venting. It, um...it looks the same as it did, sir."

Ghorek lashed out with a claw, sweeping everything off the table in front of him before spinning to punch the flimsy tent wall. *No!* It wasn't possible that he'd failed in his grand act of vengeance. Concord must suffer!

But he had nothing left; he'd played his last hand. He strode out of the tent in a daze, then cast his eyes to the orange sun above in despair. Concord ships would be arriving soon now to finish the job of exterminating his people, and the old gods weren't going to swoop in and save them.

CONCORD HQ

POWER GENERATION

David huffed a winded laugh. The ionized air was a bitch and a half to breathe. "While Miri was...gone...I know I acted as if I had my shit together. I told myself I *had* to stay in control in order to keep Concord from falling to the Anadens. To keep everything she'd built intact. To be strong for Alex. But it was all a lie. I was a wreck, half out of my mind and headed swiftly for certifiably insane."

"You could have fooled me."

"My superior officers always did say my level-headedness and calm under pressure was one of my best attributes. I'm sure I don't need to tell you what they said my worst ones were. The point is, if I'd been in the slightest bit rational, I'd have come to you with Caleb's request. I should have.

"But...I don't know. Saving Marlee felt like a proxy for saving Miri, and I would have done anything—*anything*—to make it happen. So I ran headlong off the cliff that looked to my grieving mind like salvation."

"I would have helped you and Caleb."

"I know. If I'd been thinking clearly, I would've known it then, too. Still, I have no excuse."

Richard shrugged, and his expression softened. "That makes for a pretty good one, as excuses go."

"Not good enough of one. We should have been partners, start to finish, no matter what. I am deeply, *sozhaleniyem* sorry."

The muscles around Richard's eyes twitched, and after a beat he nodded. "Okay. Apology accepted."

David shot Richard a chagrined yet hopeful look. He had ten more minutes' worth of *mea culpas* all queued up if needed. "You're certain?"

"I'm certain. I am sick of being the grumpy old curmudgeon who hauls his grudges around like a badge of honor. I'm sick of being angry and petty."

"You weren't being petty."

"It felt like I was."

David offered his hand, sweaty and covered in greasy solvent though it was. "Friends?"

Richard clasped David's hand in his equally filthy one. "Always. And you know, as I think about it, this *does* remind me a little of the mission on Radavi where we met. Mostly in how it's ended with us triumphantly flat on our asses."

"Well, you know what that means: next up, two rounds of beer on me."

"I think three this time."

"*Da,* that's fair. Three it is."

A commotion broke out around the ring to their left to announce the arrival of the hazmat team, and they helped each other back to their feet. Richard cupped his hands and shouted, "This way! Careful when you get close to the container!"

David gestured toward the bomb and the gaggle of hazmat specialists now congregating around it. "Time to clean up this mess. Together."

58

HAAFAN

Every hour that passed without a renewed Rasu incursion only ratcheted up Alex's impatience and, judging by the repeated flexing of the muscles along his jaw, Caleb's unease. It wasn't simple annoyance on their part, though—it was the fact that they were out of missiles and possibly out of tricks.

If the Rasu outside woke up or more arrived, she and Caleb could save themselves by opening a wormhole where they stood and getting the fuck out of town, and Valkyrie could undock the *Siyane* and flee in less than a minute. She'd tried to convince Wyddoniiet to let her evacuate everyone on foot. However, the locals were determined to bring along not only their personal belongings, but a voluminous amount of equipment as well as their three ships. Their demands left only one viable option.

Luckily for the Ourankeli, her mother had promised to deliver on this option soon. So long as they had time and warning, everything would be fine. They just had to get these aliens *moving.*

They stayed close to the hangar bay, with Valkyrie constantly monitoring the sensor probe they'd positioned outside for any hints of Rasu activity while she and Caleb watched the Ourankeli pack up their lives and cram it all inside their ships. Most of the items they loaded served no identifiable purpose to her scrutiny, but now was not the moment to play curious onlooker and distract them from their work.

So Alex paced ineffectually while Caleb fielded a barrage of questions from Marlee about the Ourankeli's needs and quirks, of which there were clearly many.

They were on their third circuit of the hangar bay when Valkyrie spoke up with dire news.

'I am detecting a spatial disturbance eighteen megameters from the planetoid.'

Alex grabbed Caleb's hand. "A Rasu wormhole?"

'A reasonable assumption, but...perhaps not?'

Valkyrie was rarely uncertain about anything. Alex slipped into sidespace, choosing a spot five megameters outside the planetoid. In the distance, the fabric of space split apart to form a halo of golden light.

That's not a Rasu wormhole—it's a Caeles Prism one!

So it appears.

Together she and Valkyrie watched as a stunning adiamene hull emerged through the opening, and for quite some time. When it finally cleared the wormhole, the vessel stretched for almost a kilometer in length. For all its grace and beauty, its profile was dominated by the weapons arrays lined up in rows along its belly.

I heard you might need a little assistance over here in...wherever we are. How can we help?

Her face screwed up in surprise, followed by delight. *Malcolm? I didn't realize you were back on a bridge.*

Only just now, but...yes. I am.

She wanted to ask about Mia, but as with everything else, it could wait. Thanks to several recent conversations between Caleb and Mia, they knew she was safely back in her own persona and no longer a fugitive, if nothing else.

Fantastic. Do you see those broken Rasu floating around way too close to this planetoid?

We're picking them up on scans now. What did you do to them?

Used an improvised neutron bomb to disable their regenerative capabilities, then emptied my negative energy missiles into them. But they won't stay broken for much longer.

Here's the situation: we've got five dozen and change aliens living inside this rock who need a new home straightaway. They should be ready to move in another...twenty minutes, maybe. I need you to keep an eye on those disabled Rasu, and if they start to fire up and reform, blast them with those tremendous weapons you brought along.

Also, be on the lookout for new arrivals, since they might have gotten off a distress signal. And when we finally get these aliens packed up and ready to move out, I just need you to reopen your wormhole so their ships can get to Concord space. Have you received destination coordinates from the Embassy?

We have. It should be a simple enough rescue, unless a few thousand *Rasu show up.*

You've got a nice ship there. You can handle them. She smiled to herself. *Oh, and Malcolm? I'm glad you're back.*

Caleb had been standing in front of her scrutinizing her every facial quirk for the entire conversation, and she cracked a grin at him. "Malcolm's here with his dreadnought and an express ride for the Ourankeli ships."

"Jenner, seriously?"

"It sounds as if he's returned to work, at least in some capacity."

"Hmm. Mia?"

"It didn't seem appropriate to ask him whether they've reconciled, in case they haven't."

His gaze unfocused briefly. "She's fine. She's doing community service work with the Godjans today." He shrugged. "I didn't ask whether they'd reconciled, either."

She rolled her eyes but didn't comment further. While she sympathized with both of them, if pressed, she'd come down on Mia's side. Having lost Caleb once and moved the heavens and the firmament to bring him back, she understood where Mia was coming from.

Hey, Alex? Looks like we got here in the nick of time. Long-range sensors are picking up a growing spatial disturbance on the fringes of the stellar system.

Understood. Stand by—unless you need to start shooting, then by all means.

She grabbed Caleb's hand. "Reinforcements are here. We need to move." She scanned the hangar bay until she spotted Wyddoniiet in the far left corner talking to Cyfeill, the Ourankeli who had grudgingly given them a tour of Haafan upon their arrival.

They hurried across the bay and skidded to a stop in front of Wyddoniiet, attracting curious attention from every Ourankeli in the area.

Alex started to touch one of Wyddoniiet's arms, then thought better of it. How squishy would it feel? "Time's up. We have incoming."

All of the alien's limbs seemed to tighten up around their torso. "I see. I will inform the others we must depart."

'I have confirmed with Colonel Ettore that Rasu signatures are now approaching the planetoid. Estimated arrival: six minutes.'

"Who?"

'The Denali's *Prevo.'*

"Ah." The time for subtlety and politeness was at an end. She stepped closer, into Wyddoniiet's personal space, though she still didn't touch them. "Now. You must depart now. You and whoever else is traveling on the *Siyane*, be on board in two minutes, or we will have no choice but to leave you behind."

Wyddoniiet's eyes spun in a full circle, and they and Cyfeill rushed off without further comment. Was that agreement? They'd find out soon enough.

She and Caleb sprinted *back* across the bay for the *Siyane* as the ramp extended in anticipation of their arrival. Alex fell into her cockpit chair and scanned the HUD, but Valkyrie had everything ready to go, so she pulled up the sensor readings from outside. A grouping of red dots—forty to fifty of them—grew steadily larger on the screen.

Caleb peered out the open airlock as the clock ticked down, glancing briefly at her every few seconds. They wouldn't leave Wyddoniiet here unless they ran out of all options, but hopefully she'd instilled a proper sense of exigency in the alien.

The bedrock door to the hangar bay detached and began to open as the engines of the Ourankeli ships fired up one by one. Okay, where the fuck were their passengers?

'Estimated arrival of Rasu within firing range of the planetoid: one hundred seconds.'

Alex drummed her fingers on the dash and her feet on the floor. "Valkyrie, spool up the Caeles Prism the instant we're clear of the door."

'All systems are prepped and ready.'

Caleb's fingertips flitted above the control panel that operated the ramp and the airlock. "Come on…."

At the last possible second, Wyddoniiet appeared from the left with two Ourankeli trailing behind them. Caleb waved at them to hurry, and for the first time since meeting them, she and Caleb got to see what an Ourankeli looked like when they ran. Unsurprising that it resembled low-level flying. Were they actually flying?

Malcolm, get ready to open the wormhole.

Cutting it a bit close, aren't you?

Not my preference, believe me.

Their three passengers reached the airlock, and everything happened at once. The ramp chased the Ourankeli up and finished retracting; Caleb closed the airlock; the force field protecting the open hangar bay shut down; their impulse engine purred to life, and the *Siyane* lifted out of the berth to trail the third Ourankeli ship out through the open door.

A golden glow consumed the viewport as the *Denali's* expansive Caeles Prism powered up directly ahead of them. In the distance to their port, the clumpy shadow of multiple Rasu vessels moved across the bright profile of the system's star.

We're ready, Alex. Sooner would be better.

She chuckled. Malcolm hadn't even met the Ourankeli yet, and they were already perturbing him. "Valkyrie, are the Ourankeli communication protocols loaded in the system?"

'A moment...yes.'

She activated the comm. "Ourankeli ships, you are authorized to traverse the wormhole. Go now."

The vessels accelerated past the *Denali,* little more than gray dots against its massive hull—and vanished through the wormhole.

'Estimated fifteen seconds until the Rasu are in firing range.'

Malcolm, you're clear. Get out of here.

What about you?

We're right behind you. See you at home.

The *Denali* disappeared as well, and its wormhole closed as the *Siyane's* opened. The shadow of the first approaching Rasu vessel loomed like an advancing eclipse as the *Siyane* shot through the tear in space and was gone.

59

CAF AURORA

TOKI'TAKU STELLAR SYSTEM

If there existed a Rasu command ship here today, Miriam was currently staring it down.

NO.

The leviathan didn't budge. Alas, it had been worth a shot, but nightmare rules did not apply here.

The murky aubergine hull stretched for a virtual eternity. At least twice as large as a Kat superdreadnought, the leviathan's breadth and length were devoted almost entirely to weapons delivery.

Of course, so was the *Aurora*. "Thomas, so long as we are situated between this Rasu and the planet below, negative energy missile use is authorized. Target its weapons assemblies whenever possible."

'There are many such assemblies.'

"I realize there are. Start on the port end."

*Commandant Solovy (*CAF Aurora*)(Command Channel): "Fleet Admiral Bastian, I need every Sabre targeting this leviathan's weapons assemblies."*

*Fleet Admiral Bastian (*AFS Leonidas*)(Command Channel): "Two of the Sabre squads are intercepting new Rasu arrivals—"*

*Commandant Solovy (*CAF Aurora*)(Command Channel): "The leviathan.* Now.*"*

*Fleet Admiral Bastian (*AFS Leonidas*)(Command Channel): "Acknowledged."*

She'd received a report fifteen minutes earlier stating the Taiyoks were deploying a new manner of weapon against the Rasu that had breached the atmosphere and begun attacking the surface. The Taiyoks had pulled off more than one surprise today, and early indications suggested the newest one was making significant headway against the ground incursions, which was welcome news.

But each one of this leviathan's weapons was robust enough to burn straight through the atmosphere and reach the surface from space at full strength. Such firepower could burn large swaths of the planet in a matter of minutes, and no ground-based weapon was going to stop it. It was up to her to do so, and do so quickly, which meant she did *not* have time to explain her rationale to Bastian. Whether due to her brief absence from the plane of the living or simply his long aversion to her leadership, cracks in the chain of command were making themselves visible. She would deal with those cracks, but not here.

A negative energy missile detonated mid-stream of one of the leviathan's violet beams directly in front of the viewport, and the world seemed to turn inside out. The reverse explosion created a yawning void that defied description; Miriam honestly wasn't certain her eyes were capable of processing what they were seeing. Though even these cosmic forces could not penetrate the *Aurora's* double-shielding and adiamene hull, her stomach felt as if it, too, curled in on itself and fell into its own void.

Then the beam and the missile were gone. Unfortunately, the leviathan remained.

Her XO cleared his throat unevenly. "Well, that was...strange."

"Yes, it was." She blinked away the vague feeling of disorientation. "Thomas, report. What's our progress?"

'We have destroyed five of the weapons batteries. A squad of Sabres has arrived and has thus far destroyed two and damaged one.'

"Which leaves?"

'Twelve and a half discrete weapons batteries.'

She nodded tersely. "Keep firing."

A torrent of rapid chatter erupted on the comm feed. It scrolled faster than she could follow, but it appeared to involve a Khokteh regiment tangling with a swarm of smaller Rasu vessels near Toki'taku's moon. She was about to check in with the Tokahe Naataan and see if his regiment needed any assistance when four of the leviathan's weapons batteries wrenched apart in a single blast, sending a massive crack shooting up through the center of the vessel.

"Was that us?"

'Negative, Commandant. A coordinated barrage from three Kat superdreadnoughts has struck the leviathan.'

Their AI-driven ships would be able to link their firing timing with perfect precision, she supposed. Whatever they'd done, it was damn impressive. The crack in the vessel's hull widened until the ship fell into two pieces—but almost immediately, those pieces were reaching out for one another.

Commandant Solovy (CAF Aurora)*(Mission Channel): "All ships in range, target the split in the Rasu leviathan located six hundred kilometers from the* Aurora.*"*

"Thomas, keep our fire on the weapons batteries."

Chaos descended outside the viewport, and only the vanishing infrared target markers they'd painted on the weapons batteries told her their strikes were scoring hits.

A new squadron of Eidolons arrived from the Presidio then, their holds filled with fresh negative energy bombs, and she bypassed Bastian to task them directly with seeding their bombs across the fissures on the two halves of the leviathan. This beast was *not* going to succeed in its mission today.

Craters in the leviathan's hull soon began opening up like pockmarks on a moon, and the additional damage *finally* began to take its toll on the vessel. One half cracked again, wrenching two of its own weapons batteries apart as it did so. The Rasu was down to three still-powerful weapons, but it had also lost much of its propulsion and steering control.

A chunk of the leviathan fell away from the main body and began tumbling into the atmosphere, only to have a laser from the Taiyok's crippled-but-not-dead defense array disintegrate it into tiny, harmless pieces.

*Commander Palmer (*ADV Dauntless*)(Command Channel): "Taiyok Authority is reporting eighty percent destruction of in-atmosphere Rasu. If we can keep any more from reaching the surface, we'll have this battle in hand."*

*Commandant Solovy (*CAF Aurora*)(Command Channel): "Excellent news. Let's finish off this leviathan, then try to push the battle line back and give the planet some breathing room—"*

She cut herself off as the remains of the leviathan abruptly shapeshifted its jagged, broken edges into a more uniform oval and accelerated away.

'I am detecting multiple Rasu wormholes opening ten megameters past the planet's satellite.'

On the tactical map, large groupings of dots moved in unison, like flocks of birds in advance of a storm.

*Commandant Solovy (*CAF Aurora*)(Mission Channel): "Everyone, track your current Rasu targets. If they're fleeing, we want to usher them off properly."*

The reports flooded in after that, all confirming how retreating Rasu were leaping through a sea of wormholes forming out behind the lunar body. The pieces of the leviathan that remained near the planet appeared to have lost all propulsion, and the Sabres finished them off almost as an afterthought.

In five minutes, the battlefield was empty of Rasu. The comm channels erupted into excited chatter as congratulations circled through the fleets.

'Well done, Commandant. We've proved we can defeat the Rasu without the need for protective Rift Bubbles.'

"I suppose we have, Thomas." Endorphins rushed through her body, supercharging the relief of a victory in hand. But a tiny, recalcitrant voice in her head refused to celebrate. Thus far, the Rasu had only fled a battle when it became crystal clear to them that they would not be able to achieve their goal. Here, the combined Concord, Dominion and Taiyok fleets were maintaining the upper hand, but they had not yet won the day. Not quite.

So why had they left?

'You seem disturbed, Commandant. What troubles you?'

She shook her head roughly, letting the cheers and high-fives rippling across the bridge buoy her spirits. "Nothing, Thomas. This is a well-deserved victory on our part. I need to confer with Commander Palmer about assigning a defensive force to remain behind in case the Rasu return. Then let's go home."

60

PALAEMON

(FORMERLY ANARCH POST EPSILON)
MILKY WAY GALAXY

Marlee exited the Caeles Prism from Concord HQ and stepped onto a floating platform. The files had said the entire settlement was built atop a body of water, but she'd assumed, wrongly, that it was an exaggeration. She studied the setting in interest, taking in the elevated walkways connecting an intricate network of large, square platforms. Many of them had full-sized buildings constructed on them. It was almost a little floating city!

When the anarchs had cleared out their Post Epsilon after The Displacement, they'd left all the infrastructure in working order. This facility had housing for hundreds of residents, a cafeteria-grade kitchen, generous meeting rooms and several open areas that had once been combat training space. On the whole, it was the perfect location to temporarily house the growing number of Godjan refugees when they first arrived. It was quiet, isolated, peaceful and rather humid, which maybe reminded the refugees of home.

She'd made the initial arrangements for the Ourankeli's pending arrival before leaving HQ, which had hopefully bought her enough time to check on the Godjans here first. She wandered along the spongy, tacky walkways and peered into the water in search of fish, to no avail. This was where Alex and Kennedy had invented the Caeles Prism, out on one of these platforms. The site was of historical interest in more than one respect.

She reached the first platform that hosted a real building and asked around for the onsite Confove Mission director, a Naraida named Ildaite Llawhe. As she understood past events, in the year or so after The Displacement, a lot of work needed to be done to clean up the unseemly societal wreckage the Directorate had left behind, including many displaced and mistreated aliens in need of assistance. The Erevna exobiology research labs were shut down, and their subjects required medical attention and general acclimatization, as did a shocking number of 'political' prisoners who found themselves with their sentences commuted, often after many centuries spent languishing in prison.

The Confove Mission was formed to meet these needs and take care of those who had been mistreated by the Directorate. In the years since, a philanthropic crisis was always popping up somewhere, and Confove had become the go-to group to step in with aid. Now, they were helping the Consulate properly care for the Godjans.

She found Llawhe inside the cafeteria. He was shoveling a clover-colored Naraida dish called '*sici caso*' into his mouth in between issuing a steady string of instructions to a Naraida woman and two humans sitting opposite him. Naraida were almost uniformly thin and willowy, but they also had turbocharged metabolisms; she'd never met anyone who could eat as much as quickly as a Naraida.

She waited for a pause in the orders and stepped up to the table. "Director Llawhe? I'm Marlee Marano, from the Consulate."

"Yes, of course." He gestured to the others. "I think I've covered everything. They should be coming through soon."

His underlings stood and hurried off, and Marlee eased into one of the vacated chairs. "I don't know how much Dean Veshnael told you, but I'm here this morning to finalize the approved resettlement locations and to introduce the refugees to the various mentoring programs we're implementing. We hope to start the programs here, then transition them to the new sites as the refugees are moved to more permanent homes."

"Excellent." He wiped his mouth and stood. "Come with me. I'll show you the space we've designated for the mentoring sessions, then we can go to my office and review your list."

She followed him back outside and down a winding walkway to the left.

Her steps slowed as she spotted a Prevo holding open a wormhole on one of the platforms empty of erected structures. A female Godjan emerged through the wormhole walking backward. As soon as she cleared the wormhole, a group of four more Godjans emerged as well, huddled together and looking terrified.

The female Godjan placed her hands on each of their shoulders in turn. "Good job. Come now, there's nothing to be afraid of here."

Marlee cocked her head in surprise. Was that…? "Director Llawhe, will you excuse me for one minute?" She didn't wait for an answer before jogging toward the staging area. More Godjans stumbled through the wormhole, and the female continued coaxing them onward with a soothing yet confident voice and manner.

By the time Marlee arrived, forty or so Godjans stood trembling on the platform. The female nodded to the Prevo, and the wormhole closed. The Naraida woman and two humans from the cafeteria approached the group to stand next to the female Godjan, who motioned to them. "Everyone, this is Baeloni, Angela and Rafael. They're going to take you to get some food—it's super yummy—then show you where you're going to sleep tonight. Now go right this way—" The speaker turned and caught sight of Marlee. Her eyes widened, and she practically jumped into the air as she sprinted over and grabbed Marlee around the waist.

"Miss Marlee!"

She tried not to giggle. "It is *so* good to see you, Vaihe."

"Oh, it's so good to see you, too." She let go of her vise grip on Marlee's hips to spin around toward the refugees, who were half-listening to a speech by the Naraida woman and half-gaping at Vaihe. "Everyone, this is the lady I told you about. The one who rescued me! Oh, sorry to interrupt, Baeloni. Please continue."

Marlee waved to the group, then knelt in front of Vaihe to meet her at eye level. "This is all amazing! And you look incredible. I may have rescued you, but you've rescued all these people. I knew you were destined for great things when I met you, and I am *so* proud of you."

"Oh, no, I just do what I can. My people need to be told that there's a new life waiting on them, free of violence and…." A shudder rippled through her. "Everybody is afraid to go through the hole in the world at first, just like I was. I try to show them it's safe and help them believe that what's on the other side is better."

"You're doing a wonderful job."

"How was your trip? I missed you."

"Oh, it was…interesting. I'm happy to be back home." Marlee smiled breezily. "How did all of this come about?"

"While you were gone, I went to see Senator Miss Requelme. I told her I wanted to try to help the rest of the Godjans, and she took me to meet some nice people." Her expression grew overly serious. "People from Confove. They help others who are…lost. One of them started opening holes in the world to the places I told him about, and I went through to try to convince people in the villages to come back with me. That was on the big space station, but later we moved here. I like it here. The fresh air is nice, and there's so much open space. Also, the water doesn't smell foul like it does on Savrak."

"I'm glad Mia was able to help you make a difference for all these

Godjans. I'm sorry she's gone now, but you're doing so awesome on your own."

"Gone? No, she's not gone. I mean, I didn't see her for a while, but she's here right now. Over there in the Orientation courtyard."

"What?" Marlee's gaze followed where Vaihe pointed. She saw a Novoloume woman and three humans talking by a picnic table. After a few seconds, one of the humans shifted toward her. Her hair was *way* different, as were her eyes, but Mia's elegant features were instantly recognizable.

She squeezed Vaihe's shoulder affectionately. "I need to go talk to Mia for a few minutes, okay?"

"I understand." Vaihe nodded sagely. "I have responsibilities I should attend to as well."

"Of course you do. You're an important person around here—much more important than I am."

"Oh, never!"

"Oh, yes. I'll find you again before I leave."

Vaihe hurried back over to the Prevo operating the wormholes, and Marlee walked along the floating pathways toward the courtyard. According to Llawhe, the Godjans preferred being outside whenever possible, especially during the first hours after their arrival. So they held the initial orientation sessions in the courtyard, where they gently began to educate the refugees about Concord and what they could expect in the coming days.

Mia spotted her when she was still half a walkway away, and a warm smile blossomed on the woman's face. She placed a hand on the Novoloume woman's arm and murmured something, then strode off to meet Marlee halfway.

When they met, Mia reached out and embraced Marlee warmly. "I am so relieved to see you alive and in one piece. You had everyone terribly worried."

"And you. I love the hair! It's very…."

"Rebellious?"

"Daring, for certain."

"Thank you. I might not keep it forever, but it's working for me for now."

Marlee straightened her shoulders. She'd gotten a great deal of practice at apologies by now. "I am so sorry I didn't leave Namino when you asked me to do so. I apologize for any trouble my thoughtless actions brought upon you. The responsibility all lies at my feet."

"I'm just glad you survived. And engaged in some heroics, too, I hear."

"Not really. In the end I hope I helped a little, but I learned a lot, no question. And I made several new friends. And developed a righteous hatred for the Rasu."

"Good. We'll need that in the days to come."

Marlee fidgeted nervously, but stopped herself. It wasn't a becoming trait for an adult. "I heard what all happened while I was gone. It must have been so awful for you. I can't even imagine what you've been through."

Mia's expression clouded, and her gaze drifted off for a few seconds; then she visibly shook the fugue off. Always poised, always the diplomat. "It was not my finest hour. But it's okay. I'm moving forward now—which is what brought me here. I am now on hour five of my eternal community service as part of my plea deal."

Marlee recalled what Morgan had said about this not being Mia's first time as a fugitive. She still didn't believe it, and Mia still felt too much like her boss for her to straight-up ask. "Thank you so much for helping Vaihe. For helping all these Godjans."

"No thanks are needed. You were right about them, and about our duty to help them. It's one of the few good things I did after…." Her face blanched.

"Mia, you don't have to—"

"How is working for Veshnael? Not too dull, I hope."

She let the woman change the subject without pressing her on Malcolm. "It's, um…he's not you. But he's an honorable man, and he's not too bad as a boss. He's clear as to what he expects of me, compliments me when I do good work and is only slightly stern when things go the other way. I can't complain."

"That's never stopped you before."

Heat flared in Marlee's cheeks. "Yeah, I'm sorry about that, too. I'm trying to be better at…everything."

"I was only teasing." Mia regarded her curiously. "Your harrowing time on Namino changed you, didn't it?"

"I'm endeavoring to make sure it did. If you're interested, I can fill you in on the experience sometime, when we're not both working."

"Or serving as indentured labor, in my case. I want to hear your stories. My personal situation is somewhat…" her expression flickered again "…in flux for another day or two, but I'll let you know once I get settled. We can go out for dinner and drinks—as friends rather than employer and employee."

Hey, she was definitely racking up the quality friends these days. "I'd like that very much. Now, I abandoned Director Llawhe to talk to Vaihe then pounce upon you, so I should track him down and get to work, lest I return to the Consulate to find one of Veshnael's stern looks waiting on me."

"I'll let you in on a secret. Veshnael is all bark and...actually, quite a lot of bite. He's made of sterner stuff than most Novoloume. But he'll be an excellent mentor for you. Learn from him, and you'll become a better diplomat than I ever was."

"That's not possible." She hugged Mia again before the woman could object, then set off in search of Llawhe. She had such a busy day of work ahead of her.

61

ARES

Eren strolled into the office Corradeo had set up on the top floor of the Praesidis estate. He started to collapse into a chair and throw his feet over one arm, much as he had the last time he'd been here, but he thought better of it at the last second and sat properly. He didn't respect much in this world, but Corradeo Praesidis had earned his respect.

The man bestowed a kind smile on him as a reward. "How did you and Nyx get on?"

He blew out a breath and stared at the ceiling. "Well enough, I guess. She's not exactly a good time at parties, but she does know her stuff."

"Indeed, she does. She saved us both numerous times during our journeys. Can I ask, what delayed your return after you located Ferdinand?"

Nyx hadn't told him about Kolgo? Interesting. Eren opened his mouth to spill the beans, then thought better of this, too, and decided to run with the lie instead. He couldn't say as he was sure why. "Oh, there was a quick errand I needed to run. Nyx was kind enough to indulge me in it."

"It sounds as if perhaps you two did get on well, then. I'm glad to hear it. Thank you for helping to handle the Ferdinand problem. I wish we'd been able to bring him around to reason, but he was most resistant to logic or, I suppose, reality."

"It's a noble idea, but it never would have worked. I appreciate how you're trying to be diplomatic and not speak too ill of the dead, but Ferdinand was rotten with greed, avarice and arrogance. Beyond saving."

"Is this why you would've killed him if given the chance?"

Eren bristled. This was what he got for covering for the bitch. "Did Nyx tell you that?"

"Is it true?"

He sank lower in the chair. "I don't know. The other night at dinner, I absolutely would have pressed the trigger if you hadn't stopped me. When you sent us off to find him, I absolutely intended to rectify the oversight and put a laser between his eyes. But now, I'm starting to realize that killing every villain in the cosmos isn't going to bring Cosime back." His troubled gaze rose to meet Corradeo's empathetic one. "Killing a few more might help, though?"

"It won't. I don't speak of it, ever, but I have been where you are. It was so terribly long ago, but in a matter of seconds I can recall the anguish and the fury as if it were yesterday."

The man was just full of secrets and hidden layers. "How did you get past those feelings?"

A dark smirk tugged at the man's lips. "It took hundreds of millennia, but I saw to it that the perpetrators met a final end."

"Talk about revenge being best served cold."

Corradeo merely shrugged.

"The truth is, I'm beginning to suspect I've gotten all the revenge I'm ever going to get. Torval is dead, Ferdinand is dead, Jhountar is dead, at least one hundred thousand Savrakaths are dead. Maybe I need to close the book on revenge and find a way to move on." He sighed. "It's not going to be easy."

"Of course it isn't. Listen, Eren. Things are about to change here, and everywhere Anadens find themselves living and working. I want your help in ensuring it's ultimately positive change. If you are searching for a new cause, I'm offering you one now. Help me guide our people to a better future. A worthy future." Corradeo paused. "But only if you're ready to move forward. I'll need your full commitment on this."

Eren closed his eyes, letting the vision of Cosime's sparkling emerald irises dance across his vision, drawing back to reveal her dazzling smile. She'd loved life so damn much. Loved him even more, which was the damnedest thing.

He swallowed past the ragged ache in his throat, then reopened his eyes and nodded firmly. "I have to be ready. I have to move forward. It's what she would have wanted."

RW

Eren rested one foot against the wall and watched as several Kyvern *elas* tested out the drone cam and adjusted the lighting around Corradeo for maximum presentation. Out of the corner of his vision, he spotted Nyx doing much the same, her brow creased with suspicion as she watched her lessers work.

He briefly considered going up to her and asking her why she'd kept Kolgo's assassination a secret from her grandfather yet ratted him out about

Ferdinand…but then he realized he didn't care to muddy himself with Inquisitor politics and power plays. He was forced to concede she did appear to want what was best for her grandfather and had bought into the man's audacious vision, which was all that mattered now.

Corradeo brushed away a lingering wrinkle in his jacket and squared his shoulders, a sign he was almost ready. Getting to see the performance live should be interesting, and this time Eren didn't have to jet around the galaxy overseeing dozens of system hacks in order to make the speech a reality. The Directorate's passing had brought an end to the draconian restrictions on communications, and Concord's rise had in turn brought an open and ubiquitous quantum comm network. Unlike fourteen years ago, today the man simply had to speak, and the world would hear him.

The aides scurried off into the shadows the bright lighting created, and a hush fell over the room. Corradeo locked his gaze on the drone cam. Showtime.

"My name is Corradeo Praesidis, and today I am reclaiming this name from a usurper. Some of you have known me in the past as Danilo Nisi, and you can trust that I remain that man more than any other.

"I led the anarchs in our quest to overthrow the Directorate, because for too many millennia, your leaders failed you. They took away every Anaden's most basic freedoms—the freedom to choose for yourself who you will be and what mark you will make on the universe. They did this not only without your consent but without your knowledge.

"In form and formality, those chains were cut fourteen years ago when the Directorate fell. In practice, however, freedom is meaningless unless you are given the tools to embrace it, and you were left adrift, with no rulebook and no lodestar to show you how to reclaim your rightful destiny. I should have been here for you all along, offering whatever wisdom I have gained to lead all our people to a new, better future.

"I can't go back in time and undo this mistake, but I can be here today, tomorrow, and for as long as I am needed. Not to take you by the hand and set your course for you, but to show you how the path to your own personal freedom lies right at your feet.

"I recognize full well that you, the Anaden people, have not elected me to act and speak on your behalf. One day soon, you will select your own leaders, and I will gratefully cede this responsibility to them and fade into memory once again. But until such a day arrives, I ask you to trust in me to make the best decisions I can about our future. To that end:

"Effective as of today, the Dynasties no longer exist as a component of any Anaden government. While my current advisors are of necessity chosen from among the Dynasty *elassons,* starting eighteen months from now, all government advisors will be selected on merit alone.

"This decree does not erase you who are. If you are proud of your Dynasty, you are *free* to continue to bear its name. But now, you are also free to choose your own eponym, and with it, your own identity.

"From now on, if someone born into the Erevna Dynasty desires to become a fighter pilot, there will be an open path for them to do so. If someone born into the Machim Dynasty wants to learn engineering, they will find the same opportunities. Professions will require competency and expect achievement, but their ranks will no longer be limited by genetics or title.

"When someone undergoes regenesis, they will now do so confident they will awaken the same person they were when their old body expired. There will be no more genetic manipulations without an individual's informed consent—nay, without their active direction.

"It will take time to dismantle the aged ramparts of the old social and legal structure, but the work begins right now. I'm pleased to announce that the Anaden government will be renewing its support of and participation in Concord, effective immediately. I will, for now, serve as our representative to the Concord Senate, but I look forward to being replaced in future elections."

Corradeo pressed his palms together at his chin and offered the cam a faint smile. "Most of all, understand this: the Humans are our brethren, and we should embrace them as family. The Asterions are our brothers and sisters, and we should welcome them home with open arms. The Novoloume, the Naraida—the Barisans, Dankath and Efkam—have long been our allies. We took too much from them and treated them shamefully in the past, but now we have much to offer them in a relationship of equals and allies. The Katasketousya…odd though they seem to your eyes, understand that they have done more to save Anaden civilization—to save all peaceful civilizations—than you will ever know. We owe them our gratitude and our hand in friendship.

"We will do all we can to support Concord and its efforts to safeguard our corner of the universe from the great evils lurking in the void, but we must also learn to become worthy partners. We must build a new Anaden society, one that honors our greatest achievements, intellect and discoveries but focuses our endeavors on the achievements yet to come. One that we will be proud to champion and defend. Today I invite you, all of you, to join me on this most exciting of adventures."

62

CONCORD HQ

COMMAND

Miriam cast a quick glance at the vid screen, listening to Corradeo's broadcast with half an ear. The man always could give a rousing speech, and while they hadn't always agreed on approaches, he'd proved himself to be a skilled and ultimately thoughtful leader. Hopefully his return to public prominence would bring a swift and favorable end to the Anaden conflict, and with it some real stability for Concord. God knew they needed it right now.

The door to her office opened and David and Richard staggered in, looking rather worse for wear. All thoughts of propriety vanished from her mind, and the next instant she was in David's arms, holding him tight against her chest. "Thank goodness you're safe."

His lips nuzzled her ear. "You're the one who stared the Rasu down until they fled with their tails tucked between their legs. So to speak."

She stepped back and pulled Richard into a brief embrace as well. "You two have saved Concord HQ for the second time now in my absence. I owe you everything yet again."

David shrugged broadly, but he was beaming. "I *would* say you should try not being absent, but you were protecting billions of lives. Keeping home safe until you returned was the least we could do."

"A little more than the least, I'd say." She noticed the easy, relaxed body language between him and Richard, something that had been noticeably absent of late. "I don't want to bring up a touchy subject and ruin the mood, but is it possible you worked out your differences while you were finding and defusing the bomb?"

David glanced at Richard, showing uncharacteristic hesitation. Richard adopted a weary smile as he collapsed into one of the chairs. "We did."

"Well, this is a relief. The two of you were practically unbearable." She went back to her desk to retrieve her tea, then regarded them over the top of it. "What's the thirty-second debrief?"

Richard answered first. "The Barisan body in Power Generation exploded from the inside out due to a small device sewn into his stomach cavity. We've identified him as Hohlaak Ponla-min, a member of the crew of the merchant vessel we believe delivered the antimatter bomb to HQ. My working theory is that the Savrakaths stole the vessel and kidnapped Ponla-min, booby-trapped him and presumably promised to save his life if he delivered the bomb. Then the vessel departed HQ without him on board and he was murdered soon thereafter."

"How did the antimatter bomb make it past our security measures in the first place?"

"A forensics team is still tearing apart the device—carefully, of course—but a preliminary report indicates the antimatter was encased in four layers of special-purpose shielding. The volume of commercial shipments coming through HQ every day necessitates that most containers receive a cursory scan during unloading then an additional en masse scan in the warehouse. Those screening mechanisms weren't robust enough to penetrate this degree of shielding."

Miriam frowned. "I trust I don't need to say that we should upgrade the scanning procedures. If it slows down shipping throughput by a few hours, so be it."

"Agreed. We're on it."

David reached out and touched her arm. "The Savrakath problem is getting out of hand, and it seems the Red-Flag designation isn't going to be enough to keep them from pursuing war against us. Their level of technology means the Ch'mshak solution won't work for them—not for long. So what do you have a mind to do about it?"

She sighed and set the tea aside.

Lakhes, I'm ready for you to join us now.

A sea of lights swept into the office almost immediately, as if Lakhes had been waiting right outside the station. She had no idea if this were true or not. David and Richard jumped a little in surprise, but she merely lowered her chin in greeting to their guest. "Thank you for coming, Lakhes. Am I to understand that you have a proposal for how to ensure the Savrakaths don't threaten Concord citizens or property again?"

I do. The Savrakaths are, as you have repeatedly pointed out, a problem of our own creation. Thus it is only proper that we—the Idryma—solve the problem.

"Despite this latest and most egregious action on their part, I won't see them eradicated. They must be removed as a threat, but we will not commit genocide." After the strike they had attempted to deliver at the very core of Concord, her heart wanted to see every last Savrakath dead, but her conscience would not allow vengeance to take hold.

I accept your parameters and have endeavored to design a solution which comports with them.

David snorted. "Why don't you just shove their planet into a new portal universe and leave them there?"

Shaping astronomical bodies and cosmic forces within *an enisle is routine for us, but constructing a dimensional portal the size of a planet is not. We can do it, but it would take time we can no longer afford to spend.*

Miriam scowled in growing frustration. "Then you should have started months ago."

Perhaps, but we did not, and we cannot go back and alter our plans now. However, as I said, we have devised an alternate solution. One we believe will accomplish the same end.

Miriam listened to Lakhes' proposal with her best effort at objectivity. The science behind it was beyond her comprehension, but the Kats had long trafficked in feats that were inscrutable to human understanding. David challenged Lakhes on several points, all of which the Kat answered to his satisfaction while displaying only slightly condescending patience.

It might not be a perfect solution, but it was a far better one than Concord could achieve. After a moment's pause, Miriam nodded sharply. "Do it."

63

SENECA
CAVARE

Marlee unlocked her apartment, stumbled inside and collapsed onto the futon. This being a responsible adult routine was exhausting! After meeting with Director Llawhe, she'd spent the rest of the morning helping the RAR Prevo and Vaihe scour the Savrak countryside for any remaining Godjans, then spent the afternoon greeting the new Ourankeli refugees and scrambling to attend to their immediate needs.

The aliens were mysterious and fascinating, and she was in awe of their intellect and grace. But they were also fussy and fastidious as all hell. Making them happy was shaping up to be a herculean task. Their language was beautiful, though, even if her throat thus far refused to create the more complex tonals.

She felt around on the floor for the water bottle she'd discarded this morning, then checked the private Consulate news feed for updates on the battle at Toki'taku. It looked as if the planet had been saved, at least for now, thanks to the Asterions' trademark cleverness and a bucketload of Concord warships.

She wondered if Xyche'ghael would be offended if she stopped by for a visit. She'd have to find him first, since Namino remained basically uninhabitable, but Nika or Grant would know how to find the Taiyok.

With a groan, she stretched her arms over her head and started considering a shower. Or a late dinner first? Possibly some tea in-between?

The doorbell chimed, cutting the debate short. It was probably Eosha, who she'd hardly spent five minutes with since returning from Namino. She was a little tired for guests, but she hauled herself back off the futon, ran a hand through her hair and went to answer the summons.

She opened the door and—

"Morgan?"

The woman glanced at her feet, then down the hall in both directions, then finally at Marlee. She was wearing faded denim pants over dark work boots and an oversized cream sweater. Her hair was clean and brushed, falling in a neat line at her chin, and her eyes shone brilliant lavender.

"Hi. I wanted to stop by and apologize for the other night at *Purgatory*. I'm sorry you had to see me like that. I don't...well, I don't actually remember much of what happened, but I've no doubt it was an utter shit-show on my part. I wasn't at my best."

Marlee dislodged the lump from her throat, shocked by far more than being on the receiving end of an apology for once. "No, it's totally fine. I shouldn't have dropped in on you unannounced."

"I just did."

"Right." Marlee burst out laughing; after a few seconds, Morgan chuckled as well, and the tension eased. "Do you want to come in for a minute? I just got home from work and was about to make some tea. Would you like some—or a glass of wine?"

"Tea sounds good. I don't need to aim for a repeat of the other night." Morgan followed her inside, then wandered to the far window to stare out at the street below.

Marlee scrambled into the kitchen and frantically activated the fancy tea brewer—a housewarming gift from her aunt—then counted down the seconds until it finished its cycle. She fetched two ceramic mugs from the cabinet and sloshed the steaming liquid into them, sucked in a deep breath and oh-so-casually strolled through the living room to hand one to Morgan.

"Thanks." The woman continued to gaze pensively out the window. "I used to live a couple of blocks away from here, you know. It was a crappy apartment in a run-down complex at Apennine and Monte Rosa. I didn't spend much time there, though. This was before The Displacement. Before the IDCC, even. When I stole Stanley from the military and made a break for freedom, I had to move to Romane."

"I don't know this story. Maybe you can tell me about it sometime."

"Okay. I assume the statute of limitations for theft has expired by now." Morgan gave her a whimsical little smile, and a flutter in Marlee's chest answered.

"You said Apennine and Monte Rosa? I think the building's a warehouse now."

"Ha. I think it was a warehouse before it was an apartment complex, too." Morgan turned and rested against the window, mug clutched in both hands. "I've been noodling over the Rasu. Ever since we got back from Namino, they've taken to haunting my nightmares. Nasty buggers, and so *rude*."

"Invading planets all willy-nilly like they do. No manners."

"Exactly. What are they up to? Why are they scavenging materials one minute and doing data analysis the next? These questions have been intruding on my peacefully drunken existence to the point where I think I'm going to have to do something about it."

"Oh?"

"Yeah. The trouble is, there's only one thing I've ever been any good at—other than playing *skalef*—and that's flying a ship and using it to shoot things. But I can't rejoin the fleet, not after...." Morgan's expression darkened, and her eyes dropped to study her tea.

"It's okay, I—"

"No, it's been six years. I should be able to say it out loud. Not after AEGIS and Concord ordered Brook and her squad into an unwinnable trap with no means to survive." She exhaled deliberately, her breath mingling with the steam rising from the tea. "I never was much of a team player, anyway. I tried, for Brook, but it was mostly an act. But I am good at flying. And shooting things when shooting is called for."

"I saw."

"You did. And I promised you more of that."

Marlee gulped.

"The point is, I need a change of scenery. I want to get up in the Rasu's craw, but I'm still working out how best to do it. Until I figure it out, Devon says he needs a suicidal pilot to test out his most hare-brained prototype weapons. I've volunteered to be his guinea pig."

"You're going to be working for Special Projects? What about *Purgatory?*"

"I sold it to Solstan this morning for half of what it's worth. He'll take good care of it—better care than I did. And I'll be more of an outside consultant to Special Projects than an employee. I don't do well with bosses and rules and decorum." Morgan huffed a wry laugh. "You probably figured that out already."

"I did, and I like that about you." Too much? Almost certainly too much. Exhaustion-fueled delirium was making her dizzy in the woman's presence.

"You do? Oh." Morgan looked genuinely puzzled for a moment. "I've got to configure a fighter and rig up a few other tools, but once I get up and running, I thought you might want to come by and check out some of the tests as they happen. Maybe watch me get blown up a few times."

"I'm not—"

"It's fine if you're not interested. I just thought...you fought the Rasu on Namino. You're clearly invested in defeating them, and you seemed to enjoy the fireworks we created at the Rasu compound."

The fireworks. Yes, those she *had* enjoyed. "I'm definitely interested. I was only going to say that Special Projects is locked down pretty tight. I can hardly ever sneak my way in there, and I have a lot of inside access. But I bet you could get me a pass if you call me your assistant or something. If you're serious, I mean."

"Stanley says I'm always serious. I think it's part of my charm, but he disagrees for some reason. Regardless, it shouldn't be a problem. Devon will let me do whatever I want to with his toys, because I know all his secrets."

Abruptly Morgan placed her mug on the windowsill and turned toward the door. "I'll let you know once the boring stuff is finished and I start blowing shit up. You can come by. Um…thanks for the tea."

"Of course." As Morgan walked perhaps a little slowly toward the door, Marlee's heart seized up in a panic. *Don't leave so soon….* "Hey, have you had anything to eat tonight yet? I haven't, and I'm famished. We could take a stroll down to *Fuori Barbeque.* I can point out all the new improvements the city management's made in the last few years, and you can tell me how it was better the way things used to be."

Morgan stopped in the middle of the living room; her brow furrowed, and she seemed to be trying to parcel out how much of what Marlee had said was a joke. "I am a bit hungry. But are you sure you want me to tag along? I've been told I'm not great company."

"Whoever said that was mistaken. I'm sure."

64

TOKI'TAKU

ASTERION DOMINION EMBASSY

The distant horizon remained a smoky, russet color, a hallmark of the many fires still raging across the great forests of Toki'taku. Closer, in the city that spread below Nika, flames still licked at the sky, but they were repeatedly repelled by the efforts of emergency technicians circling in the air above. Of necessity, the Taiyoks were quite skilled at fighting fires, and she suspected they'd have most of the blazes extinguished by evening.

The Rasu's attempted invasion had caused severe damage in several of the largest cities as well as across the forests, but objectively, the damage didn't begin to compare to the wreckage the enemy had wrought in its weeks of occupation of Namino. The Taiyoks would recover, if the Rasu let them.

The attacking forces had been losing, no question, when they'd elected to retreat rather than bring yet another armada to bear on the fight. It nonetheless seemed an odd choice for the Rasu to make. Perhaps they'd simply had somewhere better to be, or perhaps they'd grown tired of what had hopefully felt to them like a fruitless battle. Whatever the reason for their abrupt departure, the specter of the Rasu returning in greater numbers at any time cast a slight pall over an otherwise joyous victory.

But for today, they would all happily take the victory. Also, if or when the Rasu returned in the future, the Taiyoks would welcome them with a minimum of 10,000 Rima Grenades.

A feather-light footfall in the room behind Nika signified the arrival of her guest through the d-gate, and she went to greet him.

Xyche'ghael halted two steps into the entry room of the Dominion Embassy. He looked frozen and...well, it was always difficult to discern emotions from a Taiyok's facial expressions or comportment, but he looked *afraid.*

She stepped forward to offer him a hand. "I'm glad you decided to accept my invitation. Come with me out onto the balcony."

Xyche peered behind him, toward the front doors that led to the city. "Are the constables en route?"

"No. Though Toki'taku soil lies beneath the foundation of this building, the embassy itself is Asterion Dominion property. They can't banish you from here."

He considered her words silently, then ignored her hand to stride deliberately through the open glass doors and onto the balcony. She followed quietly.

The thick feathers covering his shoulders ruffled beyond the ash-tainted breeze, and she briefly worried he was going to take flight—an act that risked sealing his fate in the harshest terms. But after a few seconds, the feathers settled down as he took in the view from one horizon to the other. "The forests burn, thanks to the imperious stubbornness of the Elder."

"But they will not burn to the ground, thanks to him seeing reason in the end."

"You must be a most persuasive diplomat."

"It's not a difficult case to make when the lives of billions are at stake."

"One would think." Xyche glanced over at her, his compound eyes wide and bright, reflecting the vermilion flames from a nearby structure. "Does he know I am here?"

"I didn't mention it. Though if you want to speak to him, I can invite him to come to the embassy—"

"No. That will not be necessary. All the words that existed to be said between us were uttered long ago." He breathed in deeply, his gaze drifting to the sea of forests beyond the city. "This is...I do not know how to properly thank you, Nika, other than to call you my friend. Whatever boon you ask of me, I will give everything of myself in an attempt to provide it to you."

Had he ever referred to her as 'friend' before? His words warmed her heart, but she knew better than to make an emotional scene about it.

"This isn't a quid pro quo, Xyche. I don't need anything in return. Besides, you've helped me so many times already. If you hadn't shown me how to acquire a Taiyok stealth module for the *Wayfarer*, I might never have learned of the Rasu. Everything about the last year might have been different." She sighed. "I just wanted to give you a chance to see your homeworld one more time."

"And it is...all I imagined it could be." His wings stretched out, the more delicate feathers rippling as they caught the breeze. But again he did not take flight, instead seeming to revel in the feel of the air buffeting his skin. "Thank you. I did not sufficiently appreciate my home before I was exiled from it. But I vow now, here in the presence of the *puiga'atua,* that I will never forget this moment. For all of my days."

Abruptly his wings drew in tight; he spun around and left behind the balcony for the entry room. "I should depart now."

The speed with which a Taiyok, even one she called *friend,* could turn brusque always kept her on her toes. "We can stay longer if you like. The time is yours to spend as you wish."

"No. This interlude has lasted long enough for me to commit the experience to treasured memory, and it is best not to tempt fate too brazenly. Now I move onward."

65

ROMANE

Mia ran a hand along the surface of her old desk on the ground floor of Exia Spaceport. This morning, she'd repurchased the property from the conglomerate she'd sold it to twelve years ago, at a thirty-two percent markup over the original sale price. She'd earned twice the markup on investments alone in the last decade, so the cost didn't bother her. The question of whether she ever should have sold it in the first place nagged at her a little more. A lot of her choices were doing that lately.

A quick review of the historical financials told her the conglomerate had kept the spaceport well-maintained and running at a profit, but considering the entire world had changed while they owned it, they hadn't done much to grow the business.

A slight smile tugged at her lips nonetheless. This, she could work with. If she was determined to circle around to her roots, Romane was a far superior option than Pandora had been. She no longer needed to hide, and she had plans.

But in order to move those plans forward, she first had to fork over a great deal more money. She took a final survey of the office to mentally note several desired improvements, then left the spaceport behind and headed downtown to Dynamis Tower.

RW

The four square blocks to the west of Exia Spaceport had never been used to their full potential. Hotels, a couple of restaurants and some office space filled the buildings, but most people departing the spaceport were already headed somewhere else, and the neighborhood had never really thrived beyond the transportation it offered.

Mia was shown into a meeting room on the 23rd floor of Dynamis Tower. She recalled the significant damage the building had suffered during the OTS riots, but it gleamed brighter than ever now. Out the windows and across the street stood the Connova Interstellar headquarters; she considered dropping in to see Noah and Kennedy after the closing, but odds were high they were chained to Concord HQ these days.

The COO of Carina-Solar Properties and the SVP of Development for Anatoli Construction, along with attorneys for each, waited for her inside the meeting room. Together, the two companies owned or controlled the leases to every building comprising those four blocks near the spaceport—leases they'd wasted. She'd do better.

She'd frequented too many attorney-filled rooms of late, but it was more important than ever to do everything by the book. She was a convicted felon now, and she had to keep her nose clean. Besides, it felt damn good—cathartic even—to again be wearing a tailored suit, heels and pearls. To be meeting with high-class people who weren't trying to subjugate or kill her. Oh, they were sharks all the same, but at least the games they played involved money rather than lives.

One of the attorneys, a blonde woman in an emerald suit and blue diamond earrings, greeted her with a smooth but frigid handshake. "Thank you for coming, Ms. Requelme. The bank confirmed a few minutes ago that your financing has been secured, so let's sign some documents."

She gave the woman her best diplomat's smile. "Yes, let's."

RW

The idea had likely originated when she'd started noticing the utter lack of aliens on Pandora, but it had blossomed fully formed in her mind during her first community service stint with the Godjan refugees. Despite a few rough patches here and there, humanity had on the whole done an admirable job of accepting their new alien neighbors after The Displacement. Integrating them into their lives and worlds, though? This was another matter.

Most colonies of any size had an outreach program, and some were more successful than others. But even on Romane, ostensibly the most progressive and urbane human world, one rarely passed an alien on the streets. It hadn't made sense on Pandora, and it made far less sense on Romane. After spending so much of her time on Concord HQ these last years, the absence of any diversity here seemed odd to her, but also disappointing. And it had occurred to her…while she'd never hold government office again, this didn't mean she couldn't change the world for the better.

With the repurchase of the spaceport and now the leasing of the adjacent properties, she had the physical pieces in place. Just a few additional hoops to jump through.

A dozen blocks from Dynamis Tower, she climbed the Romane Government Center's wide marble stairs and let the memories the setting triggered wash over her. Breaking the news of the Kats—then Metigens—to Governor Ledesme and scrambling to prepare for the coming invasion. Founding the IDCC and taking the first steps toward growing it into the powerful inter-governmental agency it was today. Sitting at the table with the leaders of the Earth Alliance and the Senecan Federation as equal partners in the formation of the GCDA and AEGIS.

Though her heart still ached from the thousand trials of the last few months, she couldn't deny that it was good to be home.

This time she was ushered into the office of the Romane governor, a position currently held by a distinguished man named Rolph Tremblay. Tall and wiry, with charcoal skin and sharp eyes beneath a smoothly bald head, he had come to politics by way of business and, before that, medicine. They'd met several times on AEGIS affairs, and he greeted her warmly now.

"Ms. Requelme, welcome. I was sad to hear of your recent troubles, but glad to learn they've brought you back to Romane. I hope this isn't too selfish of me."

She was going to have to endure this manner of small talk for a while yet, and she'd prepared a stock response. "Thank you for your concern. I'm simply eager to put the past behind me and focus on the future."

"I'm happy to hear it, and I look forward to helping you in any way I can. To that end, I understand that as of this morning, in addition to repurchasing your old spaceport, you now own most of the property surrounding it."

"Yes, which is why I'm here. I have some exciting ideas on how to repurpose the area to the west of Exia Spaceport. I realize I'll need to acquire zoning approval for what I have in mind, so I want to involve you and any relevant government departments from the start."

"Interesting. What do you have in mind?"

"If I may." She placed a quantum cube on the corner of his desk and opened up an expansive virtual image. "I had an architect friend of mine mock up these designs. They're very preliminary, of course. But I want to transform the neighborhood into an inter-species cultural exchange, expo and mentoring center. We allow our alien allies to visit our worlds, but I fear we're not making them feel particularly welcome while they're here. It's time we do so.

"I want to build an educational center that features the history and culture of every Concord Member species, and possibly Allied species as well. We'll include ourselves in those presentations, naturally. The center can include play areas for children to interact with alien tools, art and toys, as well as study chambers for in-depth research by visiting scholars. Adjacent to the educational center, I envision an expansive resort and hotel with species-specific rooms and restaurants. Surrounding the resort will be a wide variety of shops and parks, plus outreach centers to help aliens who are interested in working and living on human worlds—and vice versa.

"In short, I want to make Romane the cultural center of not just humanity, but of Concord. It's a step we might have taken years ago, but when The Displacement happened, we had so many changes to adapt to and so much to learn. But I believe we're ready now." She smiled broadly, and this time it was for more than merely show. "So what do you say, Governor? Will you help me make my vision a reality?"

RW

Mia walked the three kilometers back to the spaceport with the beginnings of a spring in her step. Governor Tremblay had required a little convincing, but his protestations had mostly been about him testing her to ensure she would see this venture through to completion, or perhaps trying to confirm she wasn't as insane as some gossip feeds suggested. In the end, she'd won an enthusiastic if preliminary sign-off and a meeting with the Zoning Commissioner tomorrow morning.

She'd rented a small apartment a few blocks north of the spaceport for now. She didn't doubt that Malcolm would cede their home here to her—he never voiced it, but he'd always preferred Vancouver to Romane—but she wasn't ready to surround herself with a house full of memories. This was a fresh start, after all.

Half a kilometer short of the spaceport, she stopped at a park and relaxed on a bench for a few minutes. A glass fountain reflected the afternoon light of the two suns like a prism, and the weather was warm enough for several children to be playing and squealing among the plumes of water.

She'd spent an hour writing and rewriting a message to Malcolm last night, for all that it was four measly paragraphs. But she'd needed her plans for the future to be real and on-course before the words themselves could be real. Now they were, so she opened the draft and read it through for the tenth time. It felt wholly inadequate; there was more she wanted to say, wanted to do.

But she couldn't fling herself off that cliff again. Not yet. So she gave up stressing over it and hit 'send.' Then she stood, rejoined the flow of pedestrians on the sidewalk and struck out into her future.

66

THE PRESIDIO

AEGIS CENTRAL COMMAND

A lieutenant showed Malcolm into the fleet admiral's office, then excused herself and closed the door.

Until recently, this had been *his* office, and a wave of nostalgia hitched his step for half a second. But military officers weren't known for personalizing their offices or for sentimentality, and not much of the decor had been altered with the change in ownership. A single visual above the meeting table, a few framed medals on the wall. And, obviously, the man behind the desk.

Nolan Bastian stood as he entered; they exchanged salutes, then Bastian offered him a hand. "Admiral Jenner. It's good to see you back with us and in uniform."

Malcolm shook the man's hand before taking the seat opposite the desk, which only felt a little weird. Okay, fine, it felt a lot weird. "Thank you. I...about the uniform." He jerked a thumb toward the closed door. "I hear the brass has got a cage match arena set up for us downstairs. Bladed weapons, spiked armor, the whole package. If it's all the same to you, I'd prefer to disappoint them and skip out on the blood sport."

Bastian huffed a restrained laugh. "Your unexpected return has exposed some old fault lines within AEGIS. We've enjoyed a unified human military for fourteen years now, but the old loyalties aren't quite dead. It turns out they were merely slumbering."

He and Bastian had served together for years now in the upper echelon of AEGIS military leadership, and they had a good, if somewhat formal, working relationship. They weren't friends, but they hadn't been enemies since the 2nd Crux War, and he was relieved to find Bastian in an amiable mood today.

"So it seems. The Earth Alliance diehards want me reinstated as fleet admiral, while the Federation power brokers insist you keep the position. Believe me, it wasn't my intent to create this controversy." He sighed. "A lot of things weren't my intent. Listen, you earned the position, and you've comported yourself with the highest honor since stepping into the role. I don't have the right to snatch it back away from you now."

"Don't you, though?" Bastian shook his head. "I appreciate you being gracious, I do. And I'm proud of the work I've done these last two months. But the truth is, I lost the position the moment you reappeared on Concord soil."

Malcolm frowned. "Why do you say that?"

"Because you enjoy one advantage I never will: you have the trust and confidence of Commandant Solovy. It's my own fault that I don't enjoy the same, but I don't regret my actions toward her. Someone needs to hold her feet to the fire. Someone needs to ensure that she is always accountable for her decisions to the officers serving under her and to the people we protect. I appointed myself to the job the day I became the Federation Field Marshal, and I intend to keep fulfilling my duty for as long as I serve."

Bastian clasped his hands atop the desk. "But three battles against the Rasu have made one fact crystal-clear to me: we need to be united and indivisible in this fight if we are to have any chance of defeating what is shaping up to be the most formidable enemy we have ever faced. My strained relationship with the Commandant is a pain point in our chain of command, and this makes it a weakness, one that endangers the lives of countless people every time we go into battle.

"We can't tolerate weaknesses, not in this conflict. So I'll be tendering my resignation as fleet admiral this afternoon. The job's yours again. You've served us well in the past. May you continue to do so in the future."

RW

Malcolm stood in the observation room, his hands clasped behind his back and his nose a respectable ten centimeters away from being pressed against the glass. To his right, a fraction over a kiloparsec away, sat Romane, while 1.5 kiloparsecs behind him, Earth's sun shone. He honestly wasn't certain where 'home' resided any longer, so the bridge of the *Denali* would have to do for now. And the fleet admiral's office, it seemed.

The AEGIS Oversight Board was meeting four floors above him, but with Bastian willingly bowing out, the result should be a foregone conclusion. And Malcolm found he was…glad. Moping, brooding and skulking around scenic locales just didn't suit him; more relevantly, none of it had helped. He was ready to call an end to this cringe-worthy self-pity and get back to his job. He wanted to save lives and protect the innocent. He wanted a lot more, too, but duty had always been his bedrock. It would keep him afloat now.

The official communication from the Oversight Board arrived then, and he exhaled in relief. The drama was concluded, and it was time to go to work.

He pivoted and strode toward the lift. The *Denali's* quick jaunt to rescue the surviving Ourankeli had exposed a few lingering cobwebs from languishing in dry dock for two months, and he wanted to take her out for a proper shakedown run. Also, he needed to learn the ins and outs of the new double shielding system.

He was stepping onto the bridge when his eVi flashed a unique notifier—one he'd set to alert him immediately of any communications from Mia.

His heart skipped two beats, but he kept his gait steady and his expression blank as he diverted to the captain's office adjacent to the bridge and closed the door behind him. His hands trembling slightly at his sides, he opened the message. Read it, then read it again.

Malcolm,

I'm truly sorry for the things I said to you the other night. If they hurt you—what am I saying? Of course they hurt you, but this wasn't what I wanted. Or maybe it was. Maybe I wanted you to feel the tiniest fraction of what I had suffered through while you were gone. Still, I'd take many of those words back now if I could.

But I did mean some of them. I love you. I love you so much I can scarcely breathe when I think about it. Losing you destroyed me, and now the wreckage is scattered around me like flotsam.

I hope you *meant what you said about not giving up on us. It's unfair of me to ask you to keep hold of this promise, when I can't promise you anything in return, but I'm selfishly asking you anyway. I wish more than anything that you could tell me you'll always come back to me and it be true, but I now recognize this is one wish too far. And...I don't know if I can live with that. I want to try, I do.*

But I need time. I need to remember who I was and figure out who I want to be from here forward. I need to pick up these shattered pieces of myself and see if they can ever fit together again. And I need to be alone to do it. I love you, but you can't be the only reason I exist in this world. I hope you understand.

—Mia

A flutter in Malcolm's chest set his nerves tingling, spreading warmth out from his fingers to his toes to ignite a smile upon his lips. It felt like hope.

67

SAVRAK

To the small group of weary, bedraggled but surviving government and military leaders of Savrak, Lakhes appeared as a great avatar in the likeness of the Savrakaths. Technically, in the likeness of the one they worshiped as Galakharno. A fellow Idryma member, Alastor, had long played this role, but after the Savrakaths went rogue, Lakhes had felt a responsibility to don the guise himself.

They fell prostrate in front of the avatar—all except Brigadier Ghorek—and in doing so, resembled their ancestral reptiles from a time long before their artificially accelerated evolution had rendered them upright.

"Galakharno, have you come to save us?" The plaintive voice emerged from among the group's members, but Lakhes couldn't say to whom it belonged.

To save you, and to punish you.

"Punish us? But we have only ever defended ourselves."

Incorrect. You have met diplomacy with aggression, generosity with torture and defeat with vengeance. You strike out blindly, with no reasoned contemplation regarding the culpability of your targets or of your end goal. You have killed many and threatened trillions.

At root, the blame does not fall solely on you, for you are what I made you. I hastened your development and awarded you with technology and weapons you had not earned on your own. For committing these mistakes, I feel deep regret toward you and your victims. I will bear this responsibility, but now I must bring an end to your foolish, thoughtless actions. You are not ready to live among the stars and their inhabitants.

Ghorek, who had proudly stepped into Jhountar's weighty leadership role only to fall victim to his predecessor's same failings, surged forward out of the gathered group. "What do you mean by this? Would you strike us down for daring to rise up?"

No. You will live. Your world will survive. Rebuild it, if you can. Learn to stay your hand. Learn judiciousness and, in time, wisdom. One day, you may prove to be ready.

Another of the group, their voice weaker and more tentative, spoke up. "Galakharno, we don't understand. If you are sparing our lives, then what is our punishment to be?"

Do not attempt to leave the atmosphere of your homeworld again. Anyone who does so will find themselves returned to where they began.

You are now exiled from the stars. But you are also protected, for anyone who attempts to enter your planet's atmosphere will find themselves returned to where they began as well. Savrak will exist as an island in the sea of space.

Take this gift—for it is surely that—and use it wisely. Evolve. Better yourselves. Become worthy of this second chance I am granting you. I will be watching.

Lakhes vanished from their sight in a burst of blinding light, then reappeared thousands of kilometers away, deep in the chaparral wilderness of the planet's south pole. Here waited the device that members of the Idryma had spent weeks designing, testing and perfecting. Upon learning of its function and capabilities, Mnemosyne had given it the name 'Echo Rift.'

Everything seemed to be in order, so with a heavy heart, Lakhes activated it.

The first layer activated the device's own self-defense mechanism: a rift barrier that repelled any attempt to reach the internal physical workings, coupled with a cloaking mechanism to hide the device from all eyes.

The second layer rippled out across the swamps and the ruined cities to expand beyond the circumference of the planet. This barrier faced inward rather than outward: any object or energy trying to escape it would be greeted by a shockwave that swiftly returned them to the planet's surface. Though it wasn't designed to kill, injuries upon impact with either the shockwave or the ground were likely. This was unfortunate, but it should teach the Savrakaths not to toy with the barrier.

The third layer served as the promised protection for Savrak's inhabitants: a more traditional Rift Bubble that deposited any external object or energy attempting to cross it fifty megameters away from the planet. Not inside the corona of the system's star in this case, as the would-be intruder could merely be an ignorant explorer.

Finally, an additional cloaking mechanism activated around the outer layer of the Echo Rift. The void swallowed Savrak whole, and it vanished from sight.

After confirming that every element of the device was operating as intended, Lakhes left Savrak behind to rejoin the others.

RW

CAF AURORA

SAVRAK STELLAR SYSTEM

"Damn. It's as if the planet never existed." Alex shook her head at the starkly empty scene outside the viewport, suddenly absent one jungle-infested planet.

She and Caleb had arrived back in Concord space, Ourankeli refugees in tow, only to discover they'd missed a great deal of excitement during their absence. Once the Ourankeli were situated and in the Consulate's care, she'd accepted her mother's invitation to come along for the ride and witness the Kats implement their promised solution to the thorny Savrakath 'problem.'

Mesme rippled placidly beside her on the bridge. *You have seen this manner of stealth deployed in conjunction with a rift device before.*

"Of course—on Portal Prime. And I'll point out that I was able to get around it."

No. I allowed you entry.

She shot Mesme a little half-smile. "Fair enough. But this one is genuinely impenetrable?"

There is no one located inside of it capable of granting anyone entry.

"You can still get inside, though, can't you?"

The arrival of Lakhes on the minimally staffed bridge distracted everyone for a moment, and Mesme conferred with the Praetor.

When they separated, Alex cleared her throat. "Mesme? I asked you a question."

When are you not asking me questions?

"Never. So?"

Yes, we can penetrate the Echo Rift and reach the planet's surface. This device is not programmed to accept a bypass code, however, so it will be impossible for anyone else to traverse it. To answer the next question on your tongue, in the unlikely event that the Savrakaths one day discover the device, multiple safeguards surrounding it will prevent them from interfering with its functionality.

Miriam, pacing languidly atop the bridge overlook, let out an audible sigh and turned toward them. Her mother looked as if she felt sorry for the Savrakaths, even after all they'd done. She rarely allowed the weight from the burdens of leadership to show, but every so often, Alex saw the cracks. "What will happen to the Savrakaths now?"

Lakhes answered. *We will watch them, but we will no longer interfere in their development. Time and experience have taught us the perils of trying to shape sentient beings into what we wish them to be.*

Alex coughed into her hand to hide a chuckle. She and Caleb might have played a small role in teaching the Kats this particular lesson.

Perhaps one day, many centuries from now, they will evolve into a species worthy of joining the interstellar community and participating in a peaceful alliance. But first, they must survive. Then, they must learn how to thrive without our assistance. Time will tell how their story unfolds.

Miriam nodded stoically. "Very well. I trust you will inform me promptly if anything about their situation ever changes. Barring any such developments, I will close the file on the Savrakaths and turn my more fulsome attention to strengthening Concord, from within and without." She gave Alex a bittersweet smile. "Shall we return to HQ? I understand your father is making lunch for us."

A Caeles Prism wormhole opened in front of the *Aurora*, and they accelerated through it, leaving the Savrakaths to their fate.

68

CONCORD HQ

COMMAND

By the time they docked at HQ, departed the *Aurora* and made their way to Command, the ostensibly 'working lunch' in the conference room adjacent to Miriam's office had grown to include Caleb and, this time, Richard as well.

Alex was still trying to catch up on recent events, but now that everyone was safe, she absolutely loved the idea of Richard and her father mending their relationship during a crazy sprint to find and disarm an antimatter bomb buried in the heart of HQ's power core. She also assumed the story had been embellished a great deal in the short time since its resolution, of course, as was true of all her father's best stories.

She sat down beside Caleb, squeezed his hand beneath the table and allowed herself to relax. A big victory over the Rasu, renewed peace with the Anadens, riddance of the troublesome Savrakaths…it felt like they finally had a chance to catch their breaths. *But first a hush of peace*, as Emily Brontë had once so eloquently written.

She filled her salad plate from the communal bowl of spring greens, tomatoes, carrots and shredded cheese. "Is it true? Corradeo Praesidis is going to serve in the Senate now as the Anaden representative?"

Miriam looked almost mirthful. "He has officially requested permission to do so, yes."

"You don't think he'll end up bristling against the same restrictions Ferdinand did? He's not exactly used to sharing power."

"He's not, but he's also a far more principled and pragmatic man than Ferdinand ever dreamed of being. I'm optimistic that he'll take Concord as he finds it and adjust. Perhaps he can even help us change it for the better."

Caleb nodded over his fork. "I think he will."

Alex leaned closer to murmur in his ear. "Did you happen to see him while I was gone?"

"No. There will be time later."

"Okay." Today was a good day, and there was no reason to push Caleb out of his comfort zone right now. "And Malcolm's back in the fleet admiral's chair? I can't imagine Bastian is taking it well."

Miriam's smile veered toward a rare smirk. "Actually, Bastian volunteered to resign the position. Yes, it surprised me, too. Despite his willingness to cede the role, however, the Federation government still managed to extract a price for Malcolm's reinstatement as fleet admiral. It appears the next AEGIS Senator will be from the Federation's ranks."

"Oh? Do we know who it will be?"

"Rumor has it they're pressuring Aristide Vranas to leave semi-retirement and return to politics. I don't know if they'll be successful, but..." Miriam shrugged "...I would be comfortable with the choice. Even if we didn't always agree, he's a good man. We'll see."

And that marked the beginning and end of her interest in politics, so Alex steered the discussion to a more intriguing topic. "Have we snagged one of those Rima Grenades from the Asterions and reverse-engineered it yet? Between those pint-sized terrors and the Rectifier tech, the next time the Rasu reach the surface of a planet we want to protect, the ground war is going to look a lot different."

Miriam grabbed a steaming hot roll from the basket at the center of the table. "I believe the Initiative has already sent Special Projects a box of the grenades. It's impressive how swiftly the Asterions are improving on existing Kat technology. But what *I* really want to see out of them is a working renewable negative energy weapon. That technology will do more to change the game than anything we've done so far in combat engagements."

"True." David and Richard had their heads huddled close together while they shared a chuckle, and Alex watched on in amusement and a touch of jealousy. If the story they were recounting to each other was a good one, she wanted to hear it.

The door buzzed, and Miriam frowned a little, standing as it opened. Pinchu strode in, then looked over at them in surprise. "Apologies. I did not realize—"

"Nonsense." Alex leapt up and went to greet him. "You're welcome to join us, though I'm not sure you'll enjoy the food."

Pinchu embraced her, but the act felt strangely weak and half-hearted. "Thank you, but I cannot. Commandant, I apologize for interrupting, but I have a matter of some urgency I need to discuss with you."

Miriam glanced back at the table. "Whatever it is, you can share it with those here. Everyone has the necessary security clearances."

"As you wish. In the aftermath of the Toki'taku battle, one of my commanders discovered that one of our fast-attack frigates never reported in upon returning to Ireltse. We did not record its loss during the encounter itself, so our analysts reviewed the full battle report. It appears..." all four of Pinchu's eyes blinked, and he shifted his weight onto his tail "...the last communication from the frigate indicated it was being pursued by a large Rasu vessel. We must conclude that either the frigate was destroyed in the encounter or...it's possible the frigate was boarded by the Rasu and confiscated."

Her mother's expression darkened precipitously, and a gloom descended upon the room like an encroaching shadowy mist from the moors. "I see. You've been unable to contact this ship or any of its crew?"

"Correct. It was staffed with forty-four military personnel. They are all unaccounted for."

Miriam began striding across the conference room, her chin tucked and her eyes downcast but her movements energetic. "*This* is why they retreated from Toki'taku before the battle was decided! They realized they'd snatched a prize far more valuable than a single alien planet."

Alex caught her mother's arm on her next pass around the conference room. "What prize is that?"

Miriam's countenance grew darker still. "Us."

She'd been too relaxed, and it took Alex a second longer than it should have for the import to sink in.

Concord. Protocols, member species, military rendezvous points and fleet details, and most of all, the location of Concord planets. Maybe not all of them, but certainly the Khokteh worlds and nearby space stations. Concord HQ?

Miriam flicked her wrist, and a small aural materialized in front of her. A red alert flashed in the header, and text scrolled urgently beneath it. "It's almost as if they were waiting for the big reveal. Rasu signatures have been detected approaching Sector 4b of the Large Magellanic Cloud."

"They are coming for my people first. I must return to Ireltse at once." Pinchu's tail swept in a dramatic arc as he spun around and hurried out the door.

Chair legs scraped across the floor as everyone stood in a rush. Alex held her ground, demanding her mother's attention. "Well, fuck, obviously. What does this mean for us?"

Miriam's gaze darted to the viewport and the parade of ships docked on the spiraling berths surrounding HQ. As it did, her expression resolved into one of grim determination. "It means now the real war begins."

The Story Continues In

ALL OUR TOMORROWS

RIVEN WORLDS BOOK FOUR

(AMARANTHE ♦ 17)

Available Now at gsjennsen.com/all-our-tomorrows

AUTHOR'S NOTE

I published my first novel, *Starshine*, in 2014. In the back of the book I put a short note asking readers to consider leaving a review or talking about the book with their friends. Watching my readers do that and so much more has been the most rewarding and humbling experience in my life.

So if you loved ***ECHO RIFT***, tell someone. Leave a review, share your thoughts on social media, annoy your coworkers in the break room by talking about your favorite characters. Reviews are the backbone of a book's success, but there is no single act that will sell a book better than word-of-mouth.

My part of this deal is to write a book worth talking about—your part of the deal is to do the talking. If you keep doing your bit, I get to write a lot more books for you.

Of course, I can't write them overnight. While you're waiting for the next book, consider supporting other independent authors. Right now there are thousands of writers chasing the same dream you've enabled me to achieve. Take a small chance with a few dollars and a few hours of your time. In doing so, you may be changing an author's life.

Lastly, I want to hear from my readers. If you loved the book—or if you didn't—let me know. The beauty of independent publishing is its simplicity: there's the writer and the readers. Without any overhead, I can find out what I'm doing right and wrong directly from you, which is invaluable in making the next book better than this one. And the one after that. And the twenty after that.

Website: gsjennsen.com
Wiki: gsj.space/wiki

Email: gs@gsjennsen.com
Twitter: @GSJennsen
Facebook: gsjennsen.author

Goodreads: G.S. Jennsen
Pinterest: gsjennsen
Instagram: gsjennsen

Find my books at a variety of retailers: gsjennsen.com/retailers

APPENDIX

THE STORY SO FAR

View a more detailed summary of the events of the Amaranthe novels online at gsjennsen.com/synopsis.

Aurora Rising

The history of humanity is the history of conflict. This proved no less true in the 24th century than in ancient times.

By 2322, humanity inhabited over 100 worlds spread across a third of the galaxy. When a group of colonies rebelled two decades earlier, it set off the First Crux War. Once the dust cleared, three factions emerged: the Earth Alliance, consisting of the unified Earth government and most of the colonies; the Senecan Federation, which had won its independence in the war; and a handful of scattered non-aligned worlds, home to criminal cartels, corporate interests and people who made their living outside the system.

Alexis Solovy was a space explorer. Her father gave his life in the war against the Federation, leading her to reject the government and military. Estranged from her mother, an Alliance military leader, Alex instead sought the freedom of space and made a fortune chasing the hidden wonders of the stars.

A chance encounter between Alex and a Federation intelligence agent, Caleb Marano, led them to discover an armada of alien warships emerging from a mysterious portal in the Metis Nebula.

The Metigens had been watching humanity via the portal for millennia; in an effort to forestall their discovery, they used traitors among civilization's elite to divert people's focus. When their plans failed, they invaded in order to protect their secrets.

The wars that ensued were brutal—first an engineered war between the Alliance and the Federation, then once it was revealed to be built on false pretenses, devasting clashes against the Metigen invaders as they advanced across settled space, destroying every colony in their path and killing tens of millions.

Alex and Caleb breached the aliens' portal in an effort to find a way to stop the invaders. There they encountered the Metigen watcher of the Aurora universe, Mnemosyne. Though enigmatic and evasive, the alien revealed the invading ships were driven by AIs and hinted the answer to defeating them lay in the merger of individuals with the powerful but dangerous quantum computers known as Artificials.

Before leaving, Alex and Caleb discovered a colossal master gateway that generated 51 unique signals, each one leading to a new portal and a new universe. But with humanity facing extinction, they returned home armed with a daring plan to win the war.

Four Prevos (human-synthetic meldings) were created in a desperate gambit to vanquish the enemy invaders before they reached the heart of civilization; then they were given command of the combined might of the Alliance and Federation militaries. Alex and her Artificial, Valkyrie, led the other Prevos and the military forces against the alien AI warships in climactic battles above Seneca and Romane. The invaders were defeated and ordered to withdraw through their portal, cease their observation of Aurora and not return.

During the battle, hints of the consciousness of her deceased father manifested in the shared connection between Alex and Valkyrie. Alex reconciled with her mother during the final hours of the war, and following their victory Alex and Caleb married and attempted to resume a normal life.

But new mysteries waited through the Metis portal. Six months later, Caleb, Alex and Valkyrie traversed it once more, determined to learn the secrets of the portal network and the multiverses it held, leaving humanity behind to struggle with a new world of powerful quantum synthetics, posthumans, and an uneasy peace.

And in the realm beyond the portal, Mnemosyne watched.

Aurora Renegades

Following the victory over the Metigens, Alex, Caleb and Valkyrie set off to unlock the secrets of the Metigens' portal network. Discovering worlds of infinite wonder, they made both enemies and friends. A sentient planet, Akeso, that left a lasting mark on Alex and Caleb both. Silica-based beings attempting to grow organic life. A race of cat-like warriors locked in conflict with their brethren.

Behind them all, the whispered machinations of the Metigen puppet masters pervaded everything. In some universes, the Metigens tested weapons. In some, they set aliens against each other in new forms of combat. In yet more, they harvested food and materials to send through the massive portal at the heart of the maze.

But Alex and Caleb found yet another layer to the puzzle. In one universe, they discovered a gentle race of underground beings with a strange history. Their species was smuggled out of the universe beyond the master portal by the Metigens. They watched as their homeworld was destroyed by a powerful species known as Anadens; but for the Metigens, they would have perished as well.

Back home in Aurora, the peace proved difficult to maintain. The heroes of the war—the Prevos who melded their minds with AIs—found themselves targeted by politicians and a restless population desperate for a place to pin their fears. Under the direction of a new, power-hungry Earth Alliance PM, the government moved to cage and shackle them.

In desperation, the Prevos uploaded the AIs' consciousnesses into their own minds, fled from their governments' grasp and disappeared onto independent colonies. Devon published the details of the Prevo link to the exanet, unleashing its capabilities for anyone who wanted to follow in their footsteps.

Meanwhile, an anti-synthetic terrorist group emerged to oppose them, fueled by the rise of Olivia Montegreu as a Prevo. While the private face of Prevos was the heroes who defeated the Metigens, the public face became the image of Olivia killing a colonial governor and tossing him off of a building in front of the world.

Unaware of the struggles her fellow Prevos faced, Alex forged her own path forward. Rather than bringing the AI into herself, she pushed out and through Valkyrie, into the walls of the *Siyane*. Piloting her ship in a way she never dreamed, Alex was able to feel the photonic brilliance of space itself. Over time, however, that bond began to capture more of her spirit and mind.

On the surface of a destroyed planet, Mesme at last revealed all. The portal network, which the Metigens call the Mosaic, was above all else a refuge for those targeted for eradication by the Anadens. And the Anadens, rulers of the true universe through the master portal, were the genetic template upon which humanity was built. Aurora was nothing more than another experiment of the Metigens, created so they could study the development and nature of their enemy and the enemy of all life.

Alex and Caleb returned to Aurora to find a galaxy rocked by chaos. After the execution of Olivia Montegreu by Alliance and Prevo forces, Miriam had gone rogue. Under her careful planning, a resistance force, bolstered by help from inside the Senecan and Alliance militaries, moved to remove the despotic Alliance PM.

As Alex struggled with her growing addiction to an ethereal, elemental realm, she felt herself being pulled away from reality. Away from her husband, her mother, her friends. She watched as those she loved fought, but increasingly found herself losing her own battle.

When terrorists staged a massive riot on Romane, Dr. Canivon, the mother of the Prevos, was murdered in front of Devon and Alex. Overcome by her own and Valkyrie's grief, Alex unleashed the explosive power of the ethereal realm to destroy the terrorists' safehouse. Standing in the rubble of her destruction, Alex made a decision to sever the quantum connection between herself and the *Siyane*, choosing a tangible, human life. Choosing Caleb.

Miriam wrested control of the EA government away from the PM, bringing an end to the Prevo persecution. In the wake of victory, however, a shadowy Anaden hunter emerged from the darkness to attack Alex and Caleb. Caleb was gravely injured when the Anaden's power, known as *diati*, leapt into him, healing his wounds and helping him kill the alien.

Mesme revealed the ominous consequences of the attack. Soon, the Anaden leadership would discover Aurora. When they did, they would destroy it unless humanity could stand against them. Mesme told Miriam and the others to prepare, but knowing the end game was upon them, asked Alex and Caleb to come to Amaranthe. The master universe. The home and dominion of the Anadens.

Aurora Resonant

In Aurora, Miriam led the formation of a multi-agency, multi-governmental (GCDA) and military (AEGIS) organization dedicated to meeting the imminent threat of the Anadens.

In Amaranthe, Alex and Caleb discovered an underground 'anarch' resistance movement against the Anaden Directorate. They made contact with an anarch agent, Eren asi-Idoni, and he helped them infiltrate the Anadens' Machim military command and steal secret information on the Machim fleets. Alex and Caleb were captured, but not before Valkyrie uploaded the information they sought. Eren 'nulled out' rather than being captured, for when Anadens died they underwent a regenesis procedure that returned their consciousness to a new body.

Valkyrie transmitted the data to AEGIS then returned to Amaranthe. When Eren reawakened, he joined Valkyrie and Mesme on the *Siyane*, and they rescued Alex and Caleb from the prison where they were being tortured for information.

The Directorate nonetheless learned the full truth about the Metigens/Katasketousya creation of Aurora and ordered a fleet to deliver a powerful weapon known as a Tartarus Trigger to Aurora and annihilate humanity. Forewarned, Miriam led a fleet of warships into Amaranthe to intercept them.

The battle commenced with the destruction of the one known gateway into the Mosaic, and Mesme sneaked onto the lead Machim warship and stole the Tartarus Trigger. Humanity used its Prevos, Rifts and other tricks to take the Anadens by surprise and prevail in the battle. Afterward, Alex, Caleb, Miriam and Mesme were summoned to a secret meeting with the leader of the anarchs, Danilo Nisi, and a tenuous alliance was formed.

AEGIS scored several early victories but also devastating losses. While the battles raged, Alex and the other Prevos developed a method for using sidespace to open physical wormholes, enabling AEGIS vessels to travel anywhere in known space without using the Anaden gateway system.

The AEGIS fleet attacked the Machim homeworld, destroying the Dyson rings encircling its sun and blowing up their orbital military command station. At the same time, Nisi broadcast an impassioned speech across the empire setting forth the Directorate's sins and the anarch's mission to free those oppressed.

In a flashback Caleb's *diati* showed him, it was revealed that Nisi was actually Corradeo Praesidis, the former leader of the powerful Anaden Praesidis dynasty. Many millennia ago, his son tried to kill him; thinking him dead, the son stole his name, face and power, and now served on the Directorate as the Praesidis Primor.

Valkyrie and her twin, Vii, had spent months rebuilding the consciousness of David Solovy that manifested during the final battle of the Metigen War. Using the Anadens' regenesis technology, they transferred his consciousness to a cloned body, and he and Miriam were reunited after twenty-five years.

The Directorate tracked an AEGIS vessel to the primary anarch base and launched a surprise attack, and a bloody battle followed in orbit and on the ground. To stop a Machim warship from bombing the base with anti-matter missiles, Alex re-established her ethereal connection with the *Siyane* to bypass the warship's shielding and destroy it; in doing so, she found the connection no longer exerted the damaging hold on her it once did.

Alex soon discovered a way to use the supradimensional properties of the mysterious Reor mineral to access the contents of the Reor slabs used by the Directorate to store sensitive information. She uncovered the location of the Directorate's regenesis backups, and AEGIS and the anarchs devised a plan to take out the entire Directorate, permanently, in one massive strike.

For all but two of the Directorate members, the mission succeeded with minimal losses. However, the Machim Primor escaped his assassination attempt. Armed with the location of one of the Mosaic gateways, he acquired a new Tartarus Trigger and raced to wipe out the Aurora universe.

On Solum (Earth's twin), Caleb engaged the Praesidis Primor in a battle of staggeringly powerful *diati*, and the *diati* freed when the Primor died rampaged wild. Caleb couldn't wrestle it under control, and it killed millions before destroying the planet itself.

The anarchs learned that the Primors kept an additional regenesis backup stored on their secret space station, the Protos Agora, which orbited the Milky Way galactic core. The *Stalwart II* took the Tartarus Trigger Mesme stole at the start of the conflict and used it to destroy the station.

Just when they believed they had finally achieved victory, they discovered the Machim Primor's plans. The Primor had a head start, and the only way to try to prevent him from destroying Aurora was for the Kats to disconnect it from the Mosaic, rendering it unreachable forever. Caleb, however, instead used his now total control over *diati* to command the cosmic force to pull all the pocket universes in the Mosaic—including Aurora—into Amaranthe, then destroy the Mosaic.

He succeeded, but the energy the act required killed him. While Miriam and the others worked out what it meant for all of humanity to now exist in Amaranthe, Alex took Caleb to the living planet of Akeso and, via the deep connection they shared, Akeso brought him back to life.

Asterion Noir

On the planet of Mirai in the Gennisi galaxy, a woman woke up in a rain-soaked alley with no memory of who she was or how she'd gotten there. Two strangers found her and offered to take her in. When asked, she told them her name was Nika, though she didn't know why.

Fast forward to five years later. Nika, alongside her rescuers Perrin and Joaquim, led a group of rebels called NOIR against the despotic government of the Asterion Dominion. An insidious virutox was infecting people's programming, altering their personalities and causing them to commit inexplicable crimes. NOIR's investigation of the virutox brought them to Dashiel Ridani, who Nika learned was her lover in her prior life, before she lost her memory.

With her world thrown into disarray, Nika and Dashiel chased the threads of her lost identity while searching for the source of the virutox. Their search led them to the leaders of the Asterion Dominion, the Guides. Nika broke into the Guides' data vault, where she found they had ordered her psyche-wipe five years earlier after she pressed them on a series of disappearances.

Meanwhile, Gemina Kail, an Administration Advisor, traveled to an alien stronghold across the galaxy, where she delivered thousands of Asterions in stasis chambers to an alien species called the Rasu.

As the virutox spread, wreaking increasing havoc across the Dominion, Justice Advisor Adlai Weiss traced the source to the Guides' doorstep. They ordered him to drop the case and let the virutox propagate among the population. He disobeyed, developed a vaccine and contacted NOIR for help in distributing it.

Across the galaxy, Nika and Dashiel discovered the stronghold of the alien Rasu. A metal-based shapeshifting species of immense power, they'd constructed hundreds of thousands of warships and space stations. Armed with this terrifying information, Nika and Dashiel returned to Mirai.

One of the Guides, Delacrai, defied the others to help Nika. She shared how an Asterion scout ship encountered the Rasu eight years ago; the crew was captured and killed. The Rasu grew interested in the Asterions' unique bio-synthetic intelligence powered by kyoseil and quantum programming, and in return for not attacking Asterion Dominion worlds, they demanded a regular supply of Asterions to experiment on. The Guides agreed.

The other Advisors were told the terrible truth about the Rasu and the Guides' deal with the aliens. They scrambled to undo the damage eight years of the Rasu Protocol had inflicted while racing to find a way to respond to an impending Rasu deadline, when the aliens expected more Asterions to be delivered.

Nika's oldest friend from her former life, Maris Debray, revealed that both she and Nika were members of the "First Generation": Asterions who had never erased their psyches in the 700,000 years since they fled the Anaden Empire and created themselves as a new species by merging Anaden DNA, AI programming and the kyoseil mineral. Only a few dozen of the First Generation remained, and their history was kept secret from everyone else.

With time running out, Nika sought the help of the Sogain, an enigmatic species who once threatened the Asterions with extinction if they ever trespassed on Sogain territory. This time, the aliens disclosed the location of a single, stranded Rasu.

An Asterion team captured the Rasu and brought it to Mirai for interrogation. The creature revealed that the Rasu exhibited a collective intelligence when physically connected to other Rasu, but regained independent thought when they were separated. They intended to use kyoseil to control other Rasu over great distances, as kyoseil was supradimensional, deeply interconnected and one of the universe's oldest life forms.

Using this knowledge, the Asterions identified a way to link their consciousnesses together via kyoseil. They dubbed these connections 'ceraffin' and used them to develop a plan to face the Rasu.

They constructed volatile electricity bombs to be sneaked into the Rasu stronghold. The Rasu were expecting 8,000 Asterions in stasis chambers, so Nika used the ceraff structure to split her psyche into shards inhabiting 8,000 copies of herself.

The copies were delivered to the Rasu as expected, and they awoke inside the Rasu's lab on their primary space station. Chaos ensued as they fought to reach the power control center, even as they were cut down by the thousands. A mere dozen made it to the control center, and a single instance survived to override the power safeguards.

Dashiel detonated the electricity bombs, and a cascading power overload ripped through the stronghold. It destroyed the Rasu's Dyson lattice, which triggered an intense surge in solar flare activity, and all the Rasu stations and vessels were incinerated, save one vessel that escaped through a wormhole.

The Asterions recognized this was not the end of the conflict, but the beginning, and they needed to prepare for the Rasu's return. Nika was contacted by the Sogain, who informed her the Anaden Empire of old had fallen and suggested she might find allies among the new one which had risen to take its place.

Nika journeyed to the Asterions' ancestral home, the Milky Way. Before she arrived, however, a wormhole opened in the cabin of her ship, and Alex Solovy walked through it.

Acknowledgements

Many thanks to my beta readers, editors and artists, who made everything about this book better, and to my family, who continue to put up with an egregious level of obsessive focus on my part for months at a time.

I also want to add a personal note of thanks to everyone who has read my books, left a review at a retailer, Goodreads or other sites, sent me a personal email expressing how the books have impacted you, or posted on social media to share how much you enjoyed them. You make this all worthwhile, every day.

About the Author

G. S. JENNSEN lives in Idaho with her husband and two dogs. She has become an internationally bestselling author since her first novel, *Starshine,* was published in 2014. She has chosen to continue writing under an independent publishing model to ensure the integrity of her stories and her ability to execute on the vision she has for their telling.

While she has been a lawyer, a software engineer and an editor, she's found the life of a full-time author preferable by several orders of magnitude. When she isn't writing, she's gaming or working out or getting lost in the mountains that loom large outside the windows in her home. Or she's dealing with a flooded basement, or standing in a line at Walmart reading the tabloid headlines and wondering who all of those people are. Or sitting on her back porch with a glass of wine, looking up at the stars, trying to figure out what could be up there.

www.ingramcontent.com/pod-product-compliance
Lightning Source LLC
Chambersburg PA
CBHW020305030826
48979CB00027B/2120/J

* 9 7 8 1 9 5 7 3 5 2 2 2 0 *